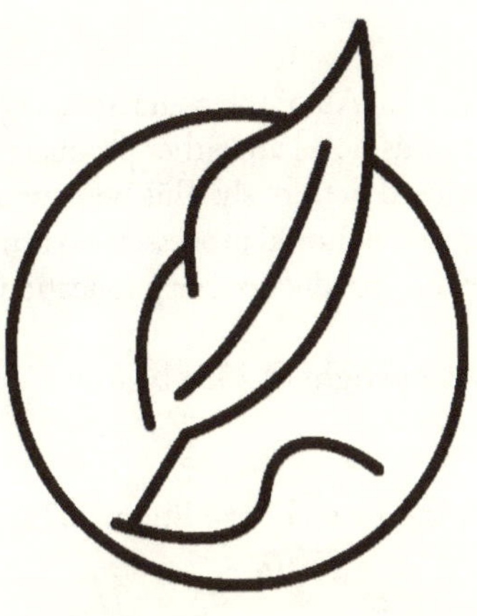

a spilt ink press novel

This is a work of fiction. All of the characters, organizations, and events portrayed in this novel are either products of the author's imagination or are used fictitiously. This book was created through human authorship and editorial processes; no artificial intelligence was used in its writing, production, or publication.

Published by Spilt Ink Press. First edition, 2026.

Spilt Ink Press is an imprint of Gordon Publishing Collective dedicated to transformative storytelling born from life's beautiful messes. We believe the stains of experience hold magic—and from every spill, a story can rise.

www.spiltink.press
www.gordonpublishingco.com
info@gordonpublishingco.com

ISBN: 978-1-970895-03-2

For the ones bound by ghosts
and those who run toward them.

"I'll find my way back home
It'll be alright
It's darkest before the dawn
But I'm heading towards the light"

Way Back Home,
Ed Prosek, Portair, Driftwood Choir

SOME SUNNY DAY

CHAPTER 1
ALEX

Love will mess you up and make you do the craziest shit you've ever done in your life.

When Mae Seasons conveyed this warning—the beginning of a parable more than advice or encouragement—at Silver Springs Health and Rehabilitation Centre two years ago, her voice was low and raspy, filled with the type of confidence one could only have if they knew the ending of the story. The words struck like a bullet I didn't see coming, and it wasn't until later—when the pieces of our worlds began to splinter—that I realized how right she was.

The proof was coming, barrelling toward both of us like a runaway train on tracks we were too proud—or too afraid—to step off. The next six months would strip us bare, unravelling everything we thought we were, dragging us to places we'd vowed we'd never go, and reshaping us into people we barely recognized.

And yet, we didn't stop it.

Oh, the crazy, reckless, beautiful things we were about to do—and the fierce, aching love that would compel us to do them.

CHAPTER 2
MAE

HAVE YOU EVER MOVED halfway across the world to chase a ghost? No? Then you can shove your smug judgment right up your arse, or "derrière" as the French say.

But then again, fuck them, and quite frankly, fuck you too. You've all given me enough headaches to last however many days I have left on this planet. And I say all this because, at ninety-three years old, I haven't got a single second to waste on anyone's petty, misguided, and likely jealous thoughts. I did what you're too scared to do, what most people are afraid of. But, if we're being completely honest, and let's assume that we're not—we hardly know each other, so you don't deserve my complete honesty—I was a little scared too.

When I picked up and left just before Christmas a few years back, leaving Alex Chambers in my wake at The Oak Bean—you remember that petulant puppy dog who made me shed a tear as I left—it was straight to the airport. The beauty of being at my stage of life is that your material belongings don't travel with you. If you're inclined, you can pick up and go at the drop of a dime.

And that's exactly what I did.

"Where to, love?" asked Dolores, as I climbed into the fabled Buick LeSabre, a car that had seen more glory than a cutout in a men's room stall at any rest stop along the northern logging highways.

"Airport, then to Caen, France," I said, a flush of excitement coursing through these old veins as I gave voice to the plan I hatched while figuring out my departure from Silver Springs.

"Meter's running," Dolores joked, knowing full well I wouldn't be paying her a cent for this trip.

Over the years, Dolores, a.k.a. Chandra of the Midnight Sun, had been the beneficiary of plenty a healthy tip from our excursions. What made her appealing to me, and Lord knows there's not a lot there to covet, was that she knew it. She never said a word about it, and our bond was cemented in the silent understanding that this was how our relationship would always be: strictly transactional.

...

The first time I met Dolores, I was drunk out of my godforsaken mind, lying hopelessly on the sticky floor of a dingy bar I couldn't name, in a town I barely remembered driving to.

The night had started as most of them usually did back then—with a bottle and a mission to forget everything that mattered, everything that weighed on me. But somewhere between my third shot of something clear and the cheap whiskey that followed, I completely lost the thread. The bartender cut me off, which was met with a slew of colourful insults I couldn't recall the next morning. Then came the inevitable tumble from my barstool to the floor, where I decided I might as well stay.

The lights above me spun and swirled, a blurred kaleidoscope of reds and yellows. Someone laughed, a booming yet distant sound that somehow felt disconnected from this world. My cheek pressed against the grimy floor, which smelled like a foul mixture of spilled beer and shame.

"You're gonna catch something if you stay down there, love," said a low and gravelly voice tinged with amusement. "But you really ought to get up before one of these boys gets the wrong idea, if you catch my drift."

I groaned in response, unwilling to lift my head.

"Maybe I want to catch something."

The voice chuckled, closer now. "Well, that's a new one. What's your name, sweetheart?"

"None of your damn business," I slurred, rolling onto my back to look at whoever was bothering me. "What's *your* name?"

"Dolores, but my friends call me Chandra of the Midnight Sun."

And there she was—Dolores. A vision of leather, piercings, tattoos, bold colour, and unapologetic attitude. Her hair was dyed a fiery shade of red, curled up in a messy bun that still looked purposeful. She had a cigarette tucked behind one ear, her hands planted on her hips like she was contemplating buying a piece of furniture at a flea market and ready to haggle with a stubborn seller.

"You're a mess," she said, her plum-tinted lips curling to a half-smile.

"No kidding," I muttered.

She didn't look like the kind of person who helped sloppy drunks off bar floors, but before I could spiral further into self-pity, she bent down and offered me a hand. Her fingers were calloused, the kind that came from hard work or hard living—or both.

"Jesus, how many lumberjacks have you jerked off to get hands this rough?"

With a burst of laughter, she reached for my hand and grasped it.

"C'mon," she said. "Let's get you up before they call the cops."

"Why do you care?" I blinked at her, confused.

"I've been where you are, honey," Dolores shrugged. "And trust me, this floor isn't where you want to spend a single moment."

With more effort than it should've taken, I grabbed her outstretched hand. She pulled me up with surprising strength, steadying me when my legs wobbled like a newborn foal.

"You got some place to stay?" she asked, her tone softer now.

I shook my head, sudden tears prickling at the corners of my eyes before I could stop them. God, I hated being vulnerable, especially in front of total strangers.

"Alright," she said, ducking forward and looping my arm around her shoulder. "You're coming with me. And no, I don't care if you think that's weird."

I didn't have the energy to argue, nor the pride to refuse. Dolores half-dragged, half-walked me out of the bar, her studded leather jacket brushing against my arm.

Her place was a tiny apartment above a laundromat, the

kind of space that would always have the faint smell of detergent no matter how many candles were burned. She plopped me onto a faded couch that had definitely seen better days and handed me a glass of water.

"Drink," she ordered, lighting the cigarette she'd been saving.

I obeyed, the cold water a jarring relief for my dry throat.

Dolores leaned against the counter, watching me with an expression I couldn't quite read.

"So, what's your story?" she asked, exhaling a stream of smoke.

I didn't answer. Instead, I stared at the water glass in my hands, trying to piece together what was left of my dignity, of which there was almost none.

She didn't push. She just sat down with me, her presence strangely comforting despite the circumstances.

That night, Dolores didn't just save me from the bar floor. She saved me from myself. And for reasons I couldn't understand at the time, she never let go.

I woke up the next day to a simple note: *Good luck.*

I left five hundred dollars on the kitchen table and a phone number. This was the first of many more meetings between us.

•••

I had tried to mimic this no-strings-attached arrangement with Alex when I realized he would be sticking around at Silver Springs, but I'll be damned if the little bugger didn't grow on me. Turns out, I needed him, though not nearly as much as he needed me. Hoped as I did, it became clear that our relationship could never have been transactional; he doesn't need to know this though. I'm sure his ego is already inflated enough from having Erica to parade on his arm when he's out and about.

The ride to the airport was silent, unless you count the wheezing and groaning of the engine as it rumbled with a healthy dose of defiance and despair. It sounded like an asthmatic accordion and I glanced to my left more than once to ensure that it was in fact the car and not Dolores on the verge of delivering us to our death. It wasn't music—no, far from it—but it was the only sound we heard, and somehow it served as the perfect soundtrack.

As we arrived at departures, Dolores gave me a look I knew all too well. Her gaze lingered just a moment too long, the faintest quiver betraying the resolve in her smokey eye shadow framed eyes. It wasn't sadness, nor anger—just a simple acceptance etched in the slight downward pull of her lips and the soft tension in her brow, both of which could be evidence of her having just endured a stroke. And let's be honest, with her lifestyle, the reaper wasn't far from paying a premature visit. But then her eyes sparked, as if taking a snapshot and committing the memory to a place it wouldn't fade.

Sentimental bitch.

As quickly as the moment had settled, Dolores looked away, not saying a word, resolved to the outcome and accepting of her fate.

Bad ass bitch.

We both knew we would never see each other again.

I slowly got out of the rust-decorated death trap, thrilled that it would be the last time I'd have to endure its guttural cries when it revved up and shifted gears, but slightly saddened by the fact this marked the end of a great adventure. I patted the roof of the car as if it were a faithful four-legged companion, which Dolores took as my unspoken signal that she was free to go. The tires squealed and the car backfired, the result of any combination of factors, including a rich air-fuel mixture, ignition timing issues, faulty spark plugs or wires, exhaust leaks, faulty valves, or poor quality or incorrect fuel type.

Wipe that look of shock off your face. Did you really think I wouldn't know a thing or two about cars?

Unfortunately for me, however, Dolores' peel out caused a ripple effect no one was prepared for.

First, I fell, ass over tea kettle, landing on my backside on the concrete. I don't have the same dump truck I did as a young lass, so I felt that impact into my bones. Second, the backfire echoed like a gunshot, so you can imagine the sudden panic such a distinct sound created at an airport of all places. Whiny little children became whinier, crying babies became even worse versions of the tiny, freeloading selves they already were, and every faux tough guy dad hit the floor quicker than their pants during a desperate Tinder date. Once the presence of actual danger was officially dismissed, those alpha male idiots proceeded to walk around with their chests puffed out, ready to defend anyone in distress, family or otherwise.

Have you ever seen a group of middle-aged men try to act brave? It's pathetic.

But, after all the hullabaloo, and once things calmed down and returned to their normal state of apathy from all parties involved—except the babies, who were as pain-in-the-ass pretentious as could be—I made my way through the airport, to my gate, and eventually onto the plane where I was seated next to a mother and, yes, you guessed it, her pretentious little prick of an offspring. The only saving grace of this situation was that this mother was dumb enough to have paid for a separate seat for her child, leaving the middle seat open. At least I'd have some room.

"Oh, I hope he doesn't fuss too much," said the mother, bouncing her child on her lap.

I ignored her, hoping that she would think I was deaf, or at the very least hard of hearing, both of which were likely for a woman my age.

"I SAID, I HOPE HE DOESN'T FUSS TOO MUCH."

"Jesus tap dancing Christ, lady," I said, startled. "I heard you the first time but chose to ignore you. I can see now that may not be an option. So, how about this? You'd better hope *I* don't fuss too much. There's not a lot of difference between this bag of bones and that bag of shit-smelling skin folds you're holding."

At this, the woman's eyes widened and her mouth fell open. Mission accomplished. I didn't hear a word from her the rest of the flight. The little bastard, on the other hand, was a different story.

I had arranged for a ground-floor apartment in the heart of the city, something that would be easy to get to and easy to access. The spring in my step was starting to squeak more often than not and the fewer stairs I had to do the better. Thankfully, making this arrangement wasn't terribly difficult, mostly because I had farmed it out to Dolores. I was surprised to discover that as much of a chauffeur as she is, she's one hell of a trav-el agent. Her methods might not fit the criteria for principled procurement, but when you don't have a lot to risk, it's pretty much all gain and reward. So, Dolores, for the right price, of course, was a one-stop shop for all my travelling needs.

Everything I needed was prepared, purchased, and waiting for me when the cab dropped me off. The driver was looking for a tip larger than he deserved, so I left him with one: "Just because you're French doesn't mean you're blessed as a lover—so quit looking at me like that."

The apartment was small—especially if you were a privileged princess type; some would even call it quaint. I chose to call it a place to be. It held no special meaning, it never would. It would simply be a place I could sleep, eat, take a bath, and move the bowels. I could have been more detailed, but it seems I'm getting more lady-like in my old age—and at a certain point, none of the aforementioned are more pleasant viewing or sounding than the other. The important thing was that it suited my needs and was an open-ended rental, month to month, and I had more than enough in the coffers to comfortably ride out my remaining days here if that's what I wanted.

I spent the first few months getting familiar with the area, figuring out who I'd need to speak to, where I'd need to go, and who I could coerce into helping me. My lack of French language skills prevented anyone worth their salt from lending a hand; I could have used Alex, as much as it pains me to say it. Not because he was particularly helpful in the French-speaking department, but rather because I could bend him to my will and have him do the grunt work that lacked appeal to yours truly.

And, as if on cue, he started sending me email updates.

To: maedayseasons@questingmail.ca
From: alex.m.chambers@questingmail.ca
Subject: greetings from Canada

Date: June 16

Hi, Mae!

How are you? I hope France is treating you well and you're finding what you're looking for. Things here are as good as expected. Erica and I are, I guess you'd say, going steady—that's the term your generation would use, right? I can't thank you enough for prompting this to happen. I was hesitant at first, as you're well aware, but things are seemingly falling into place.

After you left, I couldn't go back to Silver Springs, though I thought about it, continuing my role for another few months, but, truth be told, it just wasn't the same without you. And really, you were my role, so what would I have even gone back to? The only other reason to consider a return beyond that is Autumn, and I'd already said a proper goodbye to her, if you can call it that. It was a one-sided conversation, of course, but it was closure; I've accepted everything about the situation and am ready to move on. I'll always love her, but you know that.

I've heard that Phil and Susanne are exactly how you left them, save for the overt and abundant PDA. Sorry, that's a public display of affection—not sure if you'd know that acronym. Everyone there was sad to see you go, even if they were relieved to see you go. I'm sure you can appreciate why.

Anyways, I just wanted to drop a quick line and say that you're missed and both Erica and I are thinking of you. If you need anything, just let me know.

Alex

These emails came regularly for the next few months—you could set your watch to them. Alex was quite eager to tell me about his new life (which still didn't include a paying job; just how much damn money did he inherit?), how great Erica was (something I already knew), and even what he was cooking on a weekly basis, with photos and all (bloody millennial). But I'd be lying if I told you that I hadn't come to expect and even enjoy these missives.

To: maedayseasons@questingmail.ca
From: alex.m.chambers@questingmail.ca
Subject: wondering what's up
Date: October 21

Hi Mae,

Or should I say, bonjour! How's your French coming? Wait. Don't answer that, I know you'll only turn it into some double entendre. I'd love to hear an update on what's been going on with you and your time in Caen. Have you made any progress in finding what you're looking for?

Speaking of progress, I finally nailed that risotto dish I've been working on. See the attachment for a pic. You can't tell me it doesn't look appetizing, especially after years of the food at Silver Springs!

Do you think you'll come home soon, or is Caen your new adopted home? Like I said, lots of questions, no answers. Hoping you can help me out with the latter.

If you need anything, just let me know.

Alex

If *I* needed anything. What could I possibly need from Alex or anyone else, other than doing the work I don't want to do myself? I suppose some help would be beneficial in navigating the language barrier and some of the more challenging historical terrain. Google Translate has been helpful, but not in real time when trying to decipher what the random Pierre or Jean-Paul is telling me in rapid-fire French. They may make great wine and cheese platters, but as far as helpful hosts, the French here are about as useful as a dead-battery vibrator in a nun's nightstand.

As Alex's emails increased, so too did the web of information I was trying to untangle; documentation, photographs, and information about John, his unit, and his possible whereabouts—all the things I came here to uncover, sent courtesy of Luc Brassard, a local historian I was working with. Even though I felt thirty years younger than what my passport declared, the influx of information was mentally exhausting and I found myself napping more during the day, sleeping a little later in the morning, and losing some of my edge.

My desire to type out email responses usually maximized at zero, so when I did engage with Alex it was often over the phone. Time difference be damned, I never gave much care or thought to when I would call. He was on my schedule if he wanted information.

Then, one evening in early January, Alex sent another email, and upon reading it, I was going to tell him it should be his last. We were apart now, our story concluded—we should become memories. There was nothing else we could say or update each other on. Simply put, our story had reached its final page. I wasn't going back and I'd never see him again. It was time to put this dog to pasture.

To: maedayseasons@questingmail.ca
From: alex.m.chambers@questingmail.ca
Subject: advice for a new year
Date: January 8

Mae,

How's it going? What's the weather there like this time of year? We got another generous snowfall the other day and the city has been blanketed in the white stuff ever since. Though the holidays are over, everything still has some of that Christmas feeling. It's nothing like how green it was last year, that's for sure.

There was something I wanted to ask you, to get your advice on, or your blessing I guess. I'm not really sure. But, uncertainty aside, I was going to ask you if—

I didn't finish the email because a new message popped up on my computer from Luc. He was far from the best, but the best I could get. And neither said much.

Fucking eh.

To: maedayseasons@questingmail.ca
From: brassard.through.history@mailtime.fr
Subject: A revelation!
Date: January 8

Bonjour, Mae,

I hope you are sitting down as you read this; what I have unearthed is not at all the information I was expecting to find. I will give you the petit version in this note, but we should meet to discuss, as you say, ASAP. Why wait a moment longer when you've already waited a lifetime!

The following will change how we move forward.

I read the rest of Luc's email and could only do one thing: call Alex.

CHAPTER 3
ALEX

"You better be calling to tell me you're dead, Mae."

This would have been the only acceptable reason for her to be ringing me at three in the morning. Forget the fact she was six hours ahead in France, she's smart and can do math, this much I'm sure of.

"I'll do you one better, Sonny," she said. "I'm changing my name to Hattie Lawton because I'm uncovering more mysteries than I can solve."

"Mae, you know full well I don't know who Hattie Lawton is," I sighed. "And this seriously can't warrant a 3 a.m. phone call."

Erica stirred beside me, seemingly unphased by the middle-of-the-night disruption of a vigorously vibrating cell phone on the bedside table.

"Tell Mae I say hi," she mumbled, turning over, melting into the blankets she had just pulled off me.

I wish I could say this was the first time such a disruption had happened, but the truth is, for the last few months, Mae had been calling at all times of the day. I know that the amount of sleep required changes as you get older, but her pattern, or lack thereof, had me questioning whether she slept at all anymore. During some calls, her incoherence and re-petitiveness made it clear that she had not slept, or that some type of neurological short-circuiting was taking place. Or, conversely, that she had slept too much and was trying to play catch-up with whatever news of the day she felt compelled to provide updates on. Whatever the case, the updates were sparse in content and rich in insults.

It had been just under two years since I said goodbye to Mae at The Oak Bean, her departing plane to France whisking her out of my life, at least in the physical form. I hadn't expect-ed to feel such a degree of loneliness with her gone.

Don't get me wrong, I don't miss the nerve-racking antics, the kicks, or the verbal assaults on both my masculinity and mental capacity.

Okay, maybe I miss them a bit, even the bruises.

But, the bruise inflicted on my heart when Mae left hurt a fuck ton more than any damage her orthopedic Dr. Scholl's could deliver. And for those not familiar with that particular unit of measurement, know that it's more painful than you can imagine.

Mae left only a few days before Christmas, December 21 in fact, the first official day of winter, and I spent the rest of the holiday trying to figure out if letting her go to France alone was a smart decision or a momentary lapse of judgment. I say the latter because two years with Mae in France, or anywhere in the world for that matter, would undoubtedly include some really good stories.

But as we know, we can't change the past or go back and alter a decision when it suits us in the present, so I let her leave. Let her get into the car with Dolores and drive off. Let her board the plane and take off. Let her follow the destiny she believed she needed to follow.

Admittedly, I felt a little lost without her. Though I had gained a new partner in crime, Erica, I was mourning the departure of my best friend. Even saying that out loud to Erica soon after Mae left—complemented by her chorus of chiding chuckles—seemed slightly absurd. I was well aware that discovering a best friend at this stage of our lives, and over just a few short months, raised more questions about my mental stability than Mae's. And *that* was saying something. Maybe Mae did have every right to question my mental acuity.

Naturally, we kept in touch, but not before a period of radio silence; our lives were moving in their own respective directions, and we both needed time and space to see and understand what that looked like. For me, it was embarking on a new relationship.

Navigating new love in your thirties when you haven't truly done so since you were a teenager—and how accurate is the playbook you're calling from if that is your only iteration?—felt like stepping into a play halfway through without a script or even knowing the general plot. Most people had developed a deep well of experience by now; they recognized the cues, understood the pacing, and observed the unspoken rules. Me? I felt like I was ad-libbing my way through every conversation and overthinking every touch. Was texting twice in a row too much? Did admitting you adored their laugh sound too pathetic? I wasn't just learning how to love someone—I was learning how to let someone love me back, and that felt like fumbling in the dark for a light switch I wasn't even sure existed. It also had me constantly speaking in similes and metaphors.

For Mae, on the other hand, it was finding a new place to live, forming a circle of care that would keep her healthy and safe, and, perhaps most importantly for her, learning a new language to tell people to fuck off. It shouldn't come as a surprise, knowing Mae, that all of these perceived hurdles were swiftly and successfully overcome. Of course they were.

Once our communication resumed, it was relatively frequent but indiscriminate in delivery. Phone calls were the most typical, but FaceTime and email were also part of the mix—don't ever tell Mae seniors can't navigate technology—and there was even the occasional written letter. Each time one of her handcrafted missives arrived in the mail, I would study the stamp and postage markings and take a moment to imagine the distance and route this piece of paper travelled to reach me. It reminded me of the letters Mae's husband, John, would send her from the war. How it must have felt to receive a letter from him, to know that its arrival was an irrefutable sign that he was alive, still fighting—a hopeful possibility that letters would one day be replaced with in-person conversations upon a joyous reunion.

Mae let me read some of John's correspondence during our time at Silver Springs. The writing was beautiful. There's no other way to describe it. You could feel the warmth of his love floating off every word. Each letter was a poetic bridge across the chasm of war, a delicate thread sewing their lives together despite the intervening miles and inherent madness. Don't ask me how, but you could sense that he pressed the pen to the thin, rationed paper with affectionate care, as if his words could hold her hand through ink alone.

He described how the French countryside smelled after it rained—likening it to the violets she once planted by their favourite spot—though he knew she had never before seen a countryside so vast. Each message was full of tenderness and layered with fragments of their pre-war life: the special spots, their secret wedding, the people who shaped them. Between the sweet remembrances, he dolefully confessed small truths he could never say aloud—how the unrelenting fear tasted bitter on his tongue, how the thought of her kind smile kept him steady and resolute when shells rained down. He folded each letter with careful precision, as if uneven creases might dilute the love, and slipped it into the envelope like a prayer. If you think a letter can't hold more than mere words, you're sorely mistaken. Especially when they're sent from someone who never makes it home.

I remember feeling, as I read the letters Mae allowed me to, like I was intruding on something sacred yet impossibly intimate, as if the letters were never intended for my eyes— which, of course, they weren't—but had found their way to me by some spectacular twist of fate, some flicker in the cosmos that indicated my understanding of these letters was some kind of requirement.

But I could recognize the letters made Mae ache—not with sadness, mind you, but from the beauty of a love so unguarded, so plainly hopeful, that it felt almost impossible in this world. You could see in her absorption of them just how deep her love for John ran. In those isolated moments, it was hard to discern how Mae ended up as coarse, confrontational, and hardened on the exterior as she was, rarely revealing the warmth exhibited in the quiet moments of the letters that burned aglow deep within her.

Needless to say, this collection of correspondence alone was enough to understand why Mae took off to France and felt compelled to chase the history, the memory of John. Chasing a ghost wasn't impossible because we couldn't see them; it was impossible because they lived where we could not. Mae was determined to prove this wasn't true, despite originally coining the phrase. She was going to live where John was, where his spirit resided. She was going to chase a ghost that had long since slipped past the veil of this world.

That was Mae. She played by her own rules, and nobody could or dared tell her otherwise.

"Mae, whatever this is, whatever mystery you've solved but has somehow created more in the process, can it wait until tomorrow? Or later today? Fuck, just any time when two humans are both awake for a conversation."

"It's nine here. I've been up for hours. Don't blame me for the time zones; blame Galileo or some such schmuck. And no, it can't wait."

"Yeah, I don't think Galileo had anything to do with time zones. And why can't it wait, exactly?"

"Because I just found out that John has a daughter, and she sure as shit didn't pop out of my hoo ha."

CHAPTER 4
MAE

Luc Brassard was, without question, the last person I ever expected to rely on. He didn't look like a historian. No tweed jackets with elbow patches, no neatly pressed Oxford shirts, and certainly no air of quiet dignity that suggested he spent his days surrounded by ancient texts—or ancient anything for that matter. Instead, he looked like someone who'd wandered off the stage of a drag cabaret show and decided to give history a go for kicks; typical for someone his age with everything silver-spoon fed to him.

His hair was a mop of unruly dark curls that had clearly never met a comb they didn't hate. He wore scarves—bright ones, the kind that would've made Picasso jealous—and he insisted they were "an homage to the great revolutionaries." Homage my wrinkled ass. Why can't men just admit they like bright colours?

At forty-two, Luc carried himself with the kind of swagger that confirmed my suspicions he coasted through life on just enough charm to get by. He was tall, lanky, and had a permanent smirk on his face—suggesting the punchline of a joke only he knew was just around the corner, even if he ended up being the punchline most of the time. But I suppose when you're not as bright as the rest, life is never really that bad.

I'd found him by accident—or, more accurately, because I was desperate. After another dead end at the archives, a librarian had mentioned him offhandedly, the words spoken so quickly and quietly it was as if they were already apologizing for the suggestion before it was out of their mouth.

"Luc Brassard," said the librarian. "He knows a lot—when he's sober."

That wasn't exactly a glowing endorsement, but my options were running out, and I wasn't in a position to be picky. And really, who was I to judge the alcoholic consumption of anyone, let alone a single French man in his forties? If nothing else, it sounded like a good time.

The first time I met Luc, I regretted it immediately. But, much like the kind of regret that's on par with realizing too late you shouldn't trust a fart after shovelling down bad shrimp scampi, once you've gotten over that hump, things feel better, if not slightly less embarrassing.

He sauntered into the café fifteen minutes late, wearing an emerald green scarf that looked like it had been plucked from the wardrobe of a 1920s Parisian artist. His jacket was threadbare, his boots scuffed, and he carried himself like someone who hadn't worried about anyone's opinion since birth. When he saw me sitting at a corner table, his face lit up like we were old friends.

"Ah, you must be the desperate American," he said, loud enough for the entire café to hear.

"I'm Canadian," I corrected, trying to maintain what little patience I had left.

"Even better! The Canadians are the only people in the world who drink more than the French. We're going to get along fabulously." He dropped into the chair across from me without waiting for an invitation, setting his battered satchel on the table with a theatrical flourish. "So, what brings you to my humble city? Lost treasure? Secret love affairs? A vendetta?"

"None of the above," I said, already lamenting the librarian's suggestion. "I'm looking for someone who knows World War II history. Someone reliable."

"Ah, reliable," he repeated, leaning back in his chair and lacing his fingers behind his head. "That's a word people use when they mean 'boring.' I assure you, I'm anything but boring. But I'm reliable, make no mistake."

This was a mistake. A colossal mistake. I glanced at the door, briefly considering making a run for it, or at least a hearty shuffle.

Luc seemed to sense my apprehension, because he leaned forward, his grin softening into something that almost resembled sincerity.

"Look, I know I'm not what you were expecting. But I'm good at what I do, and I've got a knack for finding things other people miss. You need me. You just don't know it yet."

"Do I?" I asked, raising an eyebrow. "You'll quickly come to find out I rarely *need* anybody."

He shrugged, unbothered by my skepticism.

"Let's find out. What are you looking for?"

I hesitated, debating whether to walk away or give him a chance. Then I sighed and pulled out the folder of notes I'd been holding.

"I'm trying to trace a specific soldier's movements during the war. His name was John Seasons."

"John Seasons," Luc repeated, pulling a pair of horn-rimmed reading glasses from his satchel and perching them on the tip of his nose. They were crooked, of course, with one arm held together with what looked like dental floss. "A fine, sturdy name. Sounds like someone who wrestled bears in his spare time."

I opened my mouth to respond, but he was already flipping through my notes, muttering to himself.

"Normandy, 1944. Caen. Oh, I see, you're not just looking for a soldier. You're looking for a story."

He said it so matter-of-factly that I froze.

"Everyone who comes to me is searching for a story," he continued, not waiting for my response. "They want to make sense of something, connect the dots, find the missing piece. History isn't just dates and battles—it's people. And people are messy, which makes history messy. That's where I come in."

He snapped the folder shut and fixed me with a look that was equal parts mischievous and determined.

"So, Mae—may I call you Mae, Mae?" He was amused by this wordy repetition.

"What else would you call me," I said warily.

"Mae," he said, leaning in conspiratorially, "you've come to the right place. I'm going to help you find your story. But first, *un espresso*. And a croissant. Have you tried the croissants here? My people have perfected the pastry, they are simply *magnifique!*"

Before I could protest, he flagged down a passing waiter and ordered for the both of us, tossing in a compliment about the waiter's tie that made the man blush.

I stared at him, completely at a loss. This man was a carica-ture. A walking cliché wrapped in scarves and smugness. How could someone so ridiculous possibly help me with something so important? Furthermore, his pronunciation of croissant, *kwah-sahnt,* somehow mixed English and French in the most wretched way since Boris Johnson and Emmanuel Macron shared a Cornish beer and wine. And yet, as I watched him dive into my notes with an intensity that bordered on obsession, I found myself thinking that maybe—just maybe—he wasn't a mistake after all.

Luc's mind worked like a chaotic symphony. He'd jump from one topic to another, connecting seemingly unrelated events with a logic only he could follow. He'd throw out obscure historical facts like breadcrumbs, daring you to keep up. It was maddening. It was brilliant. It was a version of me fifty years ago.

And it worked.

Over the past few weeks, Luc had somehow become an indispensable part of this journey, or whatever the hell it was that I was doing. I hated to admit it, but I didn't know where I'd be without him. He had a certain knack for gaining access to things he shouldn't, whether it was a private archive or the goodwill of a museum staffer. He could charm his way into— or out of—almost anything. I wasn't sure if it was raw intelligence or blind luck, but the results were undeniable. Again, my penchant for the younger, male reflection of myself was too much to pass up.

All that being said, let's not pretend for too long that I truly understood him. Luc was a walking contradiction in every way. One minute, he'd be rattling off the precise troop movements of Napoleon's army, and the next, he'd be shamelessly flirting with a waiter half or even double his age.

Okay, not quite double, but you get the idea.

And then there were the stories, outlandish tales from his so-called youth. Like the time he claimed he'd spent a summer masquerading as a tour guide at the Palace of Versailles just to see if he could. Or the week he "accidentally" ended up on a yacht off the Amalfi Coast with the descendant of a French king.

He was absurd. He was over-the-top. He was exactly what I needed, and I hated it. But I also loved it. It was refreshing.

And so, when his email arrived in the midst of reading Alex's, the only option was to abandon my current read and jump into whatever news Luc had waiting for me.

To: maedayseasons@questingmail.ca
From: brassard.through.history@mailtime.fr
Subject: Mae, I found someone
Date: January 8

Bonjour, ma chère Mae,

I do hope—je t'en supplie!—that you are seated, perhaps with a fine glass of Bordeaux in hand, because what I am about to reveal is no less than une révélation foudroyante! The kind of thing that makes the moustache twitch and the heart do a little waltz. I had not anticipated such findings—non, pas du tout! What I expected was a drizzle, but instead I found the torrential storm!

Now, I shall give you the condensé, the essence of this tale, but ma chère, we must talk in person, face to face, with the urgency of two spies exchanging secrets under a Parisian bridge. Time, as always, slips away like butter on a hot baguette— why wait another minute when we've waited a lifetime?

But beware, madame—ce que je vais dire changera tout.

For days I have turned this over in my mind like a warm croissant in trembling hands, wondering how to serve it to you gently, wrapped in ribbon and good intentions. But alas! There is no way to soften such a truth, no silk lining for this news. I, who am normally so eloquent, so poétique, find myself blunt as a spoon. Forgive me. Pardonne-moi.

Are you ready? Ready for your world to tremble like the bed of Luc Brassard with a stunning mademoiselle, the great and lusty sculptor of Nice, when moved by the fierce joy of amour véritable?

Her name is Jacqueline Laurent. Oh là là, quelle histoire! And from what I have uncovered, the puzzle pieces—les morceaux!—they fall together with uncanny precision. Her maman, may she rest among the angels, has passed. But Jacqueline? She has stayed close to her origins, living some fifty kilometres from Caen. She has dedicated herself to the remembrance of WWII with a passion that sings of a legacy she may not even fully comprehend. For this, je la respecte profondément. This Internet, it's a beautiful thing, yes? She had a blog for many years, though it's gone dark for some time now. But the Internet doesn't forget, does it? Non!

Mae, I believe Jacqueline is John's daughter. Oui, c'est vrai. The dates, the records, the hushed secrets; they all point to this truth.

I can scarcely imagine what this means for you, mon amie. It is much to absorb, like a rich boeuf bourguignon that sits thick on the soul. I could not keep this from you another second. You deserved to know.

If you wish to speak of this—if you want me to continue, to help, to uncork a bottle and sit with you in contemplation— say the word, and je serai là, wine in hand, heart open.

Reach out when you can, though I hope c'est bientôt, for this, this is un tournant, une vérité, une bombe!

Sincerely,
Luc

I went straight for the whiskey and I poured. And poured. And poured.

This is a dangerous game for anyone, let alone someone my age. But the blindsiding mention of a daughter belonging to John was dizzying enough, so why not let the amber-hued drink propel me to the brink of a whiskey-induced coma. Fuck it if I ever wake from it.

My instinct should have been to discount Luc's findings, laughing at the unbelievable words in his email, the idea too preposterous to hold even a kernel of truth never mind be a thread worth tugging.

But somehow, something felt off. This revelation—if I could even call it that—churned in my gut like week-old deli meat on moldy rye, uneasily digesting in the pit of my stomach. I had always trusted my instincts—I never would have made it this far in life otherwise. But *this*? This was something different.

I didn't dare ask myself what it meant that John potentially had a daughter. It opened the door to not just the unknown, but to a sprawling meadow of rabbit holes, each leading directly into an abyss.

Could there be more children? Did John love me? Was he who he said he was? Was he a liar? Is this a sham? Had I been duped?

Was Luc trying to extort me? Did John truly love me? What the fuck was going on?

The questions swirled like a hurricane gathering strength, preparing for a devastating landfall that would reshape lives forever.

Especially mine.

CHAPTER 5
ALEX

I HAD HOPED to fall back asleep after Mae hung up, but given the bombshell revelation and abrupt disconnection on the other end of the line, my mind raced until the sun started rising. As morning light crept into the room, I did my best to subtly rouse Erica. I nudged her gently, my hand brushing the soft curve of her shoulder, feeling the warmth of her skin under the sheets. She sighed, shifting slightly, but didn't wake.

When I finally had enough, and couldn't bear this isolated moment any longer, I nudged her again, a little firmer this time. It wasn't enough to discernibly shake her but rather pull her from the edges of sleep. Her blue eyes fluttered open, hazy with the remnants of dreams, and I could see the confusion before she even spoke.

"What's wrong?" she murmured, her voice thick with the load of slumber.

I swallowed hard, my heart pounding. I hesitated, my chest tight with the anxiety that had set up camp since the wee hours of the morning.

"It's Mae," I said, the words coming out hesitantly, as if I was holding my breath between them.

Erica shifted closer, her hand instinctively reaching for mine, life infusing her eyes, a wave of clarity sweeping through her mind despite having just been roused. I've always believed this to be an uncanny magic only women possess, an intoxicating portrait of true beauty despite the traces of dried saliva around the corners of their mouths. Whenever I awoke, I was, at best, a lumbering bear, moaning and groaning with every movement, reacting to daylight like a vampire.

And so, as a decent hour finally struck in our time zone, I recounted to Erica what Mae had told me on the phone. Since she immediately hung up after saying that John had a daughter, my conversation with Erica, at least in terms of any specifics, was rather short.

That didn't prevent a barrage of questions from Erica, however.

"What do you mean John has a daughter? How old is she? Is Mae okay? What else did she say? How did she find out? When did she find out?"

I had nothing to offer for this cascade of inquiries.

"I honestly don't know any more than you do, and I took the damn call," I said, letting my head drop as I ruffled my bed head and rubbed my eyes.

As was customary since our courtship began, conversations of a certain scale would not, under any circumstances, begin in the morning without coffee. After rummaging through the cupboards and settling a brief argument that it was in fact my fault for not grinding more beans, the coffee grinder went to work and the unmistakable aroma of the seasonal Starbucks blend filled the kitchen. Forget that first sip feeling, that first smell feeling is sublime.

We sat silently, intently watching the coffee drip slowly as though we'd be quizzed on how many drops were in the carafe, but really we were both eyeing up how much needed to brew before we could get away with filling a cup. Each drop fell with a soft, rhythmic patter, an echo reverberating in the glass confines of the pot, accumulating ahead of what was about to happen. Finally, I made my move, grabbing two cups and filling them as evenly as possible, the aromatic steam rising in unpredictable swirls, the surface of the dark liquid rippling ever so slightly as I carried the mugs back to the table. For a moment, I lost myself in the simplicity of it, but then I realized the only simple thing here was that it was coffee and it was for consuming, not romanticizing.

As much as I wanted to talk about the phone call, in equal measure, I also wanted to run as far away from it as possible. I may be an adult according to my birth certificate, but when faced with real-life situations requiring the assured actions of an adult, well, I'm one of the last people you would want on the scene first.

In true Alex fashion, I sat still as a mouse in the midst of a cheese heist, hoping that the silence would serve as some type of real-world *Men In Black* flash stick, effectively erasing what we knew—which was next to nothing—and allowing us to get on with our day as we otherwise would have.

I knew deep down we weren't about to have a basic conversation, a straightforward relaying and reviewing of a simple fact—this would be the kind of moment where seismic shifts could occur in our foundations, especially Mae's.

And so, as the coffee maker announced the completion of its duties with a conclusive beep, this break in the silence got the conversational ball rolling.

"So, what exactly did she say?" asked Erica, sipping from her coffee, two hands wrapped around the mug and looking as if she belonged more on the cover of a Ralph Lauren catalogue than here in a residential kitchen with me.

"She said that John has a daughter. That's it. That's all she said before hanging up."

"I don't believe it. I mean, I literally don't believe it. I've known Mae for a long time. I know how warmly she spoke of John. I've read some of his letters. Those weren't letters written by someone who would ever stray outside of the relationship he had with Mae."

"I know. I've read the letters too. But, I mean, I suppose it's possible, right? You hear stories all the time about soldiers having children with women in the countries they're fighting in."

At this remark, I received an icy glare that needed no explanation. I knew exactly the line I had crossed and there was no returning from it without immediate and honest penance.

"Okay, bad example," I offered apologetically.

"Bad example? When was the last time you heard of such a thing? And let's be honest, shall we, it doesn't take a war for men to wander into sampling what's out there. So, for a solitary second, let's just pretend you didn't say that and look at this from a different point of view."

Erica was silent for a good thirty seconds before I felt the courage to chime in.

"What point of view is that?" I asked timidly, but with a hint of wryness not heard but seen in the curling corners of my mouth.

"Fuck, I honestly don't know. I hoped you would have something."

Until our coffee cups were empty, we sat in silence, trying

to ascertain not only what to do and say, but how to get Mae to tell us more. She wasn't exactly the openest of doors.

If nothing else, I'll give Mae credit for dropping this bomb on a weekend, allowing Erica and me the opportunity to zombie-walk our way through a day with little to no consequence other than our own personal plans. The only necessary thing on my docket today was to shovel a bit of snow that had fallen overnight. The lack of sound sleep was presenting hangover-like symptoms, so I knew the fresh, cool air would do me good. And moving my body was never a bad thing. When I finally moseyed outside, the cold air bit at my cheeks; I stood for a moment at the edge of our townhouse driveway, psyching myself up to complete the task ahead.

The shovel in my hands felt like an old, familiar friend, a seasonal acquaintance that faithfully arrived each year and stayed for a while—one I was introduced to at the age of ten when my father had me start contributing to the wintertime household chores. The snow on the driveway was powdery and light; a strong enough gust of wind would have blown the asphalted surface clear, saving me any effort. Today, I would have no such luck, with not even the hint of a breeze. The snow glistened in the winter sun, sparkling like tiny diamonds scattered across the ground. It was almost too perfect, too pristine to remove.

Or so I told myself in a mental courtroom argument that would absolve me from performing the task.

Your Honour, my client had no right to deface such natural beauty, such art. Should we change the Mona Lisa's smile to appease the homeowners association too?

Resigned to the fact that my chore would need to be completed, I took one tentative step, then another, feeling an icy surface slick underfoot, deceptively concealed by a thin layer of the fresh powder I was about to destroy. And then, without warning, my foot slid and before I could catch myself or even brace, I was flat on my back, the cold shock of the pavement infiltrating the thin fabric of my pants. The wind was momentarily knocked out of me, and I lay there, staring up at the sky, trying to steady my breath. From somewhere nearby, a laugh. A loud, boisterous, unmistakable laugh.

"Nice one!" said David, my neighbour who had a knack for always being witness to such embarrassing events. He was, by all accounts, an asshole, and having to endure his patronizing ridicule on this of all mornings was more than I could take. He was, as a matter of fact, Phil Doubleday 2.0. Though I never thought it possible once upon a time, I actually missed Phil, his constant ridicule and off-handed if not slightly-to-overtly racist and ignorant commentary of those at Silver Springs.

I groaned and pushed myself up, wincing as my legs sang in protest. David stood at the edge of his driveway, his face split in a grin that was all teeth and antipathy. He was leaning against his overcompensating-for-something truck—I don't have to describe it, I'm sure you can easily picture it—his arms crossed, watching me with the kind of snide amusement that made my skin crawl. The kind that only someone like him would find funny, someone who got off on the small humiliations of others.

"Should've watched where you were walking, huh?" he said, the smirk never leaving his face.

I didn't dignify him with a response, brushing snow from my jacket and trying to ignore the sting to my pride as much as the ache in my hip. David had always been this way—ever since I moved in with Erica—always finding something to laugh at, something to mock. It didn't matter who it was or whether it was something minor, like a slip on the ice, or more significant, like the time he sold the neighbour across the street a broken lawnmower and acted surprised when they returned to ask for a refund. He had that obnoxious way of being loud enough for everyone to hear, that unpleasant ability to make others feel small. And yet, no one ever said anything more than "oh, that's just David." It might as well have been the neighbourhood tagline. Whatever trauma he endured to become this way, surely it wasn't deserved, but dammit if he didn't make it nearly impossible to think otherwise. He was the kind of guy who wore his asshole status like a badge of honour. People like this pissed me off to no end.

Unfortunately, Mae hadn't instilled the courage or taught me the art of snapping back and standing up to bullies. Not that it was her duty, but she was my Mr. Miagi in so many ways, why not this one too? If only she was here now.

You might think she would be on David's side, joining in the laughter and echoing the mockery of my misstep, but you'd be wrong. You see, Mae could handily bust my chops, balls, and whatever else she so chose, but damned if she would let anyone else have a go. A knowing smile crossed my face at the thought of her ripping into David.

I stood up straighter, brushing the last of the snow from my pants, not giving him the satisfaction of a second look.

"You're a real piece of work, David," I muttered under my breath as I walked back to my front door. He only laughed again, loud and uncaring. I didn't have to look back to know the smirk on his face hadn't faded.

"You're done the driveway already?" asked Erica, waiting for me in the kitchen.

"No, I'll do it later. It's a bit slick out there."

"And David's out too."

This wasn't a question. Erica, and the rest of the street, could hear David's hyena-like laugh. He was loud for the sake of being loud and it shouldn't have surprised me his booming chortle would penetrate the walls of the house.

"Yes, the asshole of the year is out there too."

"Did you say anything to him?"

"No. What's the point? He's still going to be an asshole."

"That's true, but it's also important to stand up for yourself, Alex."

"I wish Mae was here." I didn't know I was going to say it until the words left my mouth. Then I started to laugh. "I really do wish Mae was here to put that prick in his place."

"Well, let's see if we can get her on FaceTime and you can tell her all about it and ask for some pointers, how's that sound?"

Erica, I could tell, was as interested in getting Mae on the line as I was—even though we both refused to outright say it to each other. Maybe it was because there was so much to unpack, so many unknowns within Mae's blunt admission to wait much longer. It was nearing late afternoon in Caen and we figured that Mae would be home, sipping tea—or whiskey—and turning the pages of whatever book she had on the go.

It wasn't until three in the morning in Caen—9 p.m. for us—that Mae returned our call. We had tried earlier, six times during a four-hour span, and finally gave up. The lack of response was worrying and left both Erica and me on edge the rest of the day.

"Can't you take a hint," snapped Mae when her face appeared on our iPad. "Six calls and none of them answered, what do you think that means?"

"Mae, are you okay?" I asked, disregarding what I was certain was a rhetorical question—something I had never been exceptionally good at deciphering. "You call me in the middle of the night, drop a bombshell of a statement, hang up, and then go silent all day. You had us worried."

"Mae, ignore Alex—how are you?" asked Erica over my shoulder. "He's still working on his bedside manner."

"Let's hope he doesn't have to put it into practice often," snipped Mae. "But, Erica, dear, you look stunning as always. It's not even fair."

"Thank you, Mae. Alex told me what you told him. Honestly, I'm having a hard time believing it's true. Obviously I never knew John, but from what you've told me and the letters you've shared, this just doesn't add up for me."

Mae was silent for a moment, either from a minor connection delay or simply trying to formulate a response, of which it was clear she didn't have one. Her face filled the screen—she could use technology, but a camera's rule of thirds would always be foreign—it was literally lined with decades of laughter, worry, and love, but now it was vulnerable and crumbling under the weight of something unspeakable. She didn't sob or wail—no, her grief was quieter, more devastating.

Tears slid silently down her weathered cheeks, collecting in the creases of her skin like rainwater on cracked pavement. Her lips trembled, parted slightly as if she wanted to say something but couldn't find the right words, and her eyes were glassy and unfocused, staring not at me or Erica but at some unseen corner of her shattered world. I wanted to reach through the screen, to touch her hand, to close the unbridgeable distance between us, but all I could do was sit there, helpless, as her world unravelled before me in a fragile, tear-streaked moment.

"Mae," I offered softly. "What's going on?"

"I need you to come to Caen," she said, barely audible.

"I'm on my way."

CHAPTER 6
MAE

SHITE. Was inviting Alex to come here a huge mistake?

I know I needed his help, but now I'd have no choice but to let him into the inner sanctum, so to speak. To reveal to him the deepest, darkest parts of my past—and apparently John's—so that I could find the answers I needed.

I realized I hadn't given him a date or time, just that I needed him to come to Caen. He could be here tomorrow for all I knew. And knowing him, he probably would be. I got to work moving things around the apartment, tossing boxes filled with documents from the kitchen and living room into the spare bedroom—this would be my new base for uncovering all things concerning John. Alex could sleep on the couch. I don't want him getting too comfortable anyway.

The moment I decided to move everything about John into the spare room, I felt an almost electric urgency—like I had crossed an invisible threshold and there was no turning back. Or it was vertigo. At my age, you never can tell for certain. It took me longer than it should have, each object proved to be a kind of weight I wasn't sure I could, or would want to, continue carrying. But once I started something, there was no stopping. I first cleared the room completely, stripping it down to the bare walls, twin bed, and sturdy table that I'd dragged in from the storage closet. Every piece of history that I moved—his photographs, the stack of letters bound with twine, official documents with seals I still didn't fully understand—felt monumental, like I was in *The Da Vinci Code*, collecting and arranging puzzle pieces that might eventually reveal an answer I wasn't even sure I was ready for.

How did that Tom Hanks do it? He was always prepared for everything. A national treasure that man.

By the time I was finished, the room resembled an investigator's office, though far messier. On one wall, I'd pinned every photo of John I had, along with a map I'd scribbled on to track his unit's movements and the records that pointed to places I'd never heard of. The table was a chaotic spread of papers, folders, and the leather-bound notebook he'd carried with him everywhere. I hadn't opened it since the day I found it. I wasn't sure if I was ready now. It could wait.

This room—it was no longer just a spare room. It was a battlefield of memory and possibility. I sat down on the edge of the bed and let my eyes wander over everything. My chest felt tight, not from sorrow exactly, but from the sheer magnitude of what all this meant. I had chosen to turn my home, my life, into something entirely new—a mission.

Is this what a soldier's life feels like?

This question, every question I had, swirled through my mind like a storm.

Was I ready for what I might uncover? What if I discovered something more that changed how I'd always thought about John? About myself?

And more terrifying than any of that—what if I didn't find anything at all?

I pulled the lid off a cardboard box and, amongst the many letters I had saved from John, removed one at random, hoping that his words, his voice, would reassure me and carry me through the frustration and downright confusion I was enduring as a result of Luc's email.

My Dearest Mae,

As I write this, I can hear the faint hum of life outside our makeshift barracks—men laughing at some crude joke, the distant clinking of pots from the mess tent, and the occasional crackle of the wireless. For now, it feels calm, though the tension in the air never fully disappears.

The early days here have been strange, a mix of monotony and a gnawing anticipation of what lies ahead. Training fills much of our time, though the men are restless, itching for action while also secretly hoping it never comes. The cold here bites harder than I imagined, though the camaraderie among the men warms even the chilliest mornings.

I think of you often, Mae. At night, when the world feels still, I picture you sitting by the fire, mending something that I did not get around to fixing, or reading one of your novels. I miss the sound of your laugh, the way you hum to yourself when you are walking around town. I carry your photo in my breast pocket, over my heart, and when I am feeling particularly homesick, I pull it out and remind myself of what I am fighting for—what we are all fighting for.

There is talk among the officers of things escalating soon, but no one really knows anything for certain. The waiting is the hardest part. Some of the boys joke that we will be home by Christmas, but I can see the doubt in their eyes. Still, we hold on to hope—it is all we can do.

Take care of yourself, my love. I long for the day I can hold you in my arms again, and when that day comes, I will never let go.

Yours forever,

John D. Seasons

Fuck me.

How can someone write something like this and then go stick it in some French whore and produce yet another French whore? The letter, having read and reread it several times, didn't make any sense. This was the John I knew, the John I married. Forget that we were so young. Forget that love was new. Love in the 1930s had a way of creeping up on you, subtle yet undeniable and unrelenting, like the first strains of a familiar melody on a crackling phonograph.

If you don't know what a phonograph is, look it up. Just ask your watch or something.

But *this* love? I hadn't known what love was until I stumbled into it.

•••

The hall was alive with the kind of energy I'd only ever read about in stories—laughter ringing out, heels clicking sharply against the polished floor, and brass-heavy music filling every corner of the room. I wasn't supposed to be here. I wasn't like the other girls who wore frilly dresses, twirled around in heels they could barely walk in, and looked like they belonged. My mother had barely glanced at me when I'd slipped on the worn dress that had been tossed into my bedroom, unbothered by anything that didn't fit her narrow idea of what a "girl" should be. If anything, she was glad I would be out of her hair tonight. I wasn't the kind of girl who played these dress-up games. When George—the only boy in town who showed any interest in me—came to collect me, she was as dismissive of him as she was with me on the best of days.

We walked down the street, connecting eventually to an old dirt path that I had spent more time bare foot on than in shoes. George, by all accounts, was sweet, even if he came across as a bit clumsy and even more aloof. But, even at this young age, I knew that beggars simply could not be choosers. And so, George was my first ever date.

I could tell he was nervous when he picked me up, his feet unable to stay still, tapping along to a melody that was playing in between his ears. He fussed with his matted hair and rubbed his sweaty palms together. I know the degree of their moisture because, when he took my hand in his on the way to the dance, it felt like I was holding a freshly caught fish.

"Mighty kind of you to join me for the dance tonight, Mae," he said as the dusk slowly took over the sky.

"Oh, George McIntosh," I said, giddy as the schoolgirl I was, "I hope I don't disappoint you. I'm not much of a dancer. I'm not much of anything."

"Oh, now don't say that, Mae," he said, almost excitedly, jumping a step ahead and turning to face me, walking backwards in step with my forward motion. "You? Not much of anything? Well, you're not, not much of anything. What I mean is, you're everything. At least to me."

These innocent words, upon reflection much later on, would remind me what kind of devastation I was truly capable of. I didn't know it then, but I would be the first girl who broke George McIntosh's heart.

When we arrived, we were far from being early, and nowhere near late. It seemed that George had timed our travels so we could show up at the perfect time—a moment to slip in without getting caught in the fanfare of the masses, but still noticed by the few friends George had. My friends were few and far between, with focus on the few and extra emphasis on the far between. I didn't mind, though. I enjoyed doing things on my own, figuring out how to solve my problems and make my own way, even if it was a bit lonely at times. Okay, it was a bit lonely all the time.

Once inside, George made quick work of some small talk and hurried off to get something. I couldn't quite make out what he said above the competing rhythms of the music and noise of the voices. I doubt he heard me call out that I'd wait where I was for him, but I kept my promise, at least for a few moments.

I was standing off to the side, near the punch bowl, pretending to sip my drink just to keep my hands busy. And because it was free. Without George by my side, I felt out of place and all alone. Hell, I felt out of place even with George by my side, but the loneliness wasn't as strong.

The air smelled like a mix of perfume, sweat, and something too sweet—like candy floss—and it made my head ache. My insides, too, were twisting with the anxiousness that comes from knowing when you don't belong. I could even feel it in my bones. While everyone else danced and laughed, looking like they were born for the spotlight, I stood apart like a fly on the wall, shifting from one foot to the other—my shoes pinching—my awkwardness swallowing me whole. It was clear—I wasn't a dancer, didn't really care to be one, and I wasn't part of this world.

But then I saw him.

John.

He was leaning against the bleachers, his suit patched here and there, hands in his pockets, looking like he didn't belong either. He wasn't watching the dancers, wasn't even looking at the crowd. He was looking beyond them, lost in his own world of thoughts like he didn't quite care about these surroundings. The difference between us was that I felt like I was invisible, while John seemed like he was already absent. And maybe, for the first time tonight, that felt like a relief.

I thought he didn't notice me—until our eyes met. It wasn't some enchanted movie-moment, there was no time-standing-still slow walk toward me. But something sparked in the air, a small but undeniable connection between two people who hadn't been able to find their place in this world on their own, but maybe—just maybe—could find and share some space in it together.

Before I could contain myself, before I could even think about what was happening, John started walking toward me, his steps slow but sure. His shoes tapped lightly against the floor, echoing louder in the silent parts of my thoughts than I was comfortable with. By the time he stood in front of me, I could feel my heart thrumming in my chest.

"Mae?" he asked, his voice barely rising above the swell of the music. "May I have this dance?"

I blinked, completely caught off guard. "How the hell do you know my name?" I blurted out, my tone harsher than I meant.

John held up his hands, a smile tugging at the corner of his mouth.

"You're the only girl here not wearing one of those ridiculous frilly dresses your mothers make you wear," he said. "Everyone knows who you are, and I'd be a fool not to know too. And I, Mae Olson, am no fool."

I wanted to laugh, to casually brush it off, but there was something about his tone, like he wasn't trying to mock me, just stating a plain fact. And then, just like that, he asked again, his hand outstretched.

"So, what do you say? May I have this dance?"

I should have said no. I should have stuck to my familiar routine—keep to myself, have George walk me home when it was time to go, forget this whole thing. But there was something in his eyes, something I couldn't explain. I wasn't sure if it was the music, the tension of the moment, or something about how he was standing there, offering me a way out of my own isolation. Before I could back away, I found myself reaching for his hand.

My fingers brushed against his, and my world shifted. He was solid, steady, and he gently guided me onto the dance floor. It was as though he had all the time in the world to make this moment count. As I stepped into the rhythm, I felt a weight I didn't know I'd been carrying start to lift. My shoes were still uncomfortable, my body stiff with nerves, but John's hand was warm on my waist, leading me with careful precision. I couldn't dance. I wasn't graceful. But with him, I didn't need to be

"You know," he said, his voice soft against the hum of the music, "this song has been around for ages. But tonight? It feels like it was written for us."

I glanced up at him, unsure of what he meant.

"I don't know," I muttered, "I'm not the kind of girl who believes in stuff like that. And if you think for one second that a sweet-talking line like that will get your hands any further than they are now, well, you're sadly mistaken."

He smiled, a slow, knowing smile that made something inside me flutter.

"It's not about what I want," he said.

We continued moving together, slowly, carefully, completely in sync. It wasn't fancy—no twirls, no dramatic steps, just the two of us sharing a simple, synchronous rhythm. And with every step, I felt a strange kind of peace I hadn't expected. There was no lightning strike, no grand gesture. Just the song, his hand, and the way our bodies were in time with it all.

I wasn't the kind of girl who believed in fate. I wasn't the kind of girl who thought the universe had a plan for anyone. But as the music swirled around us, and with John's hand resting lightly against my back, I realized I didn't need to believe in any of that. All I knew was that this moment—us together—was right. For the first time, I wasn't thinking about anyone, especially not George. I wasn't thinking about myself, about the other people here, no one. I wasn't thinking that I shouldn't be here. I was here—and with John. And it felt like maybe I belonged.

He wasn't anything I'd imagined and somehow everything I needed—a boy with a shy smile that hinted at mischief. In a world teetering on the brink of uncertainty, where headlines spoke of despair and futures felt borrowed, he made everything feel boundless. Before him, love had been an abstract notion, something sung about in speakeasies or scribbled on the pages of penny novels. But there, under dimmed lights smudged with dust, I understood for the first time that love wasn't some lavish, unreachable ideal. It was a soft, aching realization that life without him would be as gray and hollow as the Great Depression itself.

And poor George. He would never know what happened that night, would never know where I went or with who. I just disappeared. I heard he married Sally Murray. I guess I did him a favour.

•••

Tears filled my eyes. Goddammit, John. After all these years, you're still doing it to me.

Why? Why did you have to leave? Why did you have to die?

The room seemed to hum with uncertainty, or perhaps it was the old, unpredictable radiator choosing that moment to work, and for the first time in a long time, I let myself fall apart. How stupid of me. Whatever lay ahead, this space would be my refuge, my base of operations. This wasn't just about finding answers anymore. It was about finding him. Finding us. Finding me.

And time was not on my side.

CHAPTER 7
ALEX

ERICA STOOD IN THE DOORWAY, her arms crossed loosely, not with any tension but with the kind of nonchalant openness that she inherently seemed to possess.

"So, Caen, huh?" she said, her voice light but steady, a subtle grin tugging at the corners of her mouth. I nodded, my stomach twisting ever so slightly as I tried to explain the whirlwind idea that had taken root in my brain the moment Mae made her request.

She didn't interrupt, didn't push back, didn't even question why I'd suddenly decided and quickly agreed to Mae's unexpected request. Instead, she stepped closer, taking my hands in hers, and told me that she understood and supported me. Fuck if I wasn't the luckiest son of a bitch on the planet. That said, I still studied her, searching for any underlying sign of frustration or hesitation, but there was none to be found. Just the unwavering warmth of her gaze and the certainty that she trusted me. This trip probably wouldn't make sense to a lot of people, but I've never been one to put pleasing myself before others, well not recently anyway. Once upon a time I was a lot more selfish, but it's amazing what you learn when you take the time to grow up and pay attention to it happening.

"You're not mad?" I asked, my voice cracking slightly. "I didn't really think through the whole consulting my partner aspect before the words flew out of my mouth. I've come to understand that's generally something one does with their partner."

"Mad? No," she said, laughing gently. "And second, Sheldon Cooper, I'm actually proud of you. For so quickly heeding the call to help a friend. Yes, most normal people would sit down, have a discussion, and hell, maybe even bring out the Ted Mosby yellow legal pad of pros and cons. But I doubt I'd enjoy you as much if you were normal. So, no, I'm not mad. You're following your heart and doing what feels right. You've always been that way, even if you didn't know it yourself. You're someone who shows up. Maybe a bit late at times, but you get there eventually."

"Ouch—low blow and the referee takes a point away," I said, bending my knees and protecting my groin.

"Besides, I've got plenty to keep me busy until you're back. I'm quite the independent woman, don't you know. We can't all gallivant across the globe on trust fund money."

I knew the last bit was a joke, and I had welcomed the teasing because of the money I had inherited, allowing me not to work. It meant I could spend my time doing what I wanted: volunteering, puttering around the house, being there for friends who needed a hand with a school pick-up or babysitting gig.

But everything else? It wasn't just her words; it was the serene way she said them, like it was the most natural thing in the world to let someone you love wander halfway across it for reasons they couldn't fully explain. Erica wasn't just understanding—she was the remarkable kind of supportive that made you feel like you could do anything. The kind you want to spend forever with. As I packed my bag that night, her encouragement echoed in my mind, anchoring me even as I prepared to leave. I tossed another T-shirt into the suitcase, pausing to consider the growing pile of random clothes that I was pretty sure covered all the essentials. A hoodie, some T-shirts, two pairs of jeans, socks that may or may not match, and a mildly questionable toothbrush I couldn't remember buying but was in an already opened package.

"This should do it," I muttered, zipping the suitcase with a triumphant grin.

"Are you planning to wash your underwear in a sink in Caen?"

"What? No," I said defensively. "I packed plenty. I think."

She arched an eyebrow and unzipped the suitcase, riffling through it with the precision of someone who'd done this before.

"Uh-huh," she said, pulling out a lone pair of boxers and holding it up like it was exhibit A. "Define 'plenty.'"

I scratched the back of my neck. "I mean, that's just being efficient, it's space-saving. You can flip them, right? Front, back—"

"Stop now. Just stop," she said, cutting me off with a look that was half amusement, half horror. "This doesn't fly. You're not a twelve-year-old off to camp in the woods for a week. You don't have to pack next-to-nothing light. We live in modern times, with air travel and checked baggage. You know you can pack more than one bag, right?"

Before I could argue, Erica was pulling open drawers, folding shirts with the speed of a retail worker during a

Black Friday rush, and gathering travel-sized toiletries I'd completely forgotten about.

"You also need deodorant," she said, sniffing the air pointedly.

"Hey, I was gonna pack that!" I lied. I would have totally forgotten to pack it.

She shoved the neatly repacked suitcase toward me, no longer a haphazard assortment of garments, now an organized and easy to close piece of luggage containing the actual essentials for human travel and survival.

"Congratulations," she said, patting my shoulder. "You're now equipped to last more than forty-eight hours in a foreign country without becoming a cautionary tale."

I grinned sheepishly. "What would I do without you?"

"Pack half a suitcase and wear the same shirt for a week," she shot back, walking out of the room triumphantly. And, annoyingly, she wasn't wrong.

"I'll start looking at plane tickets to get you on the first flight out."

The earliest available departure was in two days—a seven-hour and forty-minute trip, flying from Toronto's Pearson International Airport with layovers in Paris and Lyon before finally landing at Caen's Carpiquet Airport. We don't need to talk about the round-trip cost, at least according to Erica. As she saw it, and I was wont to agree, this was one of those "it costs what it costs but let's never speak of it again" financial outputs. This, of course, would include the price of the flight and any expenses I was bound to incur while I was there, many surely involving the alcohol Erica told me not to let Mae drink.

Erica drove me to the airport, leaving in plenty of time to make my 9:30 p.m. flight. It would be approximately 5 p.m. the following day when I landed in Caen after the layovers and to-be-expected minor delays; I was mentally preparing myself for interacting with Mae on such a fucked up sleep schedule.

The red-eye from Toronto to Paris played out like every chaotic travel story, with a string of missteps that snowballed into something bordering on comical. At security, the guy ahead of me was arguing passionately about his "emotional support sourdough starter." Upon overhearing this, I had to look up what this was, as I'd never heard of such a thing.

Without getting into every detail, basically, a sourdough starter is a mix of flour and water that ferments over time, capturing wild yeast and bacteria from the environment. It bubbles and rises when active, creating a tangy smell and serving as the natural leavening agent for sourdough bread. Regular feedings of flour and water keep it alive and ready for baking.

Apparently, this starter had travelled with him to six countries so far, but today, something about its size meant it wasn't going anywhere else. The container was confiscated, its inevitable demise marked by a dramatic sigh and an impassioned plea to "take good care of Lucille." By the time I reached the metal detector, I realized I'd forgotten to remove my belt, setting off the alarms and earning myself a thorough pat-down. The agent found two loose Skittles in my coat pocket and asked, straight-faced, if they were "important to the journey." I told him they were for morale. He didn't laugh.

Boarding the plane was its own form of madness. A family of five was blocking the gate, trying to consolidate their bags at the last moment, while an older gentleman in a beret argued with the gate agent in lightning-speed French about why his seat wasn't near the window he swore he'd booked. Across from me, a group in matching Eiffel Tower sweatshirts were already deep into their duty-free purchases, the cloying scent of discount cologne wafting across the boarding area. When I finally got to my seat, I realized I was in for a long flight, and not just by the clock's say so. My seatmate was a guy who spread himself across the armrest like he was making a territorial claim, and the moment we reached cruising altitude, he nodded off and began a slow descent toward my shoulder, mouth open and snoring as softly as an overworked espresso machine.

The in-flight entertainment included all the latest must-see movies—none of which I could enjoy because my screen flickered like a dying streetlamp. I ordered the pasta instead of the chicken cordon bleu—a decision I regretted immediately—although was there really a good choice to be made here? The noodles were somehow both undercooked and mushy, their sauce resembling something between marinara and the chef's regret. A man a few rows ahead of me attempted to open a banana with a plastic knife, while another passenger spilled a glass of red wine across his tray table and proceeded to dab at it with the world's smallest napkin. Somewhere over the Atlantic, a baby three rows back began a crying marathon; I respected its assessment of our surroundings and envied its raw honesty.

By the time I landed in Paris, the first leg of my not-so-amazing race, I was jet-lagged, sticky from some mystery condensation that had dripped from the overhead vents, and smelled faintly of spilled white wine courtesy of an overzealous flight attendant. I stumbled off the plane with a crick in my neck, zero dignity, and the unwavering belief that things had to get better.

After the layovers in Paris and Lyon, my final destination was approaching by the minute. Oddly enough, the closer I got to Caen, the more my anxiety ramped up. I didn't know what state Mae would be in when I arrived. She was unpredictable at the best of times, and these circumstances were entirely new and far from placid.

And, on top of that, my relationship with Mae felt like a spirited toddler we were trying to raise together—equal parts delightful and utterly exhausting. It had learned to walk, though not always steadily, and every so often it tripped over its own innate stubbornness. It thrived on candid observations and sometimes burst into a tantrum over things neither of us could remember five minutes later. It could be demanding and require total attention at the most inconvenient times—3 a.m. phone calls bearing life-changing revelations, for example. But for every meltdown, there was a moment so genuinely pure, so gut-wrenchingly sweet, that I wouldn't hesitate to forgive the metaphorical crayon marks it left all over the walls. It wasn't perfect, but it was ours, and I couldn't imagine life without it—even when it kept me up all night.

I was adjusting to the time change awkwardly—Caen being six hours ahead of my mental state—but adjusting nonetheless. When I finally arrived, I was relieved to learn that my taxi ride into the city centre was only about fifteen to twenty minutes, depending on traffic. This was one detail I hadn't bothered to consider in my haste to fly across the ocean. As evening began to advance, the light in the sky gave way to the illuminated streets and shops that lined them. The city was wrapped in the kind of chill that seemed to muffle everything. The streets, slick from a steady drizzle, glistened under the soft glow of streetlights just beginning to flicker to life. The sky hung low and gray, which is also how I felt after spending so much time suspended in it. It certainly appeared the clouds were plump with the possibility of more rain—or maybe a dusting of snow if the temperature dared to drop just a little further.

I had never been to France before. Never been outside of North America for that matter. I felt like the quintessential tourist, taking in every sight, sound, and smell; my senses, despite their connection to my exhausted central nervous system, were alive and curious. At first glance, the city felt subdued, but not somber. Warm, golden light was spilling from the windows of cafés and brasseries—again, something I had to look up at the cabbie's remarks, learning that brasseries are restaurants that serve hearty, traditional dishes in a casual and lively setting—revealing clusters of people huddled over plates, steaming cups of coffee, or glasses of red wine.

The Orne River flowed dark and steady, its surface reflecting the twinkling lights of nearby bridges and the silhouettes of bare trees lining its banks. Pedestrians moved about briskly, wrapped in scarves and thick coats, their breath visible in the crisp air. Far from home as I was, the familiarity of this place was surprisingly strong.

Positioned along the roadway were signs pointing to the Caen Memorial Museum, a renowned site dedicated to World War II, the Battle of Normandy, and peace. A chill shot through my body upon seeing them, prompting thoughts of John and all the soldiers who fought in the war.

Since her arrival, Mae had stayed in an apartment nestled within the heart of the city, where cobblestone streets crisscrossed between cafés and boulangeries—bakeries specializing in bread and baked goods—charming establishments that breathed life into the mornings in such a way it was like a scene from a movie, and far from anything that existed back home.

I paid my driver what seemed like a reasonable amount until I remembered the exchange rate, and then I frugally scaled back his tip—evidence of me being cheap and despising tipping culture. As I stepped out of the cab and collected my belongings, I inhaled air that smelled faintly of damp stone mingling with the tantalizing scent of roasted chestnuts from a cart near the square. I was definitely not in Kansas anymore.

I double checked the information Mae gave me and proceeded toward a ground-floor apartment tucked into the corner of a narrow street, sandwiched between two older buildings with weathered façades and wrought-iron balconies covered in ivy. It's the kind of place that doesn't demand attention, but manages to convey a nuanced elegance—one that suggests a history lived in every corner, on every surface.

How fitting for Mae.

Above the front door, a small brass plaque with the building's number gleamed faintly in the dimming light. The door was solid and looked heavy, its wood darkened with time and framed by tall windows that looked onto the street. When I opened it, the door groaned with a nostalgic familiarity that made me smile. The hallway beyond was narrow, the floorboards creaking under foot as if stretching after a long day. Flickers of light sparked from a pair of antique wall sconces.

Mae's door was ajar—after buzzing me in she removed the step of me having to knock before gaining entry. I pushed the door open, struggling to avoid hitting anything with my suitcase, the entry narrower than I was used to. The apartment was smaller than I expected, but comfortably warm, so at least there was that. The walls were painted in a soft shade of cream, with a few aged pieces of art hanging here and there—brushstroke landscapes, black-and-white photographs, and one vibrant print of a Paris street scene. The honey-toned hardwood floor was worn in several places, telling you the space had been lived in, loved even, for a very long time. The kitchenette was tucked into one corner, modest but functional, with open shelves stacked with glasses and mugs, a kettle, and mismatched plates. The sofa sat along one wall, its iron frame simple but sturdy, covered by a quilt that had seen its fair share of use. There was a long, narrow window above the couch, its pane filled with the view of softly swaying tree branches outside. The interior was quiet, the sounds of the street barely making it inside; I could already see how Mae would have appreciated the intimacy of the space, settling in with an almost immediate sense of belonging.

"Mae," I called out, not seeing her in the living room or kitchen.

"In the back, Sonny," came a muffled reply.

Why Mae chose not to greet me was beyond me, but I didn't think too long about it. You don't question Mae's quirks and idiosyncrasies, it's best you just accept them and move on. Life is much easier that way. And so, I dropped my things and meandered to where I thought the voice had come from. In the back, two bedrooms were separated by the bathroom, and Mae was in what would have been considered the spare room, but instead looked more like the aftermath of a violent paper tornado. Documents, photos, and random notes were scattered across the bed, desk, and floor like a piñata full of stripper flyers exploded at a drunken office party in Las Vegas. All that was missing was a map to figure out where it all went, and maybe a search-and-rescue team to dig out the actual bed. If this was an art installation, it definitely wasn't one that would make it to the Louvre.

Sadly though, this wasn't art. It was heartache. It was sadness. It was the hardened devastation that had settled into every crevice of the room, filling the space with an emptiness no amount of paper or photographs could cover up. And Mae, hunched over amidst it all, wasn't just sorting through papers—she was sorting through pieces of herself and fragments of a life she didn't know how to find again.

CHAPTER 8
MAE

Though I knew he was coming, the look on my face upon seeing his seemed to have suggested otherwise. He looked at me as if I looked different, as if the last two years had transformed my spirit to such an extent that my exterior features were reshaped too. And perhaps they were. But I knew that my eyes were the key to it all, and within them he could still see a flicker of the Mae Seasons he knew. It wasn't burning as brightly, but it was there. I knew it was there.

"Alex, my boy," I said, barely audible. I wanted to say more, but the words didn't come.

"Mae, what's going on?" he asked, scanning the room and trying to absorb and understand what he was truly looking at. He was met with a prolonged silence.

Alex took off his coat and walked toward me, cautiously, of course, given the history of physical attacks I was prone to deliver, especially to his shins. He considered his approach, slow and steady to avoid startling me with anything I may not see coming, and was convinced he saw acceptance of his advance. What a beautiful idiot this boy is.

Crack.

"Mae, what the hell?" he bellowed, grabbing his shin and hopping up and down like a kid on a sugar rush.

"Never let your guard down, Sonny," I said with a soft smile. "Now, we'll get to all this, but not in your sorry state. You look like someone who just slept in a blender. Did they hand out turbulence as a complimentary gift, or is this what your face looks like in real life these days? FaceTime filters are your friend."

It could have been the sheer exhaustion or the truly comical way I show I care for someone by verbally demoralizing them, but Alex launched into a fit of laughter that, somewhat surprisingly, I joined in on.

"It's good to see you, Mae. It's really good to see you."

"I know. I'm a fucking delight."

I ushered him back to the living room, pointing at the couch as the humble sleeping space he'd be occupying while he was here. It was clear that the spare bedroom was in use and his presence would certainly not alter that reality. The couch, thankfully for him, pulled out into a bed, but I could see by his blank expression he was skeptical of the support it would offer.

"This reminds me of that *Seinfeld* episode where Elaine goes to Florida and sleeps on the world's most uncomfortable pull-out bed. I've gotta say, Mae, you have a real penchant for the warm and cozy."

He was, of course, referring to the cabin in Pineton, which I had encouraged him and Erica to use on several occasions, and now he was describing this quaint little apartment. I knew how to create a comfortable setting where you couldn't help but feel at ease.

As Alex studied his sleeping spot and moved some things around on the couch, I took to the kitchen, grabbing a pair of glasses and a bottle of whiskey, waving my hand for him to join me. We sat across from each other at the scarred kitchen table, the kind of table that had borne witness to years of lively dinners, intimate conversations, and drag-em-out arguments. This table—this table was me.

Fuck. This table was me.

This was the best comparison I could bring myself to make, and it only took being here for two years to figure out. I, Mae Seasons, am akin to a fucking piece of furniture. Tables get walked away from, scratched up, and covered in sticky messes nobody wants to clean, even when they were produced from love. But, if I'm a table, I hope I'm at least the kind you flip over in the heat of a bar fight—not one gathering dust in the forgotten corner of some antique shop basement.

I sat back, inching away from my inanimate self equation, my glass cradled tightly in both hands. I wasn't drinking from it so much as staring into it, my lips pressed into a tight line, gazing as if I might find the truth swirling at the bottom. I wouldn't, of course, but an old lady has got to look wise if nothing else. Or maybe it just made me look more like a table.

"So, John has a daughter," Alex blurted out with the tact of a jackhammer on a glass floor. I could see him immediately brace for impact after such a jackass statement.

"Yes, it appears so. Not wasting any time cutting to the chase, are we Sonny?" The words were suspended in the air, substantial and undeniable. I snickered, but it came out hollow, the sound sharp enough to make him wince. "A daughter I knew nothing about. So, how do you like them apples?"

I realized that my voice was laced with disbelief, anger,

and a raw edge of hurt even I couldn't quite mask, and I'm the queen of masks. I set the glass down harder than I meant to—the sound echoed louder than either of us expected in the stillness of the room, making us both shift in our seats.

"Okay," Alex said, fidgeting with his glass and swirling the amber liquid around. "Let's start with what we know. Or—don't know, apparently."

I applauded the fact that he tried to take a soft tone, careful not to stoke the fire already burning in my chest. He would subscribe to, if not write it himself, the next book on gentle parenting. Though in his case, it would be out of admitted defeat and not applied social science; he couldn't discipline a child any more successfully than he could stick it in a porcupine—both scenarios hysterical to imagine and ending with relatively the same outcome.

"What's so funny, Mae?" he asked, noticing my smile as my mind wandered.

"Nothing. Just thinking about a joke I heard," I replied without thinking. "Actually, no, I'm thinking about you fucking a porcupine."

At this, I burst out laughing. My poker face was betrayed, my guard down, my mask tossed aside. This was going to be a lot fucking harder than I thought.

"Why in the hell would you be thinking about that?" he managed to sputter after spitting a sip of his drink on the floor. "And why a porcupine? Why not a—wait, no, it really doesn't matter. There's no acceptable alternative."

I continued to laugh, needing this moment of unannounced and unfiltered joy. He must have sensed it too, because he played right along.

"So, how many dates have me and this porcupine been on?"

Once our cruder-by-the-moment scenarios and fits of laughter played out, Alex again asked what we knew. The jovial tone of the past few minutes gave way to the more serious.

"What do we *know*? Nothing. We *know* nothing, Alex. Just that John lied about how he felt about me."

My voice cracked, and for a moment, I could feel myself appearing so small and frail, my usual defiance overshadowed by the power of betrayal.

"We'll figure it out. Whatever this is. We'll figure it out," he said, leaning closer, but failing to convince me.

Maybe he couldn't discipline a child, but he did know how to be a friend. He was steady, determined. I had helped him, and it was now his time to help me. But would I let him?

He reached for my hand, but I pulled it away, shaking my head. I couldn't bear the comfort yet.

"You don't get it," I said. "This isn't just some secret. This is—everything I didn't know about him."

We sat there for a long moment, the whiskey between us remaining untouched, as if we knew drinking more wouldn't dull the sharp edges of what was unravelling. Slowly, methodically, I withdrew a collection of photos from a folder and placed them on the table.

"They're from the day of our wedding."

•••

The world around us was alive with the innocuous movement of nature—the soft sway of the wildflowers, the murmur of the breeze through the trees. It felt like we had stepped into a world all our own, separate from everything. It was just the two of us. No one else, no family or friends. Mostly because there really wasn't much to speak of in those areas, but also because there was an even greater disapproval of what we were about to do. There was something almost sacred about this wild, forgotten corner of the world, a place where we could be who we were without any expectation or judgment. Oh, to live in a world free of judgment and expectation.

John stood across from me, his eyes soft and steady, holding my gaze with a tenderness that made my heart swell and ache. Each of my rough edges was smoothed over in this moment. He wasn't a man of many words, believe it or not, but when he spoke, they were heartfelt and poetic, and the ones he had spoken yesterday still echoed in my mind.

"I didn't have the right yet," he'd said, his voice rich with sincerity, "but I made a promise. A promise to you, Mae, that I would marry you."

I hadn't questioned it then. I didn't need anything more. The promise was enough.

As I said, there were no crowds here, no one to cheer or clap. Only the birds and the soft rustling of the leaves in the distance. Only the two of us, standing in the midst of wildflowers that looked as though they had bloomed just for this moment. And perhaps they did. If ever there was a moment for me to wax sentimental, this was it.

I lied about my age to make this day happen—the only lie I'd ever tell him. Though, since he never asked, and I'd never been forthcoming, was it still a lie? There was something sacred about our love that made our age difference irrelevant, seeming as faint as a distant cry. And as kids, because that's exactly what we were, the age gap meant literally nothing. All we knew was how we felt.

He reached for my hand, and I let him take it, his fingers

warm and strong against mine. There was a formed intensity in his eyes as he looked at me, as if trying to etch this moment into his memory, to store it in a mental box that could be opened any time he needed. He knew, even then, this was a box he needed, but I remained oblivious.

"I want you, Mae," he said, his voice rough but clear. "Not tomorrow, not in a month, not when everything's perfect. Right now. Right here. I want you to be mine forever."

The earlier surge of emotion that had receded from the shores now rose to create a tsunami that finally hit me, crashing hard, wave upon wave. I swallowed deliberately to keep from completely breaking down right there in the meadow, but there was no levee that could withstand what I was feeling.

He had asked about marriage only the day before, yet it felt as if this was all I had ever known, ever wanted. That promise, that single vow spoken without pomp and pageantry, had bound us together more than any ceremony, more than any preacher ever could.

And yet, here we were, promising ourselves to each other in the only way that felt real and right for us. No rehearsed vows, no rings, no witnesses—just the steadfast and sincere promise in his eyes, the certainty in his voice, the love that wrapped itself around us like the wildflowers blooming in all directions.

"I'm yours, John," I whispered, my voice barely above a breath. "And you're mine. Nothing will ever change that. Not today. Not tomorrow. Not ever. I promise you this."

His hand moved to my cheek, the touch of his fingers against my skin sending a shiver down my spine. He leaned in, and for a moment, time seemed to stop. There was no sound, no movement, just the heat of his breath on my lips, the wildness of the world around us, and then his kiss—soft, gentle, but full of all the things we didn't need to say.

When he pulled back, his eyes were full of something I couldn't name, but I understood it. I understood the promise he had made—that he would love me without needing anything more than this.

And in that moment, I knew that the two of us standing here in the wildflowers, with nothing but the world around us and the love between us was enough. No family, no friends. Just the promise we shared, and the beauty of this place.

That was all we needed.

...

The late evening slipped by quickly in the dark night and sleep was now calling us with greater urgency. I knew it wouldn't be long before we started piecing questions together, plotting out timelines, pulling threads that might lead to answers. My eyes never stopped burning with anger and something that felt like grief, and my jaw tightened with every new piece of the puzzle that refused to fit, which is to say all of it.

None of it made sense, but dammit if I was convinced it somehow did. We didn't know where this would lead or what answers we might find, but as the night stretched on, one thing became clear: we wouldn't stop until the truth was uncovered.

CHAPTER 9
ALEX

I woke up with a jolt, the pain in my back—it felt like my spine had been twisted into a knot overnight—sending a sharp reminder that I was sleeping on a pull-out couch in a room that wasn't mine, in a city I knew next to nothing about, and for reasons I wasn't entirely sure of. In another life, this would have been the end of one hell of a story. But in this one? It was only the beginning. I groggily shifted, trying to get comfortable, but every little movement seemed to intensify the ache. My eyes were still heavy with sleep and some jet lag, but the stinging discomfort was enough to pull me out of it.

I let out a long, frustrated sigh as I sat up, rubbing my lower back as I tried to remember how I even ended up here. Not literally this living room, that much I was aware of, but the here and now of this expedition into the past and the magnitude of what was waiting for us, what was waiting for Mae. Honestly, I wasn't sure what to make of everything that was said last night, even though there wasn't a lot exchanged other than how I may or may not break whatever laws existed about fornication with a quilled rodent. There was so much to process. But right now, my only concern was how badly my back hurt.

I wasn't sure how to start the day, so I reverted back to being a child and did what they do: I stood up. The difference here was that children immediately bolt through the house with the speed of a jet-fuelled blue hedgehog, whereas I, the epitome of pitiful male health in my thirties, did so gingerly, testing my legs as I tried to brace and stand without falling over. My back wailed in protest, but I pushed through, knowing I needed to get moving. This wasn't *Seinfeld*-level back pain, but it felt close enough. What did George do again? He had to move. So I would too. Pushing forty sure made you appreciate a good stretching routine.

Add that to the list of things to incorporate into a daily practice for when I get back home.

With a sigh and grimace, I stretched, doing my best to ignore the ringing pain as I shuffled to the bathroom. Looking out the window, I saw the sun gently rising, the beginning of a new day that only God himself knew the course of. But I wasn't going to let that stop me from helping Mae. I owed her that much.

I splashed water on my face, the cold helping to clear my foggy brain. My reflection was dishevelled at best—hair sticking up in random places, sleep still crusted in the corners of my eyes, and the weary look that only a night of emotional turmoil and enduring jet lag could leave behind. But I was alive, or at least that's what I inferred from my body's simple, feeble movements.

When I walked back out, Mae was in the kitchen, a kettle going for her, a percolator for me.

"Hey, good morning, Mae," I said quietly, the sound of

my voice almost foreign after the silence of the night. "How'd you sleep?"

"A lot fucking better than you," she quipped. "And to think I thought you looked like a bag of shit yesterday. This, my boy, takes the cake."

I grinned. This was the Mae I was used to. Last night's version all too often bordered on someone different, someone darker. The dark spot on her soul revealed in real time.

"So, what's the plan for today?" I asked.

"The plan for today is for you to clean yourself up, first and foremost. From there, we're heading out on a little field trip. I hope you packed some good boots."

"We'll take it slow, right?" I proffered, stretching out my lower back to the sound of a few soft cracks. "I'm still finding my sea legs, so to speak."

"No, we will not take it slow," she said. "We don't have time to waste, so quit fucking around and get ready. And in case you didn't notice, we're not on the fucking ocean, so those little chicken legs of yours have nothing new to get used to—other than maybe some exercise and muscle gain."

And just like that, we were back to the same weird, uncertain place we'd started from.

The Bény-sur-Mer Canadian War Cemetery in nearby Reviers was a meticulously maintained burial ground featuring rows of white headstones arranged across lush green grass and framed by ornamental trees and shrubbery. The cemetery offered panoramic views of the surrounding countryside, perfectly reinforcing the connection between the soldiers' sacrifice and the liberation of the region. Arriving at the site was enough to take your breath away when you paused to allow the significance of such a place to sink in.

At the centre of the grounds stood a Cross of Sacrifice, symbolizing unity and remembrance of all those who now called this place home. The names, ranks, and regiments of the fallen were inscribed on each headstone—rows upon rows of those long gone but never forgotten. I learned later that the cemetery was situated near the Juno Beach landing site, and held the graves of more than 2,000 soldiers, most of whom fell in the early stages of the Normandy campaign.

What the hell am I doing here?

A mild breeze stirred the nearby trees, carrying with it the faint scent of earth, while floral tributes placed on the graves added vibrant bursts of colour against the still, subtle backdrop. The place was calm, almost reverent, as if the land itself had absorbed the substance of the history it held. It was a space not just for remembrance, but for reflection—where the silence seemed to dampen the echoes of those who had fought, and those who had been lost.

I could feel the importance of it all, but beside me, Mae was focused intently, her eyes scanning the rows of headstones, looking for something specific. I knew where her mind was, what had been driving her for the last few days—John. This trip was wholly reminiscent of our day trip back at Silver Springs a few years ago, visiting a memorial gravesite for John. This site, however, was revealed to Mae in her research as where John could very well be buried.

Mae had her arm hooked through mine, something I chose to believe was born from sentimentality and connection more than the slippery terrain she had to traverse to get to the grave marker. Don't get me wrong, she was still leading the way, she just needed a little stability, or so she said. She stopped by a grave, her fingers grazing the stone as she murmured something under her breath. I watched her carefully, noting the determination in her posture. On our drive over, Mae told me how she was poring over maps, studying old military records, assembling fragments of information that, in her mind, might lead to one of the most elusive answers. She'd found the cemetery where John was likely buried.

"I think this is it," she said, her voice low but steady. "I've been researching. All the details match."

I studied her, wondering if the force of her words hit her as hard as they hit me.

"Are you sure?" I asked, though I already knew what the answer would be.

Mae glanced up at me, a mixture of exhaustion and resolve in her eyes.

"Yes. I spent hours cross-referencing the military records, the photos. There's an old report I found, dated back to forty-four, that listed the names of the men from John's battalion. John's name was there—one of the last to be confirmed missing." She turned back to the row of graves. "It had to be him. This is where he ended up."

"Okay, let's see what we can find," I said, not entirely convinced we would find what we were looking for.

"I know what you're thinking, by the way," Mae said, not looking at me. "You're thinking I'm foolish for setting out on this quest to uncover truths that I may not want to know. But here's the thing, Sonny, I need to know. I need to understand why things ended the way they did. I've always wondered—if I'd known what happened to him, would it have made a difference? Would I have made different choices in my life?"

She swallowed, the rawness of her words catching in her throat.

"Maybe if I know where he ended up, it'll help me let go. Help me understand, after these many years of my life, what it was all for—good or bad."

Her voice softened as she spoke, and I could tell this wasn't just about finding a grave—it was about finding closure, a way to untangle the constricting knots that had been tying her down for so long.

"I hear what you're saying, Mae," I said, unconvincingly. "But I have to ask, what do you mean? You may not know exactly how he died, and maybe that's for the best, but you do know that he did. What choices would you have made differently had you known how he died?"

I wasn't sure if this was the right line of questioning or even the right frame of thinking, but Mae wasn't making a whole lot of sense, at least not to me.

"I get it," she said, staring off into the distance. "Or maybe I don't. I honestly don't know, Alex."

Mae was lost.

"It's okay," I said, placing a hand on her shoulder. "We'll figure it out together. But Mae, sometimes letting go doesn't come from knowing everything. Sometimes it's just walking away from the past and leaving the questions behind."

As soon as the words left my mouth, I knew I'd stepped in it.

"Oh yes, you're one to talk," she snapped. "Do you not recall your little excursion to rescue a certain auburn-haired young lady, or should I say, to redeem yourself? You know it's not that easy. Don't go projecting your dollar store psychology on me."

I couldn't argue with her. Not because she was difficult—though she most certainly was—but because she was right. I was losing sight of why I came here in the first place: to be a friend and to help.

Was I somehow making this about me? Was I discounting Mae's feelings for fear that she was wasting what little time she had left on this earth? Who was I to dictate how she spent her time?

"Listen, I'm tired. You can see that," Mae said, some tentativeness in her voice. "I've barely been crass with you since you got here, but you have to understand that ninety-three years on this earth, seventy-eight of them relatively alone, are far too many to have on your punch card without knowing a little more than I do now. For me, this is part of the process. It's like finding a missing puzzle piece; it may not be the one you need at the time, but it'll make the rest of it fit."

"Damn, Mae, that's some expensive store psychology."

"You want to say something to him?" she asked softly.

"What do you mean?"

"Well, we found it. John's gravestone."

Lance Corporal John David Seasons
The Canadian Scottish Regimen
3rd Canadian Infantry Division
Died 6th July 1944
Age 22
"He gave his life for freedom."

She pointed to the faded letters etched into the stone. I hadn't realized that while we walked, and I took in everything but the names on the stones, Mae was doing nothing but.

Based on her composed stoicism, you would have thought I was the one who pointed the gravestone out to Mae. She didn't act immediately. Instead, she inhaled a few deep breaths of the wafting sea air before slowly lowering herself to kneel in front of the grave marker, her fingers gently brushing the cold stone. She paused for a moment, her lips moving silently. Then she straightened, looking at me with a distant expression.

"I don't know what to say," she admitted. "I guess—I just wanted him to know that I never forgot. That I never will. But also that I'm pissed as hell at him right now."

And, as if a switch suddenly flipped, Mae's expression shifted and she found the words she needed to say to her husband.

"You'll want to walk away now, Sonny. John is about to hear some language that would make you blush and certainly question your masculinity."

I did as I was instructed and wandered off in no particular direction, far enough to give Mae privacy but close enough to not lose sight of her. I caught her opening remarks to John, and she wasn't kidding, she let him have it. Despite my earlier blunder about leaving the past and questions behind, I was quickly understanding this wasn't just a search for a soldier's grave; it was a search for peace. And somehow, deep down, there was no doubt whatsoever that Mae would find it.

After a few minutes, Mae motioned me back over, ready to be collected and accompanied to wherever was next for us. As I approached, I heard her say "we'll meet again, don't know where, don't know when."

We walked away from John's grave, Mae never once looking back, steadfast in her new mission. She was determined to continue moving forward even though it meant constantly looking back. We returned to the taxi that had kept the meter running—much to my financial chagrin.

"Okay, now we really get to work, my boy."

This is how Mae started the conversation once we were on the road and on our way back to her apartment. It took some convincing to get her to agree to head back and warm up and relax. Despite her protests, what she just experienced was an emotional roller coaster that required a measure of recovery.

"We will get to work, Mae. And, I also have to apologize," I said sheepishly.

"Save it, there's no time for that repentance shit."

"No, Mae, I minimized what you were doing back there. I don't know why I did it, but I did, and I'm sorry. It's not what you need right now. It's not why I'm here. I'll try and do better."

"Look at you, apologizing like you're auditioning for sainthood. Newsflash: you're not that impressive."

She leaned in, lowering her voice like she was about to reveal the world's greatest secret.

"I've been around the block a few times. If I had a nickel for every time someone said they were sorry, I'd own half of Paris by now," she said, straightening up and puffing out her chest with a grin. "So, how about you stop grovelling and start being useful, like making me a cup of tea when we get back? A 'sorry' won't fix anything, but a good cuppa might do the trick. Ya?"

"Yes, Mae. That sounds good. I can do that."

And that's exactly what I did when we got back.

CHAPTER 10
MAE

We made it back to the apartment in one piece, physically anyway, the door creaking shut behind us with that familiar, comforting groan I had come to associate with safety. The air inside was cool, if not a bit damp from the rain that had started outside, but there was always a certain warmth waiting to be felt, like the memory of a long-ago hug. Or at least I'm sure that's how Alex would've described it. I think he rubbed off on me more than I care to admit. In the sentimental way, of course. Pervert.

The woodstove in the corner called out to me, its black cast-iron surface bringing me back to the rustic days when this was a primary heating source. Kids these days would look at this marvelous antique as nothing more than that, an antique. In reality, however, this was one of the most important features a home in Canada could have when I was growing up. The fire inside had long since died down, a bed of glowing orange embers now fading beneath a layer of gray ash, and we'd have to get it going again, a challenge that Alex took on without being asked.

This oughta be good.

I watched Alex cross the room with little more than a few long strides, far less than it would have taken me, and it momentarily reminded me of how much I'd slowed down. He knelt to stoke the fire, pulling a small bundle of dry kindling from the woodbox near the stove. The smell of old wood—earthy, rich, and faintly musty—filled my nostrils as I watched him carefully arrange the sticks in a tidy pile. I was standing in the doorway, observing with muted intensity, waiting to see if he could in fact do what he was confidently attempting.

"Do you know what you're doing?" I asked him, causing him to jump ever so slightly. "So help me to whatever higher power you worship, if you burn my place down, I will end you."

"No need to worry, Mae. I've done this a few times in my day."

The pressure was on now, the performance anxiety entering fast and furious.

"Do they make a little blue pill for fire building? If so, you'll need more than one. It looks to me like your confidence is shrivelling by the second."

I heard the soft scrape of a matchstick against the box, a welcome sound in the otherwise silent apartment, and when Alex struck it, the small flame flickered to life with a soft hiss. He held the match close to the kindling, watching the tip of the wood catch fire, visibly praying that it would take and grow—he did the sign of the cross for God's sake. As the flames started to crackle and flicker, the room began to change, shadows now visible and dancing on surfaces like showgirls. The woodstove thrummed softly, a deep, low sound that seemed to vibrate through the floor. That's when he turned to look at me with a look of triumph and smug satisfaction.

"Was that good for you?" I asked. "You seem mighty pleased with yourself. Must be all that solo practice."

I let a wry grin sweep across my face, and I made my way closer to the emanating warmth, the floorboards creaking beneath each step. My final destination on this particular journey was the armchair by the window, complete with worn cushions and a faded floral pattern that was too cheerful for my taste but would suit someone else just fine. You inherit what you get in a rented apartment in a foreign country, and you learn to live with it.

The smell of burning wood filled the room, pungent and clean, mingling with the faint traces of pine from the pile of logs stacked by the door. The fire crackled louder as it caught the fresh kindling; I could feel the heat start to rise, warming my hands as Alex dutifully fed the flames. Outside, the rain tapped against the windows, a soft, rhythmic percussion, but inside, with the stove's heat and the glow from the fire, it felt like a world apart. Safe. Protected. Like time itself had slowed down, which was problematic because I didn't need time to move any slower. You might think that odd for someone my age, but I needed things to start moving at a brisker pace, even if it meant getting both feet in my grave that much quicker.

"Kind of reminds you of Pineton a bit, doesn't it?" Alex asked, referencing the coziness of the cabin and the fact we were together and getting up to shenanigans once again.

Pineton. It became a place it was never meant to become.

•••

The cabin in Pineton wasn't just a retreat; it was a lifeline—or so I thought when I dragged myself up the winding dirt path for the first time. I had purchased the place on a whim from a gentleman who was anything but and could only be described as questionable.

John and I used to talk about places like this, the kind of sanctuaries where you could unfold, catch your breath, let the noisy world hush itself for a while. But when I crossed the threshold that day, fifty years old and heavier than I'd ever been—not in pounds, but in grief and defeat—I wasn't looking to catch my breath. I was looking to stop it altogether.

The cabin hadn't changed much, or so said the aforementioned suspect character who sold it to me—someone I wasn't entirely convinced had the right to do so, but the deed appeared legitimate and our transaction was never questioned. It was the kind of place where John and I should have sat on the porch steps whiling away the time, sharing a bottle of cheap wine and the grandest dreams we could hope for. The pine walls still smelled faintly of the trees that surrounded the place, and the floorboards still groaned and creaked like the greeting from an old friend. Or it could have been me. It was probably me. I was groaning about everything and anything.

The air was fresh and brisk, biting at my face when I opened the window to let the late autumn breeze swirl inside. The woods outside were thick and endless, stretching out like a blanket over the hills.

I loved the fall, it was my favourite time of year, and the view I had in front of me was the kind that once made me believe in forever. Now it felt like a grim mockery, confirmation that the earth could keep spinning no matter how hollow it all felt to me.

I wrapped myself in one of John's old sweaters. Yes, I still had one. It was frayed at the cuffs and hung loose on me, but it was the only thing I'd brought that felt like home. The fabric carried a faint scent of cedar and something else, something I couldn't quite name but that felt like him.

I walked out to the porch and sat down on the same steps we'd have joked were our throne. I didn't bring wine this time, just a glass of something dark and biting. Bourbon. The burn of it was enough to silence the roar in my chest for a moment.

The town was alive that weekend. I'd passed the telltale signs on my way in: a wedding at the church, a big family barbecue at the Johnson farm, baby showers and birthday parties in full swing. The same kind of celebrations that had always felt distant to me, like watching someone else's life unfold on the other side of a glass wall.

But at fifty, the glass had turned into a mirror. I couldn't help but see what was missing. Friends, acquaintances really, were sharing photos of grandkids and family celebrations, their voices bubbling with excitement when they talked about who was bringing the homemade pie to Thanksgiving. And I—I had this cabin. This porch. This sweater.

And this ache.

I swirled the drink in my glass and stared out at the trees, trying to let their stillness bring me some type of peace, some type of solace. Some goddamn rationale for why this was my life. But there were no answers in these trees. The decades without John, the milestones I'd never reach, the laughter I'd never share—it was all too much.

Inside, on the coffee table, sat the small amber vial I'd brought with me. The pills rattled softly when I picked the vial up, turning it over in my hands like it was some sort of ancient artifact, something I didn't quite understand but couldn't let go of.

It wasn't sadness that brought me here. Not entirely. It was the exhaustion, the bone-deep weariness that came from carrying too much for too long. It was the stark realization that I had nothing left to offer, and no one to offer it to.

As night settled in, I pulled John's sweater tighter around me, remembering the way it used to fit him just right. My fingers traced the worn threads. He'd always been too warm, shrugging it off after five minutes and draping it over my shoulders with a wink.

"You're tougher than the rest of us, Mae. Always have been," he'd say. "Don't let the world win."

Damn him for that. Damn him for leaving me to carry it all alone.

I stared at the pills for hours, the fire in the hearth burning low. I thought about how easy it would be. How hushed. And, finally, as I reached for the pills, the phone rang.

It was Dolores.

"Don't let the world win," she said on the other end of the line.

"What the fuck did you just say?" I gasped.

"I said don't let the world win. Oh, and I'm coming over. I know you're in the new cabin. See you soon. I am of the Midnight Sun for a reason, my love."

When dawn broke, the fire was out and the pills were still on the table, untouched. I packed my bag and left the cabin, John's sweater still draped around me. The ache in my chest hadn't lessened, but the world was still spinning.

And so was I. Begrudgingly. Stubbornly.

I left Dolores a note: *I don't know who you are, but you saved me again. Please keep saving me.*

And I left her another five hundred bucks.

...

I shifted in my chair, the light from the fire catching my profile, throwing long shadows across my face. For a moment, he just watched me.

"Does the flicker of the flames make me look almost otherworldly, like a figure out of a storybook?" I asked him. "Not everything needs to be compared, you know. You've got a habit of doing that, comparing things when there doesn't need to be any correlation."

"I just thought—"

"Don't think, just be. Don't think, just be. And while you're being, go make me my tea."

The good lad he was, he did as instructed—well, the tea part at least. As for the comparative tendencies, it clearly hadn't dawned on him that he was doing this, but who was he to argue with my observation. He brought my tea over and referred to it as nothing more than "simple hot leaf juice. It's like boiling a plant, then drinking its sadness." I have never been more proud of his insulting something inanimate.

"How are you doing?" he asked, placing my tea on the table beside me. "Despite your choice words for John, a few of which I heard, and you weren't kidding about how they'd make me feel, I don't think we've processed the gravity of the discovery you just made."

"To be honest, I don't really know how I'm feeling, but I do feel a little bit better knowing his final resting place," I replied. "I probably could have found his marker sooner, but I think—and don't you dare turn this into a Hallmark moment—I was waiting for you to be here with me.

"But, I suppose it's a little bittersweet. After all these years, not knowing *exactly* where he was, there was always some irrational hope that he wasn't there, you know? I'm not exactly sure why that's a comfort, but the bastard's in the ground and I know where he is, and he should be thankful right now that I didn't put him there."

Neither of us knew what to say at this point. It all made sense on one hand, while not making a lick of it on the other. What was becoming painfully obvious, however, was the change I invariably went through these last few years, uncovering secrets and information that shocked my very being. I knew I was a different person, but I didn't know how much of that was the result of what happened in the days before calling Alex to come to France or if this change has been ongoing since the day I first arrived.

Yes, I was still coarse and rough around the edges, and that's likely sugarcoating things, but there was a significant shift in who I was at my very core. Had this news really shaken me to such a degree that I was no longer the Mae Seasons that Alex knew? Or was there something larger at play? Was it possible that mortality became a conversation I was now entertaining inside my head? And, as if on cue, the little prick read my thoughts.

"Mae, how long has this been going on? I don't mean your search for John, I'm talking about the change I can so clearly see in you, and I'm pretty sure you can see in yourself too. Is this new or has this been going on for quite some time?"

I silently stared at the fire, a blank expression painted across my face, pretending not to hear the questions at all. With advanced age on my side, this wouldn't have been surprising—I can play the deaf card and no one would be the wiser.

But the question was a valid one. A valid one indeed. If you were a trout-mouthed Neanderthal that is. How long has it been going on? *Ha!* Measuring time seemed foolish at this point, even more foolish than going back in time to perform such a hokey task. I wouldn't dignify it with a direct response, no siree. But I suppose I owed him something.

"You've got to understand—my life, or the life I thought I was living, was just torn apart, blown up, and set on fire. It feels like I don't know anything anymore, and you know me, I know everything. So, imagine how truly unsettling this is for me. I just need answers and I need you to help me find them. But more than that, I need you to not ask questions and to not be, well, *you*. Can you do that? I mean, can you really do that? Can you just not be you for a while?"

"I'll be honest with you, Mae, I'm a little unsure. But I'm here for you in the same way you were there for me at Silver Springs. I'm going to do my best to help you—just please God, don't make me do anything that's gonna get me arrested in a foreign country."

"You know I can't promise that."

"Well, there's a part of me that's happy to hear you say that. I was fearful I was losing you."

"There's no getting rid of the one and only Mae Seasons," I said, my confidence returning and edging this sad-sack, woe-is-me version of myself to the sidelines. "You should know that by now. And we're only getting started. Next up, we're going to meet this little harlot who claims to be the daughter of my John."

I knew this was only the beginning of what I needed Alex to do here, but I wasn't sure what was going to happen next. He must have known that I'd concocted several schemes he would have to play out, more often than not, as a patsy. Try as we might, we'd never be prepared for what we were about to do next. And that's saying something, since I actually knew what we were going to do next.

CHAPTER 11
ALEX

Waking up the second day on the pull-out couch left me in the same early-morning discomfort as the day before. The only saving grace keeping my muscles moderately loose was the warmth of the room from the fire I had dutifully tended to.

Mae slept in, at least by her standards, and I got to making breakfast so that she would have something waiting for her when she did rouse. I figured that a full stomach would be required for whatever we were about to do today. Or maybe, knowing Mae, a full stomach would turn out to be an ingredient in a recipe for disaster.

"What smells like it was lit on fire and ejected from the backside of a sick raccoon?" was the greeting I received as the aroma of the sausage and pancakes I was making filled the apartment. How these savoury foods could have generated such a perceived stench was beyond me; I chalked it up to Mae busting my balls for the simple sake and sheer enjoyment of doing it.

"Breakfast is ready when you are," I said, not giving her the satisfaction of any reaction to her quip.

A few minutes later she shuffled into the kitchen and silently consumed the spread laid before her. I suppose the smell wasn't that bad after all. Mae ate her breakfast slowly, the way that someone who was truly enjoying and experiencing their food would do. But in her case, it was to prevent choking or to stave off the hiccups, both of which I'd dealt with while providing some form of care for her at Silver Springs.

"You ready for today, my boy?" she asked, looking up from her plate for the first time since sitting down.

"I'd say yes under normal circumstances, but I have no clue what you've got up your sleeve today. So, no, I'm not ready. I'm certifiably terrified, which I'm sure you can appreciate."

"I can appreciate a fine wine, opening your birthday presents on your actual birthday, and long, drawn out silences from people who should know when to shut up."

If Mae was telling me to zip it, I wasn't sure, but I played it safe and kept my lips sealed for the time being. Thankfully, this tactic worked, and Mae eventually steered the conversation to Luc Brassard, a name that was, until this moment, unknown to me. Little did I know, it would be a name that would never leave the depths of my memory when all was said and done.

"Luc was the one who discovered Jacqueline," she said, a stoic expression matching the tone of her voice. "And if you can believe it, the little Frenchman gave me the information in an email. A fucking email! Apparently she had some blog once upon a time, so sending me links and snippets was easier this way. Or so *he* says."

I prodded Mae about Luc, nothing too invasive, just some softball questions to get a sense of someone I was about to meet for the first time. Mae said we'd be meeting him at a café just down the road. This was heavenly music to my ears, as the percolated coffee I'd made tasted like shit brewed with a hint of burnt disappointment. With small talk out of the way, we gathered our coats and hustled out the door.

The café bustled with muffled, animated conversations in a language I could not decipher despite being required to study French for several years just to graduate high school. The soft clink of porcelain cups and the scent of buttery pastries wafting from the counter was an intoxicating pairing, and I was damn near salivating at spending time in my first authentic French café. I felt like Hemingway, minus the proclivity for pugilism. Mae and I sat at a small round table by the window, gray morning light spilling over the streets of Caen and pooling at our feet.

Luc Brassard arrived in a triumphant manner, his leather satchel slung over one shoulder, a mauve scarf loosely draped around his neck. His eyes were keen and intelligent, calculating even, but there was a genuine warmth to his smile that hinted at an old soul beneath his insouciant exterior.

"*Bonjour, mes amis,*" he said, his voice rich and confident as he took the seat opposite us. Without asking, he flagged down a server and rattled off an order in rapid French, his accent dancing on his tongue like a rhythmic melody. Mae and I exchanged a glance—Luc Brassard wasn't the kind of man who waited for permission or wasted time. This was likely why Mae was drawn to him and kept giving him assignments.

Moments later, the server returned with a tray of treats that Luc translated for me: teurgoule, the cinnamon-flavoured rice pudding famous in Normandy; a small bowl of Caramels d'Isigny, their golden sheen irresistible; and a plate of flaky chaussons aux pommes, still warm. Luc pushed the platter toward us, drooling like a St. Bernard.

"Local favourites," he said. "You eat. I'll talk."

Mae didn't need a second invitation. She reached for a chausson, breaking it in half and revealing the sweet apple filling. Apparently my breakfast menu left something to be desired in terms of being filling. I hesitated, unsure if I was more curious about the food or the man before us.

"Hi Luc," I said, extending my hand, "I'm Alex, a friend of Mae's. Nice to meet you."

Luc leaned back in his chair, folding his arms, his eyes glinting with satisfaction as Mae began sampling the sweet delicacies.

"Ah, Alex, *mon ami*, I have heard literally nothing about you, *mais oiu*, it is nice to meet me."

Great, Mae 2.0.

I withdrew my hand and studied Luc, whom I was growing to quickly dislike.

"Now," he said, opening his satchel and pulling out a large, weathered map. He spread it across the table, careful not to let the edges graze the teurgoule. "What I'm about to show you—well, it's not in any guidebook and it's not knowledge that many in this city have. You have struck gold with Luc Brassard."

The map was a labyrinth of ink and aged paper, dotted with annotations and small, almost illegible notes in French. Luc tapped a spot near the edge.

"This is Caen as it was during the Occupation. Notice the unusual markings here and here." He traced lines with his finger, pausing to look up at us. "These were routes taken by Resistance fighters."

"How do you know all this?" asked Mae. "I expected a historian would know many things, but this seems like something beyond that."

Luc's grin widened, a flicker of pride in his expression.

"My grandfather," he said simply. "He was part of the Resistance. After the war, he spent decades piecing together stories, journals, anything he could find. I've dedicated my life to preserving it."

"Why share it with us?" I asked, intrigued but wary. "This seems slightly out of place for what we're looking for, no?"

Luc's eyes darkened, his voice softening.

"Because the history of a place is not found in museums or displayed on plaques, Albert—"

"It's Alex," I corrected him.

Shit. This guy really was *Mae 2.0.*

"It's in the whispers from its walls, the cracks of its streets, and the lives of those who walked them, alive and dead. And you—you're looking for something, aren't you?"

"I literally just told you we were," I said to him as I looked at Mae, somewhat incredulous. "But yes, to repeat, we are looking for something. How did you ever figure that out?"

Luc shrugged, leaning back again, either undeterred or simply unfazed by the sarcasm.

"Call it a historian's intuition," he replied with a smile. "You didn't come all the way to Caen for the food. Or maybe you did. *C'est magnifique.* But Alex, you are looking for something too, I can feel it, *oui?*"

Mae broke the tension with a chuckle, brushing crumbs from her hands.

"Well, we did a little, for the food, that is. As for Alex, he's always lost, so he's almost always looking for something."

Luc chuckled, the spell momentarily broken, but the significance of his words lingered. He tapped the map once more.

"If you truly want to understand this place, you need to walk its past. And I can help you do that."

"You better be able to," said Mae, between bites. "It's the only reason, and I can't stress this enough, why you're here. I've had enough ego-centric men in my life, and I certainly don't need any more. Unless they serve, as you say, a purpose."

As we made small talk, I dug into the food and was not at all surprised that it tasted as sweet and delicious as it smelled. Mae and Luc chatted about what they knew already, what they hoped was just in front of them, and even included some nods my way in terms of being helpful. Well, Mae didn't quite use those words exactly, but I've gotten pretty good at translating what she really means.

By the time our plates were cleared, we were ready to get up and get moving. Luc led us out of the café and into the crisp air of Caen's narrow streets, his satchel swinging with every confident step. Give him a whip and a fedora and I'd mockingly squeal "Indy" at him.

The buildings leaned toward each other like old friends, their stone faces etched with time. I clutched my coat tighter, the wind picking up as if it wanted to eavesdrop on Luc's stories and my stirring thoughts. Mae stayed close, her expression alight with curiosity, or maybe fear of what was about to be revealed. Those two faces looked about the same.

Luc stopped abruptly in front of a modest doorway, its wooden frame worn smooth by countless hands. A faded brass plaque hung beside it, the lettering barely visible. He turned to us, his voice dramatically low.

"This," he said, gesturing to the door, "was the meeting place for a Resistance cell during the war. My grandfather brought messages here, hidden in the soles of his shoes. Can you believe it?"

As we rounded a corner, Luc slowed and glanced at me, his expression unreadable. "Your surname—Seasons, *oui?*"

Mae nodded. "Yes, you already know this. Why?"

Luc's face clouded, a flicker of hesitation crossing his features before he spoke.

"It's—unusual. For this region, I mean. Are you sure you've never had any family from Normandy?"

"Of course it's unusual for this region," snapped Mae. "It's not from this fucking region. I'm not from this fucking wine-sipping, cheese-eating, beret-wearing croissant of a country. I'm a Canadian. John was a Canadian."

Luc paused, turning to face us fully.

"There was a man—Jean Saisons, though he often anglicized it to John Seasons—who was, shall we say, significant during the war. He worked with the Resistance, but his story is shrouded in mystery."

Mae's face went a colour of white reserved for the snow in Switzerland.

"What did you just say? And let me remind you, *mon ami,* that you're speaking of not only the dead here, but a veteran of the war who saved your pastry-eating asses."

Luc exhaled, his breath a visible plume in the cooling day's air.

"Jean was a double agent—or at least, that's what the records suggest. Some say he was loyal to the Resistance. Others believe he was playing both sides, feeding the Germans just enough to stay alive while covertly aiding the Allies."

"Which was it?" I asked, sharper than I intended. "And there's a pretty important distinction we need to make right now about the John Seasons we're talking about."

Luc shrugged, his gaze steady.

"No one knows. The truth died with him, if he ever truly lived to begin with. His name appears in records, but never with consistency. There are gaps, contradictions. Some accounts paint him as a hero, others as a traitor. What's certain is that he disappeared not long after the betrayal I told you about—vanished without a trace."

Mae gaped at me, her expression that of a child whose Christmas just got cancelled, before turning to Luc, daggers flying from her eyes and poison on the tip of her tongue.

"I'm only going to say this one time, and you better make damn sure that the next words out of your mouth are *'oui, madame'*," seethed Mae. "We are here to learn *my* John's story, not about some potentially traitorous Frenchie who played both sides like a goddamn chess master."

Luc cocked his head, his eyes narrowing slightly as he studied us.

"I don't know. But your surname—it's not common, not here. And Jean, or John, was known for having connections abroad."

You fucking idiot. All you had to do was say 'yes, ma'am.'

A chill crept down my spine as the weight of his implication sank in.

If John did in fact have a secret daughter, couldn't he also be capable of this double-sided war game?

"Let me get this right," I injected before Mae could inflict any lasting verbal or physical damage. "You're suggesting that this Jean Saisons is in fact John Seasons, Canadian soldier, husband of Mae?"

"I'm not suggesting anything," Luc replied, his tone cautious. "But history has a strange way of repeating itself, *non?* Perhaps there's a reason you're here."

"What the fuck does that even mean," asked Mae, incredulously.

"Mae, I think it's time we find ourselves a new historian. This guy is three malbecs to the wind."

Mae didn't answer me. She was lost. The information she had just absorbed, or tried to avoid absorbing, was piercing her defences regardless. That, along with the confusion of Luc's words, was enough to make even the calmest mind spiral. If my thoughts were already reeling, questions rapidly tangling into knots I couldn't unravel, I could only imagine what was racing through Mae's head.

"The journal I've found, it's said to contain notes from people across the Resistance, including Jean. If there is a connection to you, perhaps it's in there," said Luc, clearly oblivious of when to stop.

The wind picked up again, scattering leaves across the cobblestones. Mae glanced at me, her brow furrowed in thought.

"Well," she said, forcing a conflicted smile, "I guess we're going to find out."

Luc nodded, his expression grave.

"Perhaps. But I must warn you. If Jean was your John, and truly was a double agent, the truth may not be easy to face."

I didn't respond, my gaze fixed on the horizon. Somewhere in the shadows of Caen, a piece of history was waiting for us. Whether it held answers or revealed more questions, I couldn't be sure. But for the first time in a long while, I felt the pull of something greater than myself—a thread tying me to a story far older and more complex than I could have imagined.

CHAPTER 12
MAE

...

THE SUN FILTERED THROUGH THE TREES in soft golden beams, dappling the forest path that had always felt like ours, something untouched by the frenzied world beyond. John stood a few steps ahead, his back to me, hands stuffed deep in his pockets as if bolstering himself against what he was about to say. When he turned, his eyes were bright with determination and tinted with truth. In his voice, a tremor.

"Mae," he began, his words heavy and deliberate, "I've enlisted. They didn't ask too many questions about my age."

The air around me seemed to shift and stop moving, the trees no longer towering protectors but silent witnesses to the sudden ache that twisted in my chest.

"You what?" I snapped, the words sharp enough to slice the fragile calm between us. "You lied about your age? To enlist in a war that's not ours? Do you think this is some kind of game, John?"

He flinched but didn't reply, which only fanned the fire burning in me.

"You're just a boy. You think running off to die in someone else's war will make you a man?" My voice cracked, but I didn't stop. "Fine, go ahead and leave me. I hope you realize how selfish you are—how cruel it is to drag me out here just to tell me you're throwing your life away."

The moment the words left my mouth, they hung between us like a thick fog. But what did he, or I, expect from a girl of fifteen? Was such an outburst justified or irrational? Did age have to play a factor here in the same way it did for his enlisting? Too many questions swirled.

His face, usually so open and easy to read, became a mask of pain. But he said nothing—just nodded as if he deserved every bit of my fury. Maybe he did—deep down I knew he didn't. I turned away, blinking back tears, but it was no use. The hurt in his eyes was already seared into my memory. I stared at him in silence until he began walking away.

Long after he disappeared down the path, the echo of my words followed me home, haunting me. I would replay those words for decades to come, regret pooling in the vast spaces he left behind, knowing I'd thrown anger at him when what I'd truly felt was fear—acute fear of losing the only love I'd ever known. I already knew life was lonely and that my future without him would be just that. I was solitary and not the type to have wide circles of friends or the social tendency to effortlessly mix and mingle in new situations.

In reality, I was proud of him, but how could I possibly say that to him now after what I had just said? I was scared and selfish. If my fear was this paralyzing, how could I fail to consider the fear that had to be embedded deep within his heart at knowing he may never return home?

I thought I'd have time to share this revelation with him,

to wind back the clock and take back the poison I spewed. But I didn't.

John was deployed the next day. It damn well happened that fast.

Despite everything I'd said, he'd asked me to come to the station. I went. Of course I did. How could I not? I didn't sleep the night before, the venom of my words suffocating and paralyzing me in the dark hours of the night.

When I arrived, he was already there, standing on the platform with his hands in his pockets, that same determination setting his jaw. A bag was slung over his shoulder, and his uniform—oversized and slightly rumpled—made him look younger than ever. My heart ached at the sight of him, the boy I loved trying so hard to bear the mantle of a man.

"Mae," he said softly when he saw me, his voice breaking amidst the commotion of the station.

I wanted to tell him I was sorry, to pull him back into the life we were building, just the two of us; I wanted to make him understand how much I needed him to stay, to scream at the top of my lungs that he was too young, a liar, not fit for duty. But none of those things were true. All I could do was stand there, the words caught somewhere between my heart and my throat.

"You shouldn't be doing this," I whispered instead, my voice trembling. "You don't have to prove anything to anyone."

He shook his head, stepping closer until he was right in front of me, his brown eyes steady but sad.

"It's not about proving anything, Mae. It's about doing something that matters. If I stay, I'll just feel like I'm running from a responsibility. How can our kids grow up in a world knowing their father turned his back and ran away from tyranny, from the demise of our freedom, instead of running toward its preservation?"

"Our *kids?*"

"I've thought about this since the first night we met, Mae," he began, his voice low but resolute. "About what it would be like if we had forever. Our forever."

He looked at me, each individual word exploding like drops of rain in a puddle before settling deep in my chest.

"I picture us with a little house on the outskirts of town. Nothing fancy, just enough space for a garden and a swing in the backyard. You'd have that window you always talk about— the one with the morning sun pouring through it, warming your favourite chair and catching in your hair as the kids play at your ankles."

His words caught, and he smiled to himself, a touch of sadness breaking through.

"And yes, kids plural. A whole brood of them, roaming wild in the woods like we used to. Laughing, climbing trees, bringing home whatever stray animal they can find because they'd have their mother's heart, Mae—your heart, big and open."

I felt the hot sting of tears dripping from my eyes but said nothing, afraid that if I spoke, I'd shatter the fragile moment.

"And I'd work hard," he continued, his voice growing thicker with emotion. "I'd make sure you had everything you needed. Everything you deserved. I'd take you dancing on Saturday nights, even though we're not very good at it, because I'd love the way you'd laugh when I stepped on your toes, and you'd jab me in the ribs when my frisky hand wandered just below your waist."

He paused, staring down at the flower in his hand before letting it drop, his fingers curling into a fist.

"It's all I've ever wanted, Mae. A life with you. A family with you. But—" His voice broke and he looked up, his eyes brimming with unshed tears. "I can't have that if I stay here, pretending this war isn't happening. If I did that, I wouldn't be the man you think I am. I don't expect you to understand—it's okay that you don't."

I shook my head, a sob clawing its way out of my chest.

"John, don't say that. Don't make it sound like going away is the only way to deserve me. I don't care about any of that—I just care about you."

He stepped closer, taking my face in his hands, his touch impossibly gentle.

"I care about you, too. More than anything. That's why I have to go. So I can come back to you as someone who's earned the life we're dreaming of."

At that, the tears streamed, blinding and endless, but I didn't pull away. I let him hold me there in the golden light of the morning, let him press his forehead to mine and whisper, "I love you, Mae. Always."

It was the kind of love that felt too big for the moment, too big for the world, a love that couldn't be contained by promises or time. As he pulled me into his arms, I gripped him as though I could anchor him here, to this station, and nothing could take him away.

He leaned in, his lips brushing my forehead, and then he was gone, swallowed by the sea of uniforms climbing onto the train. I stood there, rooted in place, watching as the train pulled away, its wheels grinding against the tracks like a slow, agonizing goodbye.

As the train disappeared into the horizon, it carried with it the boy I knew, leaving behind an empty pain and the terrible knowledge that some promises aren't meant to be kept.

...

I wouldn't be the man you think I am.

The words floated around in my mind, dancing like dandelion seeds caught in a summer breeze, weightless and impossible to ignore as the pesky allergen prompted a sneeze. Each thought carried its own potential, its own questions, and yet none of them settled long enough to form an answer. Was this how I'd spend my final years on this earth—chasing stories and the unknown? I thought death was supposed to be the great unknown, not traversing the French countryside with Alex and Luc, a certified lunatic.

Alex had been particularly quiet since we returned to the apartment, the early afternoon now upon us. The walking was more than I anticipated and my joints were begging for rest and relaxation.

I told Alex I was going to run a bath and that he need not worry about checking on me. The bathroom in this apartment had become my retreat, a sanctuary for revival, and the old claw-foot tub at its centre felt like an anchor in my otherwise unmoored life. The porcelain was aged, with delicate cracks tracing abstract patterns over its surface, like fine veins in a marble statue. It wasn't perfect—far from it—but it had character, and in that small, isolated space, it was mine.

I turned the faucet, and the pipes groaned as they came to life, water splashing out in fits and bursts before finding a steady flow. The sound of it pouring into the tub bounced off the walls in the small room. Steam rose, curling and twisting in the dim light cast from the single bulb above, softening the edges of the room until everything felt slightly blurred, like a hazy memory.

On the windowsill, my assortment of little jars of bath salts—no, not the trippy-as-hell kind that had people in Florida going batshit all those years back—caught the afternoon's glow. Even with smudged glass and faded labels, they were beautiful in their own way. I reached for one, rose-scented, and poured some crystals into my hand. They dissolved in the running water, releasing a soothing fragrance that was a gentle, almost bittersweet reminder of better days. Nestled in the security of a locked room, with the amenities of a queen and the ingredients of a lady, I felt stripped down—and believe you me, I was, but you can save those thoughts for another time you little pervert—and I could drop the hardened masks and remove the armour that has become more of who I am than a mere costume.

The tub filled steadily, and I perched on the wooden stool beside it, distractedly smoothing my hand over the soft, frayed edge of a neatly folded towel. The brass fixtures, dulled with time, glinted faintly as I twisted the tap shut, the sudden silence making the room feel momentarily larger.

I trailed my fingers through the water, testing its warmth, and sat there for a moment, letting the steam rise around me before climbing in. Within these walls, I could forget everything else—the letters I hadn't yet read, the questions left unanswered, the burden I carried on my shoulders. This tub, with its imperfections and history, held me in the same way I regarded it—a dependable, enduring presence in a world that often felt increasingly loud.

I heard Alex's footsteps outside the door and saw the shadows of passing feet, his inability to heed my direction taking the form of curious pacing not three metres away. Only once did he give a gentle knock and ask if I was okay.

"I've been here for two years on my own, if you can count and remember," I called out, drawing closer to the brink of fully submerging myself in the water. "If you think an old bathtub is what ultimately does in Mae Seasons, you're as dumb as a squirrel trying to bury a nut in concrete."

The shadow at the gap of the bottom of the door disappeared, convinced now that this wouldn't be the way I'd go out. At least not today.

Once dried, relaxed, and warmly dressed, I joined Alex back in the living room. He had made me some tea and started reading a book that he found on the shelf, something left here by the previous occupant. He told me it had something to do with a man who golfed with God and was, as he put it, "extremely engaging and well-written." Though why someone would waste their time golfing, with God or anyone else for that matter, was beyond me. I remember hearing the stories of husbands spending all weekend at the golf course, the wives bitching and moaning about "how long can a round of golf possibly take?" Well, like anything, it takes as long as it takes and, in the case of many of those women—who were insufferable, by the way—their husbands were maximizing their reprieve from them, of this much I am sure.

A log popped in the woodstove, loud as a gunshot, and I jumped, sloshing tea onto the saucer that was supporting my cup. Alex had this way of leaning forward, elbows on the kitchen table, head dipped just enough to let his hair shield his expression, like he was bracing himself for bad news, or worse—an idea that might actually lead somewhere.

"Mae," he said softly, glancing up at me. "You don't have to do this."

"Which part?" I snapped, though my voice wavered more

than I liked. "The fact that I have to reclaim John's honour from being mistaken for some double agent, or the fact that he has a daughter traipsing about France? Seems like shitty options no matter which way you slice it, Sonny. But, either way, I have to do this. That girl, that woman, Jacqueline, if she is John's daughter, then she deserves answers. And I—" my breath caught on itself, "I deserve them, too."

Alex scratched at the table's edge, his nervous habit.

"Luc said she's only fifty or so kilometres from Caen, right? That's not impossible."

"No, it isn't," I replied, gripping the saucer like it might somehow protect me. "But what do I say to her? 'Hello, I'm the wife of a man who fucked your whore mother and who might be your father. Oh, and by the way, I've been hunting the truth down on several fronts like a hound at a fox hunt. But it's nice to meet you.'"

Alex chuckled, the sound dry but honest. He knows I'd never say those words.

Hound on a hunt. Ridiculous.

"It's not like there's a manual for this, Mae. If you do it, just—be yourself. Or maybe don't, I haven't got the faintest idea what would be best in this particular scenario. Shit, this is a tough one."

I raised an eyebrow, leaning back in my chair.

"You mean foul-mouthed, hard to impress, and deeply suspicious of strangers? I don't know about you, but I think it's a perfect introduction. And one I'd be quite impressed with should I ever be on the other end of meeting someone like me."

"Well, it worked on me," he grinned, his eyes crinkling at the corners. "I guess it's time to see if it will work on Jacqueline."

That stopped me cold; the way he said her name this time,

there was something ineffable about it. The humour slipped out of the room like a retreating tide, and in its wake, the sheer enormity of what lay ahead landed like a punch to the throat. Jacqueline wasn't just a name on paper or a face in Luc's report. She was real—living, moving, existing out there while my memories of John had fossilized into fragments.

"I'm scared, Alex." It came out before I could stop it, a bare, vulnerable murmur.

"I know," he said. "But you've spent your whole life fighting. What and who isn't always clear. Neither are the reasons, but none of that matters. Don't stop now. You're Mae Fucking Seasons."

I nodded, swallowing past the lump in my throat.

"Alright," I said. "We write to her first, maybe one of your long-winded emails. If she wants to meet, you're coming with me."

"I wouldn't have it any other way," he replied, his smile genuine. "And Mae? No matter what happens, you're not alone in this."

I foolishly let myself believe him. But, deep down, even surrounded by the population of France, I knew I would always be alone.

CHAPTER 13
ALEX

I HAD MANAGED to moderate Mae's rabid mystery-solving pace, assuring her that we had ample time to figure out our plan in a logical and organized manner, thinking through each step and, perhaps most importantly, determining what she truly wanted to achieve when all was said and done. It was helpful that she had proposed the idea of writing to Jacqueline first, buying us a buffer of time I was trying to ensure we maintained.

Partially, I was selfish about the timeline; this was my first visit to France, and it was anyone's guess if I'd be back again. I wanted to see the sights, hear the sounds, and inhale the scents. This trip had the potential to be a rich and satisfying sensory experience. Above all else, I wanted to gain a better understanding of the history that was etched on every side-walk, planted in every field, and woven through the very fabric of the city. My freedom was directly related to the sacrifices of the many who died here and throughout the region. But right now, all of that was secondary to making sure that Mae not only found what she needed, but that she survived it, that we all survived it.

As the days passed, it became clear that I had arrived in Caen without a defined timeline. How long could I actually be away from home? Would I risk alienating Erica by sticking around here much longer than I'd already stayed? So many questions, so few answers. After several days of sending brief text message updates, I called Erica, oblivious of the time change and waking her up in the middle of the night.

"Alex?! Are you okay?" came a frantic voice on the other end of the line.

"Shit, the time change. I'm sorry," I said, shaking my head. "Yes, I'm fine, everything's fine. Have I mentioned I'm sorry? I'll call you later, you know, when it's not the middle of the night."

"I'm up now," she said with just enough sweetness and condemnation to elicit a confused response and truly dumb question, even by my standards.

"So, what's up?"

"Alex, you called me."

"Right. Fuck. Did I mention I'm sorry, because I feel the frequency and sincerity of these apologies has to increase posthaste."

Thankfully, Erica was an understanding person, gracious in recognizing an honest mistake in time zone management. Moreover, she had the enduring patience to put up with all the ridiculousness that was me in a nutshell.

"So, what's going on? Have you and Mae made any headway in finding John's daughter, or anything else for that matter?"

I recounted to her how I'd recently met Luc, and that I hadn't yet made up my mind in terms of whether or not I cared much for him. He seemed resourceful and helpful in many ways, but he also had an air, not quite of superiority, per se, but of unencumbered Frenchness. If that's even a thing. There was something about him that was equivalent to a pebble in your shoe—small enough to ignore for a while but always there, pressing, reminding you of its out-of-place presence. I couldn't decide if it was his mannerisms, his tone, or my own hardwired inability to trust someone so blatantly self-assured, even if they were on the manic side.

"Well, if Mae trusts him, I think you should too," came her reply, wise and calming as always. "I can appreciate your hesitation, but remember, this isn't about you or how you feel. This is all for Mae. You're there to help her. Do you need me to have you repeat that with me so it sinks in?"

"You think you're always right, don't you?" I said, jokingly, of course.

"I don't *think* I'm always right, I just am. It's the cross I bear, but I've come to accept it. Many have tried in the past and failed, but it seems that the rightful owner is now in possession. And thriving."

"A cross you bear? Right. Like when you swore your friend Jessica was too smart for that pyramid scheme."

"How was I supposed to know she thought crypto was a Pokémon evolution?"

"And Pluto? Still not a planet?"

"It's not my fault NASA has commitment issues."

"Okay, but you were positive I'd hate pineapple on pizza, and now I don't order one without it."

"Reverse psychology. I elevated your tastebuds, you're welcome."

"You know, you're insufferable at times."

"And right. Don't forget that."

The singsong tone in her voice was a comforting sound

as our repartee played out. How I got so lucky in love would always be beyond me.

"You should come to Caen," I said, once again not thinking before making a bold declaration. As much as this notion made sense, and our relationship was a lot of things, codependent was not one of them. I'm certain that it was a flare of codependency that caused me to blurt this out. "I mean, if you want."

The soft tones of cross-Atlantic connections hummed through the phone's speaker.

"It's about fucking time!" she practically screamed. "You were supposed to ask me to come with you at the very beginning, you dummy."

"I was?" I asked, genuinely unsure of how these things are supposed to play out.

"Yes! Oh, Alex, you are magnificently unaware in so many ways, you know that?" she playfully chided. "It's a good thing you have me to help lead you through the forest and keep you from getting lost."

My chest heaved an audible sigh of relief and a grin took over my face. I didn't know when her flight would be, but I was already counting down the seconds.

Dust floated in lazy beams of sunlight slicing through the tall windows of the village's one-room post office, or I guess I should say, relic of a post office that now served as a sort of museum for visitors. Everything was a museum it seemed. A bell chimed faintly as we stepped inside, its sound swallowed by the creak of old wood and older memories. If you don't think history speaks to you, you're not listening. Artifacts lined the walls: medals in faded velvet, rusted helmet fragments, yellowing posters calling men to arms, stamp collections, carrier bags, you name it. If it had to do with the postal service and the war, it seemed to be here, which naturally felt like a good spot to search for the photograph a local had tipped us off on.

Mae was the first to spot it. Tucked beneath a cracked-glass frame of wartime miscellanea, it showed a man in uniform kneeling beside a young woman and a child no older than two. Or three? Four? Fuck, all kids around that age might as well be the same, especially in a faded photo. The child clutched a stuffed rabbit. Or was it a muskrat? No, why the fuck would it be a muskrat? The man wore a smile you only see on people who haven't yet learned the price of survival.

Luc leaned in. "That uniform," he said. "It's the same regiment Jean was listed under. And that—" he pointed to the woman's shawl, "that's provincial Normandy, *non*?"

"What the fuck are you asking me for? You're the historian," Mae snapped back incredulously.

I said nothing. I just stared at the child's face, round, wary eyes and soft curls. A tug of unease stirred in my chest. If this is true, what does it mean? What does it change? Mae was going through enough as it was, and this? This was something entirely new.

"It's them," Luc said finally. "It has to be."

Mae wasn't so sure, studying the man in the photo as if it were a portrait of only him. If anyone knew the features of John's face, it was Mae, and I could tell she was not yet convinced.

Hours passed in relative silence, at least between Mae and me. Luc, on the other hand, chattered non-stop in what may have once been French but now resembled an improv performance. He laughed and bantered with strangers in the street as though he were running for mayor of a town that didn't know him. Even back at the apartment, he kept going, spinning theories out loud like his voice alone could stitch the truth together, one speculative thread at a time.

We'd managed to snap a picture of the photo, much to Luc's chagrin. He had fully intended to steal it, citing the historical imperative as though that excused outright theft. His skills as a thief, it turned out, were rivaled only by his questionable prowess as a historian, which made the iPhone route the safer bet for everyone involved. Thankfully, the museum employee with keys and actual authority had encouraged us to take a photo, explaining that many of the old pictures had handwritten notes on the back and that we were welcome to capture them "for the archives."

Now we sat gathered around the kitchen table, each of us peering into our glowing rectangles like detectives in a noir film, zooming and squinting, tapping and adjusting. We debated whether one faint blur was a smudge or the clue we'd been searching for. On the back of the original photo, the faint outlines of cursive script teased us, names half-visible, places almost familiar. Luc had them all scribbled in the margins of his notebook, the dates aligned like train cars waiting to depart a station. Somewhere in the mess a pattern was beginning to emerge. I couldn't tell if it was the one Mae hoped for or feared.

"I say we track the unit," Luc said. "Find his comrades. Someone who will recognize him."

"I still want confirmation it's Jacqueline," Mae replied, tracing the child's silhouette with her finger.

No one argued. The trail seemed to open wide before us.

The woman shuffled into the church's back room with an easy authority. Her cane tapped lightly against the stone floor. She glanced at the photograph Luc had laid on the table, then stopped.

"*Non, non,*" she said. "That's not Jean Saisons."

Mae's head snapped up. "What?"

The woman peered closer. "That's Michel Giraud. From Brittany. He was with the 31st Infantry. Died just before the liberation of Metz. The woman is his sister, Elise. The child—Clara, I think—his niece. They used to come through here after the war. I remember *le lapin en peluche*."

Silence clamped over the group like a lid, twisted so tight it might never be lifted, suffocating us all in the disappointment of a promising lead turned cold.

Luc cleared his throat. "Are you sure? The uniform—"

"I'm sure," she said simply. "I knew Michel. I was sixteen then. He gave me my first cigarette, amongst other things."

As quickly as we had entered, full of hope and possibility, we exited with despair and defeat. No one spoke for a long while. Mae sat on the stone ledge beside the church wall, the reprinted photo still in her hands, though her care with preserving it was now waning.

"Okay, look," I said, taking charge of morale. "We hit a roadblock, no big deal, right? It's bound to happen. History is complicated. It's not easy, it's not supposed to be easy. We thought we struck gold, but it turns out it was just some pyrite. We're not the first. Let's let this settle and we can keep going, keep finding new leads."

I didn't know if my words were rallying them, but trying felt like the least I could do. Besides, I had an important pick-up to make and I didn't feel like being mopey when I did.

I was pacing near the arrivals gate at the small airport in Caen, my palms slightly sweaty despite the cool breeze filtering through the automatic doors ushering folks in and out as they went about their lives. I hadn't realized how much I'd missed Erica until this moment—an acute sense of longing rising in my chest as the minutes ticked by. I glanced at the arrivals board again, studying the minute-by-minute updates, then back toward the gate, every passing second heightening my anticipation.

Finally, Erica emerged, pulling a compact suitcase behind her and attentively scanning the crowd. When her eyes landed on me, her face lit up with a joyous, almost comedic grin.

"Well, well, if it isn't the hero of Caen, here to whisk me away," she called out as she approached, her voice ringing above the thrum of the crowd. "I thought maybe you'd rent out the whole airport just to impress me."

I blushed and chuckled, my heart soaring at the sight of her.

"I tried to pull a few strings," I replied, spreading my arms for a hug. "You know me—always going over the top. Or at the very least, inclined to give it long, thoughtful consideration. Which, in most cultures, I believe is just as genuine as the show itself."

Erica dropped her suitcase dramatically and threw her arms around me.

"So, were you planning to meet me with a marching band? Or did the trumpeters call in sick? Did your considerate thoughts extend that far?"

I beamed as I stepped back, shaking my head.

"No trumpets, but I can whistle if that helps. Actually, no, I can't. I never learned how to properly whistle."

"How will you ever hail us a cab?" she teased, giving my shoulder a playful shove. "I wouldn't want you to strain something before I even set foot outside."

As we walked toward the exit, Erica tilted her head and eyed me curiously.

"You look—different."

"Different how?" I asked, suddenly self-conscious.

"I don't know," she mused, her tone teasing. "A little less broody. Did someone finally tell you it's okay to smile?"

"I guess I've had some practice lately." I laughed, feeling lighter in her presence.

Erica smirked. "Good. You were overdue."

I slung an arm over her shoulder as we walked out to the taxi waiting at the curb, her tenderness and quick wit easing us back into the comfort of our familiar dynamic. Seeing Erica again felt like an important piece of me falling back into place—a reminder of how grounding her company could be.

"So, is Mae excited to see me?" asked Erica as we slipped into the cab.

"Mae. Is she excited to see *you*? That's an excellent question, I—"

"You want to surprise her. She doesn't know I'm coming, does she?"

Erica knew me well.

"I mean, I thought it would be a nice surprise for her," I countered in defence. "She's had a lot of ups and downs lately, and you barely know the half of it. I figured that a nice surprise from someone she likes—admittedly likes, I might add— would be just what she needs to get over the latest hurdle."

"Well, you've got me for the next two weeks," said Erica, referring to the consecutive days off she was able to score from work. "Whatever we can learn and solve in that time, and I hope it's enough for you to return home with me, I'll do all that I can."

"I thought you were Miss Independent Woman who'd keep busy without me?" I prodded, smugly.

"What can I say, I miss my golden retriever."

"I'll assume you're calling me smart and loyal."

"Or needy and aloof. But think what you will, and choose whatever makes you happy. Now, who's a good boy?"

Her smile could light up the darkest of skies.

I was smitten. No, I was in love.

When we arrived at the apartment, Erica was fidgety, almost as if she was wondering whether this was a good idea. Certainly it wasn't—when would surprising Mae ever land in the hallowed halls of good ideas?—but here we were. I had mentioned that the apartment was small, cluttered, and unapologetically Mae. Stacks of documents covered nearly every flat surface, mismatched mugs of tea sat forgotten in random places, and a faint smell of coffee, tea, whatever was recently cooked, and woodstove hung in the air. Mae hadn't bothered to tidy up before Erica showed up—not that she would have—simply because she had no idea this was happening.

As part of my planned surprise, I would come in first, with Erica momentarily remaining in the hallway. I was told I was being showy but I didn't much care. I kicked off my shoes, tossed my coat on the rack, and began moving about the space as if it were any other day. I made my way to what looked like a new stack of documents from Luc.

"Don't touch that," Mae barked, nodding toward the pile of notebooks I was inspecting on the kitchen counter.

"What's this? Did Luc drop these off?" I asked, flipping through manila folders filled with reports, photographs, and newspaper clippings.

Mae snatched the folders from my hands, her expression stormy.

"It's nothing." She shoved the bundle into a drawer, using more force than necessary.

What was in this new batch of information that had Mae hot to trot?

Hot to trot? Oh, now it was happening again.

Mae scowled. "You're about two seconds away from being kicked out."

"But if you kick him out, I'd have to leave too," Erica said with added brightness to swiftly shift Mae's mood, knowing full well that waiting any longer might mean taking me to the hospital.

"Erica?" Mae's voice was barely above a whisper, but its sharp edge had all but vanished.

Erica stood in the doorway, letting go of her luggage, her vibrant smile shining like a flashlight.

"Hey, Mae. It's been a while."

Mae blinked several times, her focused-elsewhere mind catching up to what was unfolding before her. She turned to glare at me. I was grinning like the cat who ate the canary.

"Oh, Erica, my dear, it's so lovely to see you. You're much easier on the eyes than this knobhead over here," she said, casting an obvious head nod in my direction. "Maybe now we'll make some headway on getting real answers with this whole thing. I'm sure Alex filled you in on what's been going on."

I let Erica and Mae catch up, not on *the case,* as this was how I had come to think of it, but just in general. It was good for Mae to take a mental break from all that was going on.

I could see the toll it was taking on her. It was considerable.

And so, as I slipped into the bathroom to take a shower, I could sense that Mae's presence had shifted. I couldn't tell if it had to do with seeing a beloved familiar face or if it signalled the opening of a door to where she knew she needed to go.

Either way, the next week was about to be crazy.

CHAPTER 14
MAE

THE SMALL DINING TABLE in my apartment was buried under layers of history—faded photographs, brittle documents, and yellowed newspaper clippings—each one a misshapen puzzle piece in a mystery spanning decades. Erica sat cross-legged in her chair, hair casually tied up but unravelling, as she examined a hand-drawn map of Caen from 1944. I hovered nearby, glasses perched low on my nose, carefully skimming through an old letter with handwriting so delicate it seemed to float above the page.

"This map is incredible," Erica murmured, tracing the edge of a marked zone with her finger. "Look here—this was where they concentrated the rebuilding efforts right after the liberation. You can see the notes about supply routes."

"Detailed, yes," I said, my voice dry, "but maps don't tell you how it felt to stand there, smelling ash and fear."

I hadn't realized how curt and candid my reply was, but such straightforwardness had lately been occurring more frequently as I began to give fewer and fewer fucks. I plucked a photograph from the pile, holding it up in the dim light.

"That's in their faces. Right here. That's what John would have looked like; that same combination of fear and bravery battling for superiority in his mind."

The photo in question showed a group of young soldiers slumped against the remnants of a stone wall, their set expressions a mix of exhaustion and something deeper, something harder to define. Erica took the photo from Mae, her brow furrowing.

"Do you think John could've been in a group like this?"

"Could've been," I said, my tone clipped. "Or maybe not. My ghosts aren't exactly generous in giving me answers; they just hover about until I find them myself."

Alex wandered into the room, holding three mugs of coffee like a waiter trying too hard to look competent on his first day.

"Is there room for one more investigator?" he asked cheerfully, setting the mugs down.

Erica glanced up, smirking. "Careful, Alex, this is expert-level sleuthing. You might not make the cut."

I chuckled, growing even more fond of Erica by the second. If she could bust his balls like this, I might send him home before her.

"Let him try. He can start by organizing that pile over there." I gestured vaguely to the corner of the table, which was more chaos than order. "If he messes it up, we'll send him away."

"Oh, great," Alex said, feigning hurt. "I see how it is. First, I bring coffee, and now I'm the organizational but dispensable errand boy."

"Third wheel," Erica corrected, not looking up from her map. "You're the third wheel. And frankly, you're not even the good kind. You're one of those wobbly, squeaky ones that the two of us try to slowly and quietly slip away from."

"I have feelings, you know," Alex said, pulling out a chair and sitting with exaggerated dignity. He picked up a random picture from the table. "This one seems important."

"That's because it *is* important, you lummox," I said, snatching it from his hands. "Go sit in the corner and look useful. You're dismissed already."

"You mean *be* useful?" Alex asked, grinning.

"No," I shot back, "I mean *look* useful. Lower bar, better results."

Erica's coffee spilled from her mouth, her sudden laughter brightening the quiet room like sunlight through cracked blinds. I couldn't help but smile as I carefully tucked the photo into a protective sleeve.

"You two are impossible," Alex muttered, leaning back in his chair and taking a sip of his coffee. "And I thought I was bringing in reinforcement for me. Clearly, I'm just here for moral support."

"Well, you're doing a bang-up job," Erica said, shooting him a teasing glance. "Now be quiet, Mae and I have serious work to do."

The room settled again, the hum of concentration returning as Erica and I pored over another set of clippings. Alex leaned back, watching us, a look of admiration and exasperation on his face. Despite our relentless ribbing, he couldn't deny how much he cared for both of us—and how much lighter the air felt with our shared banter. In our odd little way, we made a perfect team.

Once I caught Erica up on a few more details, I could see her mind at work. She's always been a thinker, a problem-solver, and I could tell she was turning a Rubik's Cube over in her mind.

"So, you've still not made any progress on Jean Saisons," she said, not so much a question as a statement, yet somehow still a question.

Was I having a stroke?

"You've found the photograph that proved to be a bust, a letter that you thought was from him—but a failure to translate it accurately put that to rest—and you've had countless locals lead you down dead-end paths."

Again, not questions as much as statements, but also questions.

"What if Jean Saisons isn't a real name?" asked Erica. "I mean, it's a name, sure, but could it be fake? Does that make sense?"

"Yes, dear, it makes perfect sense," I said, wishing I could burn a hole into Luc's soul.

A code name. A fucking code name. It wasn't "anglicized" as Luc suggested, it was conjured from thin air, a name that could have just as easily been Big Bird. All of this was confirmed thanks to a geriatric Frenchmen who wore too much cologne and drank not nearly enough wine.

The house was damp, dim, and smelled like old glue, which I was starting to think was the region's Febreze scent of choice given the number of downtrodden and time-forgotten places we've recently visited. Across from us sat Monsieur Delon, an old man in a cardigan that looked like it predated the war itself. He flipped through the weathered document Luc had handed him, eyes squinting behind thick, smudged glasses.

"Jean Saisons," he said at last, with a low chuckle. "Ah, *mon Dieu*. You have been chasing that old ghost?"

"We've seen the name in at least four separate records," I said. "Resistance memos, field notes, a photo with 'J.S.' on the back. Can you tell us what it means?"

Delon looked up at me, his gaze sharp despite the fingerprinted fog on his lenses.

"Oh, it means something, *bien sûr*. Just not what you think."

He set the paper down and folded his hands, deliberate and patient.

"Jean Saisons was never a man. Not one man, at least. It was a code name. An alias used by Resistance couriers and operatives, especially when passing messages between sectors—a coat several people wore, depending on the day."

Alex let out a sound halfway between a scoff and a groan. Luc blinked. I nearly fell off my damn chair.

"So it wasn't real?" I asked. "He wasn't real?"

Delon shrugged, a slow lift of the shoulders that somehow held both sympathy and exasperation.

"*C'était la guerre.* Real is a luxury. We had names for people who didn't exist so we could protect the ones who did. You think the Gestapo didn't notice when the same name popped up in five towns? Jean Saisons became a signal, not a person. If you said he was there, it meant the message was received. That the drop was safe. Or not."

I ran a hand down my face. "So every lead we've followed, every document, every location—"

"Was a message trail," Delon finished. "Not a biography. You were reading our footprints, not our faces."

Delon smiled faintly and leaned back. "But don't be too disappointed, you're not the first ones to chase him. He was good at being followed. That was the point."

"Luc, you have to be the absolute worst historian this world has ever seen," I screamed. "How? How is it even remotely possible that you could not have figured this out before sending us on this wild fucking goose chase? Of all the idiots, in all the countries, in all the towns, I end up with you."

Without another word, I got up and walked out.

The following day, I woke earlier than usual and was surprised to be greeted in the kitchen by Erica, who was also up, presumably adjusting to the time change.

"Morning, Mae," she said. "Jet lag, time change, Alex snoring, whatever. I'm out of sorts at the moment, so I figured I'd get the day started. The kettle is ready if you'd like a cup of tea."

I gently placed my hand on her forearm, about as much physical affection as I'd show anyone, and she knew what it meant.

"Why don't we forgo tea for now and take a short walk?" I asked, mostly insisting through the subtext of my tone, expression, and the lingering clusterfuck of the day before. "Caen is a beautiful place this early in the morning."

"You don't have to sell me, I'll grab my coat."

The streets were still waking up for the day ahead, the air crisp and refreshing against my skin as Erica and I walked side by side, arms linked. The cobblestones beneath our feet were slick with dew, glinting faintly in the pale light of dawn, ready to take us down in an instant. All it would take was one misstep and Mae Seasons would be this day's first victim. Above us, the sky was a watercolour of muted pinks and oranges, the rising sun brushing the tops of the centuries-old buildings with gold.

Don't tell me I can't get sentimental about a sunrise.

The city felt different in the early hours—more intimate, as though it had stripped away its extra layers for us alone. I had felt this on many early morning walks since I arrived. The faint sounds of daily life were beginning to stir. A baker pushed open the door of his shop, the warm, yeasty aroma of fresh baguettes floating into the street. Luc would no doubt be in his glory. The faintest hint of cinnamon raced on the back of the wind—probably from teurgoule cooking in the oven—its intoxicating scent dashing through the air like an elusive invitation.

Erica's nose twitched. "That," she said pausing, her head tilting slightly as she breathed it in more deeply, "is the smell of heaven." She nudged me with her elbow, her lips curling into a smile, a desperate plea if there ever was one to purchase whatever was producing such a delicious smell.

"Let's hope those bakers don't slice their thumbs and bleed into their buns," I said in return, not knowing entirely why.

The sound of distant bells chimed from a church tower, their echoes ringing through the narrow streets. I wondered if those same bells had stood the test of the war, if they rang out like literal clockwork to mark the time while soldiers like John clung to their helmets, rifles, and lives.

We passed a newsstand being set up, the vendor whistling a tune as he arranged stacks of magazines, their colourful covers vivid against the gray stone of the building behind him. A few fellow early risers wandered by—an old man walking his hideous-looking dog, its paws tapping a rhythmic beat on the cobblestones; a young woman cycling with a baguette tucked under her arm. This was so unlike life back home, across the ocean.

As we turned a corner, the faint fragrance of damp stone and aged wood greeted us, mingling with the earthy aroma of fallen leaves. I paused, my hand brushing the rough wall of a building. The stony texture felt grounding, a reminder of all the years Caen had stood, weathering lives far more complex than mine.

Did the wall feel the roughness of my hands, too? Did it give a damn what I had withstood all these years?

I needed to stop caring about things that didn't care about me in return.

"You have a habit of doing that, you know," she said, an amused lilt in her voice.

"Doing what?" I asked, though I already knew.

"Touching things. Like you're trying to feel their stories. I've watched you do it for years. Sometimes on the strangest things like cutlery wrapped in a napkin."

I exhaled and relaxed my body, not bothering to deny it.

"This place has witnessed more than we ever will. It's humbling, I guess. And, let me remind you that you shouldn't spend so much time minding the business of your elders, young lady."

She rolled her eyes, but there was no annoyance in the gesture.

"You're such a romantic, Mae. You may not think so, you'll probably deny it, but deep down, there's romance still in you."

•••

Sitting by the open window at night, a small lantern flickering beside me, I choose my writing utensil and a crisp sheet of paper to write John a letter. My world is so muted without him, every inch of me weighed down by his absence, so I fill the letters with uplifting dreams of the life we'd have once he returned; small and simple, hopes and plans that felt monumental in their own way.

I spent a good amount of time going into great detail about bringing him to a picnic down by the creek, with the gingham blanket I stitched myself. I describe the pie I would bake, the kind he loved best with the crumbly top that melted into the tartness of the apples. It wouldn't be perfect, since my mother never taught me how to bake, but he'd tell me it was the best thing he ever tasted. I could almost hear his hearty laugh as we sat there, our shoes kicked off, my head resting on his shoulder as the sycamores swayed above us.

I wanted to remind him of what was waiting for him when he returned, what he was missing, like going to a dance, similar to the one where we first met. I would tell him about the dress I'd wear—soft blue like the summer sky, with a hem that swirled when he spun me. I'd have learned to wear pretty, girly clothes by then, and perhaps even be able to dance circles around him. I imagined the way his hand would feel on the small of my back, the strength of it supporting me as we danced, his forehead touching mine when the music slowed.

Behind the farmhouse stood an enormous oak tree. This was the location I'd daydream about, the two of us sitting side by side, carving our initials into its bark. I could picture exactly what I would plant in the garden he'd always talked about, with rows of tomatoes and lettuce and peppers, and how we'd laugh about my inability to keep the soil off my face no matter how careful I tried to be.

Writing was hard, even though the words flowed like a relentless river. It was the meaning behind the words that caused me to tear up, mumble incoherently, and every now and then break down completely. Every word I wrote was a thread tying him to me, a promise of a simple life that waited just beyond tomorrow, just beyond the horizon. I went to the post office religiously, sending those letters off with trembling hands, hoping against hope that they'd reach him, that they'd be enough to remind him to survive and return home. I knew they were no match for what he was facing, but I had to believe in something when I had nothing else to believe in.

But one day, the day the telegram came—my world shifted off its axis.

Walking down the street by his house, even a passing look at it was enough to bring a smile to my face, knowing the boy, the man I loved, was raised in that very place. I heard the determined sound of footsteps on the gravel, heavy and deliberate. They didn't belong to me. My heart leapt, irrationally, thinking for one breathless moment that it was him, that John had somehow managed to come back to surprise me.

When I turned around and saw the man in uniform, my heart plummeted. He was headed straight to John's front door. Tears formed and streaked down my face. I didn't bother wiping them away; I couldn't if I had tried. I was emotionally paralyzed.

Ducking behind a bush, I was shaking but silent. The man didn't appear to say anything when John's mother opened the door. Then I heard a scream. A scream so raw and helpless that it scarred my soul, leaving a black spot imprinted and destined to grow.

I walked back to my house on unsteady legs, body and mind drunk on the potent elixir of sadness and loss. Sitting alone in my bedroom, as I always did, I stared blankly at the wall. My mind raced with desperate, incoherent prayers.

I emerged from my comatose state, everything blurred together at first. Then it crystallized and shattered into sharp, jagged shards. I clutched at the memory of John, drawing it deep into my heart, rocking back and forth as the enormity sank in—John was gone. John was gone. John is gone. John is gone.

The love we shared, the life we'd planned, our letters, hopes, and dreams—they weren't just gone or lost, they were stolen, ripped apart by a brutal war that didn't care about picnics or dances or gardens or romance.

No one even knew we were married. I was just *Mae*, not Mrs. Seasons. His parents would get the official condolences. They'd receive the medal, if there was one, and the folded flag. I'd get nothing, not a shred of recognition that we had started to build something together, that he was my husband, and not just their son.

The last letter I'd written to him sat on the table, unfinished. In it, I'd told him the tomatoes were coming in early this year, and that I'd saved the first ripe one for him. I wrote that I'd wait forever, if that's what it took, to see him come up the path again.

I folded it neatly and placed it in the box with the others, my hands trembling. I couldn't bring myself to get rid of them. They were all I had left of him, of us.

My heart, my body, felt impossibly empty, the silent thoughts of never seeing John again were deafening. I sat in my room undisturbed—my parents had no clue of the demon that had just taken my soul. The moon rose, its pale light spilling across the floor, and I still couldn't cry; the grief was too vast for tears. It felt like a part of me had been ripped out, leaving a hollow ache that would never heal.

And for the first time in my life, I understood the meaning of heartbreak—not the fleeting pain of a missed connection or a lost opportunity, but the soul-crushing, unrelenting despair of losing someone who was supposed to be your forever. Romance, love, it was a myth, a buried treasure that simply didn't exist.

...

"Oh, bugger off with that nonsense. I haven't had a romantic thought, feeling, or otherwise in decades."

"Maybe," Erica said, grinning. "But if you start waxing poetic about the cobblestones, I'm walking back to the apartment without you."

I chuckled again, and we kept moving, our steps slow and unhurried. The city was ours, its history etched in every corner, every stone, and I was happy to have Erica by my side in this moment. She didn't pry like Alex did, bless his soul. Maybe it was women's intuition. Though if it was, I think I'd have a stronger feeling.

And so, as the morning unfolded, I felt something settle inside me, and it wasn't breakfast. No, it was a tranquil kind of joy in being here, with Erica, in a place that seemed to thrive on stories waiting to be told. What was it about her presence that was causing me to feel this comfortable? Best not to overthink it lest I give myself a stroke.

"Do you ever think about how many people have walked these streets?" she asked, breaking the silence. "All their stories, overlapping and spilling into each other, like layers of paint on a canvas."

Every day since the day I arrived.

"Like layers of paint on a canvas?" I repeated. "When did Maya Angelou join me?"

"Oh shut up," she said, laughing and giving me the gentlest of nudges. "And thanks for not saying Shakespeare or some other man."

"Solidarity, sister."

I thought of John then, of his stories and the history he'd carried with him, however brief it may have been, while he took in mornings like this.

"But, to be fair and answer your question, yes, all the time," I admitted, my tone softer now. "It's like the city holds them, somehow. In the stones, in the air. Ugh, you're infecting me with your verbosity and flowery language."

We strolled on, the streets of this magnificent city awakening around us, and for a moment, it felt like we'd become part of the city's story too—two voices woven into its quiet, enduring song.

As we turned onto a barren street, the sound of a whistled tune drifted through the air, cheerful and carefree. A man emerged from a side alley, his scarf loosely draped over his shoulders and a baguette tucked under one arm. Even before I recognized him, Luc's presence was unmistakable—the way he moved, so at ease in his surroundings, it was as though he belonged to the very streets we walked.

"*Bonjour, Mesdames!*" Luc called out, his smile broad and unrestrained. His eyes lighted upon Erica first, naturally, and something in his expression shifted—widened, brightened— as though the sunrise itself had stopped to greet him.

"Luc, what a surprise," I said, returning his smile, though my tone held a trace of sarcasm and lingering frustration. "What are you doing up and about this early?"

He ignored me entirely, stepping forward with a dramatic flair and bowing slightly toward Erica.

"The real question, *mademoiselle*, is what the sun itself is doing walking these humble streets."

He straightened, a hand over his heart, his grin unabashed. "I am smitten. Truly. And now, it is forever morning in my soul."

Erica blinked, then let out a laugh, light and surprised. "I don't even know you," she said, though her cheeks were flushed with a hint of pink.

"Then I am doubly blessed," Luc replied without missing a beat, "because today I have met the most radiant stranger, *and* I have a reason to properly introduce myself. Luc Brassard, at your service."

"Erica," she said, taking his offered hand with a wry smile. "And does this over-the-top charm always work for you, Luc?"

"Not always," he admitted, grinning wider. "But it does keep my mornings interesting."

I cleared my throat, cutting through the exchange. "Luc, what *are* you doing here?"

He turned to me then, though his attention still seemed half-focused on Erica.

"Ah, Mae, you know me. These early hours are when the city truly breathes. When its secrets stretch out like shadows and reveal themselves. You can learn so much about Caen at dawn—the sounds, the smells, the patterns of life. Who delivers the bread. Which windows light up first. Who walks alone when no one else is watching. Who is getting down and dirty with who in the alley next door."

"Ah, Luc, a little creepy, *non*?" I said, mimicking his accent.

He paused, his expression softening slightly.

"It's also when you hear secrets, if you're listening carefully enough," he said with a knowing smile and a lightning fast wink.

"You know, Luc," said Erica, interjecting and giving me another reason to adore her above all others, "you're about as straightforward as a strudel trying to pass itself off as a croissant—flaky, twisted, and just a little full of air."

For a moment, Luc froze, his hand stopped mid dramatic gesture in the air. Then, slowly, he clutched his chest as though she'd pierced him straight through.

"*Mademoiselle*, you wound me! To be compared to anything but the purest French croissant is a tragedy of the highest order."

I nearly doubled over laughing at this exchange as Erica shrugged, looped her arm through mine, and started walking, leaving him to sputter behind us.

"Come on, poet," she called over her shoulder. "You've got a city to show us. Let's see if your stories can make up for your nonsense."

Luc jogged to catch up, muttering something about "ungrateful muses," but he couldn't hide his smirk.

"Jacqueline," he said simply, catching his breath, his tone suddenly serious. "The past isn't the past, not in Caen."

Erica tilted her head, intrigued. "Jacqueline," she repeated. "John's supposed daughter?"

Luc nodded.

"She's a piece of this puzzle, Erica. Her and everyone like her. Her story is like the cracks in the stones—hidden, but everywhere. If you know where to look, and when to listen. And this is why I walk early," he said, leaning in conspiratorially, his voice dropping to a whisper. "The city talks to those who rise with it."

"And what is the city saying about me?" Erica asked, raising an eyebrow.

Luc placed a hand dramatically over his heart again.

"It says, 'Luc Brassard, you fool, you were not ready for a beauty like this.'"

"Luc, you're incorrigible," I groaned.

"Only because life is too short to be anything else," he said with another wink.

"Do you have something in your eye?" chuckled Erica, the jab going right over Luc's head.

"*Non*, my dear, it is clear as glass. Now, shall I walk with you, or have I already overwhelmed you both with my brilliance?"

Erica shook her head, a smile tugging at her lips.

"You can walk," she said, "but only if you promise to tell me more about Jacqueline. The cracks in the stones, all that bullshit."

Luc's grin softened into something more sincere.

"Ah, *mademoiselle*, for you, I would show you every stone in Caen. Lead the way."

Luc was mid-monologue, gesturing dramatically toward a centuries-old wall and proclaiming its "unparalleled wisdom in silence," when his foot caught in one of the very cracks he claimed to adore. He went down like a felled oak, a flurry of scarf, baguette, and wounded pride. Before we could ask if he was alright, he groaned theatrically, clutching his ankle as though it were a mortal wound.

"The city," he gasped, wincing, "it has betrayed me. After all these years of faithful devotion, this is how it repays me. Struck down by the very history I revere."

I folded my arms, holding back a smirk.

"Well, Luc, looks like one of your beloved cracks decided

it's had enough of carrying the weight of your ego and took you down before you could flirt it to death. You'll be alright to get home on your own, *oui?*"

"Well, my dear ladies," he began, his tone dripping with theatrical sorrow, and pretending to completely ignore the insult I shot his way, "it appears fate has conspired to rob you of my dazzling company. I must limp home alone, like a tragic hero abandoned by his muses. Go on without me, explore the city, and think of me fondly when you encounter its wonders. Perhaps shed a tear or two for poor Luc Brassard, the man who gave his very footing in the pursuit of beauty and knowledge."

He pressed a hand to his chest, pausing for effect before continuing.

"But don't get lost without me, eh? This city loves me, but it might chew you up and spit you out. And if I hear you've taken advice from some second-rate historian, I'll haunt you in my recovery."

I rolled my eyes as Erica stifled a laugh.

"Don't worry, Luc," I said dryly, "we'll be sure to pour one out for your ankle at the next café."

He pointed at me, a grin breaking through his wounded expression.

"At least make it the good wine, Mae. I have standards."

CHAPTER 15
ALEX

I woke to silence, the kind that feels complete and deliberate, like the world had decided to press pause while I slept, and maybe it had. On most days, this would have been most welcome. I reached for Erica out of habit, expecting to find the tangle of her hair on the pillow or the soft pressure of her arm or leg draped over me. But the sheets beside me were cool and undisturbed, the subtle aroma of her perfume the only sign she'd been here at all.

It was ridiculous, just how much I missed her already, even though she couldn't have been gone for more than an hour. Chalk it up to her arriving only yesterday, I suppose. But it was more than that too. She had this marvelous way of making the world seem fuller, even in its emptiest moments—her unguarded laugh brightening the mood of a dull morning, her dulcet voice breaking the silence before it could become too unbearable.

I sat up and rubbed the sleep from my eyes, catching sight of the small wooden trunk near the window. Mae had told me about it, had said there were things inside she wanted me to see, eventually—things she'd lived with for years but that I hadn't yet been given the chance to understand. Erica and I had briefly spoken last night about going through it together, all three of us, when the time was right. Erica had made me promise not to be impetuous and do something stupid. Translation: don't open the trunk. But now, with the apartment empty and time stretching wide before me, the opportunity felt too tempting to ignore.

Don't do it, Alex.

I crossed the room, every footstep amplified in the stillness, and crouched down, lifting the lid carefully, like it might bite or unexpectedly release something dreadful. Inside were photos, documents, and letters, all neatly stacked but unmistakably aged. The smell of old paper and dust struck me as I reached for a photograph. I violently sneezed and doused the memory of at least four soldiers leaning on a tank in my snot.

Nice work, asshole.

The picture in my hand, however, was of Mae, younger than I'd ever seen her, sitting on a blanket in the grass, but undeniably her. Her long hair was loose, wild, and she had this laugh frozen mid-moment, her head thrown back like she couldn't contain it. Beside her was a man I'd only heard about through descriptions—a man who could only be John. He was leaning toward her, eyes fixed on her like she was the only thing in the world worth looking at. This was not at all the version of Mae Seasons I had ever conjured in my mind. The Mae I knew was never this carefree, this happy. I suppose John had everything to do with that. I wondered who was there to capture this moment.

I swallowed hard and set the photo aside, though the image lingered like an imprint. Beneath it were letters, the paper softened by time, John's name was scrawled across each of the envelopes in a handwriting that was bold, deliberate, but delicate and unquestionably loving. I didn't open them. Not yet. Doing that would be far too invasive, even though I'd already gone this far by delving into the trunk. They didn't have stamps on them. They were unsent letters.

I moved to a stack of documents at the bottom, bound together with a faded ribbon. There was a birth certificate, followed by military records with John's name. He'd lied about his age—it was right there, his real birth year scratched out and a new one inked in beside it, so obvious it almost felt careless.

I leaned back, stacks of memories and history sprawling before me. Mae had lived with all of this—these fragments, these visions—for decades. She'd touched these same pages, held these same photographs, but somehow they felt too heavy for me to hold alone.

Still, I couldn't stop myself. I picked up another photograph, this one less cheerful in tone. It was Mae again, now years older, standing in front of a crumbling stone house with her arms crossed and her expression unreadable. There was a boy beside her, maybe seven or eight years old, with messy dark hair and a wary smile. I didn't know who he was, but something about the way Mae's hand rested protectively on his shoulder told me he mattered.

I felt like an interloper, intruding on remembrances and trespassing into places I wasn't sure I was meant to go. Wait. I *was* trespassing. I was doing the exact thing that I knew I shouldn't and that Erica had strictly said not to.

But the room remained quiet, and Mae wasn't here to stop me. Neither was Erica, which somehow made it all feel lonelier and more intimate at once. So I continued, letting the pieces of Mae's story speak to me, each one adding an intriguing layer to the Mae Seasons I thought I knew.

Momentarily shifting my attention away from the trunk, an envelope sitting on the table, one of many, called to me. It was from Luc, his distinctive handwriting was impossible to miss—bold, sprawling letters that looked like they were scribbled in haste, as if his thoughts might outrun his pen. I picked it up, turning it over in my hands for an instant before sliding my finger under the seal to pop it back open.

Inside, a single folded page carried the vague scent of lavender, like everything that came from Mae's world seemed to. I unfolded it carefully and beheld Luc's familiar theatrics spilled across the page.

Bonjour Mae,

I trust this letter finds you mostly upright, though knowing the chaos that tends to follow you like a lost puppy with a PhD, I wouldn't be surprised if you were currently swinging from a tree branch—or more likely buried beneath a pile of brittle archives. But enough about your escapades, let us speak of mine.

And mon Dieu, Mae, attache ta ceinture, because I have news that might just knock your socks off, if, of course, you're even wearing any.

Jacqueline—she is alive! Alive, breathing, and if I were to hazard a wild guess, still glowing with the kind of je ne sais quoi that had people tripping over their own shoelaces in another lifetime. She's seventy-eight now, living in a small village called Beuvron-en-Auge. One of those places that seems plucked from a conte de fées. Cobblestone streets, crumbling yet impossibly charming homes. Her house? The definition of a cozy stone cottage, tucked at the end of a lane. *The jardin, Mae. It's so lovely it could bring Monet to tears.*

And of course, she runs a flower shop. But not just any flower shop. This one sells artisan linens and embroidered keepsakes. Linge de maison, Mae. Picture me walking in there. You can see it, can't you? Good. Because I looked magnifique. A tall glass of sparkling beverage of your choice to drink in.

But getting there was no promenade. You know me; give me an impossible task, and I'll turn it into a performance. This began with a photograph. You've seen it, I'm sure. Black-and-white. A young girl standing beside her maman, outside a house that had clearly seen better days. That girl? Jacqueline. The woman? Yvette, her mother.

Let me sketch the scene. Normandy. Wartime. Enter John Seasons—enigmatic, dashing, foreign, morally grey like a well-aged Bordeaux. He and Yvette meet in the midst of it all. She's a young widow. He's, well—John. And what they shared, whatever it was, clearly left a mark. Six months after their last encounter, Jacqueline is born, drifting between Resistance safe houses in her infancy.

The proof? Solide comme un roc. Her birth registry lists no father—suspiciously blank. But the dates align like stars over Provence. Then there's the locket, said to once hold a photo of a man in uniform. She never spoke of him, but the silence? It thundered. Mae, I've seen her photo—taken just a few years back—and I swear to you, it's like John's gaze is reaching through time. That same fire, the regard that could melt steel. And not just that. It's her strength. Her resolve. As though she inherited his soul. Or maybe yours, though there is no blood relation there.

Her address is on the back of this letter. Yes, lisible, I swear. I triple-checked with the care of a sommelier inspecting corks. Mae, this doesn't end with me. It can't. Jacqueline deserves to know. And I suspect she holds stories that even I, with all my digging, couldn't unearth.

The rest, ma chère, is up to you.

Avec tout mon respect et un brin de folie,

Luc

I leaned back in the chair, the letter slipping from my fingers onto the table. For a moment, I just sat there, staring at the words as if they might rearrange themselves into something simpler, something less monumental.

Jacqueline. John's daughter.

It didn't feel real yet, like it was a late-night story Luc had dreamed up, but the evidence was there, clear as daylight. A photograph, a birth record, suggestions of a man in uniform.

I exhaled slowly, running a hand through my hair. I could almost hear Mae's voice in my head, her disbelief, her cutting wit slicing through the density of it all. But Mae wasn't here right now. It was just me, alone with Luc's words and the strange, tenuous bridge they built between the past and the present.

Jacqueline.

I rolled the name over and over in my mind, wondering what it would be like to stand in front of her, to look at her face and know that somewhere, in some way, she carried a piece of John. A piece for Mae. A piece of this story that had been waiting, ever so quietly, to be found.

With no one around to stop me from getting up and leaving, I got dressed, stuffed some snacks in my pocket, and stepped outside to hail a cab to go find Jacqueline.

I make the best decisions.

The cab's brakes whined as it slowed to a stop in front of me, the driver staring at me through the half-rolled-down window with a look of mild disinterest. I gave him a nod, adjusting the bag on my shoulder as I slid into the backseat.

"Beuvron-en-Auge," I said, pulling Luc's letter from my pocket to glance at the address again, as if the name of the town might change when spoken out loud.

The cabbie gave a grunt of acknowledgement and pulled into the street, his radio crackling with static and a quickly delivered weather report. The ride started as expected, with me gazing out the window as the city slowly gave way to countryside. And then we stopped all too soon.

I frowned, leaning forward. "What's happening?"

"Ah, *un moment*," the cabbie said, waving a hand as he rolled down the window and started chatting, very animatedly, with someone on the curb.

I couldn't make out the conversation, but it was loud and lively with arm gestures. Then the door swung open, and there he was.

"Alex!" Luc beamed, his energy like a whirlwind as he slid into the seat beside me without so much as a by-your-leave.

I blinked, taken aback. "Luc? What—what are you doing?"

The cabbie was already driving again, apparently unconcerned about having picked up a second passenger without my consent.

"Fate!" Luc declared, grinning as though this were the

most obvious explanation. "I was on my way home to rest my ankle—a minor setback this morning—and then, *voilà*! I spot a cab. A perfectly empty cab. And who should I find inside but you!"

"It wasn't empty. I was already in it."

"Details, Alex, details." Luc waved a dismissive hand, positioning himself in the seat with the kind of ease that made it clear he wasn't going anywhere. "So, where are we off to?"

"Beuvron-en-Auge," I said flatly, knowing there was no point in arguing. "I'm going to see Jacqueline."

Luc's face lit up like a child on Christmas morning.

"Ah! Of course! What timing. I was going to suggest we speak again before you went, but now I can accompany you. *Parfait!*"

I sighed, pinching the bridge of my nose.

"You didn't think to call me instead of hijacking my cab?"

"This way is more fun," Luc said with a shrug. "And speaking of fun, I met the most exquisite *mademoiselle* this morning. A friend of Mae's—Erica."

My eyebrows shot up.

"Erica? What does she have to do with anything?"

Luc gave me a sly grin.

"She's delightful, you know. When I saw her this morning, bright and early, she had the most radiant smile. I understand you two are, as you say, going steady. And yet here you are, sneaking off for mischief without her. Tisk tisk, Alex."

I rolled my eyes.

"I'm not sneaking. And we're not just—" I stopped myself, but Luc was already raising an eyebrow.

"Not just?" he prompted, his grin widening.

"Not just—someone you can casually interrogate me about," I finished, though the flush of heat in my face betrayed me.

"Ah, I knew it!" Luc clapped his hands together. "*C'est officiel!* You're in love with her."

"We're not having this conversation," I muttered, focusing out the window.

Luc leaned closer, lowering his voice conspiratorially.

"But she's your girlfriend, *oui*? You must defend her honour. I think she's too lovely for you, but that's a Frenchman's perspective."

"First of all, ouch. Second, yes, she's my girlfriend. And third—wait, '*too lovely for me*?'" I turned to glare at him, but he was grinning like the Cheshire Cat, which somehow diffused things.

"Don't take it personally, *mon ami*," he said breezily. "It's simply that Erica has a glow about her. A mystery. You? You have, well, not that. But maybe charm, sometimes. You're a lucky pairing, *non*?"

I groaned, deflated and sinking lower in my seat.

"I'm regretting this cab ride already."

"Nonsense!" Luc said, patting my knee like an overly familiar uncle. "This will be a great adventure! A journey of truth and discovery. And pastries, if we pass a good *boulangerie*, which, of course we will, we're in the greatest city in France!"

The cab driver chuckled softly, clearly enjoying the show. I crossed my arms, glaring at Luc as he launched into a tale about the morning's gossip and how the town baker suspected his wife was hiding money in the flour bins.

By the time we neared Beuvron-en-Auge, I'd come to a reluctant conclusion—Luc wasn't just going to be part of this journey, he was going to narrate the whole damn thing like it was a French soap opera.

And for better or worse, I was stuck with him.

CHAPTER 16
MAE

When Erica and I got back to the apartment, the first thing I noticed was how still and quiet it was. Too quiet. The kind of quiet that announces someone's absence.

"Alex?" I called out, only to be met with a blanket of silence. "Get your skinny legs moving and your scrawny ass out here right now, you hear me?"

Erica glanced toward the bathroom door, which was open, displaying a towel draped over the rack and small puddles of water from wet feet.

"Maybe he went for coffee?" she offered, slipping off her shoes.

"There's plenty of that here. It tastes like burnt tire water filtered through the gutter whenever he makes it, but still, we've got plenty and it's suited him just fine to this point."

I wandered into the living room, scanning for signs of him. And that's when I noticed the dining table. Or rather, what was missing from it.

Erica followed my gaze, her expression shifting.

The table was covered in papers, photographs, and folders,

all of them splayed out like the aftermath of a storm. Among them were the files Luc had brought back from the archives. My files. I stepped closer, my heart sinking as I assessed the familiar mess.

"He's been going through them."

Erica tilted her head, her curiosity and annoyance piqued and mingling.

"What the hell was he doing that for? What did he think he'd find?" she asked, her face turning a darker shade of red and her tone catching like glass on a shag rug

"Probably the same thing I've been looking for," I muttered, scanning the table for clues. The letter from Luc, the one with Jacqueline's address, was definitely gone. So was the map I'd left folded neatly next to it.

I sighed.

That daring little fucker.

"I think I know where he went. Actually, I know for certain where he went."

Erica raised an inquisitive eyebrow.

"Let me guess—he figured out Jacqueline's location and decided to go without us?"

"I should have called for you at the beginning instead of him. You're a much better detective, though I suppose he's catching up."

Erica shrugged and nodded, already pulling out her phone to check for a message or missed call. Nothing. Typical Alex.

"That's bold," Erica said, leaning against the back of a chair. "I specifically told him not to do anything stupid. It may not have been in those exact words, but he knew what I meant. I couldn't have been any clearer. Does he even know where to start? I mean, you've been chasing this for who knows how long, Mae. It's not exactly connect-the-dots straightforward as far as I can tell."

"Luc provided enough breadcrumbs," I said, gesturing to the bare space on the table where the map had been. "He's probably halfway to Beuvron-en-Auge by now, armed with Luc's findings and whatever scraps he thinks he can make sense of."

Erica smirked.

"You sound almost impressed."

"I'm not," I shot back, though my tone wasn't entirely convincing.

I was irritated, that's a given, but there was something else there too, something softer—an undercurrent of understanding. Perhaps I had been dragging my feet somewhat subconsciously, not really wanting to put the next piece of the puzzle in its place for fear of what might be confirmed.

Erica crossed her arms, giving me a knowing look.

"So, what's the plan? Wait for him to return with answers, or do you need a quick minute to catch your breath before we head right back out the door?"

I stared at the table, the remnants of Alex's impromptu research session scattered before me. Part of me wanted to let him figure things out on his own, to learn for himself just how tangled this story could get. But another part of me, a louder, more insistent part, knew I hadn't come this far just to sit still now.

"We're going after him," I said firmly, grabbing the coat I had removed a moment before. "I don't need any rest. There's plenty of time for that when I'm dead."

Erica grinned, already reaching for her coat.

"You know you're going to outlive us all, right?" she said. "But, at least things are really getting interesting now. And

Alex will have some explaining to do when I get my hands on him."

Interesting. That was one word for it.

"I may not be ready to know it all, but there's no way on God's green earth that he's doing this without us."

Erica and I walked briskly through the narrow streets of Beuvron-en-Auge, the cobblestones slick—whose bright fucking idea was it to pave this entire country in slippery rock?—from a pesky drizzle that had fallen earlier.

"He couldn't have gotten far," Erica said, glancing around like Alex might suddenly step out of a bakery holding a basket of fresh goods.

"He's probably holed up in some café thinking he's Sherlock Holmes," I muttered, tightening my scarf.

"Well, I hope that's true and he's solved the case, because I'm starving."

We rounded a corner and there it was—a cozy little café beside an ivy-covered building. Through the window, I spotted Alex leaning over a small round table, speaking with someone.

"Oh, you've got to be bloody kidding me," I said, pulling Erica back before she could wave at them.

"What?" she asked, confused.

"Take a closer look for yourself." I motioned toward the window.

Luc was gesturing wildly, his expression animated; Alex sat across from him, shoulders hunched and face buried in his hands.

Erica peeked over my shoulder, her eyebrows arching.

"What do you think they're talking about?"

"Let's find out," I said, pulling her toward the café's side entrance.

We slipped inside, making as little commotion as possible, taking a table near the back where we could hear them without being seen. The smell of fresh espresso and warm pastries filled the air, pulling Erica's attention in more directions than the one I wanted her to focus on. I was only concentrating on Alex and Luc.

"You must be bold, Alex," Luc was saying, his voice carrying just enough to reach us. "You love her, *oui*? Then why hesitate?"

My breath caught in my throat. Erica blinked at me, confused. I shook my head, putting a finger to my lips as Alex groaned audibly.

"It's not that simple, Luc," Alex said, his voice low but clear. "What if she doesn't feel the same way? What if I ruin everything we have?"

Luc threw his hands up in exasperation, nearly knocking over his coffee cup.

"*Mon Dieu*, you Canadians make everything so complicated! Love is love. You tell her, she says it back. You ask her, she says yes. And then you get married. *Voilà*! Simple."

Alex laughed bitterly. "Yeah, it's not that simple."

Luc leaned in, lowering his voice slightly, but we could still hear every word.

"She adores you, Alex. Do you think she travelled all the way here because she wanted to see the French countryside? In the winter? *Non*. She came for you."

Erica stiffened beside me. Wide-eyed realization started to dawn.

"Wait, what—" she began, but I shushed her again.

"I can't just blurt it out," Alex said, running a hand through his hair. "This isn't some rom-com where everything will magically work out."

"Ah, but it *can* work out!" Luc said, wagging a finger. "You need the right setting. Something romantic. A café is too casual. A park, perhaps. And then you tell her, 'Erica, I love you. You are the reason I get up in the morning. Marry me, and let us have a beautiful life together.' You are in France, after all, how much more perfect a place are you hoping for?"

Erica's hand flew to her mouth, her face going pale before turning crimson.

I leaned closer to her, whispering, "Looks like your boyfriend has some big plans."

"Shut up, Mae," she hissed, though her eyes were sparkling.

Luc continued, clearly enjoying himself.

"There has to be a grand gesture. A ring, obviously. Something, what, two karats? And you must have flowers and music! Women love these things."

Alex sighed, his voice softer now.

"I just—I want it to be perfect. She deserves perfect."

Erica was frozen, her eyes locked on Alex through the gaps in the café's plants.

"Well?" I said, nudging her. "You gonna go in there and save him from Luc, or let this play out?"

Erica glanced at me, her cheeks still flushed.

"Let's see how much worse Luc can make it."

We stayed put, listening as Luc launched into an elaborate plan involving fireworks, accordion music, and a moonlit proposal by the Seine. Alex groaned again, and Erica stifled a laugh.

As Erica listened, all I could think about was John. Our dream wedding, everything we wanted.

•••

We sat on the hillside overlooking the valley, the sun dipping low and casting the fields in molten gold. The air was soft, infused with the scent of wildflowers; it was the kind of evening that felt like it would never end. John leaned back on his elbows, gazing at the horizon like it held all the answers.

"If we ever had a dream wedding," he began, his voice low and warm, "it would be simple. Just us. Maybe a few friends, but nothing fancy."

I looked at him, my knees hugged to my chest, and smiled obscurely.

"No big church? No long train on my dress? You're sparing yourself the whole production?"

He chuckled, the sound genuine and familiar, like the rustle of leaves in the wind.

"A field like this would do just fine. You'd wear something light, something that moves with the breeze. And you'd have flowers in your hair. No veil—your face is too beautiful to hide."

My breath caught in my throat, and for a moment, I let myself imagine it: a day filled with laughter, sunlight pouring down on us, the natural world watching patiently as we promised to love each other forever.

"And you?" I asked. "What would you wear?"

He grinned, a lopsided thing that made me smile at the same time it made my heart ache.

"Anything you want. But if it's up to me? No tie. Can't

stand the confining things. Let's have a clean shirt and my best smile."

I laughed, but it wavered as it came out.

"You'd have me walk down the aisle to wed a man with no tie? Scandalous."

John reached for my hand, his touch steady and reassuring.

"It's not the tie that matters. It's the promise, the life after. That's what counts."

The words hung between us with the truth we didn't dare say aloud. I squeezed his hand, my fingers trembling.

"You know this will never happen," I whispered, my voice barely carrying over the gentle rustle of the grass.

His grip tightened, just for a moment. "I know," he said.

I pulled my hand away, unable to meet his eyes.

"So why talk about it? Why dream up something that'll never be real?"

"Because it's ours," he said simply. "No one can take it from us. Not the war, not time, not even the world falling apart around us. It's ours, Mae. It always will be."

I wanted to believe him. I wanted to cling to the picture he painted, to the hope in his voice, but the realities of that dream were already fraying.

"You make it sound so easy," I said, my tone sharper now, a crack forming in my chest that I didn't know how to seal. "But it's not, John. It's not fair. None of this is."

He sat up, the warmth in his eyes dimming slightly.

"Mae—"

"No," I cut him off, my voice rising. "Don't tell me to hold on to something that'll never happen. Don't give me hope for a wedding we'll never have or a life we'll never share. It's cruel."

The words spilled out of me, harsh and cold, but I couldn't stop them. John's face softened and fell slightly, but he didn't speak. He just looked at me, his silence unbearable.

For the first time, I felt the world move under me, its unyielding reality seeping into the cracks of who I was. I could feel it hardening me, carving away the soft elements that once believed in fairy tales and happily-ever-afters. Love, I realized, wasn't enough. Not when the world had other plans.

We sat there in that silence for a long time, the dream of a perfect day lingering before us like smoke. It didn't vanish all at once—it faded, bit by bit, until all that was left was the proof of what would never be.

...

By the time we finally stepped out of hiding, both of us were grinning like idiots. Luc's eyes lit up at the sight of us, and Alex's face turned the colour of a ripe tomato.

"Ah, *Mesdames!*" Luc exclaimed, standing to greet us, oblivious to the fact that we had seemingly appeared from out of nowhere. "Perfect timing. We were just discussing romance."

Alex buried his face in his hands.

"Kill me now."

Alex's face, already a brilliant shade of embarrassment, somehow deepened into a shade of red I'd never seen before as Erica and I stepped closer to the table. His eyes darted between us, full of surprise and, if I wasn't mistaken, sheer panic.

"How—how long have you two been here?" he stammered, his hands gripping the edge of the table as if it might shield him from whatever was about to come.

Erica slid into the chair next to him with a breezy smile, ignoring the question entirely.

"Long enough to hear about fireworks and accordions. Sounds like someone has big plans," I said, taking the seat across from Alex and grinning as Luc's eyes twinkled with mischief. "Don't mind us. Just pretend we're not here, as impossible as that is, given who we are."

"Impossible is right," Alex muttered, running a hand through his hair again. "You weren't supposed to—I mean, how did you even find me?"

"Alex, you're as predictable as a drunkard eyeing up the taco bar in an after-hours massage parlour."

"Mae!" shrieked Erica, who was not yet accustomed to the debauchery I often gave voice to.

"They serve food at your massage parlours?" asked Luc, unaware of the double entendre.

"Luc, stop," Alex groaned. "Just stop."

"Oh no, don't stop," Erica said, leaning her chin on her hand. "This is fascinating."

Luc gave a grand shrug.

"What is there to say? I had the pleasure of helping dear Alex here navigate *les mystères de l'amour*. As his new best friend, I am giving him the wisdom of my years."

Erica shot Alex a playful look.

"Is that so?"

"Can we just focus on why we're all here? You know, Jacqueline. The entire reason for this trip," Alex said, looking like he wanted the ground to swallow him whole, and willing to use Jacqueline as a momentary scapegoat.

Shrewd.

His well-intentioned deception, and enduring a cab ride

with Luc, earned him a lifeline. One I'd throw him, though not without a smirk, and certainly not one he'd be allowed to forget.

"Fine. Now that we're all here, what's the plan, Alex? You seem to be taking the lead today."

He blinked, caught off guard. "Uh, well, I thought we'd just go find her, talk to her. Figure out what she knows."

"That's it? No fireworks? No accordions?" said Erica, tilting her head.

"Erica," Alex said through gritted teeth, his eyes narrowing at her.

Luc, thoroughly entertained, clapped his hands together.

"Ah, the tension! You two are like characters in a romance novel. Truly, I could write a book about this. Maybe I will. Yes?"

"Don't encourage him," Alex said, shooting Luc a withering look.

"All right," I said, pushing my chair back. "Let's go find Jacqueline. And Alex, remember the part about you not getting arrested in a foreign country? This is where I can absolutely not promise it."

Alex stood abruptly, his face still a mottled red but his focus was clear.

Luc folded the map on the table with a precision that seemed unnecessary and out of character, given the unbridled wildness of his personality. The corners lined up perfectly, but the grin on his face was as chaotic as ever.

And with that, we followed him out of the café, Erica hiding a smile and Luc trailing behind with a spring in his step.

Whatever happened next, I knew one thing for sure—my life would never be the same after today.

CHAPTER 17
ALEX

"Well, my friends," said Luc, tucking the map into his jacket as we stepped out into the fresh air, "it seems we are ready for the next chapter. Jacqueline awaits."

"Luc, I've got to ask," I said as we gathered for our next move. "Why do we need a literal map? I mean, we have the internet, we have GPS, hell, we could probably find a Rand McNally atlas if need be, but a map that looks like it belongs in Blackbeard's cabin—is that really necessary?"

"Do all Canadians lack the sense of adventure and lore? Or is it just you? Are you not capable of appreciating the romance that exists when following the dotted lines and dashes to the, how you say, proverbial X? Have you not—"

"Okay, okay, I get it," I said. "Let's just go before I change my mind."

The morning had already been a terrific blur—Luc's letter, the cab ride together, his dramatic romantic advice, Mae and Erica showing up—and now, the looming prospect of meeting Jacqueline, John's daughter. My throat felt tight just thinking about it. I could only imagine how Mae was feeling.

"You really think she'll talk to us?" I asked no one in particular.

Luc smirked, his eyes dancing with something I couldn't quite place.

"Ah, but of course!" he proclaimed. "This is France, *mon ami*. Conversations are our way of life. She may start with skepticism, but give her five minutes of charm, and she'll be pouring the wine."

I raised an eyebrow. "You think I'm charming?"

"*Non*," he said with a shrug, the corners of his mouth twitching. "But Erica says you are, and who am I to argue with such a delightful *femme*?"

"Careful, Luc," Erica said, laughing. "I'm spoken for."

He held up his hands in mock surrender. "*Oui, oui*, I know. But I cannot help it! You are, shall we say, transcendent. And I am French, after all."

"You're French?" we all said in mocking unison.

"Let's focus on Jacqueline," I suggested. "Okay? Erica can handle herself."

"Indeed I can," said Erica, quickly reminding me of the independence I'd do well to never forget.

"Yes, see, indeed she can," Luc agreed, rising with a flourish. "But don't worry, Alex, I will be your guide today. There is no corner of this region I have not explored, no story I have not heard. Trust me, you're in good hands."

I glanced at him skeptically as we left the café. "I hope your hands are steadier than your feet."

He winced dramatically, waving a hand as if dismissing the memory. "Bah, a minor incident! Mere pavement cannot deter my brilliance."

"So, where exactly is she?" I asked, refocusing.

"She works at a flower shop, of all things," said Luc. "Fitting, don't you think? A daughter of love and war, choosing to surround herself with beauty."

"Yes, we know it's a flower shop, but where?"

"Simply follow the *cœur* and we shall arrive where we need to be," said Luc.

It was painfully clear that Luc's comprehension of the situation as it related to Mae was masked by either staggering ineptitude or a severe lack of self-awareness. His flippant words about Jacqueline being the daughter of Mae's only true love, though likely not intentional, were wrapped with barbed wire.

The insightful, poetic turns caught me off guard from the very beginning, but every now and then, and usually for only a fleeting moment, I saw Luc in a new light. Beneath the bravado and theatrics, he was astute, observant, and dedicated. I nodded, though not so much in agreement, but because I didn't know what else to do and this seemed the appropriate physical response. Erica's elbow in my ribs suggested otherwise.

"But what if she doesn't know anything?" I asked him. "What if this is just another dead end?"

Luc clapped a hand on my shoulder, his expression softening. "If that happens, *mon ami*, then we drink wine and tell stories. But I do not think it will. Jacqueline has lived a long life, and life always leaves clues. You just have to know where to look."

I looked at him, his confidence unwavering, and felt that maybe he was right. Maybe today wasn't about reaching dead ends. Maybe it was about finding new beginnings.

"Let's go, then," I said, steadier now.

Luc smiled, his steps airier than I expected as we walked away from the café. "To Jacqueline," he said, raising an imaginary toast.

"To answers," I replied, not entirely sure what I meant, but hoping for them anyway. And with that, we were off.

The flower shop sat at the corner of two picturesque cobblestone streets, its slightly fogged windows casting warm, diffuse light onto the sidewalk. It looked like something out of a storybook, with cascading greenery framing the glass and an artfully hand-painted sign that read *Fleur de Vie*. Inside, an older woman moved about with spry energy, her hands deftly arranging a bouquet of white lilies and purple irises.

"That's her," Luc said quietly, his breath visible in the cool air. "Jacqueline."

The four of us—Mae, Luc, Erica, and me—stood awkwardly on the sidewalk, huddled close together like children peeking into a candy shop. None of us spoke. Mae tilted her head, scrutinizing the woman, her eyes narrowing as if trying to detect traces of John in Jacqueline's face. That, or she was ruthlessly plotting revenge on an innocent woman who had absolutely no hand in any of the matters we found ourselves tangled up in.

"She's got his nose," Mae murmured. "I think. It's hard to tell. Maybe if the little harlot bothered to clean her windows, we'd have a better look."

Luc leaned in toward me, his voice barely registering above a whisper. "I wonder if she's got the same fire in her belly, *non?*" he said, nodding in Mae's direction, picking up on the hostile energy she was projecting.

I elbowed him gently to shush him, though I couldn't help but smirk.

"She wouldn't have any of Mae's genes, you fool," I said.

Admittedly, there was something mesmerizing about Jacqueline. She worked with serene purpose, pausing every now and then to analyze whatever bouquet or arrangement was in front of her, deciding whether to add another sprig of something or simply let it be. She was determined, steely-eyed, and deftly focused on the task before her. I'll be damned if she didn't remind me a bit of Mae. Which was a nightmare scenario, of course. The world is only big enough for one Mae Seasons.

"She doesn't look seventy-eight," Erica said, her tone equal parts admiration and disbelief as Jacqueline stepped out of view, disappearing into any number of spots in the shop.

"She doesn't look like she'd put up with much nonsense, either," Mae added, crossing her arms. "Her hussy mother on the other hand, she'd apparently put up with infidelity."

"She most certainly would not," came a throaty voice from behind us.

We all jumped, spinning around to find Jacqueline standing there, one hand on her hip, the other holding a medium-sized pair of gardening shears. We now had a clear picture of who she was, standing two metres away from us, no longer a quasi-kaleidoscopic vision through the blurred windows. She wore a loose cardigan over a floral-print blouse, her silver hair swept back into a practical braid. Her steely blue eyes scanned us, a mix of curiosity and amusement dancing in them.

"Well?" she said, raising an eyebrow. "Are you going to keep loitering in front of my shop like vagrants, or are you coming inside to tell me who the hell you are and what the hell you're doing?"

Luc recovered first, sweeping into a bow that was only slightly sarcastic. "*Madame* Jacqueline, we were just admiring your artistry. You are a true flower whisperer."

She snorted, looking him up and down. "Save the flattery for someone who'll buy it, *monsieur*."

I stepped forward, feeling my face flush.

"*Bonjour*, uh, Jacqueline? I'm Alex. This is Mae, Erica, and Luc. We—"

"—are terrible at being inconspicuous," she interrupted, gesturing toward the shop's door. "Come. You're making my neighbours think I'm running a *société secrète* here. Not that I care much what they think, most of them reek of indignation—but still, I try to be a good neighbour. You lot may not be cultured enough to understand."

"I shouldn't, but I like you. God knows why," said Mae, sizing up her counterpart.

Jacqueline turned and walked briskly back inside, leaving the door ajar behind her. The four of us exchanged looks before following, like guilty kids caught sneaking cookies and given but one option for atonement.

As we entered the small shop, we were enveloped in the pleasing smells of fresh blooms and potting soil. Jacqueline moved behind the counter, folding her arms and leaning against it as she studied us.

"Well?" she said, her gaze landing on Mae. "You look like *le chef de bande* of this group. Start speaking."

Mae blinked, momentarily thrown, before straightening. She was not accustomed to being spoken to this way. She was the ever-confident, assertive purveyor of authority—being on the receiving end was not a position she was familiar with. But, given her remarks outside and the clear indication that Jacqueline would take absolutely none of our shit, I had to wonder if an instantaneous respect had been forged.

"We came to—well, it's a long story, I'll give you the short version, we don't know how much time you have left on this earth," Mae said, disregarding the fact she was Jacqueline's senior by nearly two decades. "We believe you might be my husband's daughter. The offspring of John Seasons."

Holy. Fucking. Shit.

It's possible the collective air gasped by Luc, Erica, and me was enough to instantly asphyxiate every flower in the shop. Mae went straight for the jugular, not wasting any time in getting to the bottom of this mystery.

Jacqueline's eyebrow arched higher. "You're not starting *petite*, are you?"

"It's true!" Luc stepped forward, his hands gesturing animatedly. "There are letters, photographs, even a birth certificate. All signs point to you, *madame*. And oh, how exciting this is! You feel that? *Oui*? And your blog! You know so much!"

Jacqueline held up a hand, silencing him. "Ah, *mon petit*, let me guess—you've come about the great-uncle, or maybe *un cousin* twice removed, some shadow from the past all wrapped up in *mystère et drame*," she said, folding her arms like someone who has opened the door to far too many dreamers with family trees and half-truths. "I've seen your kind before. Always chasing ghosts like they're *baguettes chaudes* straight from the oven. And I knew that fucking blog would bite me in the *derrière* at some point."

She let out a long sigh, the kind only a woman who has lived through wars, winters, and weddings can produce.

"Listen to me, *chéri*. He was *not* the double agent people gossip about after too much wine and a poorly baked *tarte*. That was someone else entirely. Different man, different story. Did the name, somehow, end up as John Seasons? *Mais oui*. But that's a very flimsy little basket, and you've gone and stuffed it full of eggs like it's *le matin de Pâques*. You'd do better trusting an old *roue de brouette* with a crack in it."

"He was my husband," said Mae firmly, her voice steady, allowing a long pause to truly let the words sink in. "He was also my true love. My *only* love."

Jacqueline studied Mae, the expression on her face conveying that this wasn't the typical inquisition she endured about her father. But perceived thread of empathy or not, Jacqueline wasn't about to lower her drawbridge and let us come crashing through the castle gate.

"*Très bien*," she said, almost defiantly, her chin lifting just a touch. "You've dragged yourselves all the way here, from *je ne sais où*—somewhere across the Atlantic, I suppose. This one," she said, narrowing her eyes at Luc, "is obviously *français*, anyone with two ears can hear it. But the rest of you?" She gave a shrug that could've flattened a soufflé. "*Bof.* Who cares. You're here, aren't you? Clearly convinced you've uncovered something *très important*." She turned and motioned toward the worn wooden chairs with the air of a woman issuing royal decrees from her kitchen. "*Allez-y*, sit down. Let's see if you're half as interesting as you seem to think you are."

Her tone was cutting, but her lips twitched, betraying the faint hint of a smile. As we sat around the tiny table nestled in the corner of the shop, I couldn't help but think Jacqueline wouldn't be just a passive character in all of this; she was striking in ways I couldn't fully comprehend.

And judging by the glint in Mae's eye, she knew she'd finally met her match.

CHAPTER 18
MAE

Jacqueline leaned back in her chair, arms crossed like she was ready for a prizefight, which was good, because I was about to give her one. The hardened glint in her eyes was honed, calculating, as though she was trying to figure out if I was worth her time.

Oh, you better believe I'm worth your time.

I sat across from her, mirroring her posture, my hands gripping the arms of the wooden chair so tightly I thought they might splinter under me. Had I cared what the others thought, this was the moment I would have paid it some mind.

"So," Jacqueline began, her voice as cool as the air outside. "John Seasons. *Mon père*, or supposed, anyways. What tale have you got in your heads about him? Let me guess—war hero? Dashing romantic? *Figure tragique* who went off to fight for king and country, leaving broken hearts and unanswered letters in his wake?"

I blinked, stunned by her venom. My jaw tightened.

"What do you mean, *supposed* father?" I asked. "Is he *not* your father? And he wasn't just a story. He was a real man, a good man. My husband. Show some damn respect."

Jacqueline snorted, the sound derisive.

"*Good man*, was he? Because where I'm standing, it looks like he skipped town and left *ma mère* to raise a child alone. You think that's *good?* Is that what *un père* does? *Non*, a father sticks around, a man sticks around."

Emotions fought to take over and I had to calm myself. I recognized this pain. I knew this pain—having someone so important to your life walk away. John so often spoke about what he had to do—as a man—to come back and be present, to never have to leave ever again. But here, this woman, though icy and standoffish, had nothing to do with the situation, she was merely the outcome. I had to reduce her to something insignificant, anything else would be too much to bear. I felt the words bubbling up before I could stop them.

"*Skipped town?!*" I shouted. "He was *killed*. In the war. The same goddamn war that gives you the freedom to work in this little shop and me the freedom to properly kick your ass snout to anus if you keep speaking that way. You don't know the first thing about him! You have no idea what he gave up. Do you *know* what he went through?"

Her laugh was sharp enough to cut a three-dollar steak with ease.

"Ha. We all go through things," she retorted. "And kicking my *derrière*, well, that's a crime, so no, you don't have that freedom, *mon amie*. But, assuming it doesn't come to that, let's talk about life with an absentee father."

"You don't get to say that about him," I snapped, leaning forward now. "You have no idea what his life was like—what any of it was like. He was just a boy when he went to war, when he came to this godforsaken country. He fought, he witnessed and survived horrors we could never begin to imagine, and then he died. He was killed doing things none of us could comprehend, let alone understand. You want to talk about choices? You think he didn't want to stay? You think he didn't carry the load of everything he left behind every single day?"

Her expression was implacable, but something flickered in her eyes—just for a moment. Doubt, maybe. Or perhaps a crack in her armour.

"Sounds like you have a nice fairytale to hang *your* hat on," she said. "And what about *ma mère*? What about *moi*? You want me to pity *him*? She was the one who was left behind. She was the one who had to pick up the pieces and figure out how to raise me on her own. So don't sit there and tell me he's the victim in all this."

Around Jacqueline's neck hung a locket that, until now, had been hidden under her shirt. She removed it and stared at the piece of jewellery resting in her palm, its delicate chain pooling like spilled silver.

"A gift, from *ma mère*," she said, her voice soft but firm, catching the way all our eyes had gravitated to the small object in her hand. "I've worn it for as long as I can remember—since I was a *petite fille*, really. You may think it silly, *un peu dramatique*, perhaps. But this?" She paused, pressing the pendant gently with her thumb. "This got me through times that were—not kind. *Très difficile.*" Her gaze sharpened, but her tone stayed almost wistful. "It was a promise, you see? A *petite* one, but *une promesse* all the same. A hope for something better. For *l'avenir*—something bright. And now—you arrive. You people. You come with your questions, your theories, your intentions. And somehow, it feels like you're trying to make all that light a little dimmer."

She folded the pendant into her palm, shielding it like a final word.

We were speechless, which was quite impressive given the company, especially Luc. But let's be honest, I'm not one to bite my tongue either. However, something was happening here. I don't know what, but it sure as shit had my brain working overtime.

"Okay, enough," I said, cutting through the silence like a knife through butter warmer than my soul. "You've got your sweet little trinket and your misty-eyed monologue. Good for you. Congratulations! You've officially joined the ranks of a billion girls clutching lockets and unresolved feelings."

My troops stood like they were guarding the Tower of London or whatever the hell building those statues with the tall fuzzy hats guard—not allowed to move, smirk, or make any motion that indicates they're, in fact, human. I am not a surprise to them. But Jacqueline, well, she looked shell-shocked.

"I didn't come all this way to sit through story hour. I came to find out what the hell is going on. So unless that necklace spits out information that I can understand in my native tongue, maybe try saying something useful. Something with substance. Something we can *actually* work with."

I folded my arms and stared her down, her face studying mine; two prizefighters sizing each other up. I couldn't quite get a read on her, and I'm pretty sure she couldn't get one on me either.

Good.

"Now, are you going to stop dancing around and tell us what the actual fuck happened, or should we all just go home?"

Jacqueline spent the next few minutes telling us how her thoughts turned bitter, tracing the timeline of what could have been, lamenting how John could have left the war effort behind, could have turned his back on the violence and chaos, and chosen them instead. He could have escaped with her mother and her, fleeing to some hidden corner of the world where they could have been a family, where the horrors of the war would have been nothing more than distant echoes. But he hadn't.

Instead, he had stayed, committed to a cause that, in the end, didn't save any of them. Of course he did. He wouldn't have left me to go with them. Despite my unsureness, I was sure of it. Jacqueline had clung to threads of hope, believing every day that John would appear on their doorstep, ready to fulfill the promises he had made. She had been regaled with stories of her mother and father's love, and envisioned an idyllic life they could have had together. But that door never opened, and those promises went unanswered. They were left alone in a world that demanded survival at any cost, scrounging for food, dodging dangers that grew closer with each passing day. The dream of a family—a safe, whole, and secure loving family—had been nothing but a mirage.

Even now, standing amidst the pillars of the life she had built for herself, Jacqueline still felt the lingering sting of that abandonment. It wasn't just the absence of a father that haunted her; it was the residual thoughts of what could have been, of the life they were denied because he had chosen to fight instead of protect. The locket looked weighty in her hand as she enclosed it in a tight fist. Such a tiny item held all the questions she would never get answers to, all the experiences and lives they might have lived if only John had chosen differently.

"So you see, he wasn't father-of-the-year material, not to me anyway," she concluded. "I never knew my father and, quite frankly, *ce n'est pas juste*. I'm not the only person to have suffered such a fate, I know, but I will not allow anyone to tell me I should feel otherwise."

I opened my mouth to argue back but stopped, the fight draining out of me as her words sank in. I remember fighting this fight so many years ago, so angry at the man who made promises to me and walked out.

She was right, though, at least to a certain degree. I had no idea what her mother had gone through, or what she had, for that matter. It was likely something similar to me. I was angry. But I also believed in fairness, and what I was doing now was not fair, not in the slightest. But could I back down? Did I have it in me to produce, let alone wave, a white flag?

Goddammit. My old ass is getting tricked into sentimentality.

For a long moment, neither of us spoke—no one spoke. The silence felt too fragile, the shop seemed devoid of everything except Jacqueline and me. I barely registered that Alex, Erica, and Luc were still in the room with us. Then Jacqueline sighed, her posture softening as she reached under the counter.

"Look," she said, her voice no longer combative. "I don't know what's true and what isn't. I don't know if he's the husband you claim him to be. Maybe he was the man you think he was. Maybe he wasn't. But I do know one thing—neither of us really knows the whole story. And quite honestly, pretending to won't make a damn difference."

In a brisk movement, she got up and went to the back room. When she returned, she set a small, wooden box on the table between us. Its exterior was weathered, the wood darkened with age.

"These are my mother's," she said. "Letters from him. I've been through them more times than I can count, but maybe you'll see something I missed. If you want answers, this is all I've got. I'm done looking for them. I've made my peace, whatever that is, and I'm more than happy to move on completely and never think of him again. *J'ai fini.*"

I stared at the box, my breath catching. My fingers hovered over the lid, but I didn't dare open it. Not yet. Instead, I looked at Jacqueline, and for the first time, I didn't see a stranger or an opponent. I recognized someone whose life had also been spent fighting her own battles.

"Thank you," I said softly, my white flag out, if not yet completely raised.

She shrugged, leaning back in her chair again.

"Don't thank me yet. If he was half as charming on paper as you say he was in real life, you're in for one hell of a ride."

The drive back to the apartment was mostly silent, save for the rhythmic sounds of the car and Luc's occasional muttering about the "art of a graceful exit." Erica sat up front, her gaze intently fixed on the passing scenery, her arms folded tightly, a posture suggesting that she was shutting the rest of us out. But why? Perhaps the combination of Alex's broken promise and the knowledge of a possible proposal were finally sinking in. Alex was beside me in the back seat, staring at his hands as if their lines held some secret he couldn't quite decipher.

I still wasn't ready to speak. Not yet. The encounter with Jacqueline had left me feeling hollowed out, like something vital had been scooped out of my chest and the gaping cavity left raw. Jacqueline had been fire and steel, so much like me it was unbearable. And those letters—the ones she'd offered up like a taunt—were now tucked into my bag, filled with truths I wasn't sure I wanted to read. Luc was right, no amount of his digging would have unearthed whatever was written across these pages.

By the time we reached Caen, the sun was dipping low, casting the city in shades of orange and gold. The streets were emptier now, the day's typical buzz becoming softer background noise. Erica and Luc wandered off, with Luc insisting on showing her one or another hidden gem of the city. Alex hesitated at the curb, unsure whether he should follow them or stay with me. Erica seemed all too happy to go with Luc, proving my earlier suspicion correct. Or at least I was comfortable enough assuming I was correct. Really, who gives a shit?

"Go on," I said, waving him away. "I need a minute."

But he didn't.

Instead, he trailed me into the apartment, his steps thunderous and purposeful behind mine.

"Listen, sasquatch, if you're going to walk behind me, lighten the load, you're causing the floor to jump up in front of me. You don't want to be responsible for me going down and breaking a hip, do you?"

Once inside, I went straight for the bottle of red wine on the counter, pouring a glass and downing half of it before the door had even closed. Alex watched me, his hands shoved into his jacket pockets, his frame hunched and face unreadable.

"Something you want to say?" I asked. "Now's the time. Confessions and secrets of all kinds have been spilling out today, no point in stopping now."

"No." He hesitated. "Maybe. I don't know. You're different—I've never seen you like this."

"Like what?" I shot back, setting the glass down with more force than was necessary. "Like I've been gutted alive? Because that's what this feels like, Alex. This—this *thing*—is consuming me. It's killing me."

He stepped closer but didn't say anything, patiently waiting me out the way he always did. It was infuriating, and yet it was the only thing keeping me from completely unravelling.

I slumped into my chair by the window, staring out at the narrow street. The silence pressed against me until I couldn't take it anymore.

"I keep thinking about him," I said quietly. "About John. About what I said to him the last time I saw him."

Alex didn't move, but continued to stand at attention. I could feel his eyes on me like a spotlight.

•••

The woods were rich with the scent of pine and damp earth, the sun spearing long rays through the trees. This path had always been ours—a sanctuary of sorts, something natural carved out of the chaos of the world. Here, beneath the towering trees and rustling leaves, we could be just John and Mae. No expectations, no outside world pulling us apart. But now the woods felt different, as if they too sensed what was coming. The canopy above pressed down like the weight in my chest, cloying and unrelenting.

"I have to go, Mae," he said softly, his voice layered with a conflicting mix of resolve and regret.

"You don't *have* to do anything," I shot back, quickening my pace until I was in front of him, blocking the narrow path. The pine needles crunched under my boots as I planted myself firmly, daring him to push past me. "No one's forcing you to lie about your age and throw your life away for a war that isn't even ours."

His eyes flickered—guilt, frustration, maybe both.

"You may think this war isn't ours, and maybe it isn't, not right now, but if we don't do something, if *I* don't do something, you can bet your last dollar that it will soon be ours. But it's not just about that. It's about doing what's right."

"What's *right*?" I let out a bitter laugh, the sound loud enough to make the birds scatter from the branches above. "What's *right* is staying here, with me. What's *right* is building the life we've talked about, the life we've planned. But no— you'd rather play hero and march off to God knows where for God knows how long."

John sighed, running a hand through his hair in that way he always did when he was trying to keep his temper in check. His fingers left it mussed, wavy curls sticking out in all directions, but this did nothing to soften the hard lines etched into his face.

"You think I *want* to leave? You think this is *easy* for me?"

"Don't you dare make this about how hard it is for *you*," I snapped, my voice vibrating with anger. "You're the one choosing this. You're the one who's walking away."

His jaw tightened, his teeth clenched, and for a moment, I thought he might argue. But instead, he stepped around me, continuing down the path without another word. That simple action—turning his back on me—ignited something wild and reckless in my chest.

"Fine," I shouted after him, my voice breaking under the pressure of my anger and fear. "*Go!* But don't think for a second that I'm going to sit here and wait for you like some love-sick fool."

My throat burned, but I didn't care. "You want to leave? Then leave. But don't come back, John Seasons. Don't you dare come back."

At that, he stopped dead in his tracks, his shoulders stiffening. Slowly, he turned to face me, and the unvarnished look on his face was like a sucker punch to the gut. Hurt. Betrayal. Sadness. But underneath it all, there was still that maddening calm, as though he had already made peace with my worst tendencies.

"You don't mean that," he said softly, his voice as steady as the century-old trees around us.

"Yes, I do," I lied, my voice shaking with the fire that still engulfed it. "Go to hell, John. You'll never make it out there anyway. You're not brave enough, not strong enough—"

"Stop," he said, his voice low and firm, slicing through my tirade. "Just stop."

But I couldn't. The words kept bubbling up and spilling out, intense and cruel, fuelled by a desperation I couldn't control.

"You'll die out there, John. And for what? For *nothing*. For some stupid cause that won't matter in five years."

His eyes darkened, and for the first time, I saw a flicker of anger beneath the calm.

"I thought you of all people would understand," he said, his voice riddled with disappointment. "But maybe I was wrong."

He hesitated, his gaze momentarily softening as he looked at me. "Rest assured, my dear Mae, I will come back for you. We will be together again."

And then he turned and strode away, his figure growing smaller and smaller until the trees swallowed him whole.

I stood there long after he was gone, the echo of my own words ringing in my ears.

Don't you dare come back.

The phrase clung to the air, cementing itself in my mind, bitter and unforgiving, like acrid smoke from a fire that had burned too hot.

It was only when the woods fell silent and the power of what I'd said sank in that my knees buckled. I fell to the damp earth, my hands clutching at the pine needles as if I could anchor myself to something. The tears came then, spilling hot and fast, soaking into the ground beneath me.

I wanted to run after him, to take it all back, to beg him to stay. I wanted to tell him I didn't mean it, that I needed him more than I needed air. But my pride—stupid, stubborn pride—kept me rooted in place. By the time I found the courage to move, it was too late.

The woods closed in around me, their silence deafening, and for the first time, the path felt like a place I could never walk again.

•••

"I told him not to come back," I whispered. The words felt like shards of glass in my throat. "We fought, and I told him to go to hell. I said—oh, God—I said he wasn't brave enough for war, that he'd never make it out there. I wanted to hurt him because he was leaving me. And he—" My voice hitched and broke, and I covered my face with my hands, falling to my knees the same way I did in the forest all those years ago. "He left, Alex. And he never came back."

Alex sat down across from me, leaning forward with his elbows on his knees. "Mae—"

"No, let me finish." I dropped my hands and looked at him, the tears I'd been holding back now spilling over. "I've spent my whole life chasing his ghost, trying to make sense of things, trying to give everything some meaning. But the plain truth is that *I* killed him. Not the war, not any bombs or bullets. *Me.* My anger. My words. Being here, meeting Jacqueline, uncovering what I've learned is proof of that. I can feel it."

He shook his head, but I held up a hand to stop him.

"You don't get it. You don't know what it's like to carry that kind of guilt, to wake up every day and wonder if maybe—just maybe—someone would still be alive if you'd been different."

Alex's face softened with compassion, but there was something else there too—something like realization.

"You think you're the only person who's ever felt that way?" he asked. "You think you're the only one carrying guilt around like a goddamn albatross?"

I blinked at him, thrown by the unexpected edge in his voice.

"Mae, you've spent your whole life running from what happened," he said. "But you're not the only one who's lost something, or someone. You're not the only one who's been shaped by this." He paused, his voice dropping. "Do you even realize how much of other people's lives have been spent trying to live up to you? To your stories? To the *idea* of who you are?"

The words hit me like a slap, and for a moment, all I could do was stare at him. "Alex—"

"No," he said, cutting me off. "I'm not saying this to hurt you. I would never do that. I just—I need you to know that you're not alone in this. You're not the only one who's been seriously messed up by love."

The silence that followed was significant, but it wasn't unbearable. For the first time since meeting Alex at Silver Springs, I felt like the space between us wasn't an impossible chasm but a bridge.

"I don't know how to let it go," I admitted, so low it was barely audible.

"Maybe you don't have to," he said. "Maybe you just have to let it change you."

I looked at him then, really looked at him, and felt the rare stirrings of something close to hope.

"Would it make you feel better if you yelled at me a little and kicked me in the shins?" he asked, a wry grin overtaking his features.

"As a matter of fact, it would."

CHAPTER 19
ALEX

I was still sitting at the table, nursing a second cup of the God-awful coffee produced by the percolator, when the door swung open and Erica strolled in, Luc trailing behind with a triumphant grin and a baguette tucked under his arm like a sword.

This guy and his fucking bread.

"Guess who's back, *mon ami?*" Luc declared, twirling once for no apparent reason. "And she brought the spoils of battle. Behold, the freshest croissants, éclairs, and one tale of a confused pigeon who nearly became lunch."

Erica rolled her eyes but was smiling, a flush of amusement dotting her cheeks.

"For the record, I didn't *let* him chase the pigeon. I just turned my back for two seconds, and suddenly, I'm apologizing to a very angry baker who now thinks all Canadians are lunatics. And thanks to someone's failure to blend into his own culture, we have an adopted Canuck here, though I'm not sure yet if we want to list him as one of our own."

"Sounds like a story I need to hear," I said.

"Well, it starts innocently enough," said Erica. "I'm sitting at the café table, enjoying the last bit of sunshine before the sky turns to clouds, when Luc returns from inside with two coffees. He sets one in front of me, takes his seat—and then freezes mid-sip. I follow his gaze and spot the culprit: a plump gray pigeon pecking at crumbs near the next table. It's minding its own business, head bobbing and darting in that odd, mechanical way pigeons do. Luc narrows his eyes like he's just identified his mortal enemy.

"Luc goes on to say that the bird is staring at him with some type of—and these are his words, not mine—'let's take it out and measure' look. I tell Luc that, of course, this is a pigeon and what he's suggesting is absurd. But Luc isn't convinced. The pigeon pauses its pecking and tilts its head—probably to keep a possessive eye on a dropped croissant flake—and Luc stiffens. Now fully convinced the bird has challenged him, Luc jumps to his feet, takes a step forward and again, his words, not mine, 'is prepared to whip it out.' They're now locked in some kind of silent standoff, man versus fowl, and I'm pretty sure I hear someone at the next table snort.

"The pigeon ruffles its feathers; I swear it's just adjusting itself, but Luc gasps like it's preparing for an attack. He waves his arms to shoo it away, and it flaps up to the back of an empty chair, glaring—or maybe just existing—with its small, beady eyes. At this point, I'm torn between embarrassment and the urge to record the whole thing. Luc makes a lunge, the pigeon takes off in a flutter of wings, and he crashes into a table with a tray full of pastries. The baker runs out, screaming in French and, with the confidence of a tall man, Luc returns to the table looking absurdly proud of himself. He plops into the chair across from me, swipes my coffee without asking, and says, 'I was defending your honour.'"

I tried not to, but a grin leapt to my face nonetheless. The levity ushered into the room was both palpable and sorely needed.

"I hope the whole thing was worth the international incident," I managed.

"Indeed it was," Luc replied with mock seriousness. "But we must move past this debacle. What's next in our grand adventure? Are we solving mysteries? Breaking hearts? Writing love letters to the loves of our past?"

Erica rolled her eyes again and leaned closer to me. "Did you talk to Mae? Where is she?"

"She's in her room," I said, pushing back my chair. "But before we do anything else, we need to figure out how we're handling this Jacqueline situation. I'm guessing she won't just willingly hand over answers without making us work for them. Sure, we have some letters, but do you really think that's the key to this whole thing?"

"And by *us*, you mean *you, me,* and *Mae*," Erica said, smirking. "Because I can't imagine Luc surviving another round with her."

Luc gasped, clutching his chest like she'd stabbed him. "You wound me, *ma chérie*. Jacqueline and I share a mutual respect. She insults me, and I respect her ability to do so with shrewd precision."

I snorted. "She called you a dough pile with breadsticks for legs."

"And yet," he said, raising a finger, "she could not take her eyes off me. That's called magnetism, my good friend. You wouldn't understand."

"Magnetism or not," I said, grabbing an envelope from the stack on the table, "she gave us these, a first batch of letters. Mae hasn't opened any of them yet."

Luc reached for the envelope, but I pulled it back.

"No sir, not until Mae is here. She'd kill me—all of us—if I opened them without her." I could feel Erica's eyes on me as I said this.

"Okay, yes, I did that very thing earlier, but this is different. Right? Somehow? Surely, it's got to be different."

"I suppose we'll never know," said Erica, somewhat defeated by my casual admission of guilt. "I would actually like to talk to you about that when we have a few minutes."

I didn't want to talk about it. Not because it would be a difficult conversation, though it would be, but because it would mean admitting that I had broken Erica's trust, even if it was in a way that wouldn't seem significant to most. That wasn't the point. She knew it; I knew it.

For now, however, Erica sat beside me, stealing sips from my coffee. I'd never admit just how much this drives me crazy.

"So, what's the plan then? Read the letters, hope for a revelation, and pray Jacqueline doesn't chase us out of her shop with garden shears next time? Because I think we all know there's going to be a next time."

"More or less," I said, trying not to smile at her casual caffeine theft. "But first, we need to figure out what to say to her. If these letters don't clarify anything, we're going to have to rely on—I can't believe I'm saying this—charm."

"Did someone call?" chimed Luc from the other side of the room.

"This tastes like absolute shit, by the way," declared Erica. "How do you drink this?"

"Well, now that you've spit some of it back into the cup, I'll be drinking it from a new mug and a fresh pot."

"You're not afraid of my germs, are you? You know, we've

done more than share some backwashed coffee," she said with a wink.

"Ah, sex. You're talking about sex, *oui?* It's the universal language," said Luc, taking our silence as an invitation to come over. "It's good for starting wars, ending arguments, and, in some cases, celebrating the fact that it's Tuesday afternoon. And in other cases, all three! *Trois*—it's a very sexy number, *non?*"

"What's going on?" Mae chose that moment to appear, her expression a mix of curiosity and frustration as she looked at the three of us, gathered like conspirators.

"Planning," I said. "Also, Luc nearly got arrested over a pigeon."

Mae didn't even blink. "That hardly surprises me. What's that envelope? Is it from Jacqueline's stash?"

I handed it to her carefully, watching as her eyes moistened at the sight of John's name scrawled across the paper. For a moment, the room fell silent, the importance of history pressing down on all of us.

"Well," Mae said, "let's see what he's been hiding."

Dear Yvette,

The nights here are endless, though the days are just as long. In the unbearable stretches of silence, I close my eyes and imagine you and Jacqueline—your laughter filling the air, your hands busy with the things you love. It is as though I can almost feel the warmth of Jacqueline's smile as she gazes upon a new toy for the first time.

War is a cruel thief. It steals moments we might have shared, conversations we will never have, and memories we have not yet made. But, in the cracks of this chaos, I find myself clinging to the thought of the future, of you and Jacqueline. You are the glue that keeps me together, even when the world threatens to break me.

I think often of the café near the river, the one where we would sit for hours on those rare occasions when time allowed. Do you remember that first time? You wore a soft blue scarf, the one you said did not match anything but brought you luck. I told you it matched your eyes, and you called me a liar. You were right, of course—it did not match your eyes.

These trenches are a world apart from the dreams we shared with each other. Yet even here, surrounded by mud and steel and smoke, I catch glimpses of you and Jacqueline. A patch of sky that reminds me of the shade of her dress. The way the rain falls, soft and steady, like your soothing voice when you read her a nighttime story. The two of you are everywhere, and yet, you are not here.

I will come back to you, Yvette. I swear it with every breath I take. But if I cannot, if fate sees fit to keep us apart and not allow me to finish what I have started, know this: the two of you, in a way most unforeseen, have saved me.

Keep the fire burning for all of us who carry the hope that one day, this war will end. And if I have any say in it, I will walk through your door and hoist Jacqueline to the ceiling in sheer celebration.

Until then, be brave for both of us—the three of us. And when the nights grow long, know that somewhere across this broken world, I am looking up at the same stars, thinking of people like you.

John

The room was silent. Much more so than it had been in hours. It seemed as though all of us had held our breath as

Mae read the letter, if only to avoid letting slip a gasp or a grunt at the cloudy truth being recited. Or perhaps it wasn't so cloudy. Perhaps it was crystal clear and we just hoped for a little ink spill in the water, enough to cause some reasonable doubt. The only noticeable sound was the faint rustle of the paper in Mae's trembling hands. She clutched the letter like it might crumble into dust if she released it. Staring at it transfixed, her lips were pressed tight, her shoulders curling inward like she was trying to shield herself from the crushing burden of it all.

I'd never before seen her like this. Sure, she had shared a few vulnerable moments with me in the past, but Mae was blazing fire and unyielding iron, rough edges and biting remarks. But right now? She was completely raw. And I didn't know what to say, didn't know if anything I could say would even matter.

Erica hovered near her, one hand resting lightly on Mae's shoulder, like she was afraid of pushing too hard and making things worse. Luc, for once, had nothing clever to say. He stood by the window, fiddling with his scarf, his usual swagger dialed down to an almost respectful degree.

Then Mae spoke, her voice shattering the silence like a hammer falling on glass.

"He wrote this—while I was waiting for him to come back to me."

Her words landed like an unexpected gut punch, but they weren't meant for me. Erica bent down, her hand tightening on Mae's shoulder.

"Mae, you didn't know," she said gently, her voice low and thoughtful.

Mae shook her head, her grip on the letter tightening.

"No, I didn't. But he did. He knew who he was writing to. He was writing her heartfelt promises while I was—" Her voice cracked, and she stopped herself, breathing hard like the words themselves were choking her.

I wanted to say something, anything, to pull her out of this spiral, but I didn't know where to start.

Luc, of all people, stepped in first, his voice soft but steady.

"Mae, John was a man caught in impossible times. Maybe this—Yvette—was how he survived."

Mae's head snapped up, her eyes blazing, tears streaming down her face. "And what about me? I wasn't enough to keep him going?"

Her words were daggers, sharp and jagged, laced with hurt. Erica crouched down next to her, meeting her gaze head-on.

"That's not it, and you know it," said Erica. "In desperate circumstances, people find ways to survive any way they can, Mae. It doesn't mean you mattered less."

Mae didn't respond immediately. Her fingers curled even tighter around the letter, and then the floodgates opened. "I told him not to come back," she said, her voice hoarse and barely audible. She let out a series of broken sobs, her body shaking as the tears fell. "He must have left me long before he actually left."

The air in the room shifted. Erica froze, her hand left floating like she didn't know what to do with it. Even Luc went still, his usual bravado swallowed by whatever hurt and anguish he was seeing on Mae's face.

"I was so angry," Mae continued, her words tumbling out like a confession she'd been carrying for years. "So scared. I told him not to come back—and then he didn't. I didn't mean it. I believed he must have known that. But I never imagined it would drive him to this."

Erica broke the silence, her voice soft but firm. "You didn't mean that, Mae. Of course you didn't. John must have known you were just speaking from a place of hurt, anger, and fear."

Mae looked up, her eyes red and glistening with tears.

"But I said it," she spat, her voice filled with self-loathing. "And now? Now I don't even know who he really was. I've spent my whole life chasing a memory, and I don't even know if the man I loved was real."

I felt something tighten in my chest, watching her like this. Mae had always been larger than life to me. Invincible. And seeing her break apart like this—it gutted me.

Luc crossed the room, stepping into the tension like it didn't terrify him.

"The man who wrote that letter," he said, nodding toward the paper in Mae's hands. "He was real. Maybe not in the exact way you thought, but real nonetheless. And maybe it's time to find out who he really was—not the idea of him, but the whole man."

"What the fuck does that even mean, Luc?" Mae roared. "Your clever remarks, your upbeat spirit, it all makes me sick! Read the fucking room just once before opening your foolish mouth, would you."

Luc didn't respond. He just stared at her, his jaw tight.

"Let's open the next one," Erica said, her voice balanced; it was the only thing steadying the rest of us. "We're not done with this story yet. You've come this far, Mae, let's rip the bandage off and put whatever we need to behind us."

"Rip the bandage off?" Mae's words were soaked in venom. "Then just put this behind us? It's that easy, is it? A little bit of pain as some hairs pull from your arm and then it's over? The three of you deserve each other, you know that? You're a bunch of self-absorbed assholes who have no idea what it's like to love, lose, and live in a lonely world only to have it doused in gasoline and set ablaze. But yes, dear, by all means, let's rip the bandage off."

"Mae!" I interjected. "That's enough."

"You're goddamn right, it is. Get out."

CHAPTER 20
MAE

I slammed the door shut behind them, the sound echoing through the apartment like the final note of a funeral march. I leaned against its smooth surface for a moment, staring into the silence. Alex's face had been a whirling mess of concern when he left, Erica's full of hurt and questions she was too kind to ask. Even Luc had held his tongue for once, slipping out with a sober nod that almost felt like an apology.

Now it was just me and the letters.

The pile sat on the table like a taunting dare—well-worn creases, paper brittle with age and brimming with secrets. My hands trembled as I picked up the next one, the familiar scrawl of John's handwriting making my chest tighten.

Dear Yvette,

The nights here stretch on endlessly, broken only by the low thunder of bombs on the horizon. In those long hours, I find myself remembering you and Jacqueline—not just your faces, but the way your hair would catch the sun, glowing with that strange mix of copper and gold. It reminds me of warmth, of home, of being known.

There is comfort in that memory. It keeps me connected to something soft and human while everything around me tries to grind it out.

And Jacqueline's laughter—do you know how rare it is to remember joy out here? Not just the sound of it, but the way it would roll through a room like a gust of fresh air through an open window. It did not belong to me, but I was lucky to be near it. She always made heavy things feel lighter. How do kids do that so effortlessly?

I am coming back, Yvette. To you, and to the child who calls you mother. I have to. Not because of a vow or a duty, but because if there is any world left to return to, it begins with people like you—people who reminded me what it was all for.

John

I dropped the letter onto the table, staring at it like it might explode. And if it didn't, I certainly would. My stomach churned, and for a moment, I thought I might be sick. The words on the page didn't just hurt—they were blistering torture. The sentiment, it was all John. To whom they were written to? This wasn't the John I'd known. This wasn't the man I thought I'd spent my life understanding and loving unconditionally.

And yet—it was. This was his writing, these were his words. I'd know them both anywhere.

I reached for the next letter, my fingers shaking like the paper might burn me.

Dear Yvette,

I have done things here I will never speak of, not to you or anyone else. War makes men cruel, and I fear it is carving pieces out of me I will never get back. But when I think of you and Jacqueline, of the tenderness in her touch, the kindness in your voice, I feel almost whole again.

I have written a hundred letters to you in my mind. Some full of promises I cannot keep, others filled with confessions I am too afraid to make. But this one—this is the only one that matters. Yvette, please know that I love you and Jacqueline. From the first moment that beautiful little girl looked at me and smiled like I was someone worth knowing, I knew she would live forever in my heart.

When this is over, I will find you both. I will take you to that little café you love, the one with the pastries so delicate they vanish on the tongue. We will all laugh again, like we used to. We will remember what it feels like to live, not just survive. And this nightmare will become something distant—a story we got through, together. After that, we will go home. We will build a life filled with love, with joy, and with a kind of peace that no one will ever take from us.

John

Tears blurred my vision as I read the words. The room seemed to close in around me, my world shrinking to nothing more than the space between my fingers and the paper.

Love.

John had loved her. In just a short span of time, he found love. Not in passing, not as some fleeting thing a tourist might say to seal the deal, but in a way that consumed him, that gave him something to hope for beyond the horrors of the war.

The final letter sat on the table, sure to be more significant than all the rest.

Dear Yvette,

I fear this may be the last letter I ever write to you. The fighting has grown fiercer, more merciless, and the days darker. Most of the men I once knew are either broken or buried, and I know my turn is coming.

I should tell you that I am not afraid, but that would be a lie. I think of you and Jacqueline always, and I ache for the life you could have had. I see Jacqueline in my dreams, hear her laughter echoing through a home that may never be built. I see your face, and hers, older but still radiant, and I wonder if you will smile that way for someone else.

I hope you do, Yvette. I hope you find blissful joy again, even if it is not here. You deserve every happiness this sometimes cruel world has to offer. Tell Jacqueline that no matter what she does in life, I will be proud of her and that I love her.

John

I folded the letter slowly, setting it on top of the others. Then I sat back in my chair, staring up at the ceiling as though some answers might be floating there. Instead, it proffered a network of spiderwebs boasting a buffet of whatever insects had unwittingly strayed into the sticky space.

John hadn't just loved her. He'd built a life with her in his mind, even as the war tore everything else apart.

And what about me? What was I? Someone to leave behind? The woman who would never know him the way she did? Was I a muse he needed to get through some days, and she others, the ones that mattered most?

My breath hitched as a thought lodged itself in my chest, brooding and unrelenting.

Maybe this was it—the end of my search, my decades-long obsession. Maybe the answers weren't mine to find, weren't mine to keep.

Had I wasted my entire life committed to a man who was only now, at this very late point, revealed to be a scam artist? The type of scam artist I swore would never get the better of me again.

...

The house smelled of cinnamon and mint, an odd mixture that somehow worked at this time of year, when everything was infused with the scent of the holiday season. The tree, nothing worth writing home about, still stood proudly in the corner, its mostly bare branches adorned with all the ornaments collected over the years. I sat cross-legged on the worn rug, my fingers tracing the edge of a book I wasn't actually reading.

Across the room, my parents were doting over William, my younger cousin who'd come to live with us after his parents died. He was perched on Dad's knee, laughing at some joke I hadn't heard. Mom knelt beside them, adjusting the collar of William's sweater and smoothing down his hair with a tenderness that made my stomach twist.

"Isn't he just the spitting image of his father?" Mom said, her voice warmer than I had ever heard it before.

"Strong boy, too," Dad added, playfully ruffling William's just straightened hair, something he never did to me. "Going to grow into a fine man."

I watched from the edge of the room, all but invisible except for the fact that I was technically there. William beamed under their affectionate attention, his cheeks flushed pink.

"Mae," Mom called, barely glancing at me, "why don't you make yourself useful and show William how to play that one board game you seem to love? It'd be nice for him to learn."

The request wasn't unkind. It wasn't even unusual. But the offhanded way she said it, like I was little more than an afterthought, stung worse than if I'd just been ignored completely. I nodded, forcing my lips into a small, obedient smile.

I crossed the room slowly, opening the cabinet where we kept the few games we had. My fingers hovered over the colourful boxes for a moment longer than was necessary, delaying the inevitable. Behind me, I could hear William asking Mom something about the ornaments on the tree, and her delighted laughter made me flinch.

When I finally turned around, holding the game, William grinned at me like I was his favourite person in the world. "Thanks, Mae. You're the best."

It wasn't his fault. He didn't know how his presence affected me, how his words pierced me. He would never understand that I was treated like a household helper, a guide—never the one receiving the same kind of glowing praise and affection he basked in.

As the weeks passed, the refocusing of my parents' attention was swift and undeniable. It wasn't just scattered, isolated moments like this. It was for every little thing.

When William scraped a knee falling from a tree, Mom swooped in, gentle hands fluttering, to clean him up.

"You're so brave," she cooed, planting a kiss on his forehead.

I stood nearby, arms crossed, waiting for her to notice me, but she didn't.

When my report card came home from school, I handed it over with pride. Straight As, not a single blemish. Mom glanced at it, nodding approvingly, but when William came in waving his spelling quiz with a shiny gold star at the top, Dad pulled him into a bear hug like he'd won the Nobel Prize.

"Good job, champ!" he exclaimed, his voice ringing with a pride I had never heard before.

One evening, after dinner, Mom suggested we all play cards. I loved card games—it didn't matter which one, I was good at all of them. But this game quickly turned into The William Show. Through every round we played, Mom and Dad erupted into fits of laughter, clapping their hands and hooting encouragement whenever William played a card out of turn. If I won a hand by following the rules and playing well, they would smile politely, their attention barely there, as if they were waiting for William to achieve a victory in his way.

Even on Christmas morning, the sheer magic of the day felt tainted. William's pile of gifts dwarfed mine, and though I tried to tell myself it didn't matter, deep down, it did. He unwrapped a train set, a model plane, and a brand-new bicycle, his face lighting up more than the tree itself. I opened a book—a very lovely one—but it felt so unfair.

"Mae, why don't you go set up William's train set?" Mom suggested as I sat dutifully with my book.

I didn't want to help. I wanted someone to notice me. I wanted someone to ask me what I thought, how I felt, what I wanted—but those questions never came.

I always told myself that my parents weren't bad people. They weren't trying to hurt me. They were just doing their best to care for William and to fill the gaping hole left by the death of his parents. But reminding myself of these things didn't make my life any easier, didn't make me feel any better.

In truth, my parents were awful people who didn't give a single damn about me, but somehow found it easy to love and cherish a child who wasn't even their own, and to do so based solely on anatomy.

Every laugh they shared with William, every proud look, every comforting and reassuring touch—it all built up inside me like a great wall I couldn't climb over. I started to shrink into myself, speaking less, needing less, hoping that if I disappeared completely, someone would notice the empty space I left behind.

Several years later, sitting alone in the dim light of my kitchen, the memory of those days crashed over me like a wave I hadn't seen coming. It wasn't just my parents or William, it was everything. It was the way I'd spent my entire life trying to be seen, trying to be enough, trying to fill some unspoken void in other people's lives so they'd never forget I was there.

And maybe, just maybe, I'd held on to John for the same reason. Maybe I'd poured my heart into him because I thought, for once and without hesitation, someone had chosen me fully.

•••

The tears came then, steady and thick, running down my face in rivulets. I wiped them away angrily, standing up so quickly the chair caught against the floor and I almost fell over. That would have been something—banishing my three human Life Alerts just when I almost needed them most.

I couldn't do this anymore. Not tonight. Maybe not ever.

I grabbed my coat and the letters, shoving them into my bag. If this was the end of the story, then I needed to decide whether I was willing to let it go—or let it destroy me.

I had a pretty good idea which it would be.

CHAPTER 21
ALEX

THE DOOR SLAMMED SHUT behind us, the heavy crash of it reverberating in my chest. I stood there, momentarily paralyzed, unsure what to do with myself. The rawness of Mae's anger followed us into the hallway, thick and suffocating. We'd been asked, *told*, to leave, and now we were standing in the street, half-stunned, trying to figure out where to go next.

Erica, with all her tact and understated grace, was the first to speak, cutting through the silence and lingering tension like a cold breeze.

"Well, that was fun," she said, running a hand through her hair, her voice a little too serious. I could hear the frustration in it, and I knew she desperately wanted to get the hell out of here as much as I did. But there was no escaping the searing impact of Mae's words, the finality that clung to her sudden decision. Erica was struggling with what just happened, this much was evident. Based on her current state, I don't believe she had ever been on the receiving end of a true Mae Seasons dressing down.

Luc—ever the one to find a silver lining of opportunity in

every situation—clapped his hands together as if to dispel the remaining tension.

"Well, this is not how I imagined our afternoon, but no worries, *mes amis*," he said with a sly grin, his French accent thick as ever, "I have just the place for us to gather. Come, come, I will make you both comfortable."

The idea of being with Luc any longer than absolutely necessary wasn't exactly thrilling, but the invitation felt like a reprieve. And honestly, what other option did we have? We had nowhere else to go, and besides, there was no use standing in the middle of the sidewalk like a bunch of lost tourists. So we followed him, unsure and apprehensive of what kind of comfort he had in mind.

Luc's house was nothing short of magnificent—a sprawling structure with the old-world charm of high ceilings, wooden beams, and floors so polished I could see my reflection in them. Everything about the place was grand, yet somehow it still felt lived-in and pedestrian. It conveyed the sense that someone had inherited it, cared for it, but never quite bothered with all the necessary upkeep that would make it truly timeless. It was homey, despite the refined elegance draped across every wall.

"What the hell?" Erica muttered under her breath as we stepped into the foyer.

It was certainly impressive, but it was also a little over-the-top for someone like Luc.

"Don't be *trop surpris*," Luc said with a playful grin. "This is what happens when you're born into privilege and then use that very privilege to avoid doing anything remotely responsible with your life. You end up with four dogs and *une maison* that's far too big for one person. But the dogs, *mes amis*—they are the true treasures in my life."

As if on cue, four dogs bounded into the room, their names announced dramatically by Luc in what seemed like a mix of mockery and fondness.

"Meet Napoleon, Charlemagne, Louis, and Marie Antoinette," Luc said, gesturing toward the pack. "All historic figures in their own right, though none of them behave with an appreciation of the significance of their names."

Napoleon—a tiny, fluffy, scrappy thing—darted toward Erica's feet, barking enthusiastically. Charlemagne, a considerable German Shepherd, gave a low growl before sitting down obediently, while Louis, a wrinkled French Bulldog, quickly retreated and resumed snoring contentedly in the corner. Marie Antoinette, a regal-looking poodle, gave us all a haughty look before promptly turning her back to us.

Erica bent down to pet Napoleon, though she gave him her best side-eye stare, clearly unsure of how to deal with his exuberance.

"I'm going to be honest, Luc," she said dryly, "I don't know whether I'm more impressed by the house or the fact that you've been deemed a suitable caretaker for another living thing, let alone four. And you've named them, well, so interestingly."

Luc's laugh filled the room, buoyant and unrestrained. "It's the only way to remind them that even dogs can have legacies, *non?*"

He led us further into the house, his energy infectious despite the tense situation we'd just left behind. Erica seemed to gradually relax, her shoulders lowering as she got more comfortable with the absurdity of our surroundings.

"Take a seat, *mes amis*," Luc continued, motioning to the grand dining table that dominated the room. "I'll fetch us something to drink. Today calls for wine, and I promise you, it will be better than any cup of coffee."

We settled in, still processing the tumultuous events at Mae's apartment. There was a heaviness that clung to me now—an uneasy uncertainty about Mae, about what we had just uncovered. But Luc's boundless energy, his unflagging enthusiasm, was a temporary escape, and one we desperately needed.

For the first time in days, I let myself relax. He was a ridiculous man, but I couldn't deny that Luc had a way of making everything seem a little bit unreal, a little less intense. I was loath to admit it, but it turns out the French are more than just lovers. Not that I know, or even wanted to hazard a guess, what kind of lover Luc is.

As Luc returned with a wine bottle and glasses in hand, I caught Erica's eye. We were both lost in different thoughts, but there was a brief flicker of something—something unspoken—between us.

"What now?" I asked her.

Her lips twitched, a playful glint in her eyes. "Now, we drink," she said. "And figure out how we're going to survive this mess."

Erica. Always the steady hand on the roiling sea of life. If anyone could figure it out, it was her. And for a brief moment, as the first sip of wine hit my tongue, I felt something close to peace settle over me. But it wouldn't last. We were only just getting started.

Moonlight streamed through the gauzy curtains and cast long shadows across the floor, softening the contours of Erica's face and lending her an unguarded look. She sat cross-legged on the bed, her hair loose and cascading over her shoulders. She had that look—part tired, part worried—that made me want to promise her anything just to ease the tension knitting her brow.

"Alex, promise me something," she said softly, breaking the silence.

"Anything," I replied, almost reflexively, as if she had read my mind.

She tilted her head, her lips pulling into a adorable, knowing smirk.

"Don't 'anything' me just yet. You might not like what I'm about to ask."

"Try me."

She shifted, tucking her hair behind her ear, the humour fading from her expression.

"Leave it alone."

Her words hit like a bucket of cold water. We were picking up, or starting, I suppose, the conversation that I knew was inevitable since the moment I ignored her request to not do anything on my own.

"What? Why? We're *so* close, Erica."

She sighed, her shoulders slumping.

"I know you feel that way, but I can't shake the feeling that something about Jacqueline is off. Not wrong, exactly, just—I don't know, I can't put my finger on it. I'm playing my women's intuition card, okay? I just feel like she's holding on to something more, something she's not ready to share, and pushing her might do more harm than good."

I sat back, letting her words sink in.

"You're saying we just stop? Walk away after everything we've been through?"

"That's not what I'm saying," she said quickly, leaning toward me. "I just think this isn't the right direction. She already gave us those letters, Alex. That was her olive branch. If she had more to offer, more to say, she would've said it."

I looked away, frustration bubbling up inside me.

"That's easy for you to say. You're not the one Mae looks to for answers every time she cracks open another piece of John's past."

"Don't do that," Erica said, her sharpened voice cutting through the haze of my thoughts. "Don't put this all on Mae. You want to find these answers just as much as she does—maybe more. I don't know why, but it sure seems that way."

"That's not true," I said, but the words rang hollow and unconvincing even to my ears.

Erica scoffed.

"Come on, Alex," she said, shaking her head, "be honest with yourself for once. You've been chasing this just as hard as she has, and that's got nothing to do with Mae. That's all you. Maybe you're trying to prove something—to her, to John, to yourself? What are you trying to prove, Alex? And at what cost?"

Her words were like a punch to the belly, leaving me breathless.

She reached for my hand, her grip firm but gentle.

"I care about you, you know that. And I care about Mae, even if she doesn't exactly make it easy. But if you keep pushing like this, you're going to break something that can't be fixed."

I swallowed hard, trying to find the right words to say.

"I just want to help her."

"And who's helping you?" Erica asked, her voice soft but pointed.

The silence stretched between us, flush with unspoken truths lingering.

"And why do I even have to ask you this again? Oh, right, because you blatantly ignored me the first time and went off on your own adventure. I'm willing to let it go—to a point—but you need to slow down. Promise me you won't do anything stupid tomorrow. Promise."

I nodded slowly, the promise forming on my lips before I even realized I would break it.

"Okay. I promise."

I didn't sleep, couldn't sleep. It could have been the unfamiliar environment or the fact that Louis the bulldog snored like a tanker with an unreliable engine. Or, I suppose—and this was the most likely scenario—that it was because of what happened the prior day with Mae reading those letters from John to Jacqueline's mother.

Luc was already up, puttering around his kitchen with an espresso in one hand and a pastry of some kind in the other.

Did this guy always have some kind of baked goods in his hands?

"Ah, *mon ami*, you look like you had a sleepless night," he said, his grin infuriatingly chipper. "That is not so good for the faint of heart or the aging. But it is no problem for the young and vivacious, like *moi*."

"I need your help," I said, moving straight to the point.

"That sounds ominous," he said, grin fading.

I hesitated, choosing my words carefully.

"Jacqueline knows more than she's telling us. She has to. I don't know this for sure, but Erica seems to think so, and I've learned long ago to trust a woman when she plays the intuition card. But Mae isn't in any shape to push her, and I—I don't have the time to wait for her to come around."

Luc raised an eyebrow. "And what do you want me to do? Break into her flower shop? Charm her with my irresistible ways?"

I ignored his sarcasm.

"She trusts you. Well, she doesn't trust any of us, really, but out of all of us, she probably trusts you the most. You're— French. Which is a hell of a lot more than I have going for me right now. If you ask the right questions, she might open up, even if she doesn't mean to. You're the so-called keeper of this region's secrets, so, I need you to uncover hers. I'm clearly throwing shit at the wall to see what'll stick at this point."

"Please, Alex, do not throw your *merde* around in my beautiful *maison*. We are civilized, we have bathrooms for that."

With an exasperated sigh, I pondered whether or not I should fill him in on the axiom or just drive on. Instead, I simply stared at him.

In turn, he studied me for a long moment, his usual playful demeanor replaced by something more serious.

"You are asking me to charm and manipulate a suspicious woman, Alex. For what? To chase *un mystère*? I'm all for discovering secrets and being the first to know something new, but I can feel this situation changing right before our eyes. John may not be—"

"It's not just about John," I snapped. "It's about Mae. She's unravelling, Luc. She needs answers, and I can't sit here and do nothing while she falls apart. I don't expect you to get this, to understand it, hell, even I don't understand more than half of what the fuck is going on, but I can't do nothing."

No more than an hour later, Luc and I were standing outside Jacqueline's shop, watching through the window as she arranged a bouquet of lilies. She moved with the graceful confidence of someone who'd spent a lifetime perfecting her craft, her hands swift and steady despite the recent upheaval of her past looming over her.

Erica's words felt like an apparition whispering in the back of my mind.

Don't do anything stupid. Promise.

I'd shattered that promise the second I stepped out of Luc's house this morning; it hadn't even lasted twelve hours. Part of me already knew I was going to pay for it, even if the other part desperately hoped I'd get away scot-free.

With the task of striking up a casual conversation, Luc had gone in alone, leaving me to linger just outside, half-concealed by the awning's shadow. The door gave a soft jingle as it opened, swallowed quickly by the hush inside. I couldn't make out the words, not clearly, but I watched through the shopfront glass as the moment unfolded.

Jacqueline was behind the counter, her hands busy arranging something on a wooden tray. She didn't look up right away—just called something over her shoulder with that practiced brightness that came from years of welcoming strangers. Luc responded, casually, maybe even charmingly, and for a second, everything looked normal.

Then she turned. Her gaze found him—and her smile, mid-formed, faltered. It was subtle, just the smallest hesitation. Her hands paused over the tray. The muscles around her mouth tightened, eyes narrowed not with suspicion but recognition. Luc offered that slow, easy grin he wore like armour, but her expression didn't soften. If anything, it hardened and sharpened.

She said something—I could tell by the way her mouth moved and the slight tilt of her head, chin lifted just enough to signal she was done playing along. Luc laughed in return, low and unhurried, though I saw the way his shoulders stiffened beneath his coat.

Their conversation continued in muted tones, but the mood in the shop had shifted. The warmth had drained away, replaced with something cooler, more alert. Jacqueline leaned in slightly, not in invitation, but in warning. Luc, for all his disarming charm, knew better than to push her too far, too fast. He kept his hands in his pockets, voice undoubtedly smooth, words inaudible but clearly calculated.

From where I stood, it was like watching two fencers circle—blades still sheathed, but the importance of old history pressing into the silence between every syllable.

Whatever easy excuse Luc had planned to use was already crumbling. And Jacqueline? She knew exactly who had walked through her door. The past, wearing a familiar face.

When Luc finally came out, he was holding a folded piece of paper.

"She wrote this address down," he said, handing it to me. "A house in a nearby village. She said it was a place John mentioned in one of his letters. Something about a safe haven."

I stared at the paper, my chest tightening.

"What did you say to her?"

Luc shrugged. "A gentleman never kisses and tells. Well, maybe sometimes, when the details are just too juicy to keep to oneself. But in this case, my beautiful French lips are sealed. Though, I cannot say this is always the case when it comes to the fairer sex, *mon ami*."

I threw up a little in my mouth, no word of a lie, the remnants of breakfast returning for a second tasting. It took everything I had not to wipe my mouth with the paper I was now clutching like a lifeline.

Vivid mental imagery aside—imagery I wanted to erase as quickly as possible—guilt clawed at my chest. I'd twisted Luc's arm, further exploited Jacqueline's reopened grief, and betrayed Erica's trust—all for a lead that might not even pan out.

I knew Erica would hate me for it.

We stood in Mae's doorway, the day's brightness cutting across her face and casting shadows beneath her eyes. She looked like she hadn't slept in days, but her gaze was intense, piercing even. The moment she saw the paper in my hand, her expression darkened.

"What the hell is this?" she snapped, yanking it from my grip as though it might disintegrate if I held it a second longer.

"It's a lead," I said, keeping my tone even.

Mae unfolded the paper, scanning the address scrawled across it. Her brow furrowed, her mouth pressed into a thin line. She didn't look at me, she didn't have to. Her suspicion exploded like a low-hanging storm cloud bursting over an outdoor wedding.

"And just where, pray tell, did this come from?" she asked, her voice low but laced with enough bite to make me second-guess every life decision that had brought me to this moment.

Luc, believing he could somehow diffuse the situation, stepped in before I could answer.

"Jacqueline," he said smoothly, as though her name alone would absolve us of whatever litany of sins Mae was currently compiling. "She remembered something after our first visit."

Mae's eyes locked on his, narrowing to penetrating slits. She shifted her weight, crossing her arms tightly over her chest. "*Remembered* something, did she? Or did you bat those lashes of yours and lay on that ridiculous string of overused phrases you associate with charm until she gave in?"

"*Chérie*," Luc said, grinning and unrepentant, "my lashes are a gift and a blessing, and I don't waste them. She told me willingly."

"You're about as trustworthy as fresh water from a toilet bowl," Mae sniped back.

Luc pressed a hand to his chest, staggering back dramatically like he'd been mortally wounded—always with the theatrics.

"Your words, they sting! I'm just a humble man trying to help *une chère amie*."

"Friends don't meddle, you two-bit Gaston," snapped Mae, waving the paper like a weapon. "And they definitely don't drag their friends into god-knows-what kind of trouble."

"Trouble is subjective," said Luc, grinning widely. "Besides, wouldn't you rather know than spend your days wondering?"

For a moment, Mae just stared at him, her jaw clenched so tightly I thought her teeth might crack. Then, without warning, she turned on her heel and marched into the apartment.

Luc glanced at me, his eyebrows raised in triumph. "She's going to do it."

"She didn't say that," I muttered, but I knew Mae's silence wasn't a no.

"She doesn't need to. That's the look of *une femme* who hates being left in the dark even more than she currently hates me. And believe me, I know that look." He winked and followed her inside, leaving me to sigh and trail after them.

Mae was already putting on her boots and buttoning her coat, her movements quick and deliberate.

"Let's get this over with," she muttered, stuffing the paper into her pocket.

Luc leaned casually against the doorframe, his arms crossed and his grin annoyingly fixed in place.

"I knew you couldn't resist. Do I call for a car, or would you prefer to walk and let the suspense simmer?"

"Call a cab, you idiot," Mae barked, brushing past him. "The sooner this is done, the sooner I can tell you both where to shove your leads. And what the fuck makes you think the two of you bloated fools could walk this far?"

"Ah, Mae. Your words are pure poetry," Luc chuckled as he pulled out his phone.

Mae didn't even glance back. "And yours are bullshit."

All we found was a phantom—but not the one we'd been chasing all this time. The house itself was the misdirection, the bait in a trail grown cold. It existed, yes, but not in the way we had expected. There were no signs of life, no evidence of recent habitation. Not a footprint, not a hair.

The property was maintained just enough to avoid notice. The grass was trimmed, but uneven at the edges. The hedges were clipped, but without much care. It bore the unmistakable look of something kept up out of obligation, not affection—an empty shell curated to meet the lowest threshold of oversight. Just enough to keep the city inspectors at bay. Just enough to say, "someone owns this."

But there were no fresh flowers in the garden. No footprints in the dirt. No soft clutter of life at the doorstep. It was tidy in the way a showroom is tidy—sanitized, bloodless. Not abandoned, no. But certainly not lived in. Whatever presence had once been there was long gone—or hiding in plain sight.

The address Jacqueline had provided was pencilled on the map in Mae's hand like a promise, but promises, it seemed, were as flimsy as the peeling paint on the shutters of the derelict house we stood before.

Mae paced the cracked sidewalk, shoulders hunched and hands shoved into her coat pockets, muttering a string of curses that grew louder and more offensive with every step. Luc leaned lazily against the rusting iron gate, looking about as concerned as a cat napping on a porch.

"Well," Mae snapped, spinning on her heel to glare at him, "this has been a colossal waste of time. What a surprise."

"We didn't know what we'd find, *chérie*," Luc shrugged, his grin infuriatingly undisturbed. "That's the point of a search."

Mae let out a short, bitter laugh. "The *point* of a search is to find something, you patronizing peacock! *This?* This is just wandering around like idiots, and I should've known better than to follow your half-assed hunches."

Luc opened his mouth to reply, but Mae barrelled on, her voice rising.

"Honestly, you're about as useful as a screen door on a submarine. And Alex?" Her glare shifted to me, and I braced for the stinging blow. "What's your excuse? Trailing after him like a lost puppy. What the hell were you thinking, dragging me out here on some wild goose chase?"

I tried to keep my tone calm, but my voice wavered.

"I was thinking maybe this would help you, Mae. That it might lead to answers. I can see this is killing you, the not knowing. I wanted you to find out as much as you could before you gave up."

"*Answers?* The only thing this leads to is me wasting yet another day of my life chasing a goddamn ghost! And I have answers. John was unfaithful. He loved another woman. He has a daughter. I romanticized him, our life, our love, and for what? To be made a fool? No more! Fuck him. Fuck this place. And you know what, while we're at it, fuck you too!"

Before Luc could retort, my phone buzzed in my pocket. I pulled it out, relieved for the distraction. It was Erica, texting to find out where we were.

"Erica wants us to meet her back at Mae's apartment," I said before reading the message aloud.

Mae rolled her eyes. "Good. Maybe she'll be able to talk some sense into the two of you, because I am done, in case you were too dense to catch the hint."

The ride back was a subdued one, peppered with Mae's occasional grumbles and Luc's maddeningly optimistic commentary. By the time we entered the apartment, Erica was waiting at the kitchen table, the mess of collected information sprawled out in front of her. She didn't look up right away, and when she did, her eyes were red-rimmed and puffy.

"Hey," I said softly as I slid into the seat beside her. Mae and Luc hovered awkwardly nearby, but Erica's attention was fixed on me.

"Can we talk?" she asked, her voice more hushed than usual.

I nodded, and Mae, sensing this would be something significant, muttered about needing coffee. She dragged Luc toward the kitchen, leaving us alone.

Erica stared at her hands, fiddling with the edge of a napkin.

"I've been thinking," she began, her voice wavering slightly; that was never a good sign. "You made a promise to me. You went and broke that promise. And you broke it so quickly."

"Erica, I—"

She cut me off with a shake of her head.

"No, let me finish." She took a deep breath, her shoulders trembling. "It's not just that you went against your word and went behind my back. It's that you didn't trust me enough to let me be part of it. But more than that, you went behind my back. With everything we've come to know about John, and seeing firsthand how it's affected Mae, did you ever think about how, in a roundabout way, you're now doing the same?"

"That's not true," I said quickly. "I was trying to help Mae."

She looked up then, her eyes glistening with tears.

"This may seem overly dramatic, and I'm well aware of that, but I need to go," she said softly. "I don't like what I see playing out here anymore; it's not fun anymore. It was, at the beginning, a little bit—the Nancy Drew meets the Hardy Boys mashup we were all a part of. But, I don't know, something is different. Maybe, like I said, with what we know John did to Mae, your misstep is hitting with a little more consequence."

My heart sank.

"Erica, please. Don't say that."

She wiped at her eyes, shaking her head. "I've booked a

room in Paris. I can continue to work remotely from there. In fact, it will allow me to catch up. I just need to step away from all this. I need some time, some space."

Time and *space.* The two words at the conclusion of every couples' disagreement that lead more often to removal than reconciliation.

Across the room, I noticed Mae watching us, her expression unreadable. Luc, as always, looked bemused, but even his grin seemed smaller than usual.

I turned back to Erica, my voice pleading, desperate.

"Don't leave. Not like this."

Her smile was sad.

"I'm not leaving to hurt you, Alex. I'm leaving because I don't want to spend my days in France with someone so openly and readily able to lie to me and break promises without a second thought."

CHAPTER 22
MAE

Erica was sitting by the window when I approached. Her hands were wrapped around a steaming mug, but she wasn't drinking, just staring out at the street like it held all the answers she needed. I had done this many times since moving here and knew there were no answers to be found on the other side of the smudged glass pane. I lowered myself into the seat across from her, ignoring the fact that Alex's presence lingered like a kicked dog in the corner of the café.

"You're really going?" I asked, trying to keep my tone light. She glanced at me, her eyes still red-rimmed.

"You heard all that?" she asked, a small, joyless smile accompanying the words.

"I hear everything, dear," I said. "At least when it relates to the stupid things Alex does and the resulting consequences that befall him."

I studied her for a moment. Erica had always seemed so put-together, so unshakable. Seeing her now, so frayed and vulnerable, made something within me shift ever so slightly. I felt as though this should have been me, not her.

"I have to go, Mae."

"Do you, though?" I asked, leaning forward. "You're walking away from this—whatever *this* is—because of a mistake Alex made? Now, I'm not defending him; people make mistakes, Erica. Trust me, I've made plenty. You've been witness to more than several of them, in fact."

Her lips twitched into a weak smile, but it didn't reach her eyes.

"It's not just about Alex. It's about—everything. This whole thing with John and Yvette and Jacqueline, it's a lot, Mae. And it's not my history to unravel. It's yours. And okay, yes, it's about Alex and, I don't know, it just really hit me hard when I realized he was gone off to do the one thing I specifically asked him not to do. There's too much secrecy surrounding everything right now. The thought of him harbouring secrets, doing things he agreed not to—how can I trust his words?"

I saw the realization register on her face as she trailed off.

"Oh, shit, Mae, I'm so sorry. I didn't mean to—"

I snorted, sitting back in my chair and throwing her a buoy.

"Nonsense my dear," I said, patting her leg. "Alex is not John, far from it; trust me, no offense. Well, some maybe. But history's a funny thing, though, isn't it? It doesn't just belong to one person. It weaves and tangles itself into all of us, whether we want it to or not. And I sure as shit want no part of this particular piece of it."

Erica sat still, mentally taking notes as if she was back in one of her university lectures.

"You know," I began, "when I was around your age, I had a friend, Mary. Sweet woman, smart as hell. One day, she comes to me, and she's crying so hard she can barely speak. She tells me her husband's been stepping out on her. Had an affair, bold as brass."

Erica's eyes flicked up to meet mine, curiosity swimming in them.

"I lost it," I admitted. "Told her to leave him, to kick him in the nuts repeatedly, pack her bags, and never look back. She said she wasn't sure she could do it. I couldn't believe she would even consider staying with a man like that. I yelled at her, told her how John would've never done something that disloyal, would've never betrayed what we had, never broken me that way. I said things I'm not proud of, things that ended our friendship."

Erica frowned. "What happened?"

And I told her.

•••

The kettle whistled on the stove, but I didn't move to take it off. Neither did Mary. She sat stiff as a post at my kitchen table, wringing that crumpled handkerchief of hers like it owed her money. Tears streaked her round cheeks, but they didn't move me to feeling sorry for her. Not now. Not with the anger bubbling inside me like the boiling water in the pot.

"Mae, please," she said, her voice cracking. "I just—I don't know what to do."

I spun around, glaring at her like she'd just said the most ridiculous thing I'd ever heard.

"You *do* know what to do," I snapped. "You pack a bag, take those sweet babies of yours, and you leave. You don't give a philandering man like that another second of your life."

She flinched, her shoulders hunching like I'd delivered a

slap instead of honest words. But I didn't care. Not then. Not when I was this mad.

"Do you know what I'd do if John ever tried something like that?" I asked, pacing now, my declarations rising with each step. "And before you say it, yes, I know he's dead, so he can't cheat. But if he did, I'd disown him so fast his head would spin. Hell, I'd probably strike him dead myself and save the good Lord the trouble."

"Mae, you don't mean that," Mary said, her voice barely audible.

"Don't I?" I shot back, my hands slamming down on the table as I leaned toward her. "Mary, listen to me. You are better than this. Stronger than this. You don't need a man who'd disrespect and betray you like that. Do you think John would've ever pulled something so low? There are good, decent men in this world, men who would make you their whole world. Dote on you, love you, do anything for you."

She didn't say anything, just sat there wringing that damn handkerchief, and it only fuelled the fire burning in me.

"I'll save you the trouble of thinking. The answer is no, he wouldn't. Because John loved me. He respected me. And if he hadn't—" My voice faltered. I swallowed hard, the words catching in my throat. What was I even saying? John was gone. Long gone. What did it matter now?

Mary sniffled, her tears flowing freely now.

"It's not that simple, Mae," she said, hushed.

"It is that simple," I said, throwing my hands in the air. "You're just scared to do what needs to be done. You're scared to move on."

"I am scared," she admitted, her voice trembling. "But not just of leaving. I'm scared of being alone. Of what people will say. Of what this will do to my children. Can't you understand that?"

Her words stopped me cold, like she'd slapped me back. I wanted to understand—I really did—but the anger and frustration rearing and twisting up inside me wouldn't let me.

"Open your eyes, Mary," I said, my tone lowered but no less brittle. "The world's a cruel, unfair place. Happiness? That's a goddamn mirage. You reach for it, and it's not there. You're left holding nothing but disappointment, an empty cup that should be full of something but isn't. And right now, you're sipping from a cup of sand you thought was water."

She looked down at her lap, silent, and only the kettle's shrill wail, loud and insistent, filled the room. I couldn't be bothered to turn it off.

"You know," she finally said, her voice timid and broken, "not everyone is as strong as you, Mae. Not all of us have hearts turning to stone, unable to extend kindness to those who need it."

Her words cut deeper than I expected, but I wasn't about to let her see it. My heart wasn't stone. It wasn't. Was it?

"Oh, fuck you, Mary," I spat, the seething anger flaring again, drowning out the guilt her words had stirred. "I'm amazed you can stand upright with that lack of a spine. If you can't help yourself, I sure as hell can't help you. I won't help you."

Her mouth opened, but no words came out. The kettle continued to shriek, mocking the silence that stretched between us. Neither of us moved to take it off the stove.

"You know," she finally said, finding her voice again. "Fuck you, too, Mae. And don't you dare stand there with your judgment and tell me to move on." Her eyes were wet but fierce. "You want to talk about moving on? Then why don't *you*? You talk about John like he's just out running an errand and might walk through the door any second. If it's so easy to leave the past behind, why are *you* still clinging to it?"

The air left my lungs like she'd punched me. I stared at her, stunned silent.

"That's not the same," I muttered weakly.

"It's exactly the same," she fired back. "You don't let go of John because you can't. Because you don't want to. So don't act like I'm weak for struggling when you're doing the same damn thing in your own way. John didn't cheat on you, congratulations. How proud you must be to have a husband so loyal. So dead."

I turned my back to her and yanked the kettle off the stove, letting the silence stretch on.

"Get out. Now. Or you'll be adding physical assault to the list of things you've experienced at the hands of someone else."

•••

Not everyone is as strong as you.

It wasn't a compliment. It sounded more like an accusation, and it stuck with me long after Mary left that day. I had to be strong. How could I afford to be anything else in the face of the pain and disappointment served up by the world?

"Years later, I'd think back to that moment and wonder if I'd been too hard on her," I finished. "I'd been cruel when she needed compassion. But at the time, all I could see was betrayal and her weakness, and I swore to myself that if I ever found out John was anything less than the man I believed him to be, I wouldn't hesitate to cut him loose. It was an easy promise to make. Back then, I never imagined it would be tested."

"And now, all these years later, it has," Erica replied.

"I finally get it," I said. "Love makes you do things you swore you'd never do. Makes you stay, makes you leave. Makes you cry, makes you scream. Sometimes, it makes you fight like hell for something you don't even understand."

Erica's brow furrowed, and she looked away again. "I don't know if I can fight like this, Mae. Not the way you and Alex can. The way you two can go at it, disagree, and just move on."

When Erica finally stood, indicating she was in fact departing, her bag slung over her shoulder, I didn't stop her. But as she turned to leave, I said one last thing.

"Just don't make the same mistake I did, dear. Don't let fear decide things for you. Work through those things, lest you become bitter. And bitter is only good when it comes to ordering old fashioneds and beer."

Alex found me later, sitting on the terrace of the apartment, a rarely used walkout, with a cigarette in one hand and a glass of wine in the other. The night was cool, but I didn't bother with a jacket. My thoughts were too loud for me to care much about the cold.

He eased the sliding door open and stepped out, carrying his own glass.

"Mind if I join you?"

I shrugged. "Free country. Or do they only say that in America?"

"I think it's—wait, are you smoking? Since when do you smoke?"

"Does it really matter at this point?" I asked, taking another drag of my skinny little French cancer stick.

Bewildered, but no less confused about the other revelation of the evening, Alex sat in the chair next to mine, silent as he stared out at the distant shadows of Caen.

"She's gone," he finally said.

"Erica?"

He nodded in affirmation.

I took another drag from my cigarette, the smoke curling up and disappearing into the air.

"Can't say I blame her. She's a hell of a lot smarter than we are. That's all there is to it."

"You think that's all it is? I kind of broke trust with her."

"If you recall, once upon a time, I told you that she was far out of your league, both in brains and certainly in looks. So, yes, she's smart enough to know when to walk away," I said. "We'd do well if we took a page or two out of her book."

Alex didn't respond right away; I could feel his eyes on me.

"Mae, are you saying you want to stop?" he asked quietly.

I exhaled slowly, watching the smoke drift.

"I don't know. It feels like we're chasing a shadow. John's gone. Yvette's gone. In a sense, even Erica is gone. Only Jacqueline is left, and she seems a little nuts. Determined, but nuts. And coming from me, that's saying something. Maybe it's time to let it all go."

"You don't believe that," Alex said, his voice faint but assured. "I honestly don't think you believe that, Mae."

I looked at him, frowning. "And how would you know what I believe?"

"Because if you really wanted to stop, you would've already." He leaned forward, resting his elbows on his knees.

"You wouldn't have gone to see Jacqueline. You wouldn't have read those letters. Shit, you wouldn't still be sitting out here, smoking and brooding, instead of packing your bags. There is literally, and I'm using this term correctly for once, I think, nothing keeping you here if not to find out more about John."

I laughed bitterly. "Maybe I'm just too stubborn for my own good."

"Or maybe," Alex said, "you know there's more to this story. You know that something isn't sitting right. That there's still something we haven't figured out yet. Do you really think this is how it all fits together?"

His words held a measure of truth, and I hated how much they resonated.

Fucking bastard.

"I've spent so much of my life *not looking* for answers," I said in a hushed tone. "I never thought I needed to. It all seemed pretty cut and dry. And now? Well, every time I think I'm close, I get slapped across the face with something I don't want to know. So, tell me, Alex—what the hell is the point?"

"The point," he said, "is that it matters to you. And if it matters to you, then it's worth seeing through to the end."

I looked away, my mind racing. "I'm tired, Alex."

"I know," he said softly. "But you're not in this alone. I'm here now, we've come this far. If we walk away, you'll never stop wondering. And neither will I."

"So, it's about you now, is it?" I stared at him, his face illuminated by the muted glow of the porch lights. He looked as tired as I felt, but his eyes held a glint of determination that I couldn't ignore, and couldn't help but admire.

"You really think there's more to this?" I asked. "And be honest, I don't have time for bullshit."

"I do," he said. "And I think you do, too. So, what's our next move?"

I took a final drag from my cigarette, letting the question marinate. Somewhere deep down, I knew he was right. There was more to this story—something we hadn't uncovered yet. And whether I liked it or not, I wasn't ready to walk away.

But I am so fucking tired.

"We dig," I said finally, my resolve steady despite the turmoil churning inside me. "But this time, we do it on our terms. No more games, no more bullshit."

Alex nodded, and I felt a flicker of hope.

It wasn't much, but it was enough to keep going. Enough to keep fighting to discover the truth. Whatever the fuck that might be.

And did I even want to know? Alex had convinced me I did.

CHAPTER 23
ALEX

THE NEXT FEW WEEKS were a frustrating carousel of false leads and near-misses. After that night on the terrace, Mae, Luc, and I doubled down on the search for answers. Erica's absence was a gaping hole in our group, but the silence around it forged a sort of unspoken pact: focus on the mission, don't dwell on what's missing.

Luc, for better or worse, became both our most valuable player and our default scapegoat.

"Seriously, what's the use in being a historian if you can't find a single goddamn thing?" Mae griped one morning, pacing the apartment like a woman possessed.

"Do you think I have a magic wand for archival records?" Luc shot back, waving a stack of dusty documents. "This isn't a scavenger hunt, Mae. It's history, and history is messy, *oui?*"

"Messy my ass," she muttered. "That's the excuse people give when they've got jackshit to show for their work. And you, sir, have the jackest of shits."

"You're impossible," Luc groaned, a rare moment where his ever-present optimism was seemingly snuffed out. Perhaps

Luc had finally met his match; Mae was an unrelenting force that you couldn't defeat, one you just had to endure. To his credit, he'd lasted this long, and that's saying a lot.

"Better to be impossible than useless," she retorted.

"Enough!" I shouted, stepping between them. "Mae, take a breath. Luc, just—tell us, what have you found?"

He sighed, slapping the stack of papers onto the table.

"Fine. Here's what we've got so far," he said, pulling out a faded hospital log. "This is a record from Caen during the war. It lists Yvette Martin as being admitted for an injury in May 1943."

"Injury?" I asked. "A birth complication?"

"*Non*, what you would call a shrapnel wound," Luc said. "Nothing fatal, but significant enough that she stayed for a couple of weeks, or so says the paper."

Mae snatched the paper from his hands, scanning it with a furrowed brow. "There's nothing here about a baby," she said flatly.

"Exactly," Luc replied, holding her gaze. "I have cross-referenced every hospital record I could find, Mae. There's no evidence she ever gave birth to anyone or anything."

"That doesn't make sense," she said, her hand frozen mid-air, the paper trembling slightly. "If there's no baby, then what—what the hell does this mean? We've seen Jacqueline's birth record."

"It means there's more to the story," Luc said, his voice uncharacteristically gentle, but his usual whimsy slowly returning to his cadence.

Mae's face twisted, equal parts fury and despair. "We've been chasing a goddamn ghost," she hissed, slamming the paper back onto the table.

"Not necessarily," Luc said, carefully trying to defuse her. "It just means we are missing something."

"What the hell are we even doing, then?" Mae snapped, her voice cracking. "What's the point? And boys, I'm getting very, very tired of having to ask this question out loud."

I stepped in before she could spiral any further.

"The point," I said firmly, "is that we're closer to the truth than we were a month ago. This doesn't end here, Mae. You know that."

She looked at me, her eyes accusing yet curious, but underneath the smoldering fire, there was undeniable exhaustion.

"Fine," she said finally. "But if the truth is out there, it's hiding like hell and it's really pissing me off."

Sensing an opportunity to break the tension, Luc smirked. "Then it is a good thing I'm excellent at hide-and-seek."

Mae shot him a withering glare, but the corner of her mouth twitched upward.

"You're an idiot," she said, turning on her heel.

"The Greater Fool is perhaps a more appropriate moniker, *madame*," Luc called after her.

That night, as we pored over the latest findings, a thick silence settled over us. The lack of evidence about Yvette's supposed child was a curveball none of us had expected, and it forced us to reevaluate everything we thought we knew. Did we really trick ourselves into thinking it would be easier than what it was proving to be? Could we really be that naive?

"Maybe it's time we talk to Jacqueline again," Luc suggested cautiously.

Mae snorted. "Oh sure, let's go back to the lady who practically slammed the door in our faces last time."

"Or," I ventured, "we push a little harder. There's more here—we just need to dig deeper."

Mae looked at me, her expression unreadable.

"You'd better be right about this," she said. "Because if you're not—I don't know how much more of this I can take."

This much was unequivocally true. After more than two years, this endeavour was slowly killing Mae, wearing her down like sandpaper does on wood.

Luc clapped a hand on my shoulder. "No pressure, *monsieur* Alex."

"No pressure at all," I muttered, staring at the papers in front of me.

Mae was adamant about not going back to speak with Jacqueline. Her exact words, in fact, were: "If I have to stand in that godforsaken flower shop one more time, I'm going to hurl a vase at someone's head—and I won't miss."

So, naturally, we found ourselves standing outside her shop again the very next day.

Luc was the one who insisted. He had a theory—or a hope, more like it—that Jacqueline had more to offer but just needed the right touch. Judging by Mae's skeptical expression, that touch had better involve Luc throwing himself on a sword.

"I'll handle this," Luc said, adjusting his jacket and flashing a grin as bright as the morning sun.

"Luc, if you so much as wink at her, I'm leaving," Mae warned, her arms crossed.

"Oh, come now, Mae," he replied, brushing invisible lint off his sleeve. "Charm is a tool, not a weapon. Watch and learn."

We trailed behind as Luc strode into the shop like he owned the place. Jacqueline was arranging a bouquet of roses, her movements determined and efficient, if not a little rough, as though the flowers had personally offended her. She didn't look up when we entered.

"What is it you want now?" she asked, flatly, clearly annoyed at our very presence. "And don't even ask how I knew it was you, there are cameras outside the shop, and all of you, you stand out like—how do you say—sore thumbs."

Luc placed both hands on the counter and leaned in slightly.

"Jacqueline, *ma chère*, we couldn't possibly leave without seeing you again. Your wit, your grace—*c'est irrésistible.*"

She snorted, still not looking up.

"*Irrésistible*, is it? Tell that to my husband—oh wait, I don't have one, because no man has ever been able to win me over with such ridiculous lines. Now, get to the point, Casanova."

Mae muffled a laugh behind me, and I bit back a grin.

Luc wasn't deterred. "We've come because we can't stop thinking about your story. Your connection to John, *ton père*, Yvette, *ta mère*—it is riveting. It deserves to be told in full."

Jacqueline finally looked up, her eyes narrowing with suspicion. "*My* story? Or the one you're trying to write for yourselves?"

"Listen, we're not here for your approval," Mae said, stepping forward, arms still crossed. "We just want the truth. If you've got it, great. If not, we'll stop wasting everyone's time. Lord knows I'm sick and tired of wasting the time I have left."

Jacqueline's gaze floated across us, lingering on Mae.

"Your truth," she said coolly. "Always so eager to find it, no matter the cost."

Luc smiled. "Truth is priceless, Jacqueline."

"Oh, spare me," she spat at him. "You're not charming, you're exhausting."

"And yet, you're still talking to me," Luc replied smoothly.

Jacqueline rolled her eyes, but there was a flicker of amusement in them. I can't say for certain what was going through her mind, but that flicker quickly turned into something I can only describe as diabolical, the way those who have been wronged meticulously plot their retribution. I think she knew as well as we did that our connection couldn't be severed, that we were here for the long haul, and short of calling the police for harassment, she had no choice but to deal with us.

"*Très bien*," she said, setting down the bouquet. "You want more of the story? Come back *ce soir*."

"Tonight?" Mae asked, her tone irritated. "Why do you insist on wasting our time? Why does everyone insist on wasting my fucking time?!"

"I'm hosting a little gathering," Jacqueline said, waving a hand dismissively, incredulous to Mae's plight. "Some friends, some wine, likely a few too many opinions about *monsieurs* like you. If you want the rest of the story, you'll have to earn it."

I raised a wary eyebrow. "Earn it how?"

"By surviving the company," Jacqueline smirked. "I'm not going to just hand over my life's secrets. You want them? You'll have to listen, argue, and probably drink more than you're comfortable with."

"Marvelous!" Luc clapped his hands together. "We'll be there."

Mae and I shot him a glare, offering a "we will?" in unison.

"*Oui*," he said with a grin. "You wouldn't send me to face this den of lionesses alone, would you?"

Jacqueline, already walking away, shook her head. "Eight o'clock. Don't be late. And for God's sake, don't bring flowers."

As we left the shop, Luc was practically glowing.

"See? Easy," he said.

"Easy?" Mae repeated, her voice dripping with disbelief. "You've just committed us to a night of god-knows-what."

Luc winked. "It's all part of the process, *ma chérie*."

Mae muttered something under her breath that I didn't quite catch, but I was pretty sure it wasn't complimentary—in fact, I'd bet the house on it.

Still, as much as I hated to admit it, Luc's ridiculous charm, if that's indeed what we were going to call it, had gotten us somewhere. Where, exactly, was still something of an unknown, but now, we just had to survive whatever Jacqueline had in store for us. And I had the feeling that it wouldn't be nearly as easy as Luc seemed to think.

When we walked into Jacqueline's shop later that night, it was immediately clear we'd been duped. The space had been completely transformed, or was on the brink of completion. The music was loud and lively, the decorations were pink and glittery, and the room was packed with women who were already several glasses of wine deep. A banner hanging crookedly from the ceiling read: *Bon Voyage, Chloé!*

Jacqueline greeted us at the door, her smirk even more

pronounced than usual. "*Bienvenue*," she said, ushering us inside. "You're just in time. The party's about to be in full swing."

Mae froze, taking in the scene. "What in the actual fuck of all things holy is this?"

"It's *enterrement de vie de jeune fille*, or, as you would know it, a bachelorette party. At least it's about to be one," Jacqueline said nonchalantly. "*Pour une amie.*"

My jaw dropped. "You invited us to a bachelorette party?"

"Well, it seemed like a good way to break the ice," Jacqueline replied, clearly enjoying herself in her own wicked way.

Luc, on the other hand, looked utterly delighted; I wasn't the least bit surprised.

"Ladies' night?" he asked. "Say no more."

"Luc, don't you dare—" Mae started, but it was too late.

He swept away from us and into the fray like he was the guest of honour. Within seconds, he was surrounded by a gaggle of older women, all eager to experience his charm in action.

Jacqueline nudged me toward the group. "Go on," she said with mock seriousness. "You're part of the entertainment now."

"What?" I sputtered. "No, I'm not."

"Luc is about to perform a striptease. You're his warm-up act." She grinned wickedly.

"Luc is *what*?" Mae and I said in unison, but we were drowned out by a cheer from the crowd.

Luc had somehow procured a chair and was now twirling it in the middle of the room like a Las Vegas showman. The women were eating it up, clapping and hooting as he tossed his jacket over his shoulder and started unbuttoning his shirt.

"You've got to be kidding me," Mae muttered.

"Do something," I hissed at Jacqueline, who was sipping her wine and looking thoroughly pleased.

"Why? He's enjoying himself. Let the man shine," she said, waving me off. "Let's be honest, he lives for this attention. He's in his element."

Luc winked at someone, everyone, it was hard to tell. Their faces and hysterics all seemed to sync with excitement at Luc's attention.

"*Mesdames*, you're in for a treat," he announced, shimmying out of his shirt, twirling it above his head, and tossing it into the crowd.

"Oh my God," Mae groaned, burying her face in her hands.

Then, to my absolute horror, Jacqueline shoved me forward. "Your turn," she said.

"No," I said firmly.

"*Oui*," she insisted, equally firm.

The crowd started chanting, "*Danse! Danse! Danse!*"

I looked back at Mae, who, having removed her face from her hands, was now grinning for the first time in days.

"Just do it," she said, her voice coming to life, almost brimming with glee. "If Luc can make a fool of himself, so can you. Consider this one of your many debts to me paid off. If I have to endure this circus, I might as well have my clown front and centre."

With no way out, I stepped into the circle of women, feeling like a lamb to the slaughter.

Unlike Luc, who was now shirtless and gyrating like he was auditioning for *Magic Mike*, I kept all my clothes on and did what could only be described as a disjointed series of dad-like dance moves: awkward side steps, far too many finger guns, and a moonwalk attempt that ended with me nearly falling over.

The women roared with laughter. Luc clapped me on the back mid-spin. "*Superbe*! Keep going!"

Thankfully, Jacqueline took pity on me and called for a break.

"All right, *assez*," she said, waving her hand. "Let the poor *monsieur*, how you say, off the hook. We still have to put the finishing touches on before Chloé arrives."

I slinked back to Mae, who was still chuckling.

"You're a shit dancer," she said.

"Thanks for the support," I shot back.

"You know, Erica would have loved this," she said, intimating something more than just her absence. "What are you going to do about that?"

"Mae, don't you think I know that?" I said. "I think about her every day—about how I fucked up, how I broke her trust. But I also think about how it was never in a nefarious manner, never meant to hurt her. It's not like I cheated on her."

"You still don't get it, do you, Sonny?" said Mae. "It's not about your intent, it's about your actions, the outcomes. Those are what matter. It's also about whether or not you're willing to fight like hell to get someone back."

"I know, Mae, I do, really," I said. "And it's not as if we're not texting each other, so the line of communication is still open; I just wish she could see this through my lens."

I knew I wasn't going to win this argument—and in fact, it wasn't really an argument anyway—but I still always felt the need to come out ahead, which is likely why I so often found myself in these places in the first place. Erica was my rock, there was no question. And I truly meant nothing by my actions other than to help Mae.

"Alex, listen," said Mae. "We fuck up. We make mistakes.

And then, we have two choices: fix them or leave them to be fucked up. It's entirely up to you. Not me, not Luc, not even Erica in this case. You. Only you. So I suggest you strap those raisins back in your jockeys, man up, and move toward a clear and swift resolution."

"Thanks for that visual, Mae," I said, laughing, appreciative that of all the people who could be giving me this pep talk, it was happening with Mae Seasons.

As the party-goers fell back in line with Jacqueline's instructions to finish setting up, Jacqueline's friend—an older woman with a wine glass permanently in hand—sidled up to me and Mae.

"Quite a show, *jeune homme*," she said, raising her glass.

"Don't encourage him," Mae said.

The woman laughed. "Don't worry, *mon amour*. I've seen worse—though not by much."

"So, how long have you known Jacqueline?" Mae asked, leaning in, her voice dropping to a conspiratorial whisper. She was determined that we avoid enduring any unnecessary small talk with this woman.

"Oh, my," her head tilted upwards as she searched for the answer. "Maybe thirty years now. We grew up together, but you'd never know it. I'm traditional *français*; she's, how would you say, inherited."

"What do you mean, *inherited*?" I asked hurriedly, my nerves still settling. "She's not from here?"

"Oh, *non*," the woman laughed. "Though she did pick up the accent quickly. The only thing truly French about her is her love for pastry. She did one of those DNA tests a few years ago. Turns out she's not French, not even a little bit."

"Then what is she?" I asked, feeling a strange sense of foreboding.

"Eastern European, mostly," the woman said with a shrug. "Doesn't mean much, really. Wars, displacements, you know how it is. Don't we all misunderstand ourselves a little?"

Mae exchanged a loaded glance with me, her expression hardening. "What the fuck does Eastern European mean? Isn't France in eastern Europe? This backward-ass continent. But if her mother was French—"

"France is Western Europe," said the woman, ensuring we were properly aware of our geography. "As for her mother, who knows? Who cares?"

She shrugged again, tossing back the remnants in her wine glass. "She's always been something of a mystery, our Jacqueline. Aren't mysteries fun?"

Mae didn't respond, but I could tell her mind was racing. That or she was contemplating how to make a throat punch look like an accident.

Jacqueline's friend wandered off without another word and Mae turned to me.

"Something's not adding up," she said.

"No shit," I replied.

Just then, Jacqueline clinked her glass, calling for everyone's attention.

"*Mesdames*," she said, her voice carrying over the chatter. "I'm told our dear Chloé is only *vingt minutes* away. Let's finish up so we can keep this *fête* going!"

The women cheered, perhaps for Chloé or perhaps so they could continue the party they had so enthusiastically started without her. Either way, they got to work, their reward at the tips of their fingers. As the women recalibrated, Mae leaned closer to me.

"We're not done here, Sonny," she said. "We are most definitely not done here."

I nodded. Whatever secrets Jacqueline was hiding, we were getting closer to uncovering them.

CHAPTER 24
MAE

Jacqueline didn't stand a chance. The minute her little toast was over, I grabbed her by the elbow and steered her into the back room. The noise of the party became slightly muffled as the door swung shut behind us, leaving just the two of us in the dimly lit room; a fitting setting for an interrogation, if I ever did see one.

"What are you doing?" she cried, yanking her arm out of my grip.

"Cut the shit," I snapped, folding my arms. "We need to talk about your past—about what your chatty friend out there just told us."

Her smirk faltered, replaced by a wary look.

"What are you talking about?"

"You're not *French*, Jacqueline," I said bluntly. "Your friend just spilled the beans about your DNA test. Eastern European, right?"

Her face hardened. "What does that have to do with anything? I was curious, so what. DNA doesn't change the way I was raised or the stories *ma mère* told me, what I know and what I believe."

"Well, dear, yes and no. But that's not exactly the point now," I said, stepping closer. "You told us your mother was French. That she and John had this great romance. But if she wasn't French—"

"Then what?" Jacqueline interrupted. "What are you accusing me of?"

"I'm not accusing you of anything," I shot back. "I just want the truth. If your mother wasn't who you thought she was, if the stories she told you weren't completely true, then what else could she have lied about? Did she even know John the way you think she did?"

Her expression fluctuated—anger, defensiveness, and something else I couldn't quite place but knew I'd seen before, if not shown myself.

"She told me what she knew," Jacqueline said finally, her demeanor less combative and her voice calmer. "She said the letters were from a man during the war. A Canadian soldier. His name was John, and she kept those letters because they meant everything to her—she wanted me to have something meaningful, too. Do you know how many letters reference me? This man, *mon père*, fighting this great war while I was still a child? More than you can imagine. John was a hero, and the war took him away from me."

"Did she ever say they were written to her?" I pressed, staring at her. The pieces of the puzzle were swirling in my mind but refusing to fit together in any coherent pattern. "Jacqueline, *my* husband, John, was of Scottish descent. His family had roots in Nova Scotia for generations. If your mother wasn't French and no Scottish showed up on your test results, you realize you cannot be related the way you've led us to believe?"

Jacqueline ran a hand through her hair, confusion and frustration etched into every line of her face.

"I don't know. I've told you everything I know. I've spent my whole life believing this story, and now you're tearing it apart. And for what? Why?"

"Because it doesn't fucking add up, for one," I said, my voice rising. "And if it still doesn't add up, after everything you've told me, then maybe the story you were told isn't the absolute truth either. And second, maybe there's something else—something bigger—that we're all missing. That's not out of the realm of possibility given that there are a couple of geri-atrics duking it out verbally here and a pair of much younger fools out there think they know everything about everything."

Jacqueline hesitated at the door, her hand resting on the knob as if the noise and cheerfulness of the party on the other side were too much to face. I waited, expecting her to make some quip or fire off a haughty remark to mask whatever storm was brewing inside her. But instead, her shoulders slumped.

"You don't get it," she said, her voice almost swallowed by an exuberant wave of laughter from the party. "You don't know what it's like to have next to nothing to hold on to."

I blinked, taken aback. "Don't for one second think you know anything about me or what I know."

She didn't look at me, her eyes fixed on the floor.

"I don't remember much from my childhood, just flash-es. A cold apartment. *Une mère* who was always working or too tired to talk. No siblings, no friends. No family dinners or holidays with cousins and grandparents. Just—loneliness and emptiness. My whole life, I had no one." Her hand tightened on the doorknob, her knuckles turning white. "But there were *ces lettres*, I had them. I had stories from *ma mère* about John—

the brave hero who helped liberate the city and the world. Someone who cared for her so much he risked everything. She told me that was why I was here, why I existed. Because of him. Because of his courage."

She swallowed hard, her voice trembling. "I built my whole identity around that. Around being so deeply connected to someone *extraordinaire*. Because the alternative—being no one, from nowhere—well, that wasn't something I could live with."

My heart ached, her words ringing a truer understanding than she would ever know.

"Jacqueline—"

"You won't understand," she said quickly, her voice rising as if to drown out whatever I might say. "You had John, apparently. And for a while, you had—love."

Jacqueline finally looked up at me, her eyes red-rimmed and shining.

"You've spent your life chasing his memory, *oui?*" she said. "But at least you had something real to chase. *Moi?* I had to invent mine. So, if you really want to start comparing whether or not this is fair and to whom it's more fair, I'm not sure that's a wager you really want to place."

For a moment, I couldn't breathe. The magnitude of her confession settled over me like a lead blanket, its unyielding force pressing down on my soul. I wanted to argue, to tell her she was wrong, to kick her in the shins—but I couldn't. Because, the truth was, I did understand.

I thought about my own childhood, growing up in a quiet house that always felt too big and too empty. About the way I'd gravitated to John, how I'd built my world around him because I didn't know how to stand on my own. And how, after he was gone, I'd clung to his memory with the same desperation that Jacqueline spoke of now.

"I do understand," I said finally, my voice giving way to the uncertainty of the words.

Jacqueline blinked, startled by the compassion in my tone.

"I grew up the same way," I continued, my hands curling into fists at my sides. "No siblings. No family gatherings. A house that felt more like a museum. Parents who wanted nothing to do with me. And then John came along, and he was—everything to me. The first person who really saw me, who made me feel like I wasn't invisible. When he left, I felt like I disappeared all over again."

Jacqueline's gaze flickered, something like understanding breaching her defences.

"We both built our lives around ghosts," I said. "The difference is, I've had decades to carry mine. You're just starting to realize that yours might not be real. And come to think of it, maybe mine isn't either."

Her face crumpled, and for a moment, I thought she might break. But then she straightened, her jaw tightening as she forced the sudden swell of emotions back down.

"I've always known, maybe. I think. I think, deep down, like something was too neatly wrapped with a bow," she said. "But like I said, what was the alternative? There wasn't one. The life, the history I invented was what I needed to survive."

"What I don't understand, though," I said, trying to find my bearings, "is how these letters even exist. I know the rhythm of John's words, I know his handwriting when I see it, and those letters you gave us are most definitely from him. They match perfectly to the ones sitting in my apartment that he once sent me."

"I can't believe I'm going to say this, because you and your ragtag group of loafers are really more than I can bear, but if you want to keep digging, I will help you. But don't expect me to cling to hope the way you do, Mae. I've had enough *chagrin d'amour* for one lifetime."

I nodded, even though her words stung. "Fair enough."

She turned back to the door, pausing with her hand on the knob.

"For what it's worth," she said, not looking at me, "I hope you're right. I hope he was everything you believe him to be. Because if he wasn't—what's the point of any of this?"

She didn't wait for an answer, pushing the door open to shouts of debauchery descriptive enough to make a nun drop dead, and disappearing into the ruckus of the party.

I stayed behind, leaning against the counter as her words echoed in my mind.

If John wasn't who I thought he was—if his story wasn't what I'd built my life around—then what was the point?

•••

The living room buzzed with the low murmur of voices, cigarette smoke and the tang of spiked punch wafted in and out of my nostrils. I sat in the corner of a worn-out floral-print couch, the drink in my hand untouched as I listened to the heated conversation unfolding across the room.

"I'm telling you, it's another Korea," a man in a tweed jacket declared, his voice raised to compete with the scratchy record playing on the stereo. "We have no business getting involved in Vietnam. It's a bloodbath waiting to happen."

Across from him, a woman with cat-eye glasses sat perched

on the edge of her seat, her hands clasped tightly. "But what choice do we have? Communism is spreading like wildfire. If we don't stop it now—"

"You think sending our boys over there is the answer?" the man interrupted, his tone incredulous. "You want to send your son to fight a war we can't possibly win?"

The woman faltered, her lips pressing into a thin line.

My stomach turned as I took in the tense faces around the room, the palpable fear thick enough to choke on. A young man sitting near the window, no older than twenty, rubbed the back of his neck anxiously. Someone passed him a drink, but his hand shook so badly he nearly spilled it.

"I just don't get it," someone else chimed in from the kitchen. "What're we even fighting for? How many more wars do we have to go through before we learn anything?"

This is the same old conversation with the same old people. It doesn't matter what war it is or who the people are—the places and names are all interchangeable—but the opinions? They always remain the same.

I couldn't stay silent any longer. The words burned on my tongue, desperate to escape.

"We never learn," I said, my words cutting through the noise of competing voices like a whip.

The room fell silent, all eyes turning to me as if a prophet had just entered. I was flattered, even if I was the only one who saw me in this way. I set my drink down on the coffee table, leaning forward in my seat.

"You all sit here and talk about wars like they're some distant nightmare, something that's easy to debate because they happen to other people's sons, other people's husbands. But let me tell you something," I looked directly at the young man by the window, his wide eyes meeting mine, "war is not distant. It's not abstract. It's hell. It's pure fucking hell on earth."

My hands clenched into fists, my nails digging into my palms as memories flooded my mind. John's youthful face, smiling and strong, as he promised he'd come back. The tone of his voice in his letters, his early letters, so full of hope and determination. And then the unbearable silence that followed when the letters stopped coming.

"You think you're scared now?" I continued, my voice rising. "Try sitting at home, day after day, waiting for a letter that might never come. Try answering the door, wondering if it's the postman or praying it's not someone with a telegram telling you your whole world has ended."

The young man swallowed hard, his face pale as a sheet.

"And when it's over, if you're lucky enough to have them come home," I added, my voice shaking now, "they're never the same. They carry it with them, the things they've seen, the things they've done. And you carry it too, because you can't take it away from them. All you can do is try to love them through it, and hope it's enough."

A heavy silence settled over the room.

"I'm sorry, Mae," the woman with the cat-eye glasses said, her tone uneasy. "I didn't mean to—"

"No one ever does," I said, waving her off and standing abruptly. "And don't apologize. Just don't sit here and pretend this is a debate about politics. It's not. It's about people. Real people. And if you don't understand that, you've got no business talking about sending anyone to war."

I grabbed my coat from the front hall rack and left without another word, the sound of the door banging behind me as jarring as a gunshot.

The voices on the inside immediately resumed, just as heated and animated as before, my words clearly not making a meaningful mark. They simply waited me out. They'll never learn. None of them will ever learn.

Outside, the cold night air nipped at my skin, but I barely noticed. My mind was spinning, my heart racing, and thoughts of downing a bottle of Jack Daniel's and calling it a day were begging to be acted on. I pulled my coat tighter around me, the tails flapping against my legs in the brisk wind. My heels clicked against the pavement as I walked aimlessly, the noise sharp and hollow on an otherwise quiet street.

I didn't look back. I couldn't. Here we were again, ready to lose those we loved, and for what?

This was the question that would haunt me forever: for what?

I stopped at the edge of the sidewalk, staring at the empty street ahead. For a moment, I let my guard down, allowing the memories usually kept at bay to rush in. I remembered the first time I heard about John's deployment. How he'd stood in my kitchen, so sure of himself, so resolute. It was only the day before that he told me he had enlisted. How quickly it all came tumbling down for me.

"It's my duty, Mae," he'd said, his voice stoic in a way that had both infuriated and terrified me. "I'll come back. I promise."

Promises are funny things. Fragile and fleeting, like leaves caught in a gust of wind. I'd clung to his words for months, rereading his letters until the ink smudged beneath my forlorn fingers. But then the letters stopped, and the hopeful light in my life dimmed to a flicker.

I blinked away the tears threatening to spill, forcing myself back to the present. The world hadn't changed. It was still spinning in the same old way, pulling people into wars that didn't belong to them. Young men with dreams of their own, sacrificed for a conflict and cause that someone else believed in more than they did.

I dug my hands into my coat pockets and turned down an even quieter street, the noise of the party now nothing more than a distant echo rattling in my brain. Maybe I was wrong to think I could escape it. Maybe this was the enduring curse of loving someone who fought in a war—you never stopped fighting too.

...

The next morning came up gray and uninviting, the sky thick with dark clouds and a low-hanging fog that seemed to mirror my ability to form coherent thoughts. I slipped out of the apartment for a walk before Alex woke up and any of the day's guests arrived, which I knew would be anytime now.

Upon circling back to my modest dwelling, I watched through the kitchen window as the group was now up and moving; Luc studied a map spread across the table, his usual theatrics tamped down by concentration. Alex sat nearby, his eyes darting between Luc and his coffee cup, while Jacqueline stood by the counter, arms crossed, looking like she'd rather be anywhere else. I was surprised she kept her end of the bargain. She had agreed to help—albeit reluctantly and perhaps only to rid herself of us as quickly as possible—so she was welcome to be here, as miserable as the rest of us.

Good for her.

As I followed the hallway to my door, my thoughts turned

to Jacqueline. She didn't have much to say after I confronted her last night, but the crack in her usual guarded demeanor was evident—faint, but unmistakable. She might have been prickly as hell, but beneath that hardened exterior, I could see a woman who had spent her life clutching at the threads of a story she didn't even know was hers.

Solidarity, sister.

I caught an exchange of differing ideas between Alex and Jacqueline as I stowed my coat, smiling despite the obvious frustration in Alex's tone.

"Are you sure about this?" Alex asked.

Jacqueline let out a derisive snort. "Of course not. But it's not like we have better options, do we? And the sooner I can get all of you out of my life, the better. No offense. Well, some maybe. I don't really care."

I stepped into the room.

"Let's just cut the chatter and go wherever it is you think we should go next," I announced, drawing their attention and causing a whiplash-like reaction. "And let's do it quickly. We're wasting too much time talking in circles."

"Good morning to you too, Mae," Luc said, looking up from the map, his expression a mix of surprise and amusement. "Coffee not strong enough this morning?"

"Not strong enough for your bullshit, that's for sure," I shot back, snatching the map from the table, feeling a familiar rush of adrenaline that I'd been sorely missing.

"Ah, but my bullshit is what gets results, *non?*" Luc grinned, undeterred.

"Let's hope your results don't lead us to another dead end," I muttered, but I know everyone caught the trace of a smile tugging at the corner of my lips.

I focused on the address scribbled in Luc's haphazard handwriting, the same address we chased last time—a house that Jacqueline's mother had lived in after the war. The possibility of finding anything useful there felt slim, but this whole escapade was slim. Jacqueline said it had remained practically untouched since her mother's passing, save for just enough work to keep too many questions or interruptions from occurring. And maybe this time, with Jacqueline in tow, we'd have better luck at finding something, anything.

As we piled into the car, Jacqueline kept her distance, sliding into the back seat with her arms folded; apparently this was her trademark now. Luc took the passenger seat, leaving Alex to drive, which suited me just fine.

The ride was quiet, except for the occasional directions from Luc and the thrum of the engine. I stared out the window, my mind revisiting all the things Jacqueline had said last night—how she'd clung to the idea of John, my John, as a hero, how she'd built her identity around it. Her words were few, but the significance they carried was monumental.

I couldn't judge her for it, not really. Hadn't I done the very same thing—clung to the memory of John as a way to anchor myself in a world that often felt too chaotic to bear? The difference was, I'd known him. Loved him. And lost him.

Jacqueline had been chasing shadows her entire life. She never *knew* him. She may have seen his face or heard his voice, or even felt his generous, tender touch. But the whispers of a love so deep and true it made your legs quiver and heart beat faster, that was for me, and for me only.

When we finally pulled up to the house, I felt a pang of disappointment. It was just as small and unremarkable as the last time. It still didn't look like the kind of place that held answers to today's questions, let alone a lifetime of the enduring fuckers.

"This is it," Alex announced, his tone dubious.

Luc turned in his seat to face Jacqueline. "Shall, we?"

She hesitated, her eyes scanning the house. "I suppose. It's been a long time since I've been here."

"Well," Luc said, unbuckling his seatbelt, "let's see what secrets it is hiding."

As we stepped out of the car, I felt a chill run through my core. Isn't that what happens when you feel a ghost pass through you? That, or my blouse was open. Both were entirely possible at my age. It wasn't just the cold air or the eerie silence of the dilapidated neighbourhood. It was something else. I wouldn't tell the group this. Not for fear they'd think I was crazy, but I simply didn't want to give them any ammunition. But I'll be damned if, standing there on the sidewalk, I didn't feel the tiniest sense we were on the verge of uncovering something that could change everything—again. And quite frankly, I was getting very tired of this damn feeling.

Jacqueline lingered by the car, her arms still crossed tightly.

"This is probably a waste of time," she muttered, but her voice lacked conviction.

"Probably," I said, brushing past her. "But we won't know until we try, will we? And why wait until now to share this revelation with us?"

Luc shot me an approving look as we approached the front door, but I ignored it, focusing instead on the task at hand. I wasn't in the mood for his overblown antics or Jacqueline's cynicism.

Fuck them both.

Deep down, I knew this wasn't just about my answers anymore. It was about finding a way to make sense of everything that had come before—and everything that still lay ahead.

CHAPTER 25
ALEX

Looking again at the weathered house, it was evermore clear this place had been maintained only to the barest degree—just enough to avoid attracting troublesome attention, but far from cared for. Time had worn it thin, and any gesture toward charm or warmth—fresh paint, tended flowers, a light in the window—had long since been abandoned as luxuries not worth the effort or expense. The porch sagged beneath our feet, groaning with age, its boards soft and tired. It didn't sing welcome, it muttered warning. Jacqueline stood at the door, digging through her purse with growing frustration before letting out a sigh that seemed older than she was.

"I don't have a key," she admitted.

Mae raised an eyebrow. "It's your mother's house, and you don't have a key? More importantly, you didn't bother to double check before we came all this way?"

"Honestly?" Jacqueline asked, arms crossed defensively, curious to see whether or not her remark would be taken as rhetorical.

"If it wouldn't put you out too much, dear," Mae sneered, her words oozing with sarcasm.

"Well, in that case, I had a good idea I would regret having raised my hand as a willing participant in these games you all want to play. I figured that if I didn't bring a key, and things felt off, which they most certainly do, we could all just go home and save ourselves the hassle of doing whatever it is you plan on doing. Which I know can't be good, and I haven't even known you that long."

Jaqueline spoke like someone who was scared. Of the truth, of reality, of her whole world imploding in on her because of our A-Team antics to crack the case.

Luc chimed in, stepping forward and audibly cracking his knuckles.

"But not to worry, no key is no problem for Luc Brassard," he said, pulling a lock-picking set out of his pocket. "This is where I shine."

"Breaking and entering is where you shine?" Mae deadpanned.

"Entering and *liberating, ma chère*," Luc corrected, retrieving a paperclip from his pocket with a theatrical flourish. "Observe a master at work."

Jacqueline looked appalled. "You're not seriously—"

But Luc was already crouched in front of the lock, muttering to himself.

"A little finesse here, a touch of persuasion there—*et voilà!*"

The lock clicked and he straightened up, grinning like he'd just solved world peace. At the very least, he brought peace to the inhabitants of the porch, and for the time being it seemed as though Mae and Jacqueline wouldn't be duking it out.

Mae shook her head. "How is it you're not in prison?"

"Charm and good looks," Luc said, stepping aside and gesturing grandly. "And a great deal of luck, I'm sure. After you, *Mesdames* and Alex, the treasure trove of mysteries untold awaits us just inside this door."

"You're insufferable," Mae muttered, brushing past him. "And if charm and good looks have kept you out of prison, just imagine where they would get you *in* prison, sweetie."

Inside, the house was exactly what you would have expected based on the exterior—a snapshot of a forgotten era. Dust blanketed every surface and there was a pungent mustiness hanging like a London fog. It was as if the walls themselves were holding their breath; I know I certainly was, watching the agitated dust particles dance in the light. Faded wallpaper with what I'm sure was a once-vibrant floral pattern now peeled at the edges, and the furniture, mismatched and worn, seemed to have given up under the passage of years gone by.

"Charming," Mae said dryly, her eyes scanning the room.

"It was," said Jacqueline. "Once upon a time, anyway. Admittedly, after *ma mère* died I figured I'd come back to stake claim, but I never returned. It was paid off, so the only thing I had to worry about was the *taxe foncière*. You'll notice the lights don't work—I haven't paid that bill in who knows how long. And so, here it sits in all its nearly unattended glory."

Luc immediately headed for the kitchen, declaring, "If there's anything edible left in this place, it'll be a divine sign from the heavens."

Jacqueline sighed heavily. The same sigh we had grown accustomed to hearing from each other whenever Luc made such absurd announcements.

"He's like an impetuous child," she said. "Should we coax him to eat whatever he finds? See if he'll do it?"

"A clever child with a makeshift key to your mother's

house," Mae pointed out. "Maybe let him do his thing. It's more than you're doing."

Jacqueline glared at Mae with contempt, but as long as these exchanges continued with visual daggers and not real ones, we might get through this relatively unscathed—physically at least.

We spread out to search, though the house didn't seem like it held much promise at first. The upstairs bedrooms were small, their few pieces of furniture shrouded in ghostly white sheets. In one room, a crib stood against the wall, its paint chipped and its mattress bare. I lingered for a moment, staring at it. It felt odd to see a crib; whose could it possibly be? There was an echo of something important, though I couldn't put my finger on why. That, or the dust mites were infiltrating my senses and wreaking havoc on my ability to think.

Downstairs, however, Mae struck gold. She'd opened an old wardrobe in what must have been Jacqueline's mother's bedroom, and behind a row of moth-eaten garments was a stack of neatly labeled boxes.

"Files," she said, pulling one out. "And photos."

Luc appeared in the doorway, holding a chipped mug.

"No sign of heavenly morsels, but I found this. Very vintage. Very chic. It could fetch a decent price on eBay."

Jacqueline groaned again, her patience with Luc clearly wearing thin.

Welcome to the club. We have jackets.

"Can you take this seriously for *cinq minutes*?" she pleaded. "If I have to endure this tragedy, the least you can do is the same."

Luc raised his hands in mock surrender. "*D'accord, d'accord.* No need to get snippy. Now, what have we here?" He peered over Mae's shoulder, his eyes igniting. "Documents! Photos! A historian's dream! Let's pack it all up and sort through it later."

Mae shot him a withering glare. "This isn't a treasure hunt."

"And yet, here we are," Luc said, striking a mock-pirate pose. "Arrrgh, matey, we're pillaging the past!"

"This is who you brought to help?" asked Jacqueline, pinching the bridge of her nose. "Seriously, this is a joke, *oui?* He can't be real. Tell me he's not real."

"It's too late to send him back," Mae muttered, handing me a box. "And he's proving to be useful here and there, which is leagues more than I can say for you."

We worked quickly, carefully loading the boxes into the car. The photos were black-and-white, their texture worn, showing glimpses of lives that felt impossibly distant. A woman in a plain dress holding a child. A man in uniform standing proudly beside a flag. Each image was a fragment, a puzzle piece whose significance we could only guess at.

As we carried the last box to the car, Luc insisted on narrating our every move in an exaggerated announcer's voice.

"And here we see the fearless adventurers, braving the treacherous ruins to recover priceless artifacts!"

"Priceless dust, more like," Mae muttered, though I caught the thinnest flicker of a smile.

When we finally packed the last box into the trunk, I leaned against the car, wiping my hands on my jeans. "What now?"

Mae crossed her arms, her gaze fixed on the house as if willing it to give up its secrets.

"We go through it all. Every file, every photo, every scrap of paper," she said, determined. "There's something in these boxes—we just have to find it."

"Excellent plan," said Luc, clapping me on the back. "But first, a toast to our success. Who's got the wine?"

"Now's not the time, Luc," I said, but he was already rummaging through the trunk, pulling out a wine bottle and holding it aloft.

"To history!" he declared, taking a dramatic swig before promptly choking on it.

As we drove away, the haul of boxes stacked in the trunk, I couldn't help but feel a glimmer of hope. We had a long road ahead, but for the first time in weeks, it felt like we were moving toward something real.

We decided to convene at a nearby pub to start going through the boxes. Jacqueline had been silent on the drive over, her face set in a way that made it impossible to tell whether she was reliving memories or trying to repress them entirely—either would have been a suitable course of action given the circumstances. Luc had chattered the whole way, undeterred by her silence, which I'm sure only played a larger role in her not saying a word.

The pub wasn't like anything I'd ever experienced before, it felt like stepping into another century. It wasn't one of those modern, over-polished gastropubs, nor was it a new-age pub that tried desperately to be vintage; it was a place with authentic history—and a fair amount of alcohol—absorbed into the very walls. The low ceilings were supported by solid wooden beams, their surfaces worn smooth and etched with time. The walls were decorated with clusters of black-and-white photographs, tin advertisements, and assorted hunting trophies that stared down at us with glassy eyes. In one corner, a fire crackled in a large stone hearth, its heat a welcome contrast to the chill of the outside air.

The bar was polished but scuffed, its surface carved with years of scratches and initials from patrons with time and a knife in their hands. The place smelled of wood smoke, fried food, and the faint tang of spilled beer; a nostril's symphony if there ever was one. It was the kind of smell that instantly made you thirsty, even if you weren't when you arrived.

Luc took a deep inhale and sighed dramatically.

"Ah, the aroma of bad decisions and good memories. This, *mes amis*, is where revelations happen."

Mae rolled her eyes. "Can we just sit?"

We claimed a table in the corner, its top permanently covered with stains and scuffs, which, given the state of most things in here, would have made for a fitting name to light up on the sign outside: Stains and Scuffs. The chairs creaked in protest as we sat down, their joints as tired as ours. The bartender, a broad-shouldered man with a face like a weathered cliffside, ambled over. Luc ordered a round of pints and a platter of "*tout ce qui est chaud.*"

"You sure you don't want to see the menu first?" the bartender asked, raising an eyebrow.

"Menus are for cowards," Luc grinned.

The bartender smirked and walked off shaking his head.

Mae shot Luc a blistering look. "Do you always have to be the most excessive person in the room?"

"Not always," Luc said, leaning back with a smug grin. "But all the time, *oui*. And I do like to keep my skills sharp."

As soon as the drinks arrived, we got to work. The boxes were packed with a medley of papers—some neatly folded and well-preserved, others crumpled and discoloured with age. There were letters, photographs, documents, and even a few random trinkets, like a brass button and an empty matchbook. We spread it all out across the table, the flickering firelight casting shadows over the chaotic assortment.

"This is going to take hours," Mae said, rubbing her temples. "And as you know, I'm clearly too old for this shit. All of it."

"Good thing we have *la bière*," Luc said, raising his glass in a mock toast.

"Yes, because tying one on is going to help a woman approaching the century mark of her life. Although, it may put me to sleep a little quicker while you all work this out."

The photographs drew our attention first. They were faded and grainy, but they carried an undeniable importance. A man in uniform, standing stiffly with his comrades. A young woman holding a baby, her smile faint but full of something unspoken. Rubble-strewn streets with children playing amid the wreckage.

Mae lingered over one particular photo of a soldier standing in front of what looked like a hastily constructed barricade.

"This could be John," she said. "The face is too blurry to tell, but—" She trailed off, her fingers brushing over the image.

Luc leaned over her shoulder. "If that's John, he's got excellent posture. I bet he had no trouble getting promoted."

"Do you ever shut up?" Mae snapped.

"Not unless I'm unconscious," Luc replied cheerfully

"I can arrange that," said Mae.

We worked in relative silence after that, methodically sifting through the letters and documents. Most of it was mundane—logistical notes, ration updates, and a few generic messages of encouragement from commanding officers. Every so often, one of us would pause to share something interesting, like a photograph of a place we recognized or a letter that hinted at something more personal.

It was well past midnight when I found it.

I'd been sorting through a stack of letters, each addressed in the same neat, slanted handwriting. At first glance, they seemed as unremarkable as the rest. But then I noticed something odd. This particular letter wasn't addressed to Yvette, as we'd come to expect.

It was addressed to Jacqueline.

"Mae," I said, my voice tight. "You need to see this."

She looked up from her pile, her exhaustion giving way to a narrow focus as she took the letter from my hands. Her eyes scanned the page, her brow furrowing deeper with every line.

"What does it say?" Luc asked, leaning forward eagerly.

Mae read aloud, her voice even but low.

My dear Jacqueline,

I hope this letter finds you safe and happy—playing in the sunshine or watching the clouds drift by, as all little girls should. I think of you often, picturing you with that spark in your eyes and a giggle that could make even the gloomiest day brighter. You are so young, so full of wonder, and yet the world around us feels anything but.

I need you to know something, even if it is hard to understand right now. Every step I take, every sacrifice I make, it is for you. For a future where little girls just like you can laugh freely, dream without fear, and grow up in a world that is kinder and safer than the one we are in now.

I wish I could be there with you, reading you stories or holding your hand as you learn to skip stones on the water. I wish I could protect you from every hurt, every worry. But the truth is, sometimes we have to face difficult things so that the people we love can have something better.

You might not understand why I am writing this letter or who I am, and for that, I am sorry. But I promise you, Jacqueline, I am doing everything I can to make sure you will never have to know the kind of fear or uncertainty I have seen. My hope, my dream, is that you will grow up surrounded by love and laughter, with the freedom to chase anything your heart desires.

Please, hold on to that spark inside you. Hold on to your dreams, your kindness, and your courage. You are so much stronger than you know, and one day, when you are older, I hope you will understand how much you have inspired me.

If I could wrap the whole world in my arms to keep you safe, I would. But since I cannot , I will fight for the next best thing: a world where you and every other child can thrive.

Be good for your mama, and do not forget to smile. That smile is your superpower, Jacqueline. It can brighten even the darkest of days, just as it has for me.

Always remember, you are loved more than words can ever say. I will carry you with me in my heart, no matter where this path takes me.

With all my love,
John D. Seasons

The room fell silent.

"Wait a minute," Luc said, breaking the silence. "Jacqueline? As in *Jacqueline*, Jacqueline? The cranky old bat sitting at the bar over there? Not Yvette?

Mae nodded slowly, her fingers tightening around the letter.

"He wrote this to Jacqueline," said Mae, a puzzled, if not completely bewildered look taking over her face.

"So John did know Jacqueline?" Luc scratched his head, a rare moment of genuine confusion crossing his countenance. "But is it this Jacqueline? Or is this something, or someone else entirely?"

Mae shook her head slowly, her expression hard and un-readable.

"I don't know. But this certainly puts another fucking wrinkle in this whole godforsaken escapade."

As things untangled, only to be tangled again, I couldn't help but wonder what Erica was doing, what angle she would approach this information from, what calming presence she would provide us. I knew the pain of missing someone, but this felt just a little different. Maybe that's what love is. It's the feelings you know to be real but still can't believe they are. That someone can occupy your world while they're who knows how many miles away.

We sat there, staring at the letter as the fire crackled in the hearth. The past had just become a lot more complicated, and none of us had any idea where it would lead.

CHAPTER 26
MAE

THE PUB SEEMED TO HAVE CALMED DOWN, the reverberations of other conversations fading into a dull background noise as I stared at the letter Alex had discovered. It was the kind of unforeseen revelation that knocked the air out of you, even when you thought you'd already seen it all, already absorbed every cosmic punch to the ovaries possible. My fingers brushed over the paper, the edges brittle but the words alive with a mystery I wasn't sure Jacqueline—or any of us—was ready to fully deconstruct.

I glanced at Jacqueline, now seated across the table, an untouched pint in front of her. Her expression was tight, her shoulders squared as if bracing for a blow.

"Did you know about this?" I asked.

Her head jerked up, her eyes narrowing. "Know about what?"

"This letter," I said, holding it up. "John wrote this to you. Did you know him?"

"Of course not," she snapped, cutting me off. Her face flushed with something between anger and disbelief. "I didn't even know *these* letters existed until you dragged me into all this."

The edge in her voice softened something in me. For all her haughtiness and disdain, Jacqueline looked lost, as though the cracks in her foundation were suddenly too wide to ignore and the impending collapse was mere moments away. I recognized this look; it was me not too long ago. Hell, it was me for most of my damn life.

"Then we need to find out if there are more," I said.

Jacqueline's laugh was flat and humourless. "Oh, sure. Let's just wave a *baguette magique* and conjure up every letter *ma mère* ever received and kept hidden from me."

"Not magic," Alex interjected. "Just persistence."

Luc, always at the ready—or perhaps just drunk enough to believe in miracles—leaned back in his chair, stretching his arms wide.

"Ah, the thrill of the hunt. Let us find some more love letters, shall we?"

"Shut the fuck up, Luc," we all said in unison.

"We're not trying to hurt you," I reassured Jacqueline, ignoring Luc's faux look of anguish, keeping my tone level. "But if John was writing to your mother about this, to give you this letter, then there could be more here. Things maybe you deserve to know. Things we might all deserve to know."

Jacqueline's jaw tightened, but she nodded reluctantly.

"Fine," she said. "But if this blows up into some soap opera, don't expect me to stick around for the finale."

Luc clapped his hands together. "Spoken like someone who secretly loves *le drame*."

"Spoken like someone who's one snide comment away from dressing you with *une pinte*," Jacqueline shot back, her glare serious enough to turn someone to stone.

"I'm beginning to like you," I said to Jacqueline, raising my glass to cheers hers.

I now turned to Alex, who had gone back to digging through the box.

"Anything else?"

He shook his head, his brow furrowed as he flipped through papers with growing urgency.

"Not yet. Oh, wait—hold on." He pulled out another letter, this one drafted on official-looking stationery.

"It's from John to, let me see—his commanding officer," Alex said, scanning the page. His eyes widened as he read. "It's about Jacqueline."

I leaned in as Alex read aloud.

To Lieutenant Colonel James Pickney
3rd Canadian Infantry Division Headquarters
Normandy, France

Sir,

I write to you with a matter of great urgency and with personal conviction. While I understand the delicate balance between duty and the chaos of war, I find myself at a crossroads where one must inform the other.

During our sweep of the village today, amidst the devastation and heartbreak, I found a child. A girl, no more than four years old, separated from her family—if any of them still live. She was hiding in the rubble of what was once a bakery, clutching a charred piece of cloth as though it were her entire world. Sir, I cannot leave her to fend for herself.

I have seen too much on this front—too many innocents mercilessly left in the throes of cruelty. And while we march forward with orders to liberate, I am haunted by the faces of those we cannot save. I cannot, will not, consign her to that fate.

I am asking for your assistance in securing her safety. She needs a place to live, someone who can raise her with the dignity and care she deserves. If there is any network we can leverage, any way to ensure she finds sanctuary, I beg you to help me make it happen.

I know this is not standard procedure, and I do not ask lightly. I ask as a man who dreams of returning home one day to hold my own children in my arms—children I do not yet have but whose future I fight for every day. If I am to call myself a father someday, I must act as one now. What kind of man would I be if I allowed her to fall into enemy hands or to be left to the wolves?

If there is any humanity left in this war, it must influence choices like this. She is more than collateral in this hell; she is a person, she is someone's daughter. I implore you to help me ensure she finds a home where she will be loved and safe.

I will take full responsibility for this action, whatever the consequences may be. Please, Sir, do not let this be another life we let slip through the cracks.

Respectfully,

Lance Corporal John D. Seasons
C-84104
The Canadian Scottish Regiment
3rd Canadian Infantry Division
Canadian Army

The words were there in black-and-white, thin and raw. Jacqueline looked like she'd been slapped. Or saw a ghost. Or slapped by a ghost she just saw. Either way, all colour drained from her face.

"He wrote this—about *me*?" she asked, her voice barely above a whisper.

Alex nodded. "He must have. The timeline fits. But—it's not just about you. It's like he's trying to figure something out about himself."

Luc leaned forward with a grin. "Sounds like the makings of another mystery, doesn't it?"

"Luc, seriously, you have to stop," said Alex. "Just let us take a moment to unpack what the hell we're looking at."

Jacqueline didn't dignify him with a response. Instead, she fixed me with a look I couldn't quite read. "If *ma mère* was so important to him, why didn't I know about any of this? Why didn't she tell me?"

I didn't have an answer. None of us did. But one thing was clear: the past wasn't done with us yet.

•••

The sun was just beginning to rise over the dusty streets of our small town when I caught sight of John. I was walking back from the butcher, a cloth-wrapped bundle of lamb chops tucked under my arm, when I spotted him coming down Main Street. He had two children in tow, one perched on his back like a sack of potatoes and the other clinging to his hand. The little girl on his back was giggling uncontrollably, her laughter ringing out against the still morning, competing for position over the birds chirping in trees and bushes, heard but not seen.

The boy, maybe seven or eight, was dragging his feet and pouting, his head tilted forward as though the weight of the world was on his shoulders.

I stopped in my tracks, pretending to adjust my bag so I could watch.

"Come on, Charlie," John said to the boy, his voice warm but firm. "Mrs. Simmons makes the best flapjacks this side of the county. You don't wanna miss out, do you?"

The boy shrugged. "I guess not."

John crouched down, balancing the girl carefully as he looked the boy in the eye. "I know it's not home, and I know your ma's been working long hours, but Mrs. Simmons is good people. And I promised your ma I'd make sure you two were looked after. Can you do that for me, buddy? Help your sister settle in?"

Charlie hesitated, then nodded reluctantly.

"That's the spirit." John ruffled the boy's hair and stood back up, shifting the girl higher on his back. "Now, no more dragging your feet, alright? We've got a big day ahead."

I felt my body tighten as I watched him lead the children away, his voice carrying on the breeze as he teased the girl about eating her weight in flapjacks.

I wasn't the only one watching. Mrs. Willoughby, who was sweeping the wooden porch of the general store, paused to rest her broom against the railing. She leaned out and squinted in John's direction before chuckling.

"That boy," she said, shaking her head. "Always has a way with the little ones. He'll make a fine father someday, yes he will."

I tried to shrug off the comment, but my cheeks burned anyway.

"He sure will," I said as sweetly as if a songbird had lodged itself in my throat.

"Uh-huh." Mrs. Willoughby gave me a sidelong glance, the corners of her mouth twitching. "And you're just standing here for the morning breeze, I suppose?"

I shot her a bashful look, and the older woman just laughed.

As John passed by, he caught sight of me and tipped an imaginary hat, his smile as easy as a summer morning.

"Morning, Mae," he called out.

"Good morning, John," I replied, clutching the bundle of lamb a little tighter. He always made me feel a certain way— you know the kind.

He didn't linger, but as he walked away, I felt the strangest blend of longing and possibility settle over me. Is this what the rest of our life could be?

"Good boy, that John," Mrs. Willoughby mused, resting her hands on her hips. "Not like most these days, running off when times get tough. He sticks like glue on paper."

I nodded absentmindedly, still watching the small group disappear around the corner.

All day, the image of John with those children lingered in my mind—the gentle way he spoke to them, the way he knelt down so the boy wouldn't feel small, the way he carried the little girl like she was a queen riding into town. He was playing the role of brother, father, protector.

That night, as I lay in bed, staring at the cracked ceiling of my parents' farmhouse, I couldn't shake these thoughts. I'd grown up watching men shirk their responsibilities, leave their families, and abandon what mattered most. I'd seen what it did to women like my aunt, left to scrape by on their own.

But John wasn't like that. John was unfaltering. Solid. Kind. Devout.

And as I closed my eyes, I realized that somewhere, deep in my heart, I already knew I'd never meet anyone like him again. One day, he'd be the father of my children. And it would be perfect.

...

I never imagined I'd find myself in this situation—breaking into a museum, sneaking through corridors, and risking it all for the sake of answers we'd all been chasing for God knows how long. But there we were, slipping through a back entrance to one of the most famous museums in the region. It felt ridiculous, but it also felt necessary. Jacqueline was the puppet master now, and her determination was infectious. We, her marionettes, were all in, for better or worse.

"There must be more here," she said when we arrived, unknowingly making our way toward a destination Jacqueline willfully failed to disclose. Had she told us, she knew we'd be unlikely to join her.

Luc, however, was clearly in charge of morale.

"Who says you can't learn *un peu d'histoire* by breaking the rules?" he joked, pushing the door open with exaggerated care after picking the lock, once again showing his prowess more as a thief than a historian. His voice was full of too much confidence for someone who was blatantly committing a crime.

I rolled my eyes.

"We're not breaking anything. We're just—testing the door. Yes, that's right. Testing the door for security purposes," said Alex, predictably cautious in such an unlawful situation, and already working on the story he'd tell himself over and over again should we get pinched.

Jacqueline wasn't paying attention to us. She was all business, scanning the area for any sign of a guard. She was determined, and I understood why. This museum was where we'd likely find the most important pieces of the puzzle. More letters. More photos. Proof that John's life—and the truth we were searching for—was preserved within these walls.

Luc, sensing that we were on borrowed time, leaned into another door with exaggerated care, muttering to himself like it was a complicated lock or something of the sort.

"I've got this," he said with a wink that looked far too rehearsed. "I just need to work a little magic."

And perform magic he did, because after a few seconds, the door creaked open. We stepped inside, doing our best to move quietly. But then, just as we were about to start into the real business of searching, a voice cut through the silence.

"*Excusez-moi! Arrêtez!* What do you think you're doing?"

We froze. My heart, at a younger age—a much younger age—would have skipped a beat, but now, I could feel an adrenaline rush surge. Luc, of course, turned around like he was the star of some spy movie. He didn't stutter a word, didn't even break a sweat, once again proving more skilled as a criminal than a man of history. Maybe he was the next mystery that required solving.

"Ah, just admiring the fine craftsmanship of *la porte*," Luc said, offering the security guard a smile that could only be described as pure smugness. "You know, nothing impresses me more than good historical architecture. This really is a solid door. Well-maintained. You wouldn't want anyone just waltzing in, would you?"

The guard, a tall woman with an air of seriousness that matched the situation, stared at Luc for a moment. Then she raised an eyebrow, unimpressed by his ostentatious charm.

"Really?" she asked, crossing her arms. "A door enthusiast? You're standing here in the middle of the night trying to open something that's always locked, and you expect me to believe it's because you're a door expert?"

Luc's grin only widened, a glint of mischief in his eyes.

"Well, it's not just the door I'm interested in, *ma chère*. I was simply making sure your museum's secrets stay safe. You know, some people don't appreciate *l'histoire*, but I do. You see, *je suis* Luc Brassard, this country's most decorated historian."

Jacqueline hissed under her breath, clearly not impressed. "Luc! Don't say your name, you idiot. And this clearly is not the time to—"

But Luc wasn't done.

"I mean, think of it this way: I'm here to protect history, protect the artifacts, protect *les lettres*—" He let that hang in the air, clearly expecting her to buy it. "*Par exemple*, the letters from the war—the personal ones. Those must be kept safe, *oui*? And you, *mademoiselle*, I can protect you as well if you need it."

The guard just blinked at him. I was sure she was wondering whether she was dealing with an idiot savant or the most simple-minded man in the whole of France, both of which could honestly be true depending on the lens in which you viewed Luc. Noticeably, and favourably for us, she hadn't sounded an alarm or called the police—yet. She glanced at us and then studied Luc for a long moment, before shifting her eyes back to the door, and finally smirking.

"*Bien essayé*. But you're not fooling anyone. And you're definitely not getting into *le musée* at this hour. Not to protect *les artefacts* or history or anything else. In fact, that's what I'm here for. So, I suggest you leave before I call *la police*."

Luc, not missing a beat, bowed dramatically, holding his hand over his heart like he was acting in a play.

"Ah, *mademoiselle*, you wound me! I was simply trying to preserve the sanctity of this fine establishment. I only wish to contribute to the greater good of history—"

At that, the guard sighed heavily and removed something from her belt—something shiny and loud. A high-pitched alarm blared through the building. My ears rang with the piercing sound, and I felt a small piece of my soul die. We were officially and properly screwed.

The guard didn't flinch, looking at Luc like she'd known it would come to this point eventually.

"You're good, but you're not that good," she said, smirking at him as the alarm continued blaring. "And you, *monsieur*, need to learn when to quit."

Jacqueline's face was turning a shade of red that told me she was moments away from either screaming in hysterics or passing out from the absurdity of it all.

Luc, unfazed by the chaos, gave the guard a slow, exaggerated clap.

"Bravo, *mademoiselle*, bravo. You've won the day," he said with a deep bow. "But you haven't won the war. I'll be back."

The guard didn't say anything else, just shook her head and walked off, leaving us in stunned silence, the alarm still sounding. Jacqueline shot me a quizzical look that could melt steel: why was she walking away?

"Well," I said, trying to keep the mood light despite the fact that our mission was rapidly falling apart, "I guess Luc's charm only works on certain kinds of women."

Luc, completely undeterred, moved to the side window of the museum.

"Alright, alright," he said, dismissing the tension. "Let's not lose our heads. We've still got work to do, and now we only have but a few minutes to do it. You go, I'll stay with *mademoiselle*."

"Luc, what the hell are you talking about?" asked Alex. "We have to go. Now. In case you've lost your hearing, there's an alarm going off. And—I'm no expert, mind you—when an alarm goes off in a locked museum, it usually means the authorities are on their way."

"It's a ploy, I think," said Luc. "Trust me, *non?*"

"Oh fuck it," I said. "Why the hell not trust the man. He's gotten us this far. So what if we end up in prison. It'll make for a good story."

The group conceded, and after a few more quick moves and some careful maneuvering, we slipped into a small room—thankfully, no one else was around to hear the thudding of our collective heartbeats. Once inside, we started riffling through boxes, pulling out letters and photographs like racoons on speed, looking for anything that might reveal the truth about the life we were all trying to piece together.

Jacqueline found a box full of old photos and started flipping through them like it was nothing, making ridiculous comments about the fashion of the time.

Alex was lost in his own world, sifting through pages of documents, each one seemingly more cryptic than the last. I could tell he wasn't paying attention as closely as usual, understandable given the still-ringing alarm and the certainty his premonition of prison in a foreign country would come to pass.

"Chambers!" I bellowed. "Get your head out of your ass and get to work. That is, unless you want to find out what a French prison has in store for a pretty boy like you."

CHAPTER 27
ALEX

THE SHRILL ALARM ECHOED THROUGH THE MUSEUM, and my pulse quickened as I tried to process what was happening. Here we were, essentially searching for needles in a haystack without the luxury of time.

As quickly as it had pierced our ears, the shrill sound of the alarm stopped. We all froze, looking at each other as if to confirm we were hearing the same silence, and that it wasn't just the aftereffect of tinnitus.

I maneuvered back toward the door and carefully stepped out, Jacqueline and Mae shuffling slowly behind me, yet still managing to bump and push into me.

"Are you seeing this?" I said to Mae, who was now hunched next to me behind a bust of someone I didn't know, but their bronze likeness suggested historical significance.

Luc, leaning against a display case, was passionately kissing the security guard who had, not ten minutes ago, busted us. I suppose underestimating his charm was no longer an option when it came to enduring his antics.

"If we all end up in jail because of Luc's libido, I'm going to skin him alive before the little blue pill wears off," she threatened.

"Careful, he strikes me as the type that might find that kind of dominance a mood enhancer," I said chuckling, unable to help myself.

Meanwhile, Jacqueline stood by the door, arms crossed, glowering at the entire scene. She looked ready to combust, and really, who could blame her? She never wanted any of this, and now she was neck deep in the shenanigans that only befell those closely associated with Mae.

"This is absurd," said Jacqueline. "We're supposed to be finding answers, not watching The Luc Show."

I didn't disagree. Though Luc was often our biggest liability, ironically, he was our best distraction right now.

"Alright," I said, trying to formulate a plan. "We've got to get him away from there. Cops are definitely on their way, they have to be."

"Don't look at me," Mae said, gesturing toward Luc. "He's your friend."

"I didn't ask for him to seduce the security guard!" I hissed back. "And he's not *my friend*, he's your historian, your responsibility. Whatever brothel you found him in, you can send him right back to. But for now, let's just figure out how we're all getting out of here without a French rap sheet."

"Can we *focus*?" Jacqueline said, throwing her hands up. "Someone grab him before she decides to arrest him herself. She'll be quick to wise up sooner or later."

"Fine," I muttered. "I'll handle it."

I slinked out from behind the statue and moved toward Luc, who was now whispering something into the guard's ear that made her giggle. The same woman who had threatened calling the police not ten minutes ago, and abruptly put an end to our mission, was giggling like a schoolgirl.

"Luc," I hissed, waving him over. "What the hell is going on?"

He turned to me with an infuriatingly calm expression. "Alex, *mon ami*, can't you see I'm in the middle of something important here?"

"Important?" I gestured emphatically at the guard, the flashing lights of police cars now visible through the door behind them. "The only thing important right now is getting out of here before the cops come in!"

The guard—whose name tag read Claire—glanced at me, her smile faltering. "*La police* won't be a problem," she said, glowing. "I will handle them, but you will have to get out of sight."

We did as we were told, scurrying back into the room we'd come from. I cracked the door just wide enough to watch Claire stride to the front entrance and greet two men in uniform, both of whom wore the strained expressions of people who would rather be anywhere else. A flurry of French followed—quick, clipped, and beyond my grasp. Just as suddenly as they had arrived, the officers abruptly turned and left. For now, it seemed, we were in the clear.

As the flashing lights from the patrol car vanished around the corner, we stepped out cautiously from the darkened gallery, our shoes squeaking against the polished tile. We were still trespassers, still at risk, but now had time to find something—*anything*—before another patrol car possibly showed up or Claire's goodwill ran dry.

"What exactly did she say to them?" Mae asked, voice tight.

Luc, adjusting his lapel with that same maddening calm, replied, "Claire informed the officers I was her boyfriend. Albeit eager, impulsive, and apparently a bit dim. I had come by after hours to surprise her and ended up getting myself locked in. The alarm? Just an unfortunate consequence of my romantic timing."

"And us?" Jacqueline asked, brow furrowed.

"Conveniently omitted," he said with a smile. "Apparently, I'm the kind of man who breaks into museums alone in the name of love."

"Charming," Jacqueline muttered, already walking off. "Let's not waste the mercy she just handed us."

We dispersed into the shadowed corridors, tension rippling through every movement. The space stretched out before us in silence—tall ceilings, looming exhibits, and halls that twisted back on themselves like a maze designed to confuse even the most determined visitor. Add in the after-hours darkness, and it was a veritable clusterfuck.

The next few hours were a blur of dim lights, dusty files, and mounting frustration. We scoured offices and back rooms, archives and storerooms, anything that wasn't bolted shut. The museum was well-organized on the surface, but beneath the official veneer, things quickly became chaotic. Boxes were misfiled, labels faded or missing. Entire collections seemed to be half-catalogued, misnamed, or simply crammed into corners and forgotten.

In one room, we found a collection of uniforms from the 1940s. They were well-preserved, but useless. In another, crates of medals, plaques, ceremonial weapons. Each item came with a story, but none of them were the one we were desperately looking for.

We read through brittle newspaper clippings, appointment ledgers, even guestbooks—hundreds of names, hundreds of signatures, none of them meaningful, at least not in this particular search.

Jacqueline scoured letters in French so archaic and looping they may as well have been written in code. Mae found an entire cabinet filled with blank forms and photocopied inventory sheets. I spent half an hour unpacking a box of miscellany ambiguously labeled "1952" only to discover it contained nothing but tax documents and donation receipts.

The dust got into our noses and throats. Our fingers grew numb from rifling through cold metal drawers. At one point, Luc sat down on the edge of a display platform and simply sighed.

"This place is like a tomb," he muttered. "A beautiful one, but still a tomb."

He wasn't wrong. The museum felt less like a place of knowledge and more like a mausoleum—grand, dignified, full of buried things.

Fatigue began to settle into our bones and take its toll. It became harder to focus, harder to keep track of what had already been searched and what hadn't. Tempers frayed. When we spoke, we snapped at each other; otherwise, we worked in silence.

And then—just as hope began to wear paper thin, Jacqueline's voice broke through the silence.

"*Attendez*," she said, crouched beside an old steel filing cabinet. Her fingers were pressed along the seam of the lowest drawer.

"There's something off," she murmured. "This doesn't sit flush."

"Of course it doesn't sit flush, it's fucking ancient," said Mae, exhausted. "Nothing in this godforsaken place sits flush. The wood is as swollen as Luc's pecker in a room full of dim women."

Lost in the search for whatever it was we were actually searching for, I had failed to check in on Mae—not only to see how she was holding up under the emotional strain, but how she was managing the physical exhaustion of someone her age. Sure, she was still spry as hell, but ninety-three is still ninety-three.

I managed my way over to Jacqueline as she jimmied the drawer loose, pulling it fully from its track, revealing a shallow compartment tucked behind the frame. Hidden. Deliberate.

"Ha!" she exclaimed. "I told you."

No one had it in them to get into a pissing match, so we all stayed silent as Jacqueline procured a thin leather folder, its surface scuffed and flaking, the colour long since faded. No catalog number; no reference. Jacqueline handled it carefully, as though it might dissolve in her hands. She opened it, slowly, reverently.

Inside were a dozen brittle pages. Typed reports. A map. A list of names. Correspondences, mostly coded, some in French, others in short, formal German. Jacqueline let out a defeated sigh.

"Who told who now, missy?" said Mae in a tone that conveyed it was time to go home.

Claire, sensing the same, quickly announced, "You should probably leave," her tone short and her delivery more direct, though her eyes lingered on Luc with a mischievous glint. "Well, maybe not *all* of you. This one might stay."

Luc, ever ready to capitalize on charm, dipped into a slight bow. "What say we bid you all *adieu,* and the *mademoiselle* and I continue unravelling the mystery of two beating hearts?" He turned back to Claire, lowering his voice to a whisper.

I couldn't hear what he said, but whatever it was, it landed like an anchor on the ocean floor.

Claire's smile vanished. She gave him a sharp knee to the groin and, without hesitation, slapped him hard across the face. Luc doubled over, gasping.

"I've changed my mind," Claire said coldly. "I *will* be calling *la police maintenant*."

None of us waited to see if she was bluffing.

In a sudden scramble of urgency, we grabbed a few of the documents we'd managed to dig up—unsorted, half-deciphered, possibly useless—and stuffed them into our coats. We offered Claire a rushed, awkward chorus of thank-yous, which she did not return, and slipped out before Luc's stupidity could cost us more than just bruised pride.

"If you ever pull something like that again, I'll personally make sure you never see daylight," Mae said to Luc, grabbing his arm, dragging him toward the road.

As we hurried down the dark street, Luc glanced back at the building and said, "Shame to leave so suddenly. Claire and I really had a connection."

Jacqueline moaned. "If you mention that woman's name one more time, I swear—"

"Alright, alright," Luc said, holding up his hands in mock surrender. "I'm just saying, she has great taste in men."

"Keep walking," Mae snapped, hurrying her pace toward the car.

By the time we returned to Mae's apartment, I was completely drained, we all were. We stumbled inside, dumping the boxes of documents and photographs onto the kitchen table. The magnitude of what we'd just done hit me all at once, and I collapsed onto the couch, running a hand through my hair.

"That," Mae said, pointing at Luc, "was the single dumbest thing I've ever been a part of—and I've been around. Oh, let me tell you, I've been around."

"Again, *de rien*," Luc said, dropping into a chair like he didn't have a worry in the world. "Admit it—you were impressed, even if only a little bit."

"I was impressed you didn't end up in handcuffs," Mae shot back.

"I would have been," Luc winked, "had there been more time."

Jacqueline, already digging through the documents, ignored the trivial squabbling. She was laser-focused now, flipping through letters and photos with an intensity that made it clear she wasn't stopping until she found something new.

"We'll sort through everything tomorrow," I said, massaging my temples. "Right now, I think we all need to sit down, breathe, and figure out what the hell just happened."

Despite everything, including bone-deep exhaustion, I couldn't help but laugh. It was one of those instances where, once you started laughing, you couldn't stop. You weren't drunk or high, no, you were just so engrossed in the absurdity of it all that laughter was the only reasonable reaction. It was ridiculous. The whole night had been ridiculous. But somehow, against all odds, we'd managed to pull it off. This group, this unlikely group, had managed to band together to pull this off.

And as I looked at the new piles of artifacts and letters on the table, I knew we were one step closer to the truth. What truth that was exactly, I had no idea, but whatever it was definitely felt a little closer.

The next week unfolded in a strange, subdued rhythm. We all needed the break. After the mayhem at the museum, the team moved in different directions, each of us processing everything in our own way. Luc claimed he needed time to recover from his "daring heroics" and spent most of his days lounging around Mae's apartment, charming her neighbours for free pastries and coffee. Jacqueline buried herself in the documents we'd retrieved, sorting through decades of history with a fervour that spoke to her now-desperate need for answers. I spent many solitary moments thinking of Erica. Despite the chaos we'd been enduring, a large part of me felt it would be far more satisfying, not just in our finds but in our near-misses, if she were here. I continued to think about and practice what I would say to her when I saw her again. How I was sorry. How the grip of this trip had clouded my better judgment. How I would work to make sure it never happened again. I hoped it would matter, but wasn't sure if any of it would. Only time would tell.

And Mae? Mae grew quieter.

I noticed it immediately, even if no one else did. The seasoned, biting wit she wielded like a weapon dulled ever so slightly. She wasn't withdrawn exactly, but there was a distance in her eyes, like she was somewhere else entirely. Most days, she sat in her armchair by the window, staring out at the street with John's unopened letter resting on the side table beside her. It was always within reach but never held and not yet opened.

I'd catch her glancing at it on occasion, her expression drifting between curiosity and dread. But then she'd shake her head, pick up a magazine or a crossword puzzle, and pretend it wasn't there.

Mae was a fortress, always had been. And yet, something about that letter clearly unnerved her in a way nothing else ever had.

CHAPTER 28
MAE

TODAY IS THE DAY.

Each morning, this is what I'd tell myself. And each night, I'd set the unopened letter back down, dismissing the day for what it was: another waste of time.

What could this lone letter possibly say that I didn't already know? John was a good man, a great man; this much was undeniably clear from every word we'd uncovered here and from back home, every story Jacqueline or Luc or hell, even Alex, had pieced together. He was selfless and brave, someone who couldn't bear to see a child left alone amid the ruins of war. A tenderhearted person who loved and felt so deeply that he had no business fighting when he could have been loving instead. But he was also intense, not only in his battles, but in his convictions, his promises—though he couldn't keep some of them.

But this letter wasn't about any of that. It was addressed to me. And for the first time in my life, I was terrified of John's words. Never had I seen a letter from him with my name on it that made me feel so uneasy, so scared.

What if there was something I'd missed? Some unknown truth that would reframe the man I'd built my entire life around? It wasn't implausible. Up until very recently, this is what I thought had happened. Or worse, what if the letter didn't reveal anything at all? What if it was just one more sad goodbye from a man who always seemed to be saying sad goodbyes?

I thought back to the days when we were young, before the war, when John would round up the neighbourhood kids for games of baseball in the summer or building snow forts with them in the winter. The way he'd hoist little Billy Thompson onto his shoulders after a scraped knee or carry groceries for Mrs. Howard when her arthritis acted up.

He was precisely the type of man you fall in love with, fast and hard, something I was most certainly guilty of. He was dependable and kind, so different from the other boys who bragged about their conquests or the grown men who thought family responsibility ended with bringing home a paycheque. John wasn't like that. He was a man who showed up, who stayed, who cared.

And then the war took him. Not all at once, but piece by piece. Every letter he sent home was evidence of a sad reality that grew heavier with time, until the man who never returned changed from the one I'd fallen for to a hollowed out shell, a man scarred and traumatized by the brutality of war. Like so many who did come home, he would have carried ghosts I could never see, burdens that would never be shared or spoken aloud.

And now, sitting in this foreign apartment all these years later, with his ghost folded neatly into an envelope on my side table, I wondered if I was finally ready to meet the man he'd become in my absence. I always prided myself on being strong, but was I strong enough for this?

Everyone gave me space, for which I was grateful. Luc, with all his incessant theatrics, seemed to sense that this wasn't the time for one of his charm offensives. He spent most afternoons amusing himself with Jacqueline's discoveries, occasionally offering commentary like, "This handwriting? Definitely not his best work," or, "What's the deal with this guy's moustache?"

But these letters. These fucking letters. I'd had enough of them.

•••

The coastline stretched endlessly before us, rugged and wild, the white-capped waves crashing against the jagged rocks with a ferocity that matched the tension simmering in the car. Dolores was behind the wheel, her sun hat tipped back, oversized sunglasses perched on her nose, fingers drumming absently against the steering wheel. In her lap sat the letter. That damn letter. It had been burning a hole in my bag since the day we left, but now, somehow, it had made its way into her hands, or more specifically, resting above her lady parts.

"You know," she began, her voice deliberately light but carrying that distinct edge she always wielded when she was gearing up to make a point, "you've been hauling this thing around for weeks. If it's going to be your emotional baggage, you might as well rip it open and get it over with. Either way, it's dead weight."

"It's not dead weight. It's just a letter," I scoffed, leaning my head against the window.

"It's not *just* a letter, Mae. At least not to you." Dolores briefly flicked her eyes in my direction, her tone calm but pointed. "It's a whatever the fuck this is that you're dragging around like a ball and chain. And, personally, I'm running out of patience for such buzz killers."

"Well, then don't you worry about it. This is my baggage, not yours," I snapped, glaring at the expansive blue of the Pacific, the same vast ocean where fierce battles raged, dirt graves traded for watery ones. But what did it matter? Death is death. Does it really matter how or where or when?

Dolores let out a short laugh, not unkind but certainly lacking sympathy.

"You're damn right it's your baggage. But here's the thing: I don't care what you do with it. Read it. Don't read it. Burn it. Wipe your ass with it. Throw it out the goddamn window for all I care. But, Mae, you've got to make a decision. Life's up ahead, not in the folded creases of some piece of paper from the dead."

Her words were like a sudden slap, sharp and stinging. I turned to face her, anger flaring in my chest.

"You don't get it. You didn't know my parents. They barely said anything to me when they were alive. Not anything that mattered, anyway. So why the hell should I care what they have to say now? As if now, only in death, they've realized they had a daughter who was worth a damn?"

"Maybe you shouldn't care," she said with an indifferent shrug, her eyes fixed on the road. "Maybe it doesn't matter. But it's not about them anymore, is it? Like you said, they're dead and gone. It's about you now, Mae. Whether or not you decide to face it, deal with it, and then move the hell on. And honestly? That's your call. I'm just here for the view, babes."

I clenched my fists in my lap, the anger bubbling up in a way that felt both all too familiar and utterly unbearable.

"You know, for the care-free hippy you're supposed to be, you seem to have some strong opinions. So, I must ask, why do you even care, Dolores?"

"I don't," she said flatly, her voice steady but unapologetic. "I care about *you*. But this letter? This thing you keep holding over your own head? It's nothing to me, love. If you want to waste your time playing tug-of-war with a bunch of scribbled words on a page, that's your business. I'm just saying it's a hell of a lot easier to let go."

I hated how calm she was, how matter of fact. She wasn't judging me, wasn't trying to convince me or force me into anything, and that only made it worse. She was cutting through my defenses with her no-nonsense attitude, leaving me exposed to the ugly truth I didn't want to admit.

"They didn't care enough to say anything important when they were alive," I muttered, more to myself than to Dolores. "They didn't care enough to talk to me then, so why should I care now?" I was stuck in a repetitive cycle of thoughts.

Dolores glanced at me, her expression unreadable behind her sunglasses.

"Maybe you shouldn't. Maybe they don't deserve it. But here's the thing, Mae: holding on to it like this—letting it sit there, unopened, like some kind of poisoned apple—that's not hurting them. It's just hurting you."

"Okay, we're getting nowhere, at least in terms of this conversation," I said, raising my verbal white flag. "So, how about we focus on where we're going and get there in peace, before we rip each other's heads off."

"Sounds good, love," she said. "And even better news, we're here."

We arrived at this bizarre little hippie play in some coastal town, the kind of place where the air smelled like sea salt and weed, and somehow, even more weed, and everyone seemed to drift rather than walk.

Dolores dragged me into a converted barn with mismatched cushions for seats and a stage made from driftwood. The play itself was an eclectic mess—a jumbled whirlwind of interpretive dance, flower crowns, and rambling dialogue about the universe and inner peace that didn't make a lick of sense to me. Dolores, of course, ate it up, clapping wildly and nudging me every time someone said something vaguely profound. I rolled my eyes, but a part of me couldn't deny the uninhibited charm of it all. The sheer audacity of people baring their souls like that—it was raw, fearless, and annoyingly magnetic.

It was fucking hippies.

After the play, which seemed to both drag on and fly by, Dolores led me to a party on the beach, where firelight flickered against the waves, and strangers freely passed around guitars, joints, and bottles of wine as if they'd known each other forever and germs weren't a thing. Given my circumstances, I let myself get swept up in it, sitting on a log near the fire and watching Dolores charm her way through a circle of people, spinning a wild story about a road trip to Mexico that may or may not have been entirely true. The stars were impossibly bright, scattered across the sky like they'd been spilled there by some cosmic mistake, and for the first time in weeks, I felt something close to peace.

It was in that moment, with the crackle of the fire and the distant strum of a guitar in the background, that I finally pulled the letter from my bag. Dolores was off laughing with someone near the water, her silhouette framed by the moonlight, and I felt safe enough, small enough, to finally confront the remnants of my parents in the words I'd been carrying.

Their words crashed over me like a tidal wave. I didn't notice when my hands started shaking or when the tears began blurring the ink on the page. The message wasn't profound, not in the way Dolores might have hoped. There was no grand apology, no confession of undying love or regret. Just—words. Simple words. Words that I hadn't known I needed until they were staring back at me. Words that conveyed the things my parents couldn't say when they were alive—things about their fears, their hopes, their love for me, as camouflaged as I perceived it. It wasn't perfect, but it was enough.

And that was when the realization struck me. Words—no matter how imperfect, no matter how late—have immense power. Even words I didn't want to hear. Even words from the dead. They mattered. They carried consequence. They changed things, and they changed people and perceptions. Sitting there on that beach, surrounded by laughter and music and life, I made a silent promise to myself—from that moment on, I would read every letter ever addressed to me. I wouldn't leave another one unopened, wouldn't let another mystery linger and fester in the shadows. Because words deserved to be read, and maybe, just maybe, I deserved to read them.

When Dolores finally made her way back to me, cheeks flushed from wine and laughter, she didn't say anything. She just plopped down beside me, leaning her head against my shoulder, and together we watched the firelight dance on the waves.

...

Jacqueline, for her part, seemed energized by the puzzle we'd uncovered. She was still an irritable old bat, but at least she was being helpful. She pored over the artifacts we'd looked at what seemed like a thousand times with dogged determination, occasionally dragging me into her research with questions about dates or locations I barely remembered. It was good to see her so invested, though I could tell she was struggling in her own way. The story we were unravelling wasn't just history for her—it was identity. And that was a burden I could relate to all too fucking well.

But for me, the days were quiet. Too quiet. I went through the motions—preparing tea, tidying the apartment, reading the news—and all the while, the letter sat there, waiting.

On the seventh day, I finally picked it up, like I was God herself, doing something sacred for one day of the week.

The envelope was crisp, somehow well preserved through the years, the paper inside carefully folded, as if John had known even then that it might be decades before I'd read it. My hands trembled as I unfolded the letter, the familiar scrawl of his handwriting pulling me back to a time when my world was both simpler and infinitely more complicated.

I took a deep breath, bracing myself for whatever would come next. The words blurred for a moment as tears filled my eyes, but I blinked them away.

This was John's voice, his truth, and I owed it to both of us to listen intently.

My Dearest Mae,

There are moments, even in the midst of all this chaos, when I find clarity. Moments when I understand what it is I am fighting for. Those moments are rare, but when they come, they are sharp as a knife, cutting through all the noise. Today, it was Jacqueline who brought me that clarity. Now, before you get your back up, Jacqueline is not a love interest—that will only ever be you. Jacqueline is a young girl, maybe four or five years old, and I have been working to find a home for her, somewhere far from this shattered place.

There is a woman—a kind and caring soul—who has agreed to take Jacqueline in when the time comes. She lives in an unassuming village, untouched by the worst of this war. It is a place with green hills and wildflowers and fresh air, a place where a little girl can run and laugh without fear—the way it should be for all little boys and girls.

I have been writing letters to Jacqueline's adoptive mother, writing her name nearly as often as I do yours. I do this not out of pretense, but because in some unexplained and unexpected way, she has become family to me. There is something about our shared love for Jacqueline that binds us—two adults, young as we may be, tethered by the same fierce devotion to a little girl who has already known too much loss.

Jacqueline is still so young, but not a baby anymore. She asks questions. She watches everything. She feels deeply. And I want her to grow up knowing that she was never alone. So I write to her adoptive mother like a brother might write to a sister he does not see often. I recount stories and memories about Jacqueline—the way she lights up when she is anywhere new, how she laughs with her whole body, how she clenches her jaw when she is trying not to cry. I write about the ways she is brave without even knowing it.

These letters are not fiction, though the true relationship of the characters certainly is. They are meant as a kind of lifeline.

A way to share the wonder of raising a child who is learning to feel safe again. When Jacqueline is older, maybe she will read them. Maybe she will see how people held her in their hearts, even in the hardest times. Maybe she will understand that love can exist outside the usual shapes, that family can be something we make deliberately, tenderly, out of care.

I do not pretend to be her father. But I do love her, as silly as that sounds. And I love the woman who is raising her now, not romantically, but in that rare, unspoken way people sometimes come to love those who show up for the people they themselves cannot protect.

This is what I have to give: my attention, my care, my words. And maybe, in the long run, that will be enough.

And maybe it is selfish, Mae. Maybe I do it because I cannot bear the thought of her growing up feeling abandoned, feeling like the world does not care. I cannot give her much in this life, but I can give her that. I can give her a memory of being loved, even if it is not the absolute truth. I do not know why I feel this pull, but I do. You know me when it comes to kids.

Sometimes I wonder if I am wrong to do this. If giving her hope in something that is not real is cruel. But then I see her smile—even just a flicker of it—and I know I would do it all over again the very same way. Because for that moment, she believes. She believes there is something good waiting for her on the other side of this war.

Jacqueline has started to hum that song, the one I told you about that plays for the soldiers when we move on and head to the front lines. She does not know the words, but she hums the melody, and it breaks my heart and heals it all at once.

> *So will you please say hello to the folks that I know*
> *Tell them I won't be long*
> *They'll be happy to know that as you saw me go*
> *I was singing this song*
> *We'll meet again, don't know where, don't know when*

Mae, I do not know if I am making the right choices. I do not know if what I am doing will help her or hurt her in the end. But what I do know is this: if there is even the smallest chance that she will hold on to that hope, that she will believe she was loved, then I have to try.

You, too, Mae—you are my anchor in all of this. I think of you with every step I take, every decision I make. And if I do not make it back to you, I hope you will forgive me for leaving a part of my heart here, with a little girl who deserves the world but has known only its cruelty.

All my love, always,
John

I dropped the letter on the table, in front of Alex, Luc, and Jacqueline, and my body went limp, struck with fear and paralyzed by uncertainty and all the tormenting things that had never before been my kryptonite.

CHAPTER 29
ALEX

I HELD THE LETTER IN MY HAND, the ink slightly smudged, the paper tinged from the passage of time. My heart pounded as I read John's words again, each sentence growing in desperation and love. I could almost hear his voice the way Mae described it to me; the calm, measured way he spoke when he had something important to say. But now, it was just coming through as words on paper, words that delivered a more impactful blow than anything I could have imagined.

Mae just sat there, stoic and still as a statue. But I could perceive her unspoken readiness to erupt. The silence was deafening, suffocating. She didn't say anything, but I knew she was waiting. She was waiting for me to take action, to speak, to make sense of things even if all I could feel was the swirling storm. But what could I say? What could I possibly offer as a balm to make this any better

"Mae—" I started, voice cracking despite my attempted composure.

She didn't respond at first, but I could see her hands shaking—her only sign of movement—and I wondered how she was holding herself together. The woman who had always been so strong, so determined, now seemed to be barely balancing on the edge of something fragile.

"You're going to say something, right?" she asked, finally speaking, her voice determined and firm. "You're going to tell me something prophetic and wise about how this is all part of some larger plan from the lady in the sky? How life isn't fair? How we've got to play the hands we're dealt? If so, just save it."

Her eyes were fixed on me, searching and seeming to implore me to make sense of it all despite her remarks. I felt a pit in my stomach. I wasn't sure I could do or say anything.

"I don't know what to say," I admitted, letting out a heavy sigh. My hands were clammy as I folded the letter and placed it back into the envelope. "I mean, how do you even—how do you even process this?"

Her eyes narrowed, but she didn't seem angry—just weary. She stepped forward, and I was struck by how fragile she looked at that moment. There was something about the way she held herself now, like she was ready to submit to a storm that hadn't hit quite yet.

"That's the million-dollar question now, isn't it?" she said. "Since I got here, since I paired up with Luc and pieces of the puzzle began to reveal themselves, all I've been doing is trying to *process* it, Alex. But this—this is something entirely different. This was never imagined as being part of the plan—I mean, how could it be?—this wasn't part of what I came here for or what I was hoping to find. I simply wanted to find John. To know where he was laid to rest, to visit him, to get closure. It should have never taken me this long to get here, I know that. But I couldn't do it before. I just couldn't ever bring myself to travel to the place that took so much away from me, even if it held the very thing I always wanted to get back."

I swallowed hard, unsure of what to do next. Mae was breaking in a way I hadn't seen anyone come apart before, and the force of it all threatened to crush me. But I couldn't let her go through this alone. I couldn't stand by and watch her fall apart. I wouldn't let that happen.

"Mae," I said, moving toward her slowly, my hand outstretched. She didn't pull away when I touched her arm, but I could feel the tension in her body. I took a deep breath, trying to brace myself. "I think we may have reached the end of this; we've solved the mystery."

Her eyes flashed with something—a mix of pain, frustration, and maybe a sliver of hope. "You really think that's enough? To just say with finality that it's over?"

The unmasked vulnerability in her voice hit me on the chin like an uppercut from a prizefighter, and I could see that she wasn't just talking about the search anymore. She was talking about everything—the secrets, the deceptions, the heartbreak. She wasn't just fighting for answers; she was fighting to keep herself from completely falling apart.

"I think you can," I said quietly. "But you're not alone, Mae, and you don't have to face a single aspect of this on your own. We'll figure out what comes next together."

For a long moment, she didn't say anything. Then, slowly, she nodded. There was a glint of something in her eyes—maybe the first hint of actual relief in weeks, or even longer.

"Alright," she said, her voice stronger now. "What do we do next?"

I was sitting at the kitchen table, staring at the stack of papers from Jacqueline's house, still trying to make sense of it all, when I heard the knock. At first, I thought it was just noise in the hallway or the wind. Or maybe the neighbour's cat was messing around with the door and using it as a scratching post again. But then, another knock, this time more insistent.

I didn't have to look through the peephole; I knew who it was.

Opening the door, I was elated, prepared to hear the sweetest voice, but not the sour words that came next.

"Alex, can we talk?"

My heart stopped, and for a split second, I wondered if I imagined what I'd heard. Maybe the stress of the last few weeks had finally caught up with me. But no, those were Erica's exact words, the same ones that no man ever wants to hear from the woman he loves. When has "we need to talk" ever led to anything good?

Her eyes were dimmed, still full of hurt, but there was also a shimmer of determination. She was holding herself in that way I had come to recognize and admire. The way she stood tall even when the world around her seemed to be crumbling.

"Just listen for a moment before you say anything, please," she said before I could in fact say anything, her voice catching slightly, though she tried to keep it calm. "I'm here because—because I realized something. I can't fix everything, Alex. Not with you, not with Mae, not with me. But I can still try. And I know that I can't just up and run away when things get hard. It's easier, don't get me wrong, but I don't want easy anymore. Easy comes with too much baggage and loneliness and wasted time. We have some work to do, but that's part of it all. There will always be work. The moment it gets easy, that's when we know we're in trouble."

I opened my mouth to say something, anything, but no words came out. I wasn't sure if I should say I was sorry, say I loved you, or say nothing at all. So, I just stood there, frozen, my chest tight with too many emotions to process at once, my legs growing weaker by the second.

After a beat, I took a step forward and decided to deliver everything I'd been practicing in my head. I figured that if I thought too much, I would likely land myself in more trouble than before. Now was the time to recite what I had so often rehearsed in her absence, hoping to all that is holy it didn't come across insincere or trite.

"I know I hurt you, betrayed your trust, and put my own whims and self-interest above anyone or anything else," I said. "And I know that once trust is broken, it's an incredibly difficult thing to get back. I don't want easy either. I want the difficult. I want to do the work."

"I've been thinking," Erica replied. "I've been thinking a lot. And love—love is messy, Alex. It's not easy, but ours is real. I know I left when you needed me, and I regret that. But I also couldn't stay and pretend that you breaking your promise didn't bother me. I couldn't just sweep that under the rug and treat it as a conversation to be picked up later. My fight or flight response kicked in, and I took flight quicker than a dog around a vacuum. I don't know if it was the right thing to do, but it was the right thing for me in that moment. Seems a little silly, I'm sure, to a lot of people, but we all react differently, feel differently, put emphasis on certain things differently. That's what happened here. I made a choice based solely on me. I didn't care to put anyone else's feelings or opinions near the top of my list."

The impact of her words hit me like a freight train, and for a moment, everything felt like it was spiraling out of control. But then, like a beam of light cutting through the fog, I saw the honesty in her eyes. The vulnerability that had always been there, but this time, wasn't guarded.

Again, I didn't know what to say—a far too frequent occurrence today—and I didn't know what forgiveness looked like for either of us, at least not yet. But I knew, in that moment, that I wanted to try. Oh, did I want to try. I wanted to give us the chance to find the pieces of ourselves that had been misplaced in this mess.

"I don't know what else to say," I whispered, my voice thick with emotion. "But I'll start with that fact that I'm glad you're here."

Erica smiled warmly, and for the first time in weeks, the unrelenting tightness in my chest finally shifted and lightened. She was here. That was enough—for now.

"I'm glad too," she said, her voice steady now, no hesitation in it. "And I'm not going anywhere.

There was a moment of silence between us, a drawn out pause where neither of us knew what came next. But that was okay, we didn't have to figure it out all at once.

Sometimes you just have to trust that love—real love, messy love—will lead you where you need to go. And in that moment, I felt like we were on the right path, even if it was just the beginning.

CHAPTER 30
MAE

It started with a smirk.

I could feel it creeping up, pulling at the corners of my mouth as if by some invisible thread. The implications of John's letter, the ramifications of Erica's unannounced return, of every single thing we had been digging up and discovering—it was all still there, pressing down on me. But as I stared at the steadfast group around me, I felt less overwhelmed. Instead, I was feeling something that had been absent for far too long: amusement. And, my dears, it felt wonderful.

"Mae," Luc said warily, leaning back in the rickety kitchen chair, balancing it precariously on two legs. "Why are you smiling like that? It's unnerving. You're scaring me."

"Me?" I said, raising an eyebrow. "I'm not smiling. This is just my face, darling. You're scaring yourself."

He tilted his head like a dog hearing a strange noise. "*Non, non.* That's definitely a smirk on its way to being a smile. *C'est sinistre.* Almost like you're devising plans—evil plans. What are you up to? And, more importantly, how can I be of service?"

I glanced at Alex and Erica, sitting across the table, their faces mirroring each other in mild concern. It was sweet, really, how they both worried about me, but it was also unnecessary.

"I'm just thinking," I said, trying to sound innocent, though such a thing hadn't been true since I was sixteen.

"That's even worse," Luc snorted. "Whenever you start thinking, people end up emotionally bruised. Or physically bruised. Or sometimes both. This much I have come to know about you. And you better believe it will be remembered *dans l'histoire de Caen!*"

"Are you going to keep yammering, or are you going to shut up and help me figure out where we go from here?" I shot back, crossing my arms.

Alex cleared his throat. "Well, you're not wrong, Luc. She has been a little *different* lately."

"Different how?" I asked, narrowing my eyes, scrutinizing him.

"Not *bad* different," Erica said, stepping in quickly, trying to soften the blow. "Just—not the Mae we're used to. You've been so—calm."

"Calm?" I scoffed. "Well, don't get used to it. I tried it on for a while, and it suited me about as well as a thong on a nun."

Luc, returning all legs of his chair to the floor with a graceless thud, leaned forward like he was about to share some insightful piece of wisdom.

"You know, some nuns—"

Mae cut him off immediately.

"*D'accord, d'accord.* You know what the problem is? You're bottling it up," said Luc, pivoting from whatever disgusting anecdote he was about to regale us with. "You've got all your fiery Mae energy inside, and you're just suppressing and suppressing it. It's not right. It's unnatural. It's like—it's like watching *un tigre* pretending to be *un chat domestique*. Sooner or later, you're going to pounce, and when you do, it's going to be spectacular. Terrifying for all involved, but spectacular nonetheless, *ma chère*."

I stared at him, unimpressed.

"I don't bottle things up, Luc," I said amused. He had gotten to know me some, but clearly not well enough. "I'm not some cheap soda you shake up and spray on unsuspecting bystanders."

"Could've fooled me," he muttered.

I rolled my eyes and turned to Alex. "He's your friend. You deal with him."

"Oh no, I'm not getting in the middle of this," Alex said, holding up his hands. "You two can sort it out. And friend is a bit of a stretch, let's be clear about that."

Erica, bless her heart, tried to mediate. "Maybe everyone just needs a break," she suggested. "All of you have been going at this nonstop for weeks. A little downtime wouldn't hurt, right?"

"Now we're talking," Luc grinned. "How about a pub crawl? Mae, you can release all that pent up fiery energy on some poor bartender who doesn't know what's coming."

"Luc, I would love nothing more than to watch you make a fool of yourself. Again," I replied.

"Oh, *madame*, I plan to," he said, winking. "*C'est ma spécialité.*"

Despite myself, I wholeheartedly chuckled. That idiot had a keen way of breaking through even my darkest moods, and I had to admit it: I needed that levity right now.

As the group fell into a lighter rhythm, I felt the onslaught of the past few weeks start to shift. It wasn't gone—not by a long shot—but for the first time since I could recall, it felt manageable. And dammit did I need at least that.

And maybe, just maybe, letting loose a little of my fiery energy wouldn't be the worst thing in the world.

Hence the smirk.

Our pub crawl started as all good pub crawls do: with lofty promises, questionable, clarity-lacking plans, and an idiot—in our case, Luc, naturally—leading the charge like a deranged pied piper.

"First stop, *mes amis*, a little place to set the bar—low, of course, it is only the first stop after all," Luc announced, throwing an arm around Alex and gesturing grandly toward a dimly lit establishment with a crooked sign swinging and creaking precariously in the wind.

"Home to the finest pints of mystery beer and women this side of the Channel," said Luc fondly.

It was clear this bar wasn't the kind of place you intentionally visited; it was the kind of place you stumbled into when your standards had reached rock bottom for the night, and your math looked something like bringing home two threes and calling it a six the next day. The crooked sign looked like it might drop on an unsuspecting patron at any moment, and the heavy wooden door groaned like it hadn't been oiled since Napoleon's last sexcapade.

The atmosphere inside was exactly what you'd expect: dim lighting, a jukebox wheezing out scratchy blues tunes from a distant era, and several patrons who looked like they'd been there since the end of France's temperance movement and were determined to outlast this century too.

Luc strode in like he owned the place, arms wide and grin wider.

"Ah, the smell of history!" he declared, inhaling deeply.

"Nope. It's mildew or mold. Or some other unhealthy thing that starts with the letter M," Alex muttered, stepping around a suspiciously sticky patch on the floor.

The bartender was a wiry man in his sixties with a face like a dried-up riverbed. He looked up from polishing a glass, narrowed his eyes at Luc, and then sighed deeply, as if foreseeing the ridiculousness about to ensue. He must have already been well acquainted with Luc.

"What'll it be, Luc?" the bartender asked, voice rough as sandpaper and just as thin.

So he did know him. That was either good news or bad news for us. We'd have to wait and see.

Luc clapped his hands together.

"Claude, *mon bonhomme*, I'll have your finest—"

"Don't," Alex interrupted, already bracing for Luc's unpalatable idea.

"—mystery beer!" Luc finished, undeterred.

"You sure about that?" asked Claude, raising a bushy eyebrow. "Last time you did that, I was the one stuck carrying your sorry ass into *un taxi*. At my age and with my health, that's a recipe for a *crise cardiaque*. And you, Luc Brassard, are not worth dying for. You don't even pay your tab half the time."

"Ah, but every time, you get paid in stories, captivating stories you can tell your loyal patrons, enticing them to fill another glass—and put more euros in your pockets," said Luc, his hands as animated as his voice. "So *oui, absolument*. Mystery is the spice of life!"

"It's also how you end up regretting your entire life," I said, sliding onto a barstool, a little less gracefully than I used to.

Alex leaned on the bar beside me, shaking his head. "One pint of lager, please. No mystery for me."

"I'll take a cider," Erica said, smiling politely.

"And you, *mademoiselle*?" Claude asked, turning to me.

"Water," I said.

Luc gasped as though I'd committed some grave offense. "Water? In a place like this? Mae, you are killing me! And the water might too! You must believe me when I say filtration is not as high a priority as a well-tapped keg."

"I'll survive," I said dryly. "And so will you"

Luc turned back to Claude, tapping the counter. "Throw in a shot of whatever's in that bottle with the peeling label. *J'aime vivre dangereusement.*"

Claude shrugged and poured him a shot of something the colour and consistency of motor oil.

"*À l'aventure!*" Luc proclaimed, lifting the glass, examining it with the air of a connoisseur before knocking it back. "Sweet *merde*!" His face immediately twisted into a grimace, his eyes watering. "What is this, paint thinner?" he coughed.

"Close enough," Claude said, smirking, clearly enjoying a bit of payback for unpaid tabs and God only knows what else.

Alex and Erica erupted into laughter, and even I couldn't help but crack a smile.

It wasn't long before Luc found his next audience and soon-to-be victims—a table of tourists chatting animatedly in the corner. Not wanting to miss an opportunity to show off, he approached with all the swagger of a man who had no idea how off-putting his so-called charm really was.

"Bonjour, *mes amis*!" he greeted them, leaning theatrically on the edge of their table.

The group fell silent, gaping at him in bewilderment

One of the women, a petite brunette with a bright red scarf, raised an eyebrow. "You are—how do you say—ridiculous."

The rest of her tablemates burst out laughing, and so did I, though I tried to hide it behind my hand.

"Ah, but a *charming* kind of ridiculous, *non?*" Luc said, flashing his most disarming smile.

"No," she said flatly, and the laughter doubled.

As expected, Luc clutched his chest as if she'd seriously harmed him. "*Mon cœur!* How you wound me!"

"Keep talking," Alex cried from the bar. "She might actually finish the job. And if she does, we'll buy the next round!"

Undeterred, Luc launched into a story about how his great-great-something-or-other had once charmed a duchess in Paris, complete with exaggerated gestures and comical accents that shifted wildly between French, Italian, and something that might have been a Russian penguin.

The tourists were in tears by the time he finished—not from awe or emotion, but from laughing so hard at him they could barely breathe.

"Another round for our *nouveaux amis!*" Luc called to Claude, triumphant.

"I think he's finally found his audience," Alex said, smirking.

"Don't encourage him," I said, shaking my head.

By the time we left, Luc was practically floating and glowing with self-satisfaction, Erica was giggling uncontrollably, and Alex was muttering something about prohibiting Luc from speaking to tourists ever again.

"You, *mon ami*, are just jealous of my international appeal," Luc said, slinging an arm around Alex's shoulders as we stepped into the night.

"I'm jealous of your complete lack of shame," Alex replied.

"And Mae!" Luc called, turning to me. "Admit it—you had fun."

"I admit nothing," I said, though I couldn't entirely hide my smile.

The night was just getting started, and I had a feeling it was only going to get more ludicrous from here. I was contemplating my exit plan. I was tired and rest was finally calling my name.

The next establishment was everything the first one wasn't—polished, refined, and infused with a tasteful charm that practically proclaimed romance. It also included one more guest. Jacqueline was outside, waiting under the stylish sign above the entrance. The accoutrements of the place—gilded and scripted door glowing under the streetlamps, windows decorated with delicate lace curtains, flower boxes brimming with violets—offered a far more welcoming sight than the full-of-contempt seventy-eight-year-old French woman.

"*Assurément*, I was not going to miss out on whatever this is," Jacqueline said, waving her hands toward us.

After a small round of what can best be described as pleasantries, we moved inside, the ambiance inviting and sophisticated, with warm golden lighting, dark wood paneling, and shelves lined with wine bottles that I'm sure cost a small fortune. French music played in the background. The melodies were those that made you feel like you were in a black-and-white film where someone was about to profess their enduring love or confess to a scandalous betrayal. One of those things was going to be true, and it really was a coin flip based on our recent history.

"Now this," Luc declared as we stepped inside, "is where I truly belong."

"Let me guess," Alex said, smirking. "You're going to claim it smells like history again?"

"*Non*," Luc replied, straightening his jacket. "It is much more than that. It smells like destiny."

"I'm pretty sure that's just the cheese plate," Erica said, nodding toward a server walking by with an elaborate tray of brie, camembert, and what looked like a wheel of something with a rind older than me.

"We'll take one of those," Luc said, catching the server's attention with a confident snap of his fingers.

The man barely glanced at him. "Table first, *monsieur*."

Luc feigned indignation, placing a hand over his heart. "I'm being oppressed! In my own city!"

"Let's find a table before you get us kicked out," I said, steering him toward a corner booth near a window.

Once seated, we ordered a round of drinks—white wine for Erica and Jacqueline, some fancy-pants beer for Alex, and sparkling water for me. Luc, of course, insisted on being his extra self.

"*Un verre de votre meilleur vin rouge, s'il vous plaît!*" he announced, loud enough for half the place to hear.

The server raised an unimpressed eyebrow. "You want the house red?" He asked this with a degree of uncertainty as to whether Luc was indeed a traditional Frenchman, or if he was some obnoxious foreigner who had picked up just enough of the language to come off as a complete douche canoe.

"*Oui!*" Luc said, unbothered. "But say it *en français*—it sounds so much better."

"*Le vin de la maison*," the server replied flatly.

"*Magnifique!*" Luc exclaimed, beaming.

When the drinks arrived, so did a plate of hors d'oeuvres—slices of baguette topped with pâté, cured meats, and slivers of cheese. Not the cheese plate Luc had originally had his eye on, but something that would no doubt stir the stomachs of my band of blubbering fools.

"I feel like I should be wearing pearls," Erica said, delicately nibbling on a crostini.

"You would look *fabuleuse*," Luc said, raising his glass to her. "Cheers to pearls, pâté, and *je ne sais quoi!*"

"Well, I can't do pearls—" said Alex, looking about as comfortable as a nun in a strip club.

Just as we were about to raise our glasses, a distinct, elegant sound drifted toward us. A string quartet, subtly entering from behind a velvet curtain, began to play a beautiful rendition of "Clair de Lune", their delicate violins and cello filling the air with a romantic ambiance that heightened the significance of what was unfolding before our eyes. The music enveloped us like a warm embrace and set the perfect tone for what was happening.

That sly devil.

From the corner of the room, a server emerged with a bouquet of violets and white roses—Erica's favourites, as I remembered. The bouquet was placed gently on the table, its sweet fragrance mingling with the music and enhancing the moment. The pale purple and pure white petals seemed to shimmer and glow under the lighting, making everything feel like a heartfelt scene out of a movie.

I glanced at Jacqueline, and she gave me a knowing look that said, "of course they came from my shop. I am a florist."

Alex, whose nervousness had not disappeared but rather intensified with each passing second, stood up, his face an in-the-works canvas of determination and love. He cleared his throat, his gaze sweeping across all of us before settling on Erica.

He lifted his glass, but this time he didn't drink—he began to speak, his voice more assured and affected by the significance of this moment, a moment that if he got right, would be the only one of its kind he would ever experience.

Please let him only have to go through this once.

"I've watched Mae, day after day, in the most difficult circumstances, giving everything of herself—her devotion, her energy, her heart. And, through his letters and his actions described within them, John has shown me that love isn't this easy thing that simply exists without fear, trepidation, and unsureness. Love is not just about grand gestures or perfect words." Alex paused, eyes glistening for a moment, the words seeming to be more than just his own. "Love is about the small, simple things. The sacrifices. The way we forgive, the way we offer support and work together. Even when it feels impossible, even when everything else feels like it's falling apart, love gives us something to hold on to."

Erica's wide eyes gleamed, her hand resting gently in Alex's.

"Mae taught me that love isn't just for the good moments," Alex continued, his tone growing more impassioned. "It's not just for when the sky is clear and the sun is shining. It's what reinforces us when the dark clouds roll in and the storm is raging. It's what helps us rebuild, even when we feel like we've lost everything."

I could see the emotion building inside of him as he looked intently at Erica; I knew this wasn't just a proposal—it was the culmination of everything he had come to understand about love, sacrifice, and hope.

"Mae also taught me that love is not always easy," Alex

went on, his gaze never leaving Erica. "But if we fight for it, if we hold on to it no matter what, every single moment is worth it. This has been a crazy adventure that has shown me that real love endures even through the hardest moments, the most unpredictable, challenging, and uncertain times. And that's why, being here right now, I can't imagine anything more important than spending my life with someone who I know can endure everything this life will throw our way."

The music swelled, the room seemed to pause in anticipation; everyone was watching, their eyes focused on these two young people in a moment of profound connection. There was no mistaking it—this was a declaration of love that would carry Alex and Erica forward, no matter what life had in store. I could clearly see John in Alex in this moment—the resolve and the passion, the love and the vulnerability. And yes, even the endearing stupidity that envelopes a love-struck man.

Alex squeezed Erica's hand, the bouquet of violets and roses resting between them. He smiled, a hint of mischief playing at the corners of his lips, and finally, dropping to one knee, he asked her.

"Erica, will you marry me? Will you build a life with me, even when it's messy, even when it's difficult?"

Erica, eyes bright and wet with tears, nodded without hesitation.

"Yes, Alex. I would want nothing more."

The string quartet began playing a new tune, something more upbeat to match the celebratory moment, and the room erupted into applause, the sound resonating around us as Alex stood up and pulled Erica into his arms, his lips finding hers in a kiss that sealed the promise of their union.

And in that sliver of time, I knew that love, as John had

always said, had the power to transcend and conquer everything. It had conquered doubt, distance, and fear. It had created something beautiful and enduring, no matter the odds. And dammit if that son of a bitch didn't make me shed another tear.

As the night progressed, we moved from pub to pub and Luc managed to charm—or annoy—almost everyone at every place.

At one stop, he struck up a conversation with a group of older gentlemen playing cards at a nearby table, regaling them with what he called his "French lineage."

"My *arrière-grand-père* fought alongside the French Resistance," he claimed, gesturing dramatically.

"*Vraiment?*" one of the men asked, leaning forward.

"Well, not directly *alongside*," Luc admitted. "He supported them from—afar. *Avec des lettres*. And moral encouragement."

The men burst out laughing, slapping the table, and one even offered him a cigar.

At another location, Luc spotted a group of women at the bar and decided it was his duty, his *responsibility*, to mingle. He strutted over, wine glass in hand, and introduced himself with a theatrical bow. With Alex and Erica lost amid the blissful waves of their engagement, Luc seemed to turn things up several notches, now playing for the whole table instead of just himself.

"*Bonsoir, Mesdames. Je suis* Luc. But you may call me *mon héros.*"

One of the women, a chic blonde in a beret, turned to him with a raised eyebrow. "And why would we do that?"

"Because tonight, I will rescue you from boredom!" he declared, grinning.

The group exchanged glances, and the blonde smirked. "All right, *mon héros*. What's your plan?"

Luc faltered, clearly having not thought that far ahead. "I will—I will dazzle you with—my dance moves!"

Before any of us could stop him, he climbed onto an empty section of the bar and began to sway awkwardly to the music.

"*Mon Dieu*," the bartender groaned, looking unamused.

Alex buried his face in his hands. "Why do we let him out in public?"

"I live for this," Erica said, tears of laughter streaming down her face. Nothing was getting in the way of her sheer happiness.

"And I could live without it," said Jacqueline, though there was a faint betrayal of enjoyment flickering in her deep brown eyes.

Luc twirled dramatically, nearly knocking over a row of glasses, and ended with an exaggerated bow that sent him tumbling off the bar and into the arms of the blonde, who caught him with surprising agility.

"You're insane," she said, laughing despite herself.

"*Oui*," Luc agreed, brushing imaginary dust off his shirt. "But in a charming way, *non?*"

The blonde shook her head but still handed him a napkin with her number scribbled on it.

Luc returned to our table triumphant, waving the napkin like a trophy. "Ladies and gentlemen, *je suis irrésistible!*"

"You're lucky you didn't break anything," I said, though I couldn't contain my smile.

As the night wore on, even I couldn't help but relax. There was something about watching Luc make a fool of himself in such an unselfconscious way that was oddly therapeutic. For a little while, everything—the letters, the history, the questions I still had—seemed almost nonexistent.

"This was a good idea," Erica said, leaning back in her chair and sipping her wine. "And not just because it gained me a fabulous new piece of jewellery I can show off."

"Even with Luc?" Alex asked, smirking, caressing her hand.

"Especially with Luc," she replied.

"Well, *les enfants*, my night has come to an end," said Jacqueline. "This was, admittedly, more fun than I expected, and I will be honest, I'm truly *enthousiaste pour les nouveaux fiancés*, but please don't take it the wrong way when I tell you I hope this is the last we'll ever see of each other."

"Jacqueline," said Alex, "thank you for everything, truly."

"*Oui*," said Luc. "Who would have thought I would discover a new friend during *cette aventure*."

"Well, I don't know about friend, but I won't call *la police* the next time you happen to enter my shop," said Jacqueline. "And that counts for something."

"Thank you, Jacqueline," I said, properly putting a bow on this goodbye. "I didn't know I'd need you—or even want you—to be a part of all of this, but when life gives you lemons, you take a sour piss."

"A sour piss? I am sorry, I am not familiar with that saying, but I will certainly use it when I can. Perhaps a new bouquet, *pisse aigre*, just for Luc's *amours*."

I allowed myself to laugh without reservation. And with that, I too said goodnight and sidled off back home, leaving the young ones to have their fun. Their stories would be told the next day, and forever more.

That's the thing about stories. They live long after you do.

CHAPTER 31
ALEX

THE NEXT MORNING, I woke up feeling like I'd been the Hulk's punching bag, and then dragged across the floor for good measure. My mouth was dry as a desert, my head throbbed with a consistent, merciless rhythm, and with every movement I made, it felt like my body was punishing me for crimes I couldn't quite remember committing. The faint light filtering through the curtains was still too bright, and the half-empty glass of water on the nightstand mocked me for not finishing it before falling asleep.

But then I remembered: I'm engaged.

Suddenly, the hangover didn't seem quite as harsh, the world not nearly as loud. I was still wandering somewhere within the seven circles of hell, but knowing I now had a partner by my side made it easier to endure.

Across the apartment, I could hear Luc's melodramatic groans. His muffled voice floated from the couch. "My tongue feels like it's wearing a wool sweater."

Erica was already up, sitting at the kitchen table with a mug of coffee in hand, scrolling through her phone and glancing at the ring now at home on the fourth finger of her left hand. She was the picture of grace and composure. She raised a curious eyebrow at me as I stumbled in.

"How are you alive and functioning right now?" I asked, collapsing into a chair.

"Because I didn't drink my body weight in cheap booze," she said without looking up. "Also, hydration. It's a magical thing. You'd be amazed how your body feels when you drink a little water. In case you didn't notice, and I know that you didn't, in between each slowly consumed drink I had, I alternated with a glass of water."

Mae breezed into the room moments later, looking annoyingly well-rested and being equally annoyingly smug about it. She had a self-satisfied look about her—like she'd spent the morning solving crossword puzzles in pen and drinking tea while the rest of us were trying to remember our own names.

"Good morning, schmuck," she said, smirking as she placed a steaming cup of coffee in front of me.

"Don't," I groaned, clutching the mug like a lifeline.

Then Luc shambled over, completing the duo of hungover misfits. He was still wearing his shirt from the night before, though it was half-untucked, wrinkled, and featured a suspicious red lipstick stain on the collar. His hair stuck up in every possible direction, defying gravity and all accepted standards of good grooming.

"Why do you look like you got dragged out of a nightclub by a tornado?" Erica asked, barely containing her laughter. "I'd swear you weren't out of our sight all that often, and yet I can't conceive how you ended up like—like this."

"I regret nothing," Luc said, flopping into a chair with a groan.

Mae smirked and raised an eyebrow. "Not even dancing on the bar?"

"Especially not that," Luc replied, his grin only slightly diminished by the pain it clearly caused him.

We all fell into an easy rhythm after that—coffee, mild teasing, and slow, peaceful recovery. I was starting to feel half-way human again when there was a knock at the door. Mae rose to answer it, her expression shifting from curiosity to confusion as she opened the door.

"Uh, Alex? You might want to come here," she called over her shoulder.

My stomach clenched, then flipped. Was it the police? The museum staff? Someone to collect on any of Luc's outstanding bar tabs?

When I joined Mae at the door, I froze. Standing there in her uniform was Claire, the security guard from the museum.

"*Bonjour*," she said, holding out a small, battered folder. "You dropped this on your way out."

The atmosphere in the room suddenly shifted, taking on a note of cautious expectancy.

"What's this?" I asked, staring at her like she'd just handed me the Ark of the Covenant.

She shrugged, her expression unreadable. "I found it near the exit. I was going to put it back, but bringing it here gives me a chance to see *monsieur* again."

Luc appeared behind me, his grin wide despite his obvious hangover. "Ah, Claire! Did you miss me already?"

She rolled her eyes. "Not in the slightest."

"Harsh," Luc said, clutching his chest like he'd been dealt a blow. "But fair. Give it time. Absence does make the heart grow fonder. All you need is a little more time."

Claire took a step forward, kissed Luc square on the mouth, and then promptly slapped him twice—once forward, once back. I was deeply jealous. Not of the kiss, but oh, how I'd love to slap Luc.

"*T'es une cochonne*! I can smell the perfume all over you."

"Can I get a translation?" I asked.

"She called me a pig," said Luc, rubbing his right cheek but smiling voraciously.

Mae stepped forward, her tone careful.

"Why didn't you just return this to where it belonged?" she asked. "And, maybe more importantly, how did you even know where to find us?"

Claire hesitated, trying to decide which question to answer first.

"I saw some of what was inside," she admitted, lowering her voice. "It didn't seem like material anyone had thought about, let alone cared about, for a long time. But you—" She glanced around the room, taking it all in, her gaze returning to Mae, "you seemed to care. You spent hours in *mon musée*, and only someone truly searching for an answer would do that."

She handed the folder to Mae and turned to leave.

"Wait!" Mae called after her. "You didn't answer the second question."

"Well, before Luc fled, he slipped an address into my pocket. He told me it wasn't *chez lui*, but that I could often find him there. It seemed a little odd, but I kept it anyway. I've checked this place out a few times and recognized the three of you—*et qui est-elle, Luc*? And did you *propose* to *her*?"

All eyes shifted to an unsuspecting Erica, the focal point of this misinterpretation.

"Me?" asked Erica, pointing a finger back in her own direction and laughing. "No. No, no, no, no, you can't be—no, just no. Ha. No, no, no."

"Ouch," said Luc. "That's a lot of no's."

I was starting to develop an inferiority complex. Was it really that unimaginable this stunning woman could be interested and committed to me instead of Luc? Surely, that couldn't be the first logical option. Mae was getting a good kick out of it.

As Claire gave Luc a disgusted then sultry look, she pivoted and headed out the door—and out of his life.

"*Attends!*" he shouted. "Before you go, at least tell me when I'll see you again."

She didn't look back. "Maybe tomorrow. Maybe never," she said over her shoulder before disappearing down the hall. It couldn't have mattered less; they were made for each other.

"Claire. A name as beautiful as the woman herself," Luc sighed dreamily.

"Focus, Romeo," Mae said, clearing her throat.

Erica took the folder from Mae's outstretched hands, spreading its contents across the kitchen table. Inside were half a dozen letters, the paper yellowed and brittle with age, but the handwriting was unmistakably John's.

"What are the odds?" Erica murmured, carefully smoothing one out.

Mae hovered close to the table, her expression tight. "You've got to be kidding me," she said, not with pleasure but rather in defeat. "How many more fucking letters did this man write? I swear to God he's lucky he's not here to feel my wrath. But I suppose we should get on with it. Let's see what he has to say."

I leaned in, and as I started reading, a familiar ache settled upon me. These letters weren't like the others we'd previously seen. They weren't written to Yvette or Jacqueline. They were reports—letters to John's commanding officer, each one detailing the horrors he'd witnessed and the impossible choices he'd been forced to make.

One letter—one paragraph—in particular, caught my eye.

The girl—Jacqueline—is alone now. Her mother has died, and there is no one else. I cannot, in good conscience, leave her here. If we are to call ourselves liberators, we must act like it. I am requesting permission to escort her to safety, to find her a place where she can live without fear. If I am to be a father myself someday, I must prove worthy of that title now. I await your orders.

I leaned back in my chair, John's words and convictions pressing down on me. "He really couldn't turn his back and leave her behind," I said.

"No," Mae said, her voice barely audible. "He couldn't."

The room fell silent, the gravity of John's actions and intentions sinking in. Then, of course, Luc broke the tension.

"Well," he said, leaning back with his signature grin. "It looks like my daring escapades have once again paid off and saved the day."

Erica threw a balled-up napkin at him. "Claire saved the day, you idiot. Though I'm not sure how. How was this day saved exactly?"

"Semantics," he replied, dodging the napkin with exaggerated flair.

Despite everything, I laughed. It was absurd, all of it. But somehow, in the midst of the upheaval, we were piecing together a story that had been lost for decades.

And as much as Mae had convinced us we were done,

that there was nothing left to find, nothing more to know, I couldn't shake the nagging feeling that we hadn't definitively written *The End* on this whole thing.

The cemetery was silent, the kind of silence that allowed you to hear things you normally wouldn't notice elsewhere: the soft rustling of leaves, the distant breath of the wind, the sound of your own thoughts as they paraded through your head. Mae walked a few steps ahead of me, her hands stuffed in her coat pockets, her eyes fixed on the path that twisted through the rows of weathered headstones.

We'd been here before, but no two days with Mae are ever the same, and when you throw in a deceased war-hero husband that she's been searching for her entire life, well, then it definitely won't be the same as any other day. Maybe it was the accumulation of everything we'd uncovered, the assembled fragments of a life that had been hidden away for so long. Or maybe it was my dawning understanding of the magnitude of it all—for Mae, for John, hell, for everyone.

When we reached John's grave, Mae stopped and stood in silence for a moment, her head bowed. The headstone was elegant in its simplicity, engraved with his name, his rank, and the years of a life that had ended far too soon. In a lot of ways, it was no different than any other stone here. But, to each connection still living, these markers were as unique as snowflakes. Mae crouched down, brushing some leaves and other natural debris away, her fingers lingering on the cool stone.

Not knowing what to say, I blurted out, "What now?" not realizing how harsh and insensitive such an abrupt question was given the circumstances.

She didn't answer right away. Instead, she stared at the grave like she was searching for something she couldn't quite articulate.

Finally, she stood up, dusting off her hands.

"I'm not sure," she said. "I thought I'd feel—something. I don't know what exactly. Closure, maybe? Like there'd be some sense of finality to all of this."

"And you don't?"

"No." She shook her head. "If anything, I feel more restless. Like there are still pieces missing. And before you start, yes, I know that is crazy. I know we've closed the book on this one, my dear boy. Just let this old lady have her crazy thoughts without question, would ya?"

At that, I wandered off, letting her ruminate at the grave while I leaned against a nearby tree, watching her. After a few minutes, and mostly because she hadn't moved and I wondered if perhaps she had frozen in place, I wandered back over to check on her.

Upon noticing that she was still with me, I couldn't help but ask, "Why, Mae? Why does it matter so much to you? What are you really trying to get out of this?"

She turned to look at me, her expression unreadable at first. Then she sighed, crossing her arms.

"At first, it was about finding John—being able to come here and talk to him, to be with him until my time ran out. It's a frantic world out there, but look around, this corner of it—this place—is beautiful. The food is delicious. The people are—well, people. I've got everything I need to live a nice little life. Hell, you and Erica even showed up. What more could I ask for?

"And then it became about the letters. About finding out who Jacqueline really was—what her connection to John was and whether she was in fact his daughter. Of course, we know now that she's not, but those letters provided me with a strange, renewed sense of purpose and life. They made me feel again. Sure, the feelings were laced with anger and hate, misguided as it all was, but to not feel the acute pain of sadness and loss was a welcome reprieve. As tiring and disheartening as it became, it was nice to feel something else for a short while. I don't need to recount it all, you were here for it, you saw everything play out in real time.

"But now, I don't know. Something is still missing. Not a piece of the puzzle, that bugger is sewed up tighter than a nun's cooter. There's just this unsettled, uneasy feeling I have—can't name it, can't place it. And, at my age, that could be anything from an existential crisis to constipation, neither of which I'm much in the mood for. To put it plainly, it just feels bigger."

"Bigger how?"

She hesitated, her facial expression signalling she was unsure how to properly convey the scale of it with words. This much was clear from her rambling recounting of what had taken place over these last few months.

"I've spent so much of my life trying to move forward, trying to build something stable for myself. But no matter what I did or how far I went, there was always this pull from the past—this need to look back and understand the parts of John's life I never got to know. I wanted to fill in the blanks so I could know him better, even if it happened decades too late. Maybe it was selfish and juvenile and foolish of me to think I could make up for lost time with someone who no longer existed, except in memory."

"Mae, just remember who you're talking to," I said, smiling kindly. "You're describing the catalyst for our whole relationship. And, I'll remind you as you once did for me: it's not selfish. This is human nature, it's how we're wired. And honestly, I'm not sure I'd have it any other way."

She smiled, her gaze drifting back to the grave.

"And now that I do know more, I'm not sure what to do with it. Part of me wants to stop here. To let it be. But another part of me—I don't know, I feel like I owe it to him to keep going. To make sure his story, and Jacqueline's story, don't get lost again. How many other children might he have saved? How many of them are still here, living a life because of his brave and noble actions?"

I stepped closer, dropping my voice.

"Mae, the fact that he came here in the first place and made the ultimate sacrifice means that what he gave to Jacqueline he also gave to generations of other kids. It may not have been in such a direct and intentional manner, but we're here because of him. And that's pretty damn special. But, what about you? What do you want for yourself in all of this?"

"I don't know," she admitted, looking down. When she met my eyes, and for the first time, I saw a flicker of uncertainty in her. "I thought that by doing this, I'd have figured that out too. Ah, the grand delusions of an old lady."

We stood there in silence for a while, the wind picking up around us.

"You know," I said, trying to lighten the mood, "Luc would probably suggest we hold some kind of grand presentation of the letters. Like rent out a theater, sell tickets, and have him narrate the whole thing in his so-called 'sexy museum voice.'"

Mae laughed, the sound breaking through the heaviness like sunlight through clouds. "His *sexy museum voice*? Is that what he calls it?"

"Apparently," I said, grinning. "He's convinced it's his greatest asset. Personally, I think it's his ability to talk his way out of trouble. Or into it, depending on the day."

She shook her head, still smiling. "He's absolutely ridiculous."

"That he is," I said, putting my arm around her. "But he's also part of this story, whether we like it or not. We all are."

"I guess that's true," she agreed. Her smile faded a little, but there was still a glow in her eyes. "Bloody hell, how do I end up with the people I do?"

As we turned to leave, I glanced back at John's grave one last time. There was so much history buried here, so many stories that would never be fully known and told. But maybe that was okay. Maybe it was time for us to let some of that history settle back into the earth, our hands having dug up and disrupted it enough for a long while.

"Mae," I said as we walked back to the car.

"Yeah?"

"You'll figure it out. Whatever you're looking for, you'll find it. And if you don't, we'll keep looking until you do."

She didn't say anything, but the look she gave me said enough.

"Oh, and another thing," I said. "Have you ever noticed that you're always so much nicer to me when we're in a cemetery? If it's not too much to ask, and I'm not talking about a full transition, what do you say we carry some of that forward to other locations?"

"Watch yourself, Sonny," she said. "The dead may be watching but I'm not above delivering some pain to those skinny shins of yours in front of all these ghosts."

"Message received," I said, appreciating that she would never change.

CHAPTER 32
MAE

YOU'LL FIGURE IT OUT. We'll keep looking until you do.

As we walked back to the car, Alex's words echoed like they were supposed to mean something—like they were supposed to reassure me.

The truth was, I had already figured it out.

I knew exactly what my next steps were, and that's precisely why I couldn't tell him. He would have tried to talk me out of it. He'd say it was too much of a gamble, too impulsive, too risky, too final. But that's okay, he was still young enough to think he would live forever; all young men do. But I didn't need Alex's approval or blessing, not for this. And hell, maybe he'd have been right, but you can bet your ample ass that I wouldn't give him that satisfaction.

There comes a time in our lives when what's next is less of a big picture plan and more of a literal next minute decision. I was at that point. There was nothing grand left for me, not in the scope of my life, and my nexts were whatever was waiting for me at the conclusion of each breath, each thought. I was finally starting to come to peace with this, and truthfully, it was calming—and that was reassuring.

It pained me to admit it, but somehow, this young man, who in many ways reminded me of John, was the only person I had truly let into my life in a very, very long time. And having him here with me now was exactly what I needed—though I'd never admit it aloud lest he get an inflated ego and develop a completely misplaced sense of self-importance.

When we reached the car, Alex tossed his jacket in the back seat and leaned against the driver's side door, stretching his arms like he was shaking off the morning, which he probably still was.

"You good to go?" he asked.

"Yeah, Sonny," I nodded, trying to keep my expression neutral. "I'm good."

We climbed in, and as he started the engine, I caught my reflection in the side mirror. I looked calm, composed, maybe a little tired—but inside, beneath the surface, my mind was racing the way it does when processing big decisions you're not entirely sure of. Even if deep down you are entirely sure of them.

Alex's questions in the cemetery had hit closer to home than I'd let on. What *was* I really trying to get out of all this? For months, I'd been telling myself it was about John, about Jacqueline, about piecing together all the fragments of a tangled story that had been lost to time.

But that wasn't the whole truth.

The whole truth was something I hadn't even admitted to myself until now. This wasn't just about uncovering the past of others; it was about confronting my own. About proving something to myself. About finally doing the one thing I'd spent my entire life avoiding: taking a leap without a safety net.

As Alex drove, I stared out the window, watching the countryside blur past. I could feel him glancing at me every so often, probably wondering what I was thinking. But I wasn't going to give him the gratification of asking.

Instead, I said, "Thanks for coming out here with me. I know this isn't exactly how you planned to spend the day after your engagement."

"It's fine," he shrugged, his eyes on the road. "I wouldn't have come this far if I didn't want to be here."

And that was quintessential Alex. Always loyal, always reliable. Always the voice of reason.

And that's exactly why he couldn't know what I was planning.

Back at the apartment, I made an excuse to slip away, telling Alex I needed some air. He didn't question it, just nodded and accepted the spare key, letting himself in while I took off.

The city was coming alive in a way that felt almost mocking—couples strolling hand in hand, street performers drawing small crowds, occasional bursts of laughter floating from a nearby café.

I ducked into an empty side street, pulling out my phone. It rang twice before a familiar voice answered. "*Allô?*"

"Hey, it's Mae," I said, keeping my volume low. "I need a favour."

There was a pause, and then a chuckle. "*Un service?* From me? This should be good."

I ignored the teasing tone. "I need you to get me into the archives at the museum again. Tonight."

"*Ce soir?*" Luc's tone was incredulous. "You know we're already on thin ice with the lovely Claire, *oui?* Or did you forget the part where I was almost arrested and, even more recently, when I had *mon cœur* stomped on at your apartment?"

"I didn't forget, and you can dial down the drama just this once," I said, somewhat annoyed. "This is important."

"More important than me staying out of jail?"

"Yes," I said without hesitation.

Luc sighed, and I could picture him rubbing his temples with faux frustration, all the while giddy with delight at the mere thought of another clandestine caper.

"You're lucky I'm a sucker for *une bonne aventure.* Meet me there *à minuit.*"

"Thank you," I said, relief flooding through me.

"Don't thank me yet," he muttered. "And for the record, Claire scares me now. If this blows up in our faces, and I fully expect it will, you're the one explaining everything to Alex."

I hung up without replying, slipping the phone back into my pocket.

Alex didn't need to know about this. Not yet.

For now, I had a plan. And nothing—not Alex's skepticism, not Luc's complaints, not even my own nagging doubts—was going to stop me from seeing it through.

It was a surreal feeling, carrying these pieces of history in my arms as I walked through Caen's empty streets after hours. The satchel hung bulky over my shoulder, filled with the letters, photos, and mementos we'd unearthed—each item a fragment of someone else's life, someone else's story. As much as they were John's, so much time had passed that they no longer felt closely connected. They had become the stories of other people.

But not mine. I no longer needed them.

By the time I reached the museum steps, the city had settled into its nighttime rhythm: muffled music and laughter from a nearby bar, the occasional burst of a scooter passing by, the murmur of a radio spilling through an open window. It was the kind of tranquility I'd been chasing for a long time, and tonight it felt like the ideal backdrop to something significant.

I climbed the steps deliberately, each one reminding me of what I was about to do. At the entrance, I paused, glancing at the bag slung over my shoulder. Luc met me at the top of the steps, emerging from behind a concrete column, and absolutely scaring the shit out of me.

"Jesus H. Christ," I squealed. "What the fuck is wrong with you? Why can't you be mostly normal and just be patiently waiting here at the top?"

"What do you think the H stands for?" he asked, his voice sincere with curiosity, even as he ignored my questions.

"I don't know, Harold?" I said. "Our father who art in heaven, Harold be thy name? Does it really matter?"

"*Non*, I suppose it doesn't," he said, amused. "But I like that—Jesus Harold Christ."

Luc went to work picking the lock, brazen in his attempt to do so at the front door. I'm sure we were all over the security footage, but that was something Luc could deal with. I had no intention of facing whatever breaking-and-entering charges might come my way. And besides, we were breaking in to put something back, not to steal anything. That had to count for something. Would they really be that upset?

Inside, the museum was completely silent, the exhibits resting in their curated stillness. I made my way to the room we first stumbled into while trying to escape conviction—or at least I think it was the one; they all looked alike. Just outside, Luc had nearly charmed his way into permanent trouble. He'd likely dodged a bullet with Claire; there was something a little too combustible about her. And her judgment? Well, it left a heaping spoonful to be desired.

But I smiled at the memory. How many more like it would I get the pleasure of retaining from here on out?

Setting the satchel down on a large wooden table, I began unpacking its contents. The letters went first, tossed casually on the table near some boxes they likely would have been stored in before we'd scattered them across pub and apartment tables. Then the photographs, each one slipped back into its protective sleeve, their edges worn with age, the faces staring out from a distant time.

The weight on my shoulders lightened with each item I returned, figurative and literal.

All except one.

At the bottom of the bag, tucked carefully in a side pocket, was the letter I couldn't let go of, the letter that would set me free and help everyone understand what I was about to do.

It wasn't for me to keep. But it wasn't for the museum either.

Tomorrow, I'd clear the apartment of everything else not belonging to this place—the letters, the photos, the artifacts we'd collected. They didn't belong with me or Luc or anyone else anymore. And as much as I hated to admit it, neither did I.

For the first time in a very long while, I knew exactly what I needed to do. And nothing—not Alex, not Erica, not Luc, not Jacqueline, not even my own doubts—was going to stop me.

CHAPTER 33
ALEX

THE NIGHT UNFOLDED exactly how it should have. After days of tension and discovery, it felt like everything had finally shifted into its rightful place. Erica and I laughed over dinner—a delicious treat that accompanied a night in a suite at a nearby hotel—letting the hum of the restaurant and the clatter of cutlery and plates fade into the background. It was a rare, peaceful evening where we weren't chasing down ghosts, delving into old secrets, or dealing with unfinished business. It was nothing short of blissful. It was how life was supposed to be lived: in the present.

Mae had finally found the peace she needed, and I could see it reflected in her eyes—an unspoken serenity that had eluded her for, well, pretty much all her life. She had come to terms with her past and the past of others, accepting the outcomes of everything we'd uncovered—and I was proud of her. Proud of us all. Somehow we came together and managed to get through this relatively unscathed, at least by our group's standards, and now had more to look forward to than ever before.

By the time Erica and I found ourselves at the small hotel overlooking the river, the night felt like a perfect punctuation mark on the tumultuous adventure we'd survived. The room was simple yet elegantly tasteful. The city lights twinkled just beyond the windows, casting an ethereal glow over us as we moved with ease in and out of each other's space. I pulled Erica close, our bodies swaying together in the rhythm of a loving dance, more intimate than anything we'd shared before.

Everything was just right.

I led Erica to the bed, and we spent the next few hours talking about nothing and everything—about life, the future, what we wanted next. I could tell she was happy, but there was something deeper there too, something that I knew I needed to address before the night ended.

As she brushed her hair away from her face, her smile softened.

"You've been on the quiet side, you know. Everything okay?"

"Yeah," I said, meaning it. "I guess I've just been reflecting, really absorbing all that's happened this last little while. Especially the replay of you saying 'yes.'"

"Well, you're not alone there," she said, smiling more with her eyes than her mouth. "That's one of those core memories you never forget. And to be honest, I didn't know you had that in you."

It was true, I didn't have that in me, but thankfully Luc did. It wasn't just a proposal; it was a moment orchestrated with thoughtful care, designed to be everything Erica deserved and more. Luc, of all people, was the very person I needed to help me plan it and pull it off. He insisted on flowers, music, and a setting that was steeped in romance.

"Trust me, *mon frère*," he'd said with a beaming grin that could have charmed a stone. "You cannot do this halfway. Take it from me—love is a performance."

Luc had been right, of course, and the string quartet had been the perfect touch. The soft strains of the violins had floated around us like a warm breeze, and Erica's eyes had shimmered with joyful surprise as I knelt before her.

I didn't just ask Erica to marry me—I told her everything I'd learned from observing Mae's resilience and John's unwavering love. I recounted how love could survive anything, even the very worst the world had to offer. How love, despite its flaws and failings, had a way of finding its footing. It was literally the greatest speech I had ever given in my life. And what's more, for the first time in my life, I truly believed that love wasn't just an abstract idea or a fleeting feeling—it was a choice. A promise. I thought I had that with Autumn, and maybe to some degree I did, but considering how completely different this felt, I wasn't so sure anymore.

"So, what does life look like now?" she asked, running a finger down my arm.

"What does life look like? Well, it looks like Sunday mornings spent tangled in bedsheets, the smell of freshly brewed coffee filling the air, coaxing us to get up. It looks like silly squabbles over paint colours for walls we'd eventually love. It looks like road trips to nowhere in particular, laughter over shared memories, and holding each other's hands when life inevitably throws its punches. It looks like kids running around and driving us the right kind of crazy. It looks like family—not picture-perfect, but undeniably ours."

"Wow," said Erica, gazing at me intently.

"Is that a good wow?" I asked, somewhat unsure and with

a hint of anxiety scratching to creep in.

"It's a very good wow," she said before kissing me gently. "A very good wow indeed."

Later that night, as we lay in bed, wrapped in each other's arms, I thought about Mae. She'd found her peace at last. And now, I was finally on the path to finding mine. The road ahead wouldn't always be easy, it never is, but Erica and I had each other and that was more than enough to get started. We'd weathered so much already, and now, after what felt like forever, everything was moving in the right direction.

We stood in the doorway, staring at the emptiness before us. The silence was all-consuming, the stillness downright oppressive. Everything Mae had carefully cultivated—the pictures, the mementos, the maps, the letters—was gone. All of it. The apartment, once filled with countless fragments of her past and her heart, now felt hollow, erased as though it had never existed. The furniture remained, but the shelves were stripped of all traces of Mae. Even the kitchen counter was wiped clean, not a coffee mug or teacup in sight.

I felt the air catch in my throat as I haltingly stepped further inside, a feeling of dread riding up my spine.

"Mae?" I called again, though I already knew there would be no answer.

My words bounced off the walls, weak and lonesome. I glanced around the room, hoping against reason that she might be hiding somewhere, just messing around and trying to give us a twisted scare. But there was nothing—nothing but emptiness.

Erica moved to the window, looking out at the street as if expecting to see Mae's figure walking away. "What the fuck is going on?" she said, her voice so quiet it registered as little more than a soft breeze in an open field.

My stomach twisted. It felt like the last puzzle piece had been ripped from my grasp, leaving the picture incomplete.

Where the hell had she gone?

And then I saw it.

On the table in the center of the room, lying in stark contrast to the emptiness, was a letter. Its solitary presence was disconcerting—how could something so simple and ordinary feel so out of place?

I approached it slowly, Erica's footsteps trailing behind me. The letter was addressed to me, with a note stuck to it: *Alex, if you couldn't fully understand before, this should help. Mae.*

My heart pounded in my chest as I picked it up, noticing an envelope underneath.

"Alex," Erica whispered, clearly sensing my tension. "What's going on?"

I didn't answer immediately, I couldn't. I just stared at the letter, tracing my fingers over the paper, trying to control myself. And then I opened it, noticing the long-dried bloodstains and remnants of battle-tested earth along its edges, and began to read.

My Dearest Mae,

I do not know how to start this letter because I do not know how to say goodbye to you. I have sat in this dirt for hours, with nothing but the sounds of gunfire and the smell of smoke, trying to find the right words. But there are no words for this—no words to describe what it feels like to know that you will not get to hold the person you love ever again.

The truth is, Mae, I will not be coming home. I am pinned down, and there is no way out. I do not want to frighten and upset you, but I must be honest because honesty is all I have left to give you now.

You have been my constant light in the darkest moments, Mae. Your letters—they were more than words on paper; they were life. I carried them in my breast pocket, close to my heart, and when I was scared, I would read them over and over, imagining your voice saying those words to me. You do not know it, but you have saved me a hundred times over just by being you.

I hate that this is the last thing I will ever write to you. I hate that I will not get to see you smile again, that I will not get to kiss you goodbye or hold your hand one last time. I hate that I will not get to grow old with you, to wake up and fall asleep beside you, to watch the seasons change with you by my side.

But more than anything, Mae, I hate that this pain will be yours to carry. I know you—how your heart aches for others, how you love so deeply it feels like the world might break you. But, Mae, I need you to do something for me. I need you to find a way to keep going, even when it feels impossible. I need you to live.

Do not let the weight of my absence pull you under. You are too bright, too beautiful, and too full of life to let the darkness win. Love again, Mae. Please. Find someone who will make you laugh the way I did, who will dance with you in the rain and hold you through the storms. And when you do, do not feel guilty. My love for you does not end here—it will follow you, always. I promise you that.

I wish I could hold you right now, just once more. I wish I could tell you how much you have meant to me, how every breath I have taken since I met you has been for you. I wish I could kiss you and whisper in your ear that everything will be alright. But I cannot. All I can do is hope that you will feel me with you—in the wind, in the stars, in the quiet moments when the world stands still.

You are, and always will be, the love of my life. You made me better, stronger, braver. You gave me something worth fighting for, even if I will not make it back to you.

I have to stop now—the light is fading, and so am I. But, Mae, please know this: you were my greatest joy. Loving you was the best thing I have ever done, and I will carry that love with me, even into the unknown.

Forever yours,
John

I stood there for a long moment. It was, without question, the single most earnest and beautifully unreserved thing I had, or ever would, read in my lifetime. This letter, this final goodbye, was all the explanation anyone would ever need to understand how Mae's life turned out the way it did. How does one ever recover from such devastating loss, such heart-shattering pain?

"Where did she go?" Erica asked, her voice trembling, the question seeming to be more for herself than for me.

"The letter was—" I stammered. "It was from John. His last letter to Mae."

Paralyzing panic surged inside me as I began to comprehend the depth of Mae's decision. She was always intentional and so meticulous when she chose to do something. She was capable of leaving without a trace if that suited her chosen plan.

"Alex, what are you thinking?" Erica asked, her voice threaded with concern.

"She's stopped searching," I said, my thoughts moving faster than I could process them. "She carried unknowns and unanswered questions about John for her entire life, and now she has finally stopped searching."

I ran my hand through my hair, frustration starting to creep in.

Why didn't she tell me? Why didn't she just talk to me?

"Alex, I—"

"No. No, I'm okay, I've got it." I could feel the rush of adrenaline, that surge of sharpened focus I got when things were most urgent.

Mae had left clues. She didn't want us to find her right away, lest we try to stop her, but she still wanted us to know and trusted we would follow the trail she'd left behind.

"But where do we even start?" asked Erica.

I knew exactly where Mae was. We had reached the end of the story.

"She's at the cemetery," I said, firm and with unwavering certainty. "She needs the final piece of closure. She's going back to where it all started."

CHAPTER 34
MAE

I sat down at the small desk in the corner of the apartment, the steady rhythm of the city outside muffled by the walls and the silence within. My pen hovered and hesitated over the paper before I began to write.

Jacqueline,

I hope this message finds you well. Or maybe I don't. The jury is still out on you as far as I'm concerned. But you have grown on me, so know there's that. And that in itself is no small feat. I need you to understand something that I didn't say before, something I couldn't—because it's not just about you or me. It's about your father. John. For all intents and purposes, in all the ways that matter—yes, he is your father.

Among the letters I've found, the ones he wrote all those years ago, there's a story that's yours to know. John was the kind of man who would have made the perfect father for you, for anyone. He was kind, joyful, deeply committed, and so full

*of love. When I read the words he wrote about you, about find-
ing you and keeping you safe, it moved something in me. He
wanted nothing more than to protect you and to ensure you
had a life filled with love. You were everything to him, Jacqueline, even if you never knew it.*

*I know your mother, Yvette, kept things from you—about
your past, about your real family—but I want you to understand this: John would have been there to support and love
you, would have been the father you imagined. He was a noble
man who fought for his family, for freedom, for you. I hope you
know that, I hope you understand that you are the daughter of
a man who would have been proud of you regardless of biology
or adoption papers.*

*If nothing else, I want you to revere him as the father he
was meant to be for you. You deserve that. You are not just a
piece of someone else's history, Jacqueline—you are a legacy in
your own right. And John was part of your legacy too. Carry
him with you as you move forward. Tell stories of him. Make
him your own.*

Mae

I set the pen down, carefully folding the letter into a
stamped envelope. It felt strange, concluding this part of the
journey, but there was nothing more to say. Jacqueline had
all the pieces she needed to build the complete story of her
past—I had given everything I could.

Standing up, I looked around the empty apartment for
one last time. There was nothing left for me here. I grabbed
my coat, wrapping it tightly around myself, and slid the envelope under a letter already on the table. It was a letter for Alex.
Not to him, but *for* him—the last letter John ever wrote me. I

was sure he'd be back to the apartment soon and was leaving it to him to send Jacqueline her letter.

The wind howled through the cemetery, a fitting and bitter reminder of how final everything was. The burden of the world felt lighter now, as if all the years of questions, pain, and sorrow had been carried away in the unseasonably cold night air. Everything felt distant, muffled. My breath was laboured and shallow, the cold seeping deeper into my weary bones, but I welcomed it. I was ready to embrace it and let it fill my lungs.

As I knelt down, my hands pressed against John's headstone, I realized just how much I had held on to for far too long. Memories of him, of our too-short life together—everything I thought I knew—had become distorted in my mind over the years. The longing for answers, the determined search for meaning—it all came crashing down in the end. I had spent my entire life looking for peace, when, in truth, I had been carrying it within me all along. I had just buried it under decades of self-pity, self-righteousness, and perhaps more than a little stubbornness.

I rested my forehead on the cold stone, the chill numbing my skin. The absence of any sound but the wind was all-encompassing, and in it, I could almost hear John's voice. It was so real and present; I almost believed he was there beside me, a gentle hand on my shoulder, reassuring me.

"It's okay, Mae. You've done your best. You've fought for everything you wanted. You can rest now."

My chest tightened. I hadn't said goodbye—to Alex, to Erica, or to Luc. I didn't even have the courage to explain myself. But deep down, I knew it was something I had to do, and in just this way. They would never understand, it was too much for them. It was too much for me.

My thoughts turned to Alex. All the experiences we had shared, all the things he'd said to me, all the moments that had brought us closer together. From when I first met him at Silver Springs, to trying to get him to run for the hills, to his surprising willpower to stay and endure everything I threw at him. Sure, at the time, it wasn't for me, it was for Autumn, but look how far we'd come. In our moments together, we bonded, forming a friendship that transcended generations. He'd been kind, steady, patient. He had seen me at my worst; I had seen him at his worst. And yet we never stopped believing in each other's ability to make something of our future. He might be the only person who would fully understand why I had to do this. And despite the understanding, I couldn't bear the thought of him trying to change my mind, of him stopping me. And he most certainly would try to stop me. And that's why I loved him unconditionally. But that love would have to go unsaid.

I wished I could tell him, just once, that I was sorry for leaving like this. That it wasn't his fault, it wasn't anyone's fault. But I wouldn't have been able to explain why I had to walk away, not just from them, but from everything that had kept me chained to a past I couldn't outrun. That this was my only way of letting go, of finally finding peace.

And then there was Jacqueline. I left the letter for her, knowing she'd eventually receive it, believing she would carry John's memory in a way she never had before. I hoped she would honour him by remembering the man he was, not the absent stranger she had always believed him to be. But now, as I sat shivering in the advancing darkness, I wondered if I had made the right choice for her. Could she accept a new reality uncovered only through the disruptive efforts of others? Would she be able to move on and find the same kind of peace I had?

I didn't have the answers, and I had to accept that was okay.

The cold was unbearable now, my limbs stiffening, my breathing a shallow wheeze, but I didn't care. The longer I stayed, the more the pressure of the world seemed to ease and slip away. This was where it had all begun, where everything I had loved and everything I had lost had come together in the end. I was no longer running from anything. Not from the past, not from the pain, not from myself. I closed my eyes, and at that moment, everything was quiet. The wind continued to whip and whirl, but I couldn't feel it anymore. All I could feel was the peace that had settled into my bones, the peace I had always been searching for. It wasn't just about John. It wasn't just about the past. It was about me, finally understanding who I was and what I needed.

The world around me disappeared entirely. I was alone in this vast, sweeping space, but I wasn't afraid. I had found what I was looking for. I had found him.

John.

"Until we meet again," I whispered, the words barely audible as I wrapped my arms around his gravestone in an embrace that said I'll never let you go again. *"I know where, I know when."*

And then, the quiet became absolute.

The last breath I took was filled with finality, and as my body grew colder, settling into the weight of silence, I knew I had made my peace. The world would move on without me, and I was okay with that. In my heart, I had bid farewell. To Alex. To Erica. To Luc. And even to Jacqueline, whose past I had tried to piece together, whose story I had hoped to enhance with the truth. But most of all, I had said goodbye to myself.

This was how it was meant to end.

I would never know the sunny day that rose just a few hours later.

CHAPTER 35
JOHN

THE DEAFENING SOUNDS OF BATTLE raged around me, the constant crackle of gunfire, the thunderous explosions, the bitter taste of smoke in my mouth, and the agonized screams of men. We were pinned down in the fields of Caen, in the same woods I'd once walked without a care, now a war-torn wasteland. The ground shook beneath me as another bomb dropped, sending debris flying in every direction. My hands shook, but it wasn't from fear. It was from everything that was happening, from what was waiting, from what I knew was about to happen.

This was the end.

I wasn't sure how many more of us were still standing—how many of us would make it out of this hell alive—but as I crouched in the dirt, my rifle gripped tightly in my hands, I knew that I would not be one of them. My thoughts weren't on the enemy or the mission any longer; both felt futile. They weren't on the bloody scene around me or the men I was serving beside, yelling orders and signalling movements. No, my thoughts, as they had been for so long now, were on Mae.

Mae.

Her name sounded as sweet in my mind as it did when it rolled off my tongue. I would never tire of saying it. "Mae."

Though I thought of her every day, I was suspended in a state of blissful reminiscence. I couldn't stop thinking about her. Her face. Her laugh. The way she had held me in her arms and kissed me gently, as if I might break. She was so full of life and hope. I thought about how we had dreamed of a future that now seemed impossibly distant, slipping further and further away with each bullet blasting through the air. The war had changed everything. It had stolen so much—and yet, Mae remained the one thing I clung to. She had been my rock throughout it all. Of course she was. Who better to hold on to in times of uncertainty and downright fear?

I had spent years trying to keep her safe in my heart, in my mind, even from all these miles away. But now, I knew that even all of that wasn't enough. I had to leave something for her. Something that might one day reach her. A final, imperfect goodbye.

I pulled out a scrap of paper, my hands bloodied and trembling as I fumbled with the pen. Daylight was not on anyone's side, and my only wish was to be granted just enough time to complete this letter, seal it in an envelope, and ensure it was safely stowed on my person. From there, it would be up to the fates to see these words and sentiments travel from my pocket to her hands. But what else did I have if not one final glint of hope? Not the hope of surviving, no, but of having Mae read my declaration of love one last time.

The air was thick with acrid smoke, and the sounds of the battle were growing louder, more urgent. There was no way I could continue hiding here, waiting for the inevitable. The end was close, and I could feel the sting of death creeping ever closer with each passing second.

But I couldn't die without writing this letter. Without giving Mae something. She needed to know the truth that was in my heart.

My Dearest Mae, I wrote, my pen scrawling across the paper as the world shook and shattered around me. I wrote furiously, hoping to get down everything I needed to say before I became a casualty, a memory, a ghost.

I folded the letter carefully, tucking it into the front of my jacket as the madness continued around me. I knew this was the last meaningful thing I would do before it all ended.

The air seemed to thicken, the gunfire grew even louder, more intense. The familiar fear and adrenaline coursed through me in waves, but as I sat there, surrounded by the roar of war, there was only one thing left in my heart.

Mae.

What a beautiful and perfect final thought as the brightness of the fading sun brought me home. I closed my eyes and began to sing.

Let's say goodbye with a smile, dear
Just for a while dear we must part
Don't let this parting upset you
I'll not forget you, sweetheart
We'll meet again
Don't know where
Don't know when
But I know we'll meet again some sunny day

The End

ACKNOWLEDGEMENTS

As always, my first and deepest thanks go to you, the reader. When you choose to spend your time with a writer's words, there is an unspoken magic in that exchange. An unseen ripple that travels back to us in ways you may never know. From the bottom of my heart, thank you for reading this story.

To my grandfather, a World War II veteran who passed away just shy of his 104th birthday in May 2024; you were the embodiment of bravery, honour, and sacrifice. You will always be loved, and never, ever forgotten. Your life and stories inspired segments of this novel, and this book is but one small way I will keep your memory alive.

This story would not exist in its current form without Ryan Jones. As a trusted friend, reader, and sounding board, your conversations sparked the idea that became the book I didn't plan on writing next, but needed to. Your insight and encouragement shaped its every chapter, and I am forever grateful. My simple thanks will never be enough.

I have been fortunate to work with Hannah Gordon, whose keen editorial eye and steady guidance shepherded this novel from its earliest draft to the book you now hold. Her clarity, care, and belief in the story made every rewrite a joy rather than a burden.

Likewise, to Paul Orlando, whose many passes through the manuscript sharpened the rough edges and brought to life characters and scenes that were lacking.

As a sequel, it mattered deeply that this book carried the same spirit and style as *Between Two Seasons*. My thanks to Leanne Persichini for her thoughtful, skillful work in creating a cover that feels like a natural companion to the first. The John to his Mae. The Erica to her Alex.

For all of you mentioned here, and all of you reading, this book is as much yours as it is mine.

ABOUT THE AUTHOR

Marc MacDonald is an author who believes every great story starts with a spark—whether it's a single sentence, an unforgettable character, or an idea that won't let go. As a writer, Marc weaves heartfelt narratives that linger long after the last page is turned.

When he's not crafting compelling fiction, Marc applies his storytelling skills as a seasoned communications professional, proving that every message—whether in a book or a press release—deserves to be engaging. He's also a fierce defender of the Oxford comma, an unapologetic pun enthusiast, and someone who firmly believes that coffee is the most essential writing tool.

Find him deep in his next manuscript, chasing inspiration, or justifying "research" as an excuse to buy more books. Catch up with Marc on his personal website: MarcMacdonald.ca

ABOUT THE PUBLISHER

Ink is black, sticky, and stubborn. When spilled, it stains—leaving behind a mark that lingers, a reminder of the moment it escaped its container. Whether we knocked it over ourselves or someone else did, we all find ourselves sitting in spilt ink at some point.

But it's not the ink itself that defines us—it's what we do with it. At Spilt Ink Press, we embrace the chaos and mess of life's spills, transforming them into works that illuminate the human condition. We are a genre-crossing imprint devoted to literary works, magical realism, science fiction, historical narratives, poetry, and collections of short stories and novellas—stories that dive deep into the complexity and resilience of the human spirit.

For us, spilt ink is more than a metaphor; it's a call to action. It's the reminder that even in the mess, there's magic waiting to be discovered. We champion bold, imaginative voices that find beauty in the chaos and authenticity in the scars. Our mission is to bring these stories to light, creating a space for works that challenge, inspire, and connect.

Life's stains are inevitable, but they don't have to be wasted. Let's craft stories that linger, art that endures, and wonders that rise from the spills. At Spilt Ink Press, we don't just clean up the mess—we create from it.

www.ingramcontent.com/pod-product-compliance
Lightning Source LLC
Chambersburg PA
CBHW020905060726